THE BROTHERS FLICK

THE IMPOSSIBLE DOORS

WONDERBOUND.

WRITTEN BY **Ryan Haddock**

ILLUSTRATED BY **Nick Wyche** COLORS BY **Whitney Cogar**

LAYOUTS BY **David Stoll** LETTERS BY **Jim Campbell**

EDITED BY RebeccaTaylor

DESIGNED BY Sonja Synak

PUBLISHER, Damian A. Wassel

EDITOR-IN-CHIEF, Adrian F. Wassel

SENIOR ARTIST, Nathan C. Gooden

MANAGING EDITOR, Rebecca Taylor

DIRECTOR OF SALES & MARKETING, DIRECT MARKET, David Dissanayake

DIRECTOR OF SALES & MARKETING, BOOK MARKET, Syndee Barwick

PRODUCTION MANAGER, Ian Baldessari

ART DIRECTOR, WONDERBOUND, Sonja Synak

ART DIRECTOR, VAULT, Tim Daniel

PRINCIPAL, Damian A. Wassel Sr.

WONDERBOUND

Missoula, Montana

readwonderbound.com

@readwonderbound

ISBN: 978-1-63849-104-0

LCCN: 2022905819

First Edition, First Printing, September, 2022

1 2 3 4 5 6 7 8 9 10

BROTHERS FLICK

THE IMPOSSIBLE DOORS

HADDOCK WYCHE STOLL COGAR CAMPBELL

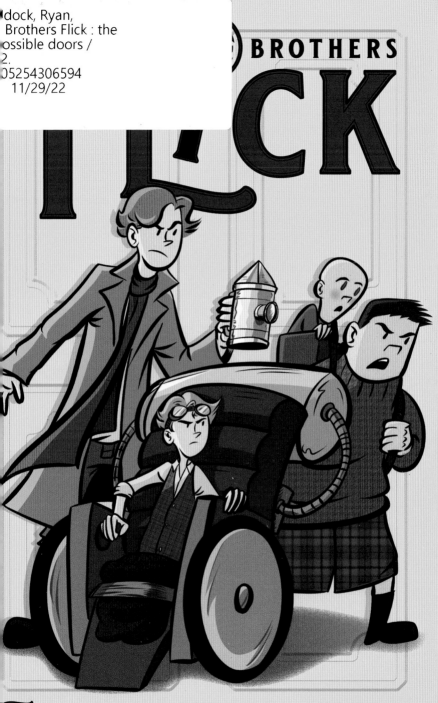

To Liam, Dexter, Rory, and Salem: I love you so much, I had to share you with the world.

To Michelle, for hot chocolate and everything after.

RYAN HADDOCK

To Ryan for the idea, the partnership, and helping an old dude make his 12 year old self proud of him.

To Liam, for being the flame that keeps us burning the midnight oil.

To Suzanne, for always & forever.

NICK WYCHE

PROLOGUE

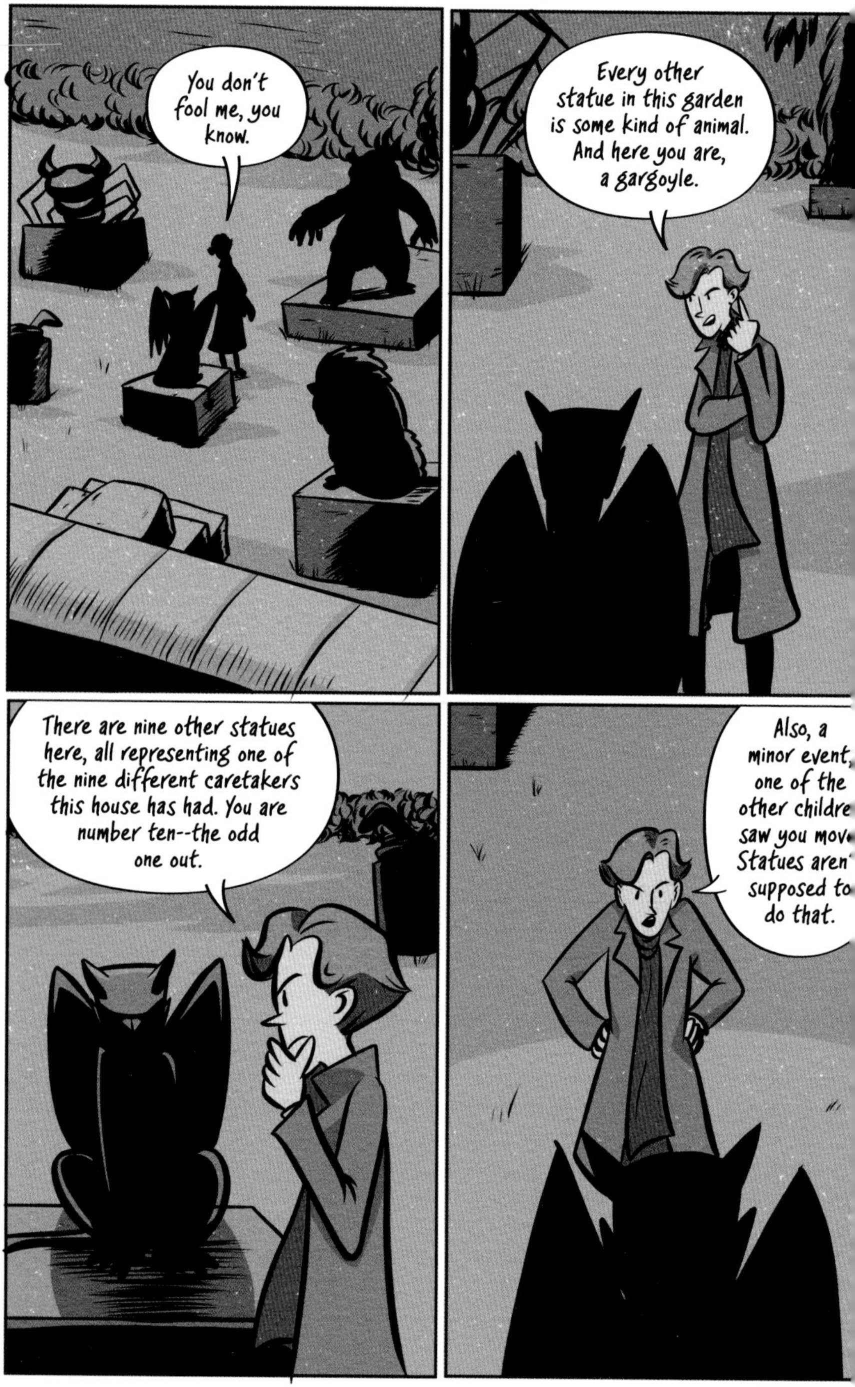

You don't fool me, you know.
Every other statue in this garden is some kind of animal. And here you are, a gargoyle.
There are nine other statues here, all representing one of the nine different caretakers this house has had. You are number ten--the odd one out.
Also, a minor event, one of the other childre saw you mov Statues aren' supposed to do that.

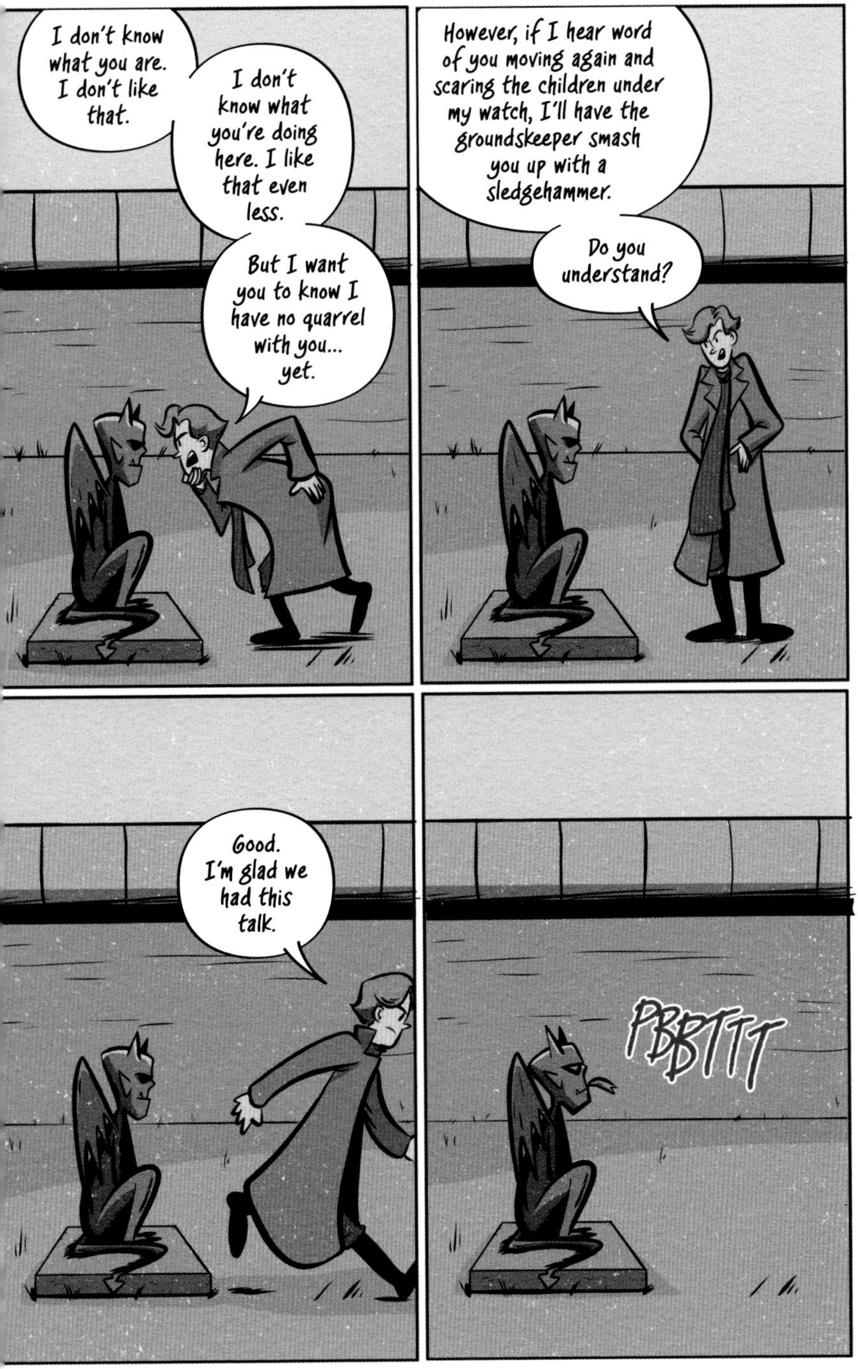
I don't know what you are. I don't like that.
I don't know what you're doing here. I like that even less.
But I want you to know I have no quarrel with you... yet.
However, if I hear word of you moving again and scaring the children under my watch, I'll have the groundskeeper smash you up with a sledgehammer.
Do you understand?
Good. I'm glad we had this talk.
PBBTTT

CHAPTER

1

THE BOY WHO CRAWLED OUT OF THE WEL

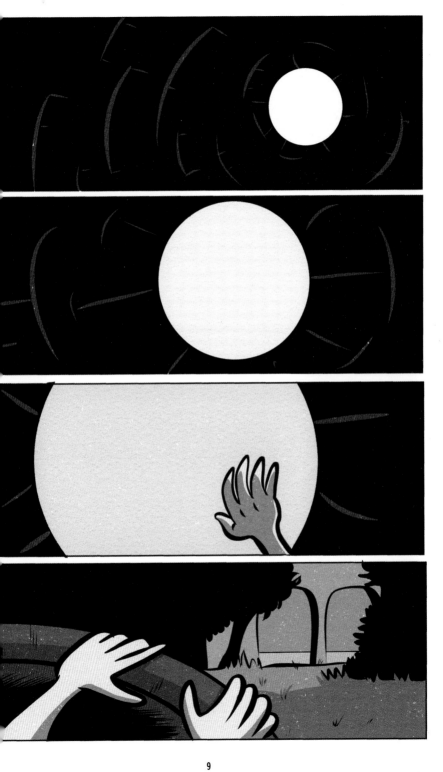

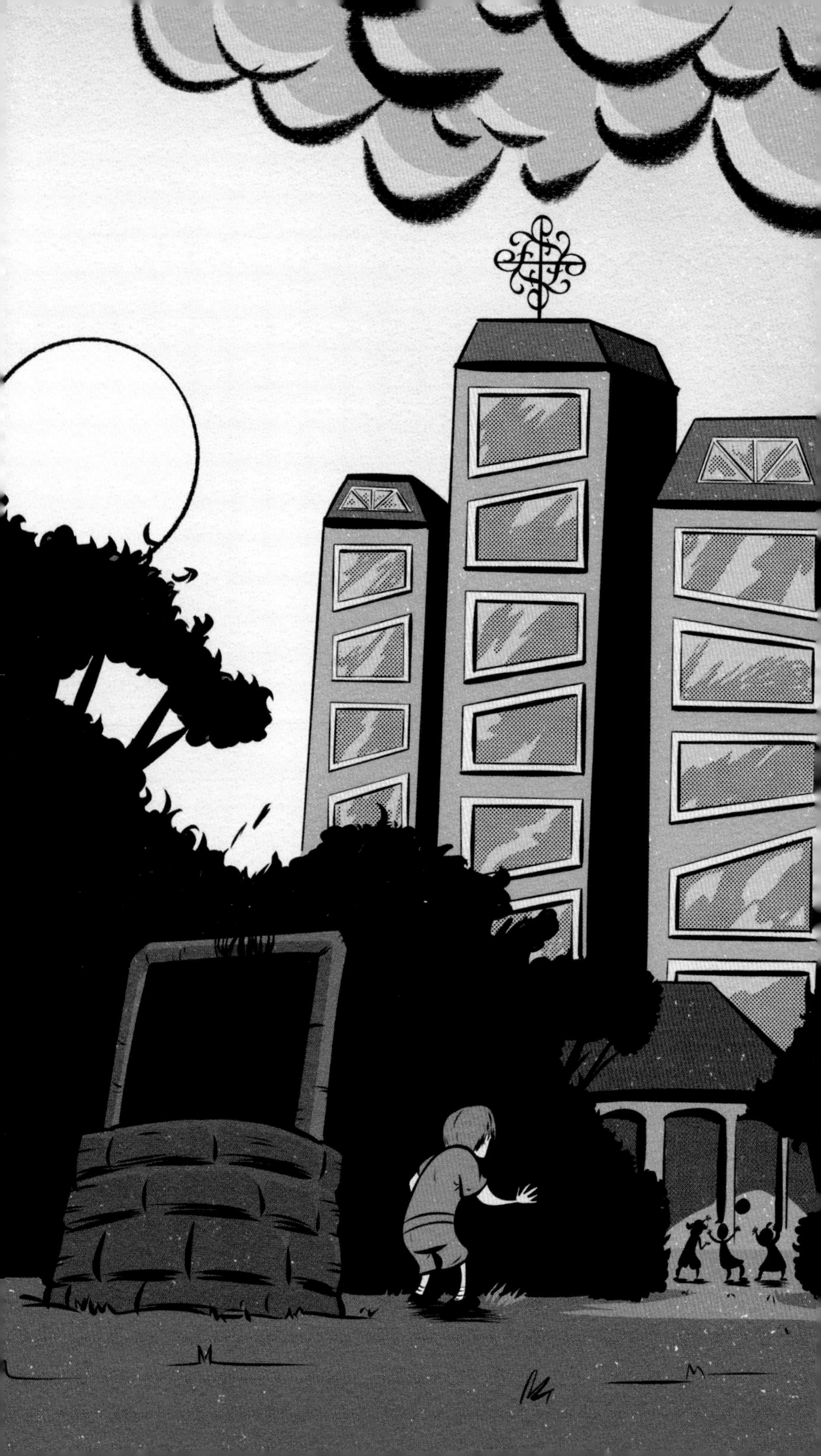

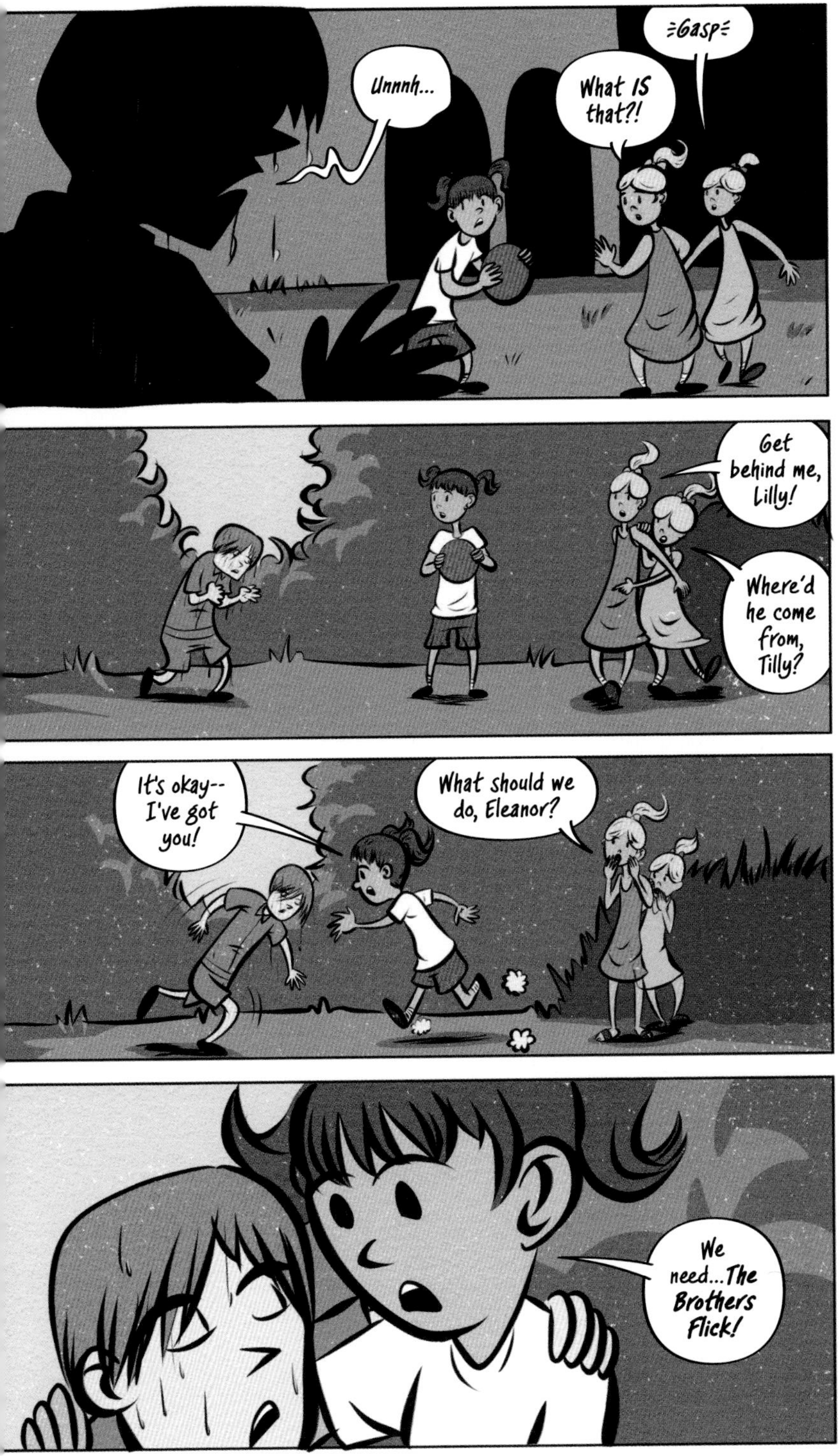
≡Gasp≡
Unnnh...
What IS that?!
Get behind me, Lilly!
Where'd he come from, Tilly?
It's okay-- I've got you!
What should we do, Eleanor?
We need...The Brothers Flick!

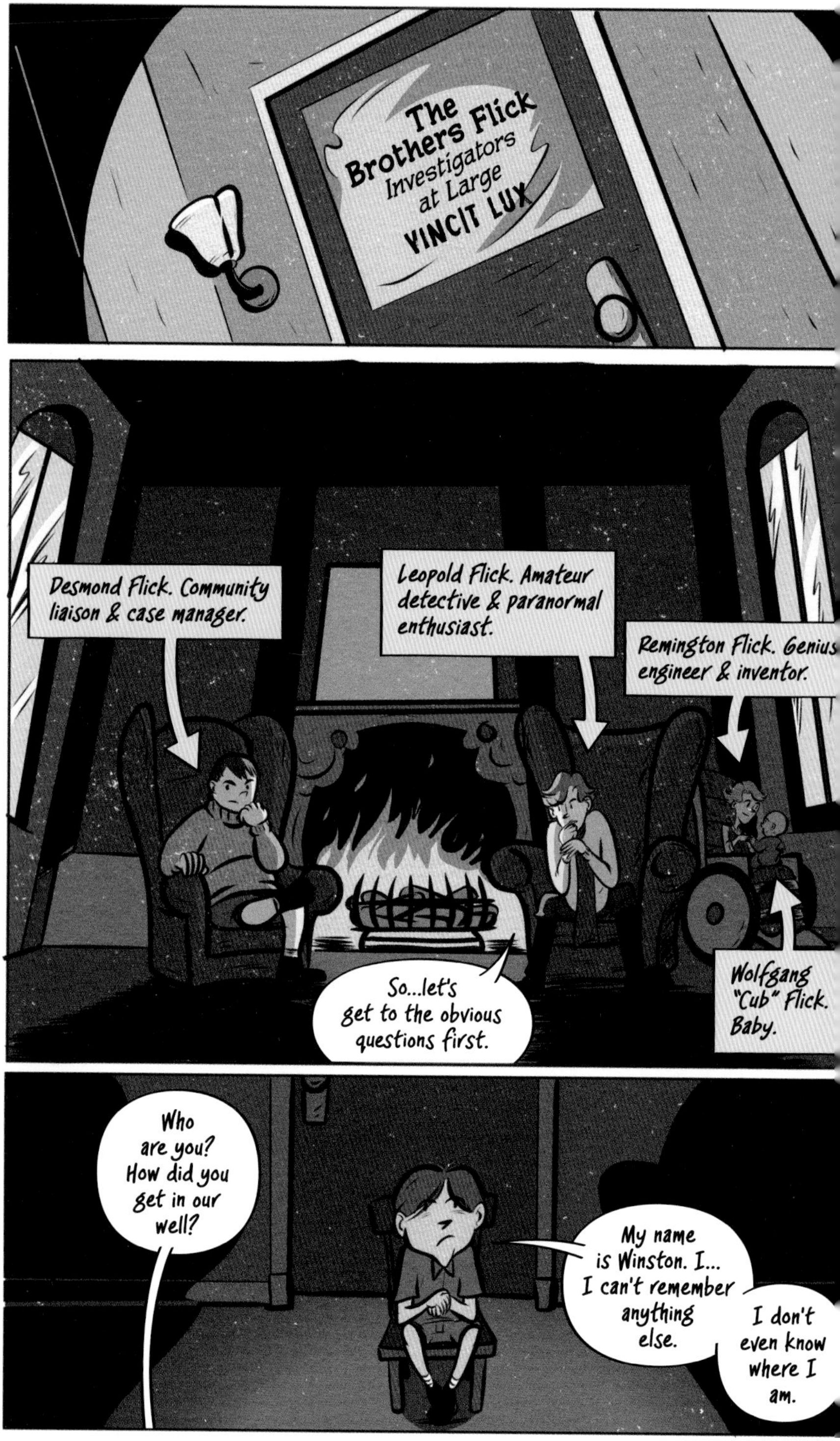
The Brothers Flick
Investigators at Large
VINCIT LUX
Desmond Flick. Community liaison & case manager.
Leopold Flick. Amateur detective & paranormal enthusiast.
Remington Flick. Genius engineer & inventor.
Wolfgang "Cub" Flick. Baby.
So...let's get to the obvious questions first.
Who are you? How did you get in our well?
My name is Winston. I... I can't remember anything else.
I don't even know where I am.

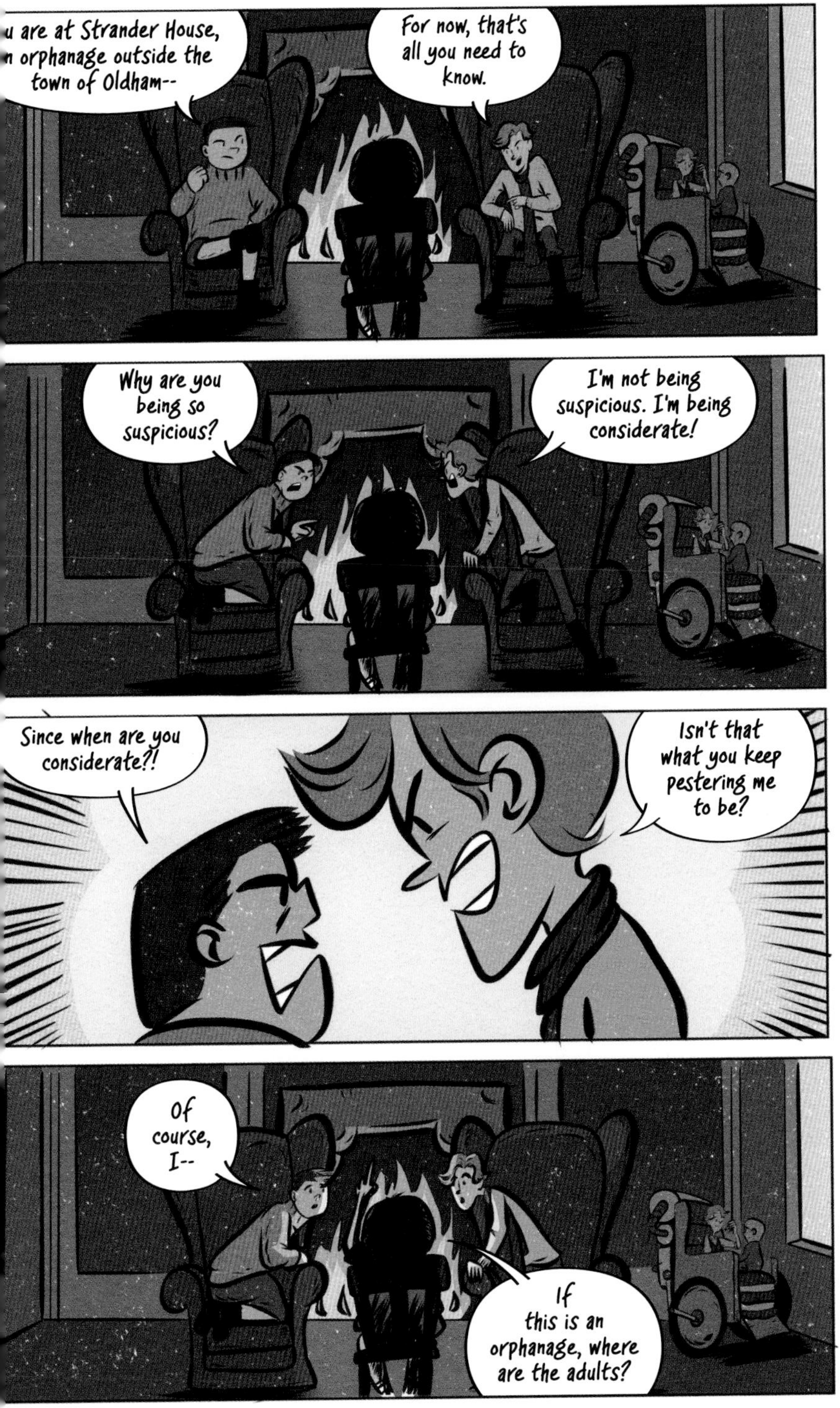
u are at Strander House, n orphanage outside the town of Oldham--
For now, that's all you need to know.
Why are you being so suspicious?
I'm not being suspicious. I'm being considerate!
Since when are you considerate?!
Isn't that what you keep pestering me to be?
Of course, I--
If this is an orphanage, where are the adults?

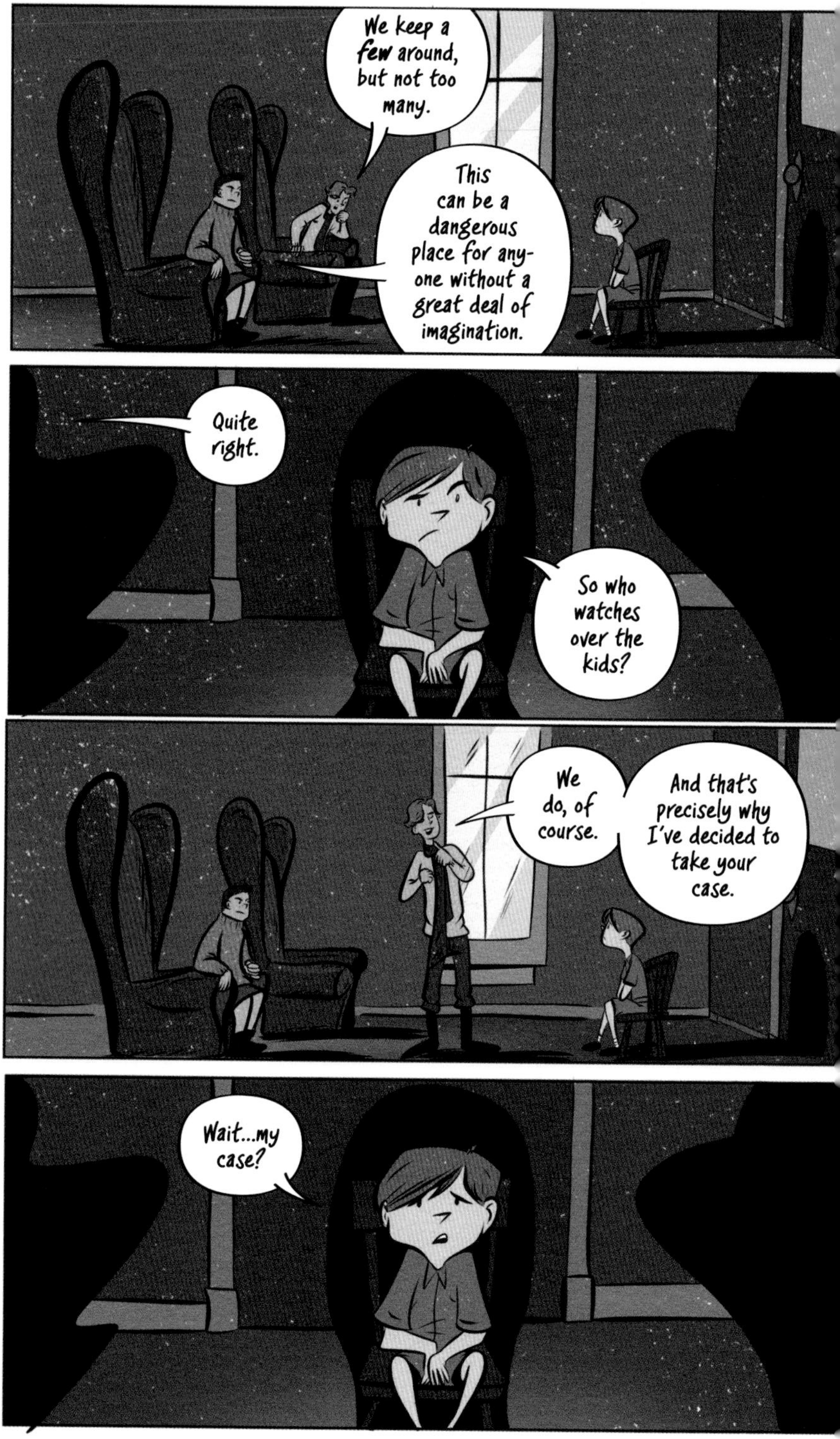
We keep a *few* around, but not too many.
This can be a dangerous place for any-one without a great deal of imagination.
Quite right.
So who watches over the kids?
We do, of course.
And that's precisely why I've decided to take your case.
Wait...my case?

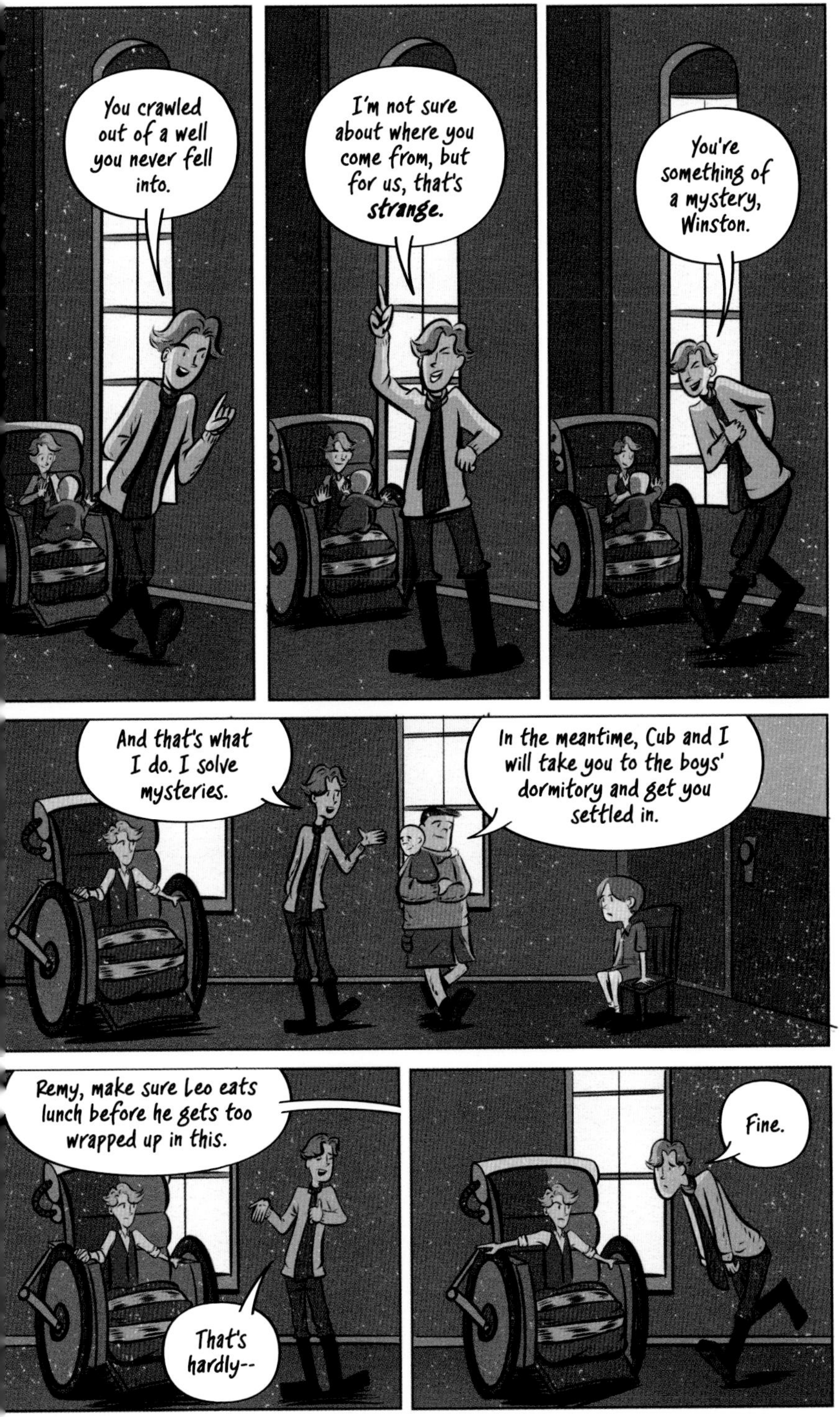
You crawled out of a well you never fell into.
I'm not sure about where you come from, but for us, that's *strange.*
You're something of a mystery, Winston.
And that's what I do. I solve mysteries.
In the meantime, Cub and I will take you to the boys' dormitory and get you settled in.
Remy, make sure Leo eats lunch before he gets too wrapped up in this.
That's hardly--
Fine.

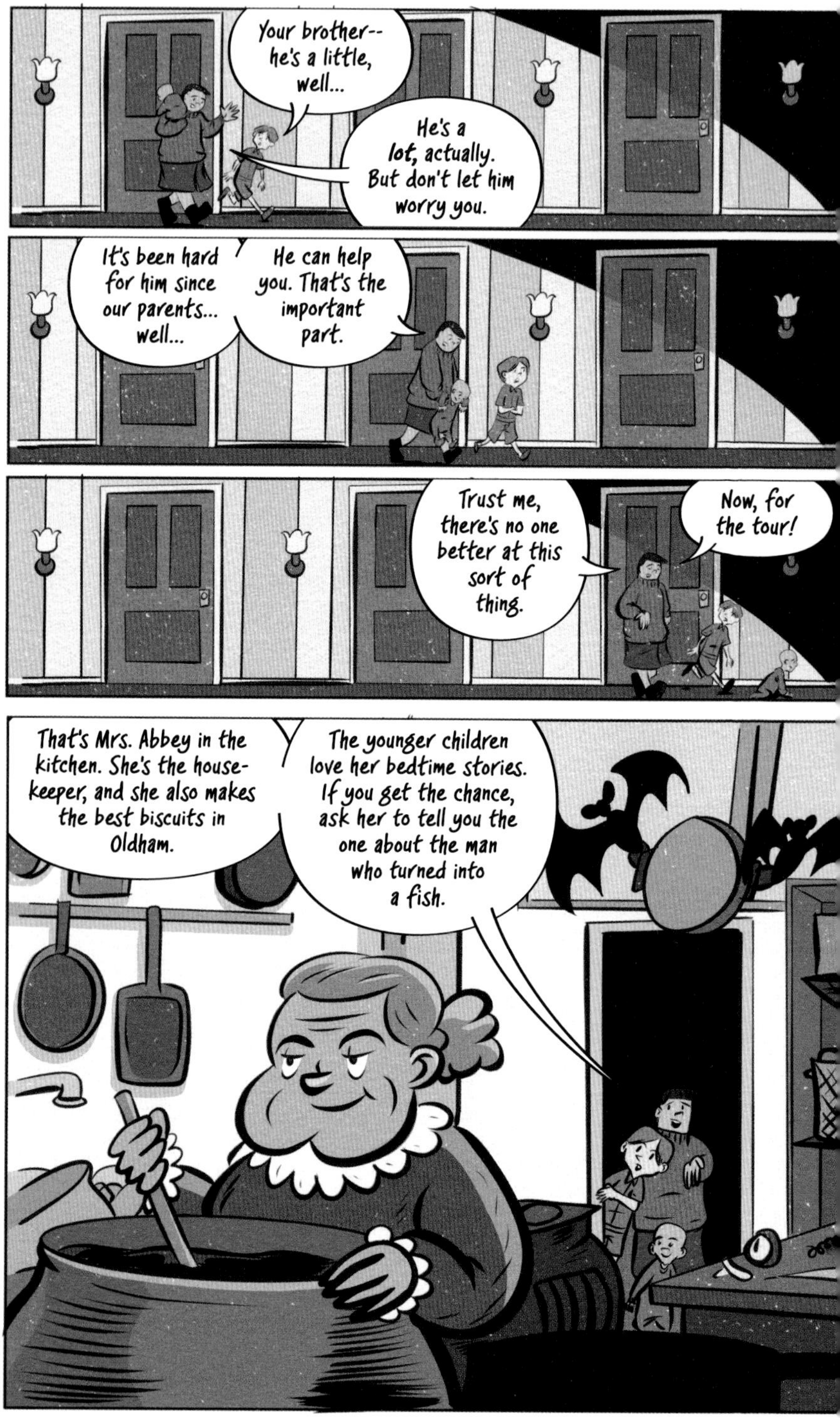
Your brother--he's a little, well...
He's a lot, actually. But don't let him worry you.
It's been hard for him since our parents... well...
He can help you. That's the important part.
Trust me, there's no one better at this sort of thing.
Now, for the tour!
That's Mrs. Abbey in the kitchen. She's the house-keeper, and she also makes the best biscuits in Oldham.
The younger children love her bedtime stories. If you get the chance, ask her to tell you the one about the man who turned into a fish.

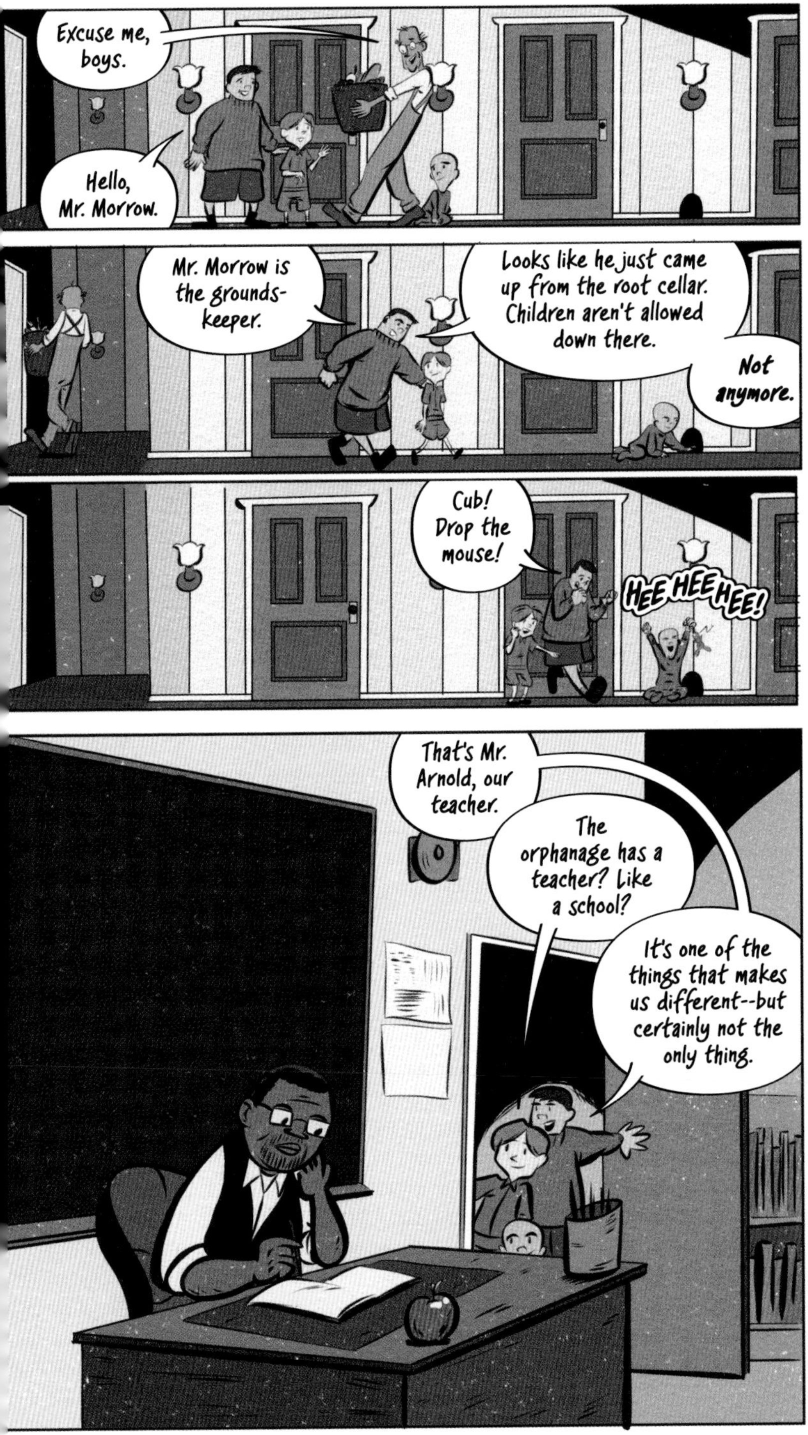
Excuse me, boys.
Hello, Mr. Morrow.
Mr. Morrow is the grounds-keeper.
Looks like he just came up from the root cellar. Children aren't allowed down there.
Not anymore.
Cub! Drop the mouse!
HEE HEE HEE!
That's Mr. Arnold, our teacher.
The orphanage has a teacher? Like a school?
It's one of the things that makes us different--but certainly not the only thing.

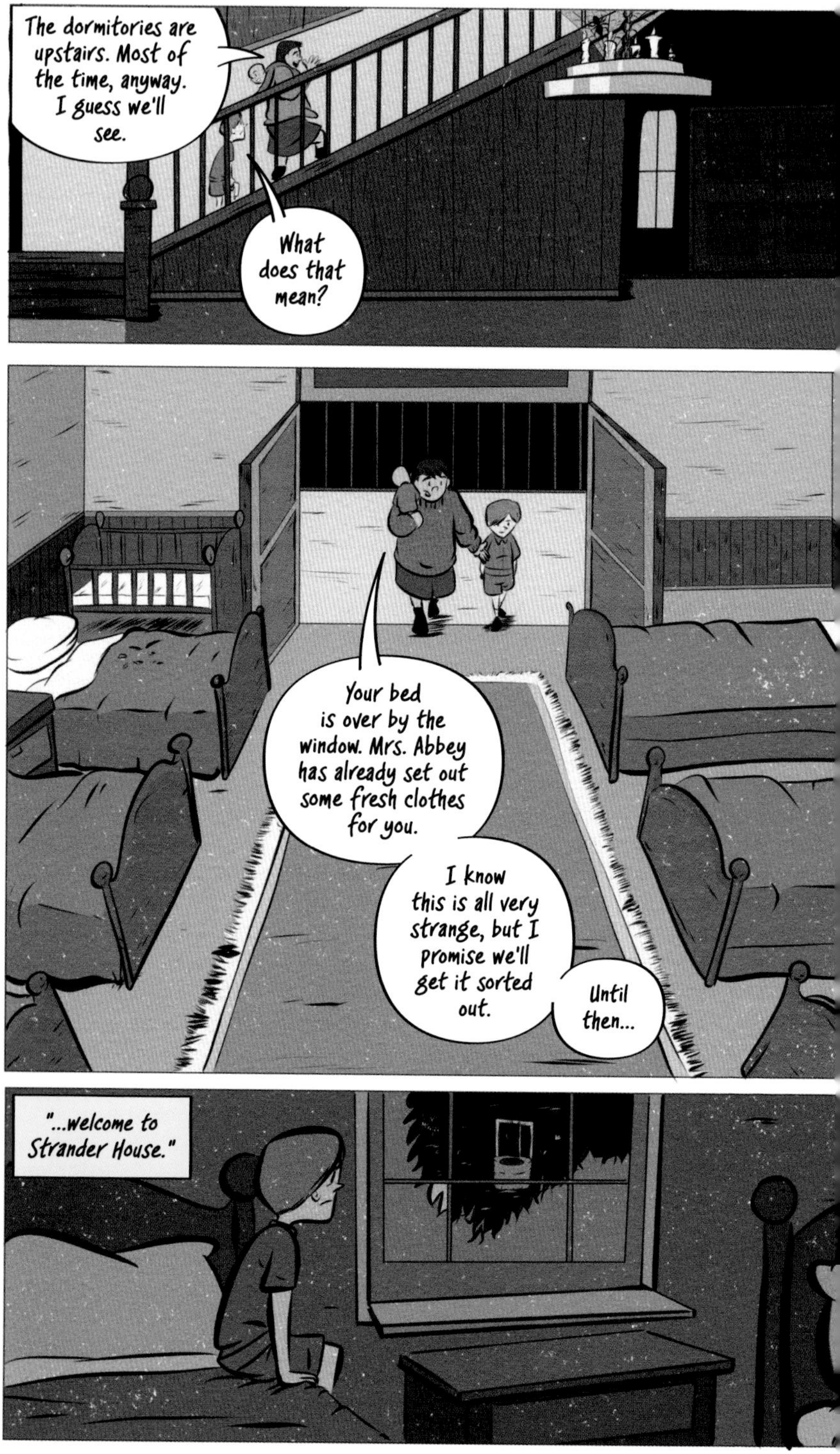
The dormitories are upstairs. Most of the time, anyway. I guess we'll see.
What does that mean?
Your bed is over by the window. Mrs. Abbey has already set out some fresh clothes for you.
I know this is all very strange, but I promise we'll get it sorted out.
Until then...
"...welcome to Strander House."

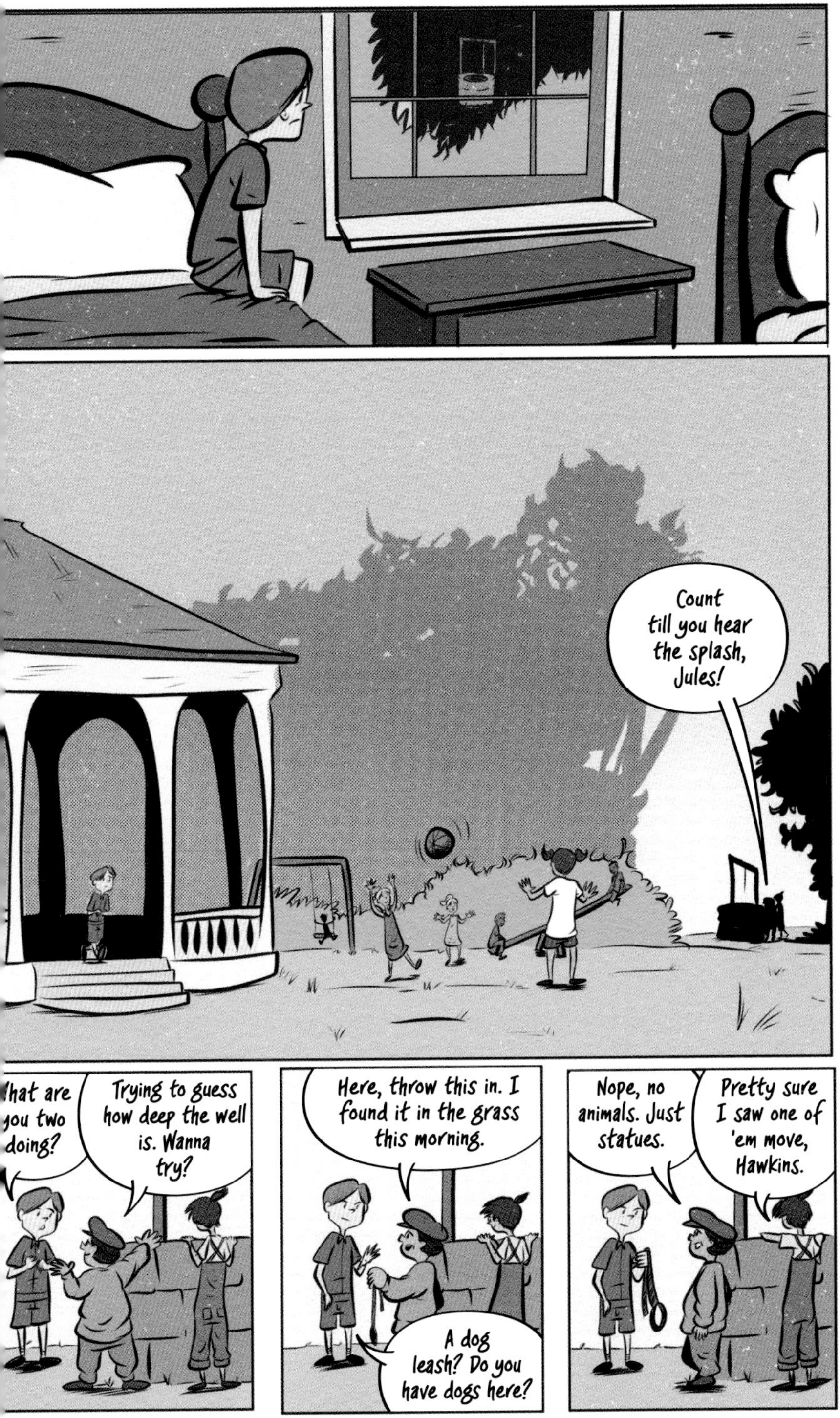
Count till you hear the splash, Jules!
hat are you two doing?
Trying to guess how deep the well is. Wanna try?
Here, throw this in. I found it in the grass this morning.
A dog leash? Do you have dogs here?
Nope, no animals. Just statues.
Pretty sure I saw one of 'em move, Hawkins.

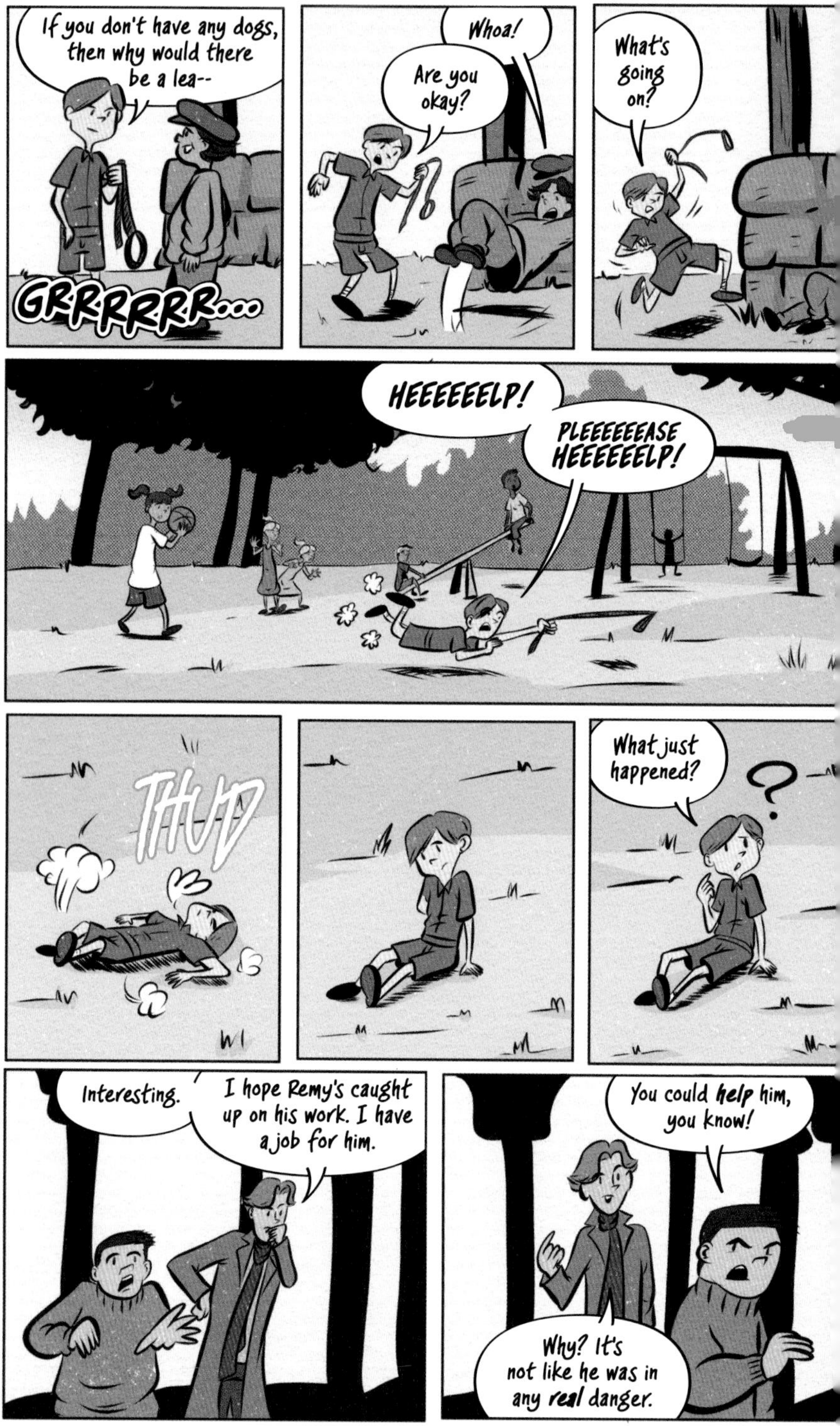

If you don't have any dogs, then why would there be a lea--
GRRRRRR...
Whoa!
Are you okay?
What's going on?
HEEEEEELP!
PLEEEEEEASE HEEEEEELP!
THUD
What just happened?
?
Interesting.
I hope Remy's caught up on his work. I have a job for him.
You could *help* him, you know!
Why? It's not like he was in any *real* danger.

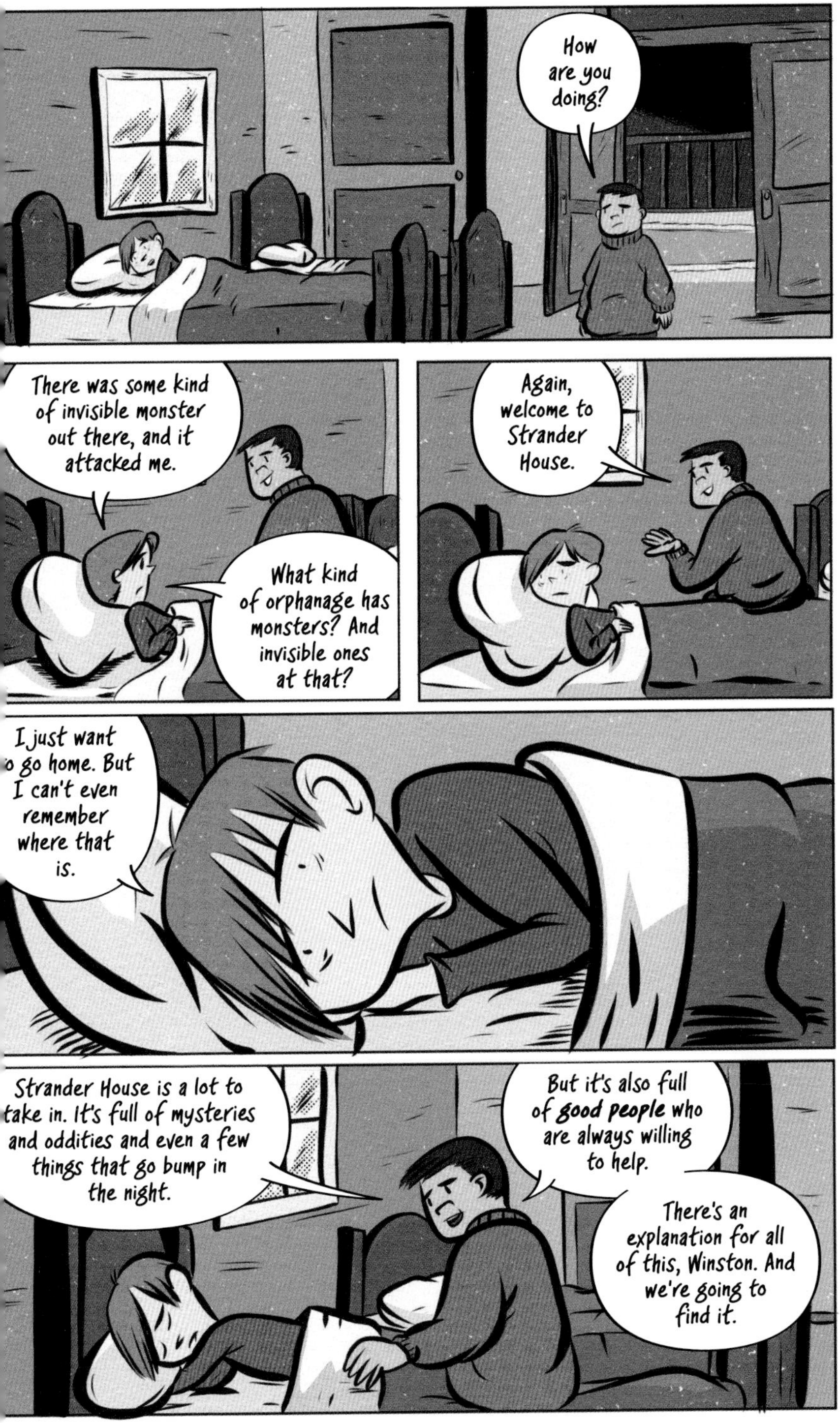
How are you doing?
There was some kind of invisible monster out there, and it attacked me.
What kind of orphanage has monsters? And invisible ones at that?
Again, welcome to Strander House.
I just want to go home. But I can't even remember where that is.
Strander House is a lot to take in. It's full of mysteries and oddities and even a few things that go bump in the night.
But it's also full of good people who are always willing to help.
There's an explanation for all of this, Winston. And we're going to find it.

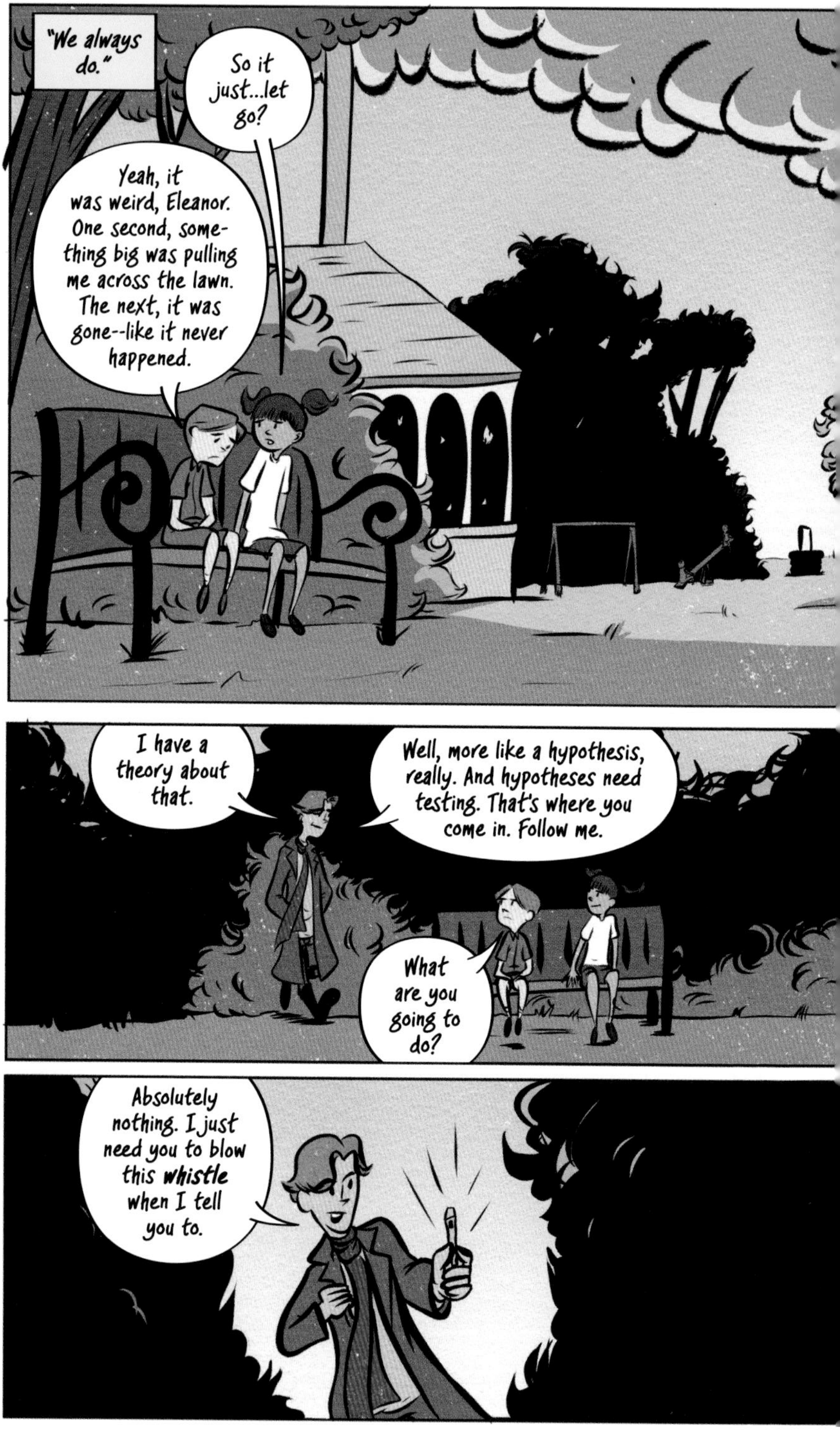

"We always do."
So it just...let go?
Yeah, it was weird, Eleanor. One second, something big was pulling me across the lawn. The next, it was gone--like it never happened.
I have a theory about that.
Well, more like a hypothesis, really. And hypotheses need testing. That's where you come in. Follow me.
What are you going to do?
Absolutely nothing. I just need you to blow this whistle when I tell you to.

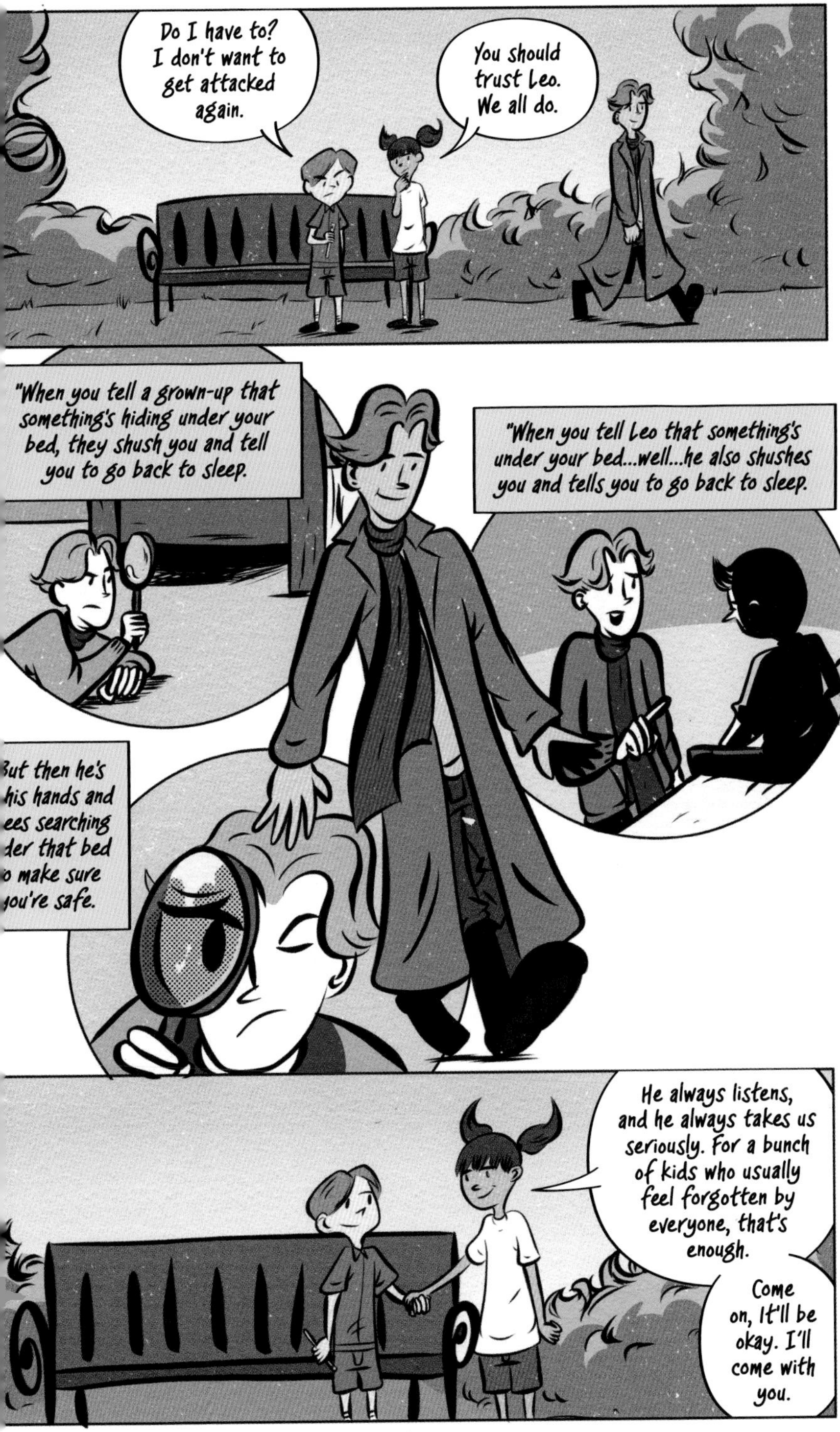
Do I have to? I don't want to get attacked again.
You should trust Leo. We all do.
"When you tell a grown-up that something's hiding under your bed, they shush you and tell you to go back to sleep.
"When you tell Leo that something's under your bed...well...he also shushes you and tells you to go back to sleep.
ut then he's his hands and ees searching der that bed o make sure you're safe.
He always listens, and he always takes us seriously. For a bunch of kids who usually feel forgotten by everyone, that's enough.
Come on, It'll be okay. I'll come with you.

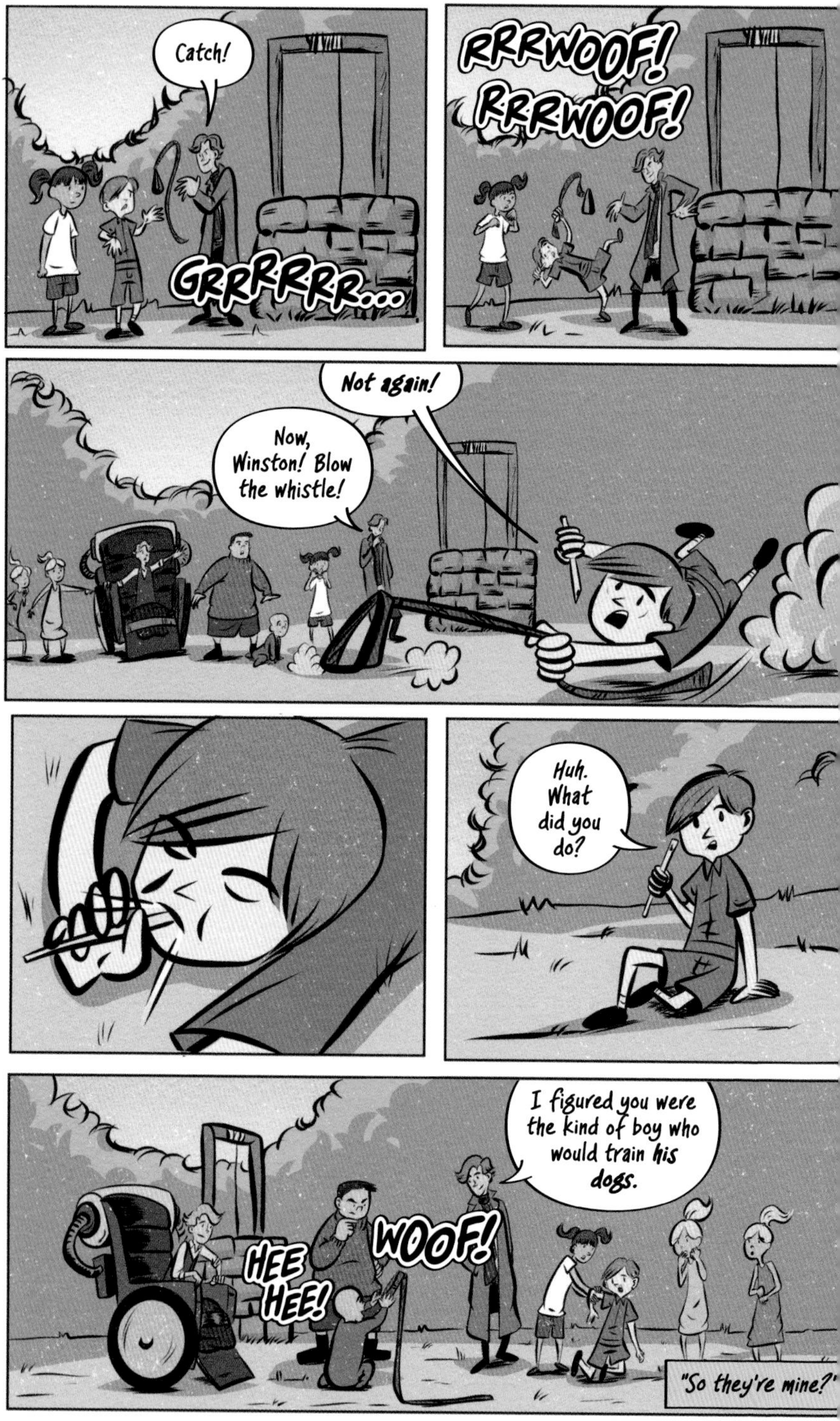
Catch!
GRRRRRR...
RRRWOOF!
RRRWOOF!
Not again!
Now, Winston! Blow the whistle!
Huh. What did you do?
I figured you were the kind of boy who would train his dogs.
HEE HEE!
WOOF!
"So they're mine?"

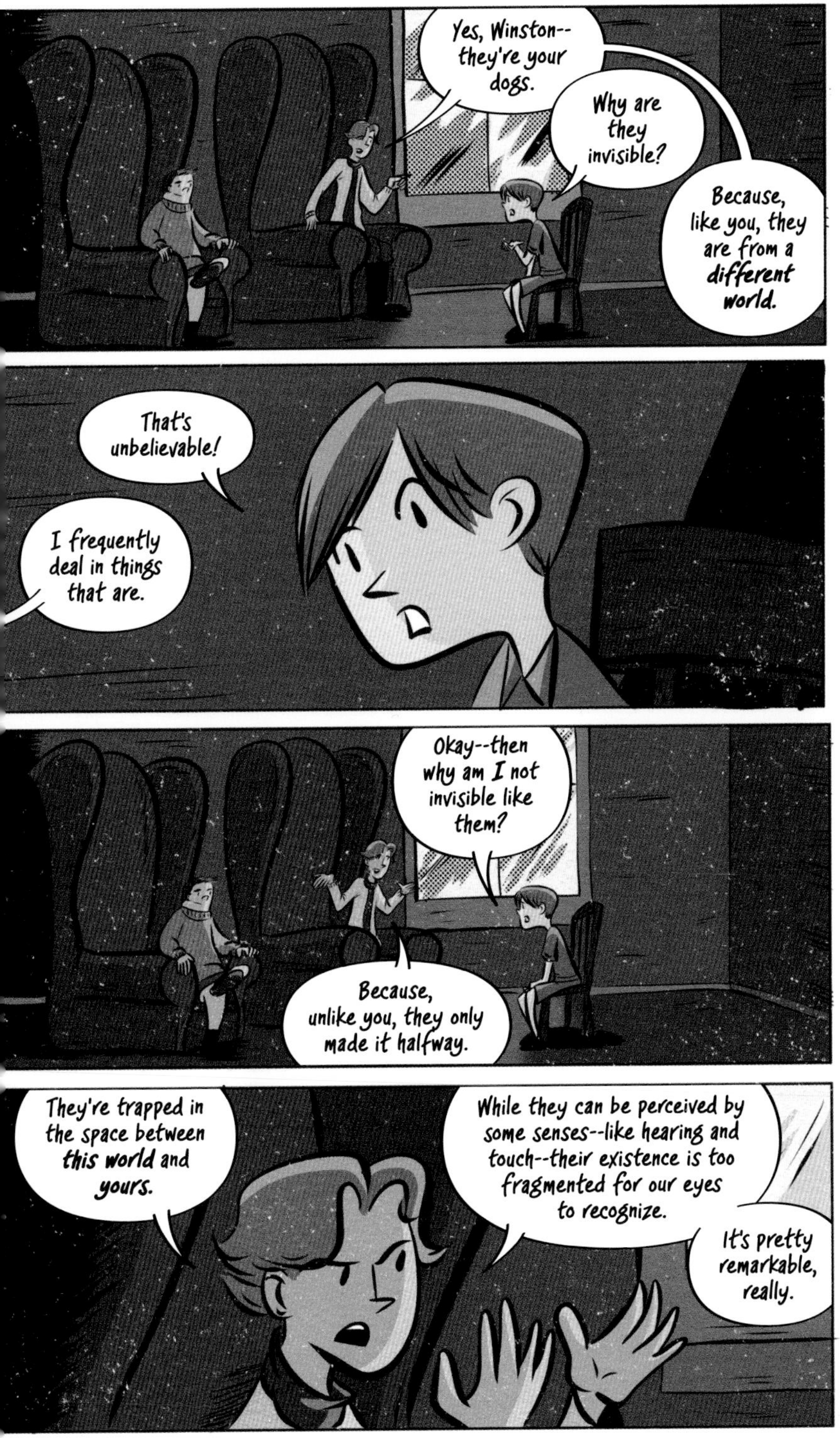
Yes, Winston--they're your dogs.
Why are they invisible?
Because, like you, they are from a *different* world.
That's unbelievable!
I frequently deal in things that are.
Okay--then why am *I* not invisible like them?
Because, unlike you, they only made it halfway.
They're trapped in the space between *this world* and *yours*.
While they can be perceived by some senses--like hearing and touch--their existence is too fragmented for our eyes to recognize.
It's pretty remarkable, really.

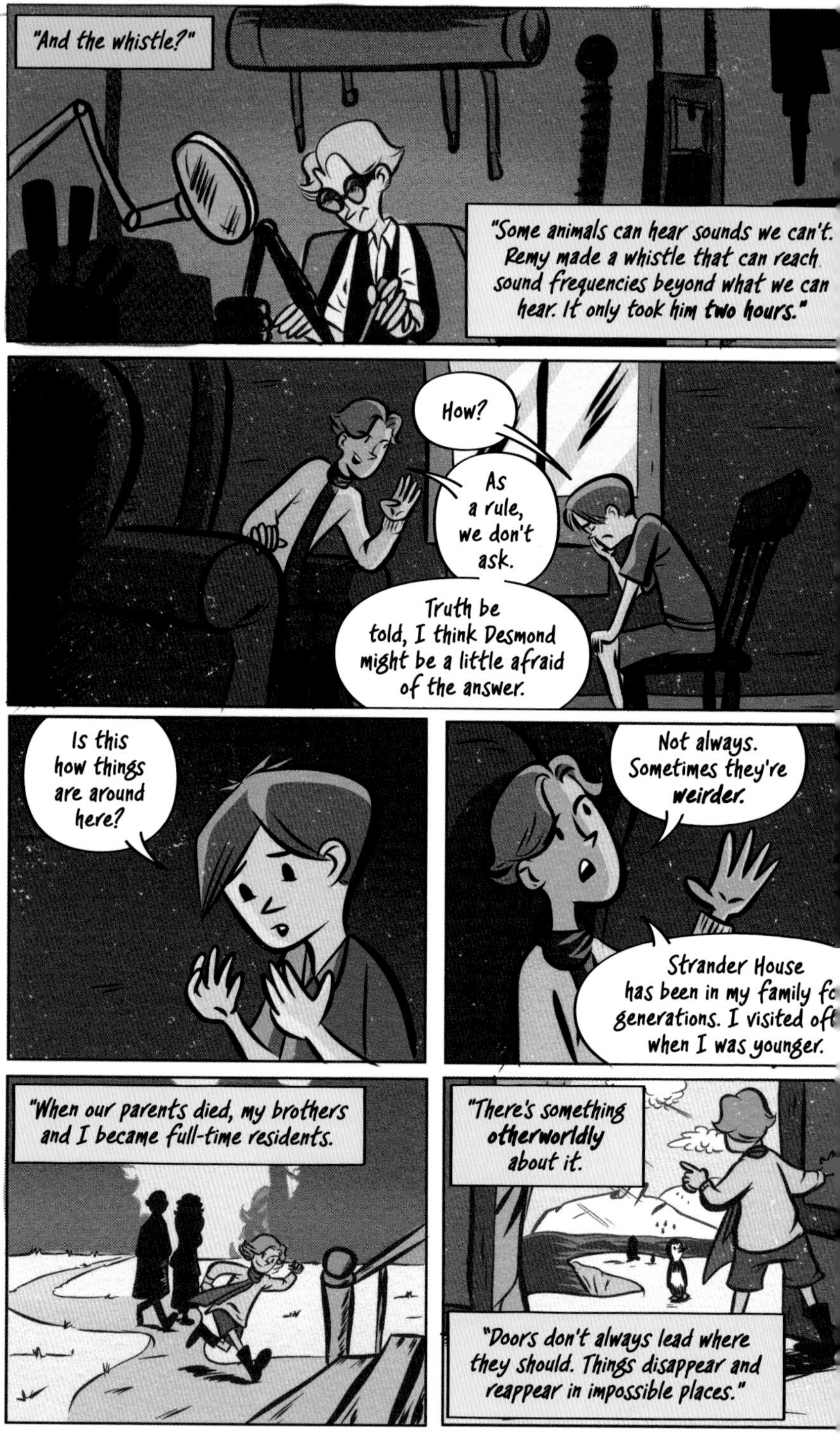

"And the whistle?"
"Some animals can hear sounds we can't. Remy made a whistle that can reach sound frequencies beyond what we can hear. It only took him **two hours.**"
How?
As a rule, we don't ask.
Truth be told, I think Desmond might be a little afraid of the answer.
Is this how things are around here?
Not always. Sometimes they're **weirder.**
Strander House has been in my family fo generations. I visited oft when I was younger.
"When our parents died, my brothers and I became full-time residents.
"There's something **otherworldly** about it.
"Doors don't always lead where they should. Things disappear and reappear in impossible places."

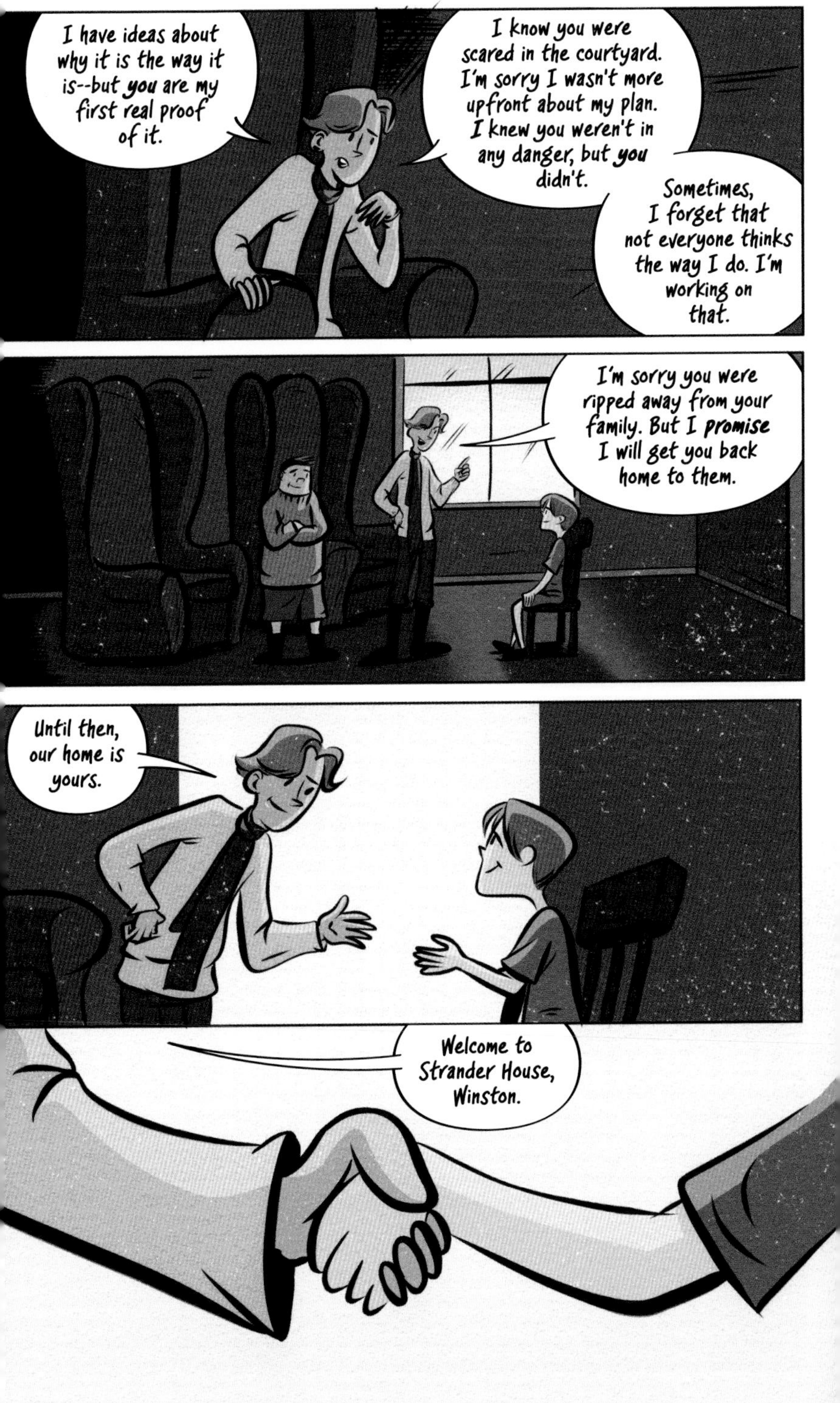
I have ideas about why it is the way it is--but you are my first real proof of it.
I know you were scared in the courtyard. I'm sorry I wasn't more upfront about my plan. I knew you weren't in any danger, but you didn't.
Sometimes, I forget that not everyone thinks the way I do. I'm working on that.
I'm sorry you were ripped away from your family. But I promise I will get you back home to them.
Until then, our home is yours.
Welcome to Strander House, Winston.

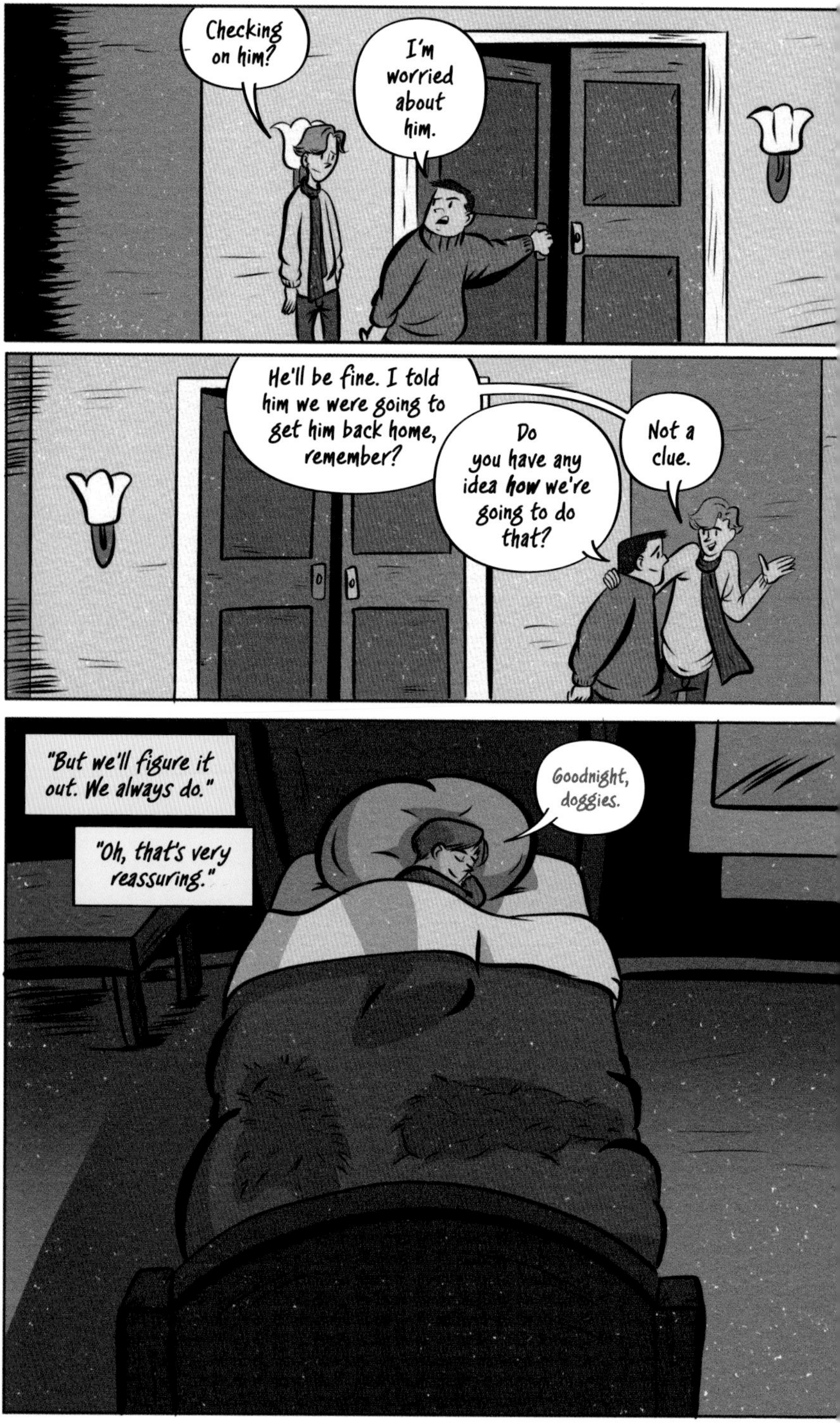

Checking on him?
I'm worried about him.
He'll be fine. I told him we were going to get him back home, remember?
Do you have any idea **how** we're going to do that?
Not a clue.
"But we'll figure it out. We always do."
"Oh, that's very reassuring."
Goodnight, doggies.

CHAPTER

2

THE OCEAN IN THE ATTIC

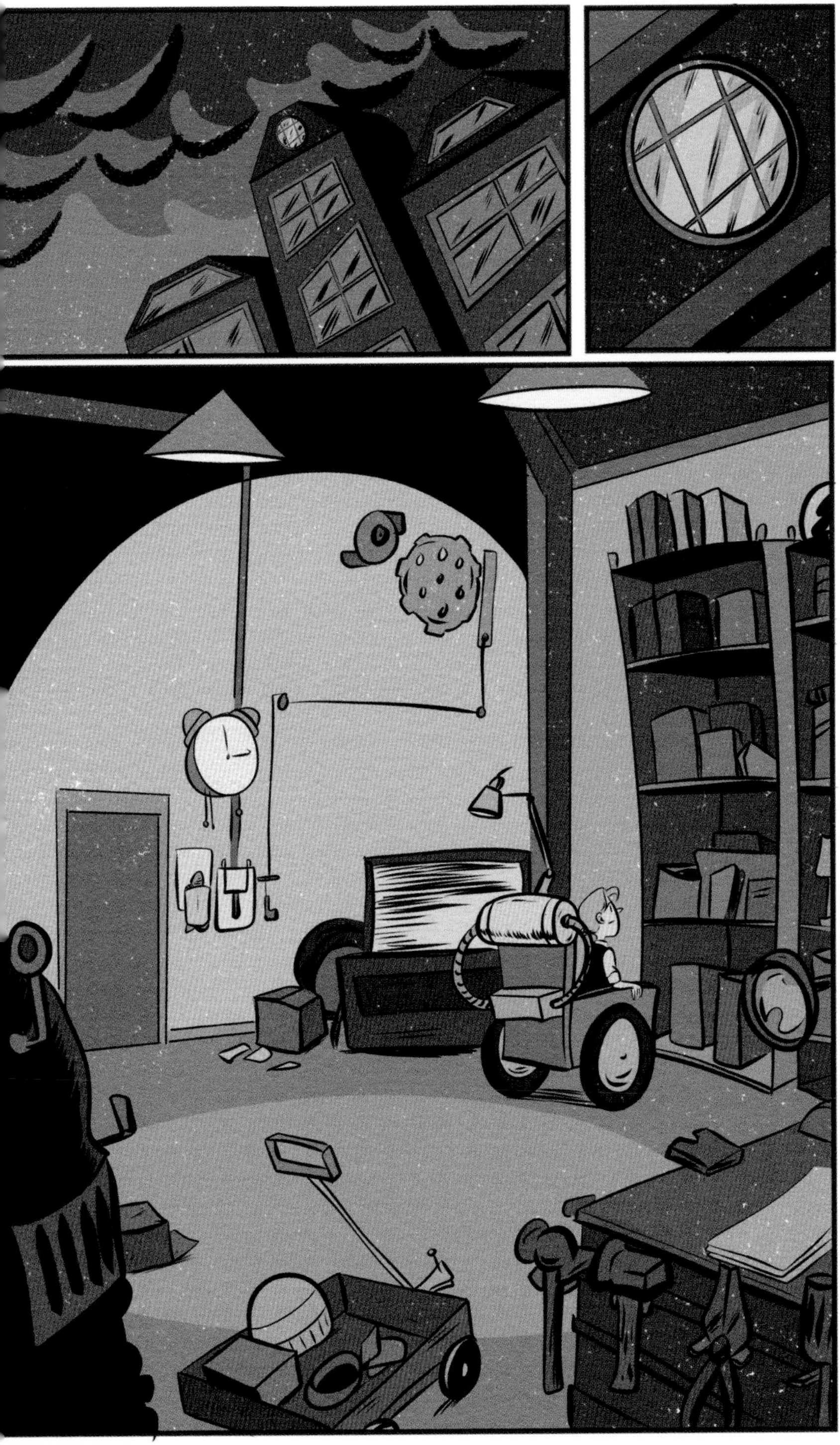

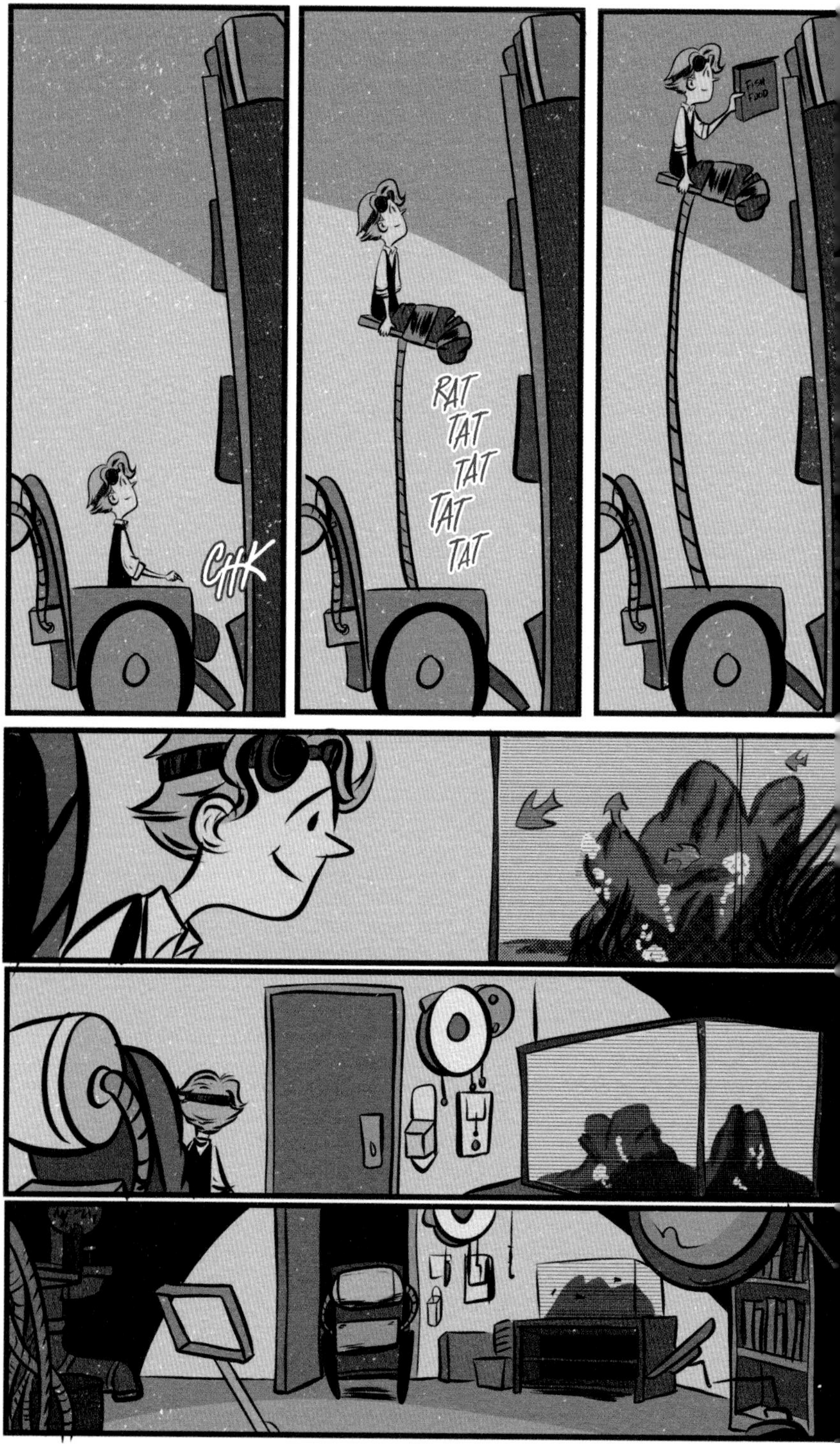
CHK
RAT TAT TAT TAT TAT
FISH FOOD

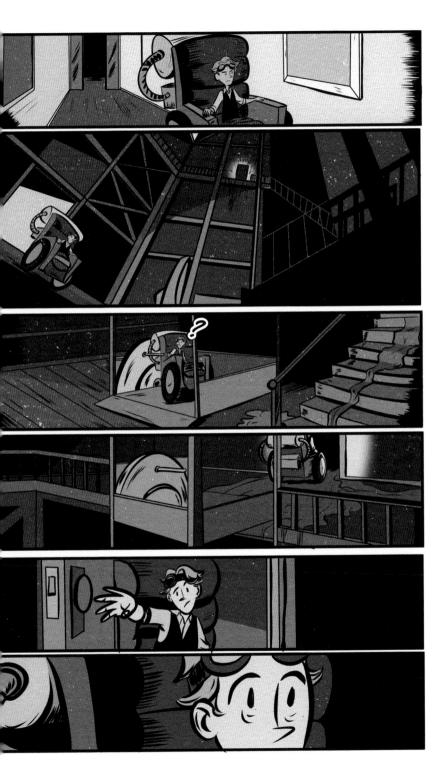

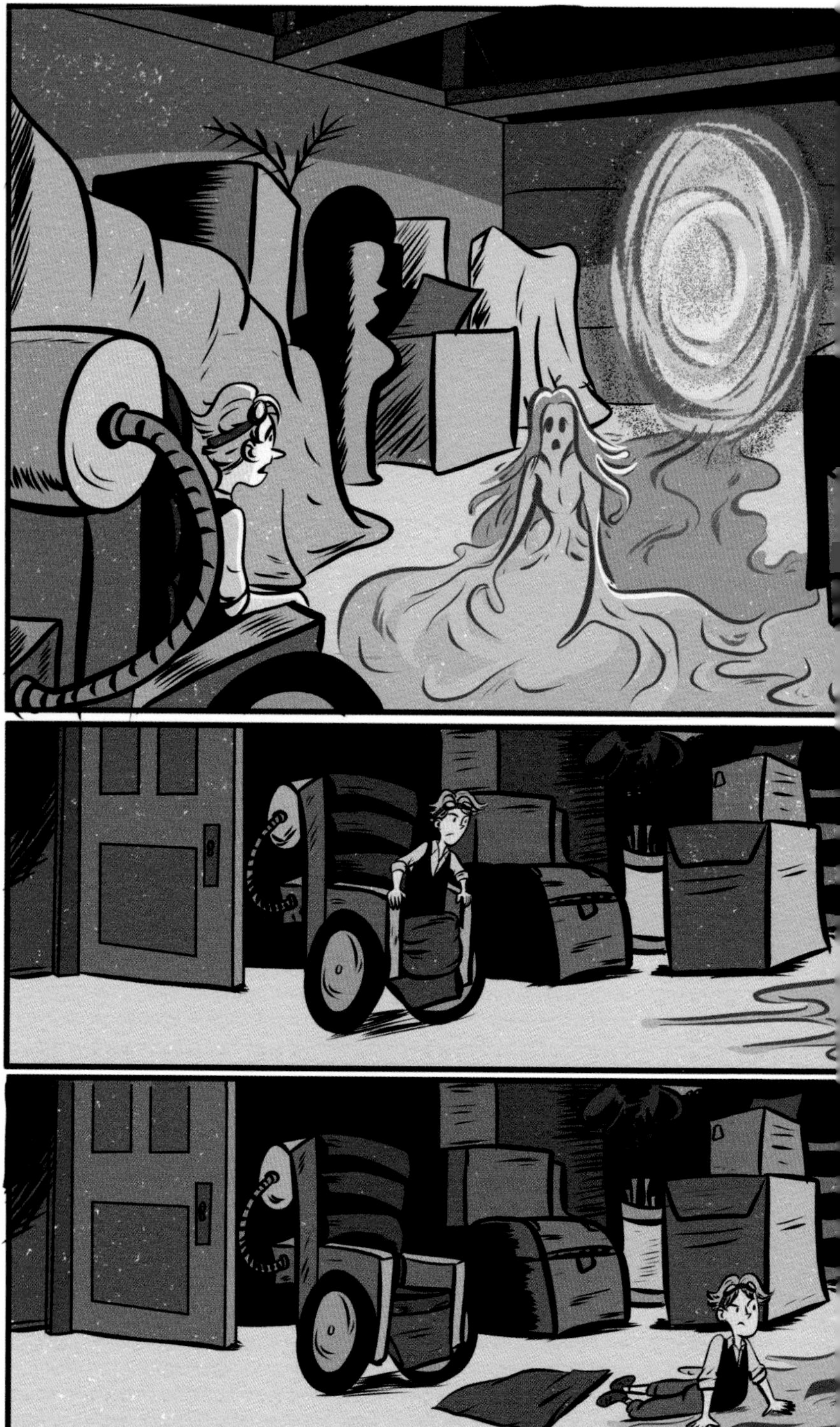

SsSHHHsSSHHH

SpsSSHHH

WOOMP

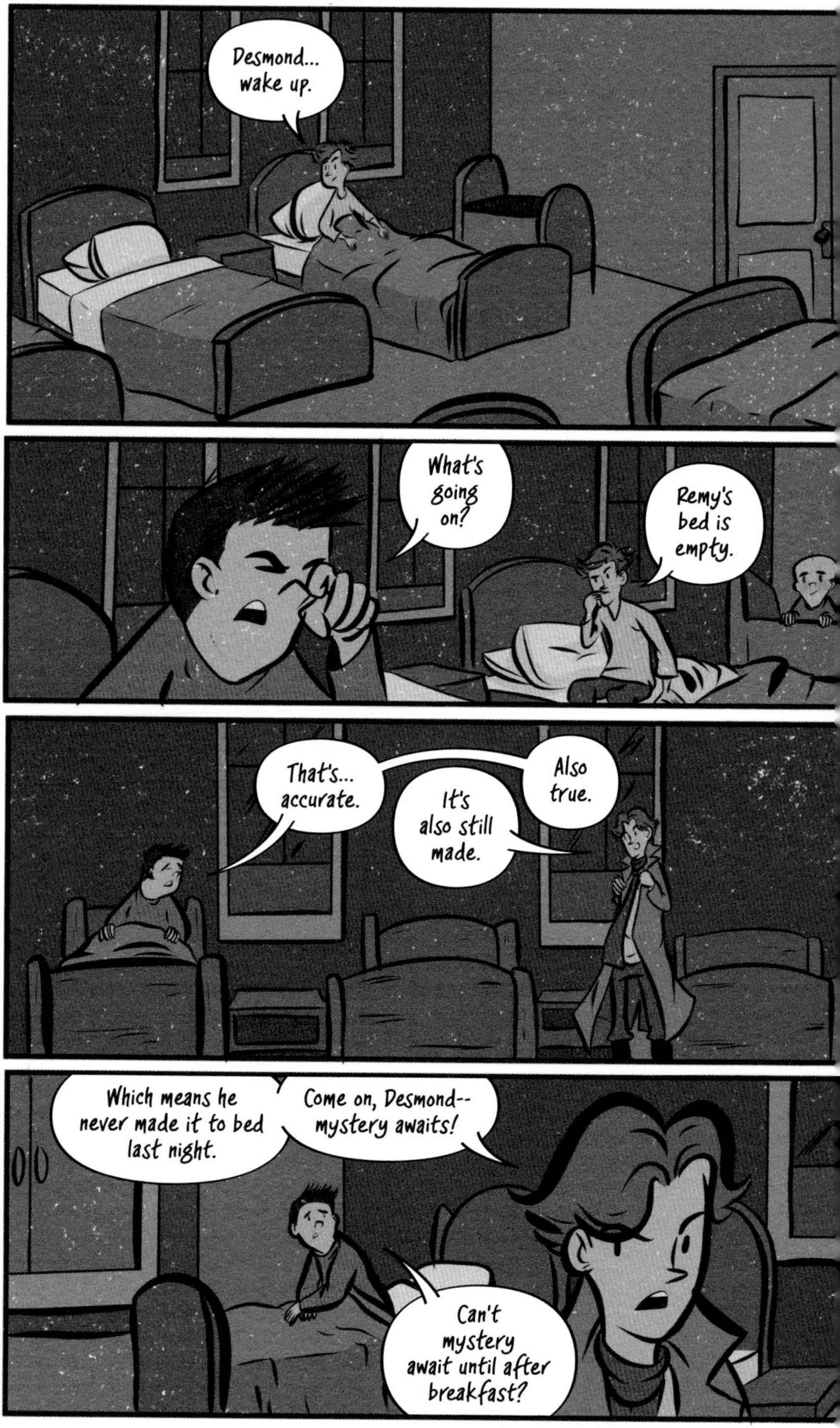
Desmond... wake up.
What's going on?
Remy's bed is empty.
That's... accurate.
Also true.
It's also still made.
Which means he never made it to bed last night.
Come on, Desmond-- mystery awaits!
Can't mystery await until after breakfast?

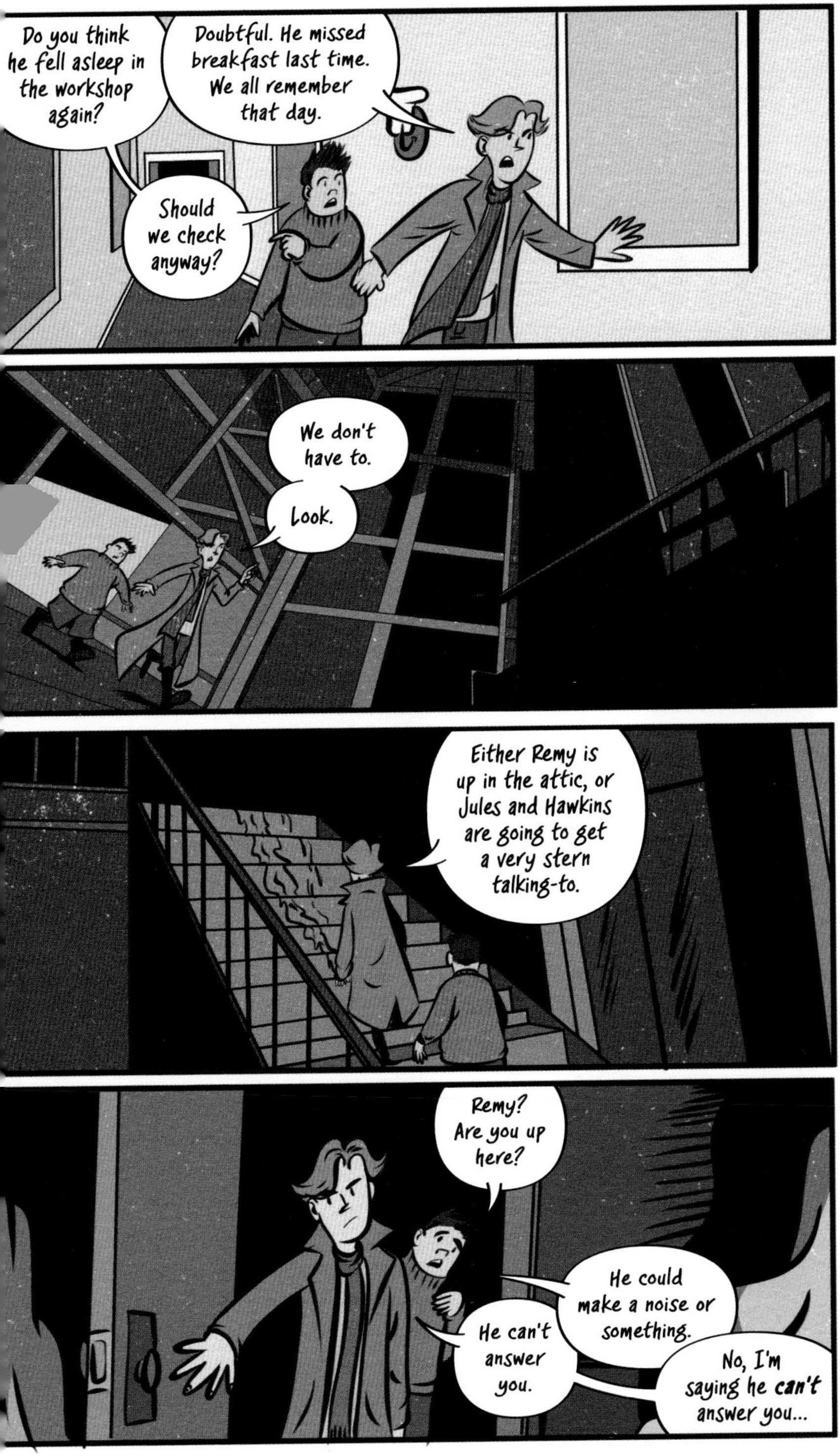
Do you think he fell asleep in the workshop again?
Doubtful. He missed breakfast last time. We all remember that day.
Should we check anyway?
We don't have to.
Look.
Either Remy is up in the attic, or Jules and Hawkins are going to get a very stern talking-to.
Remy? Are you up here?
He could make a noise or something.
He can't answer you.
No, I'm saying he **can't** answer you...

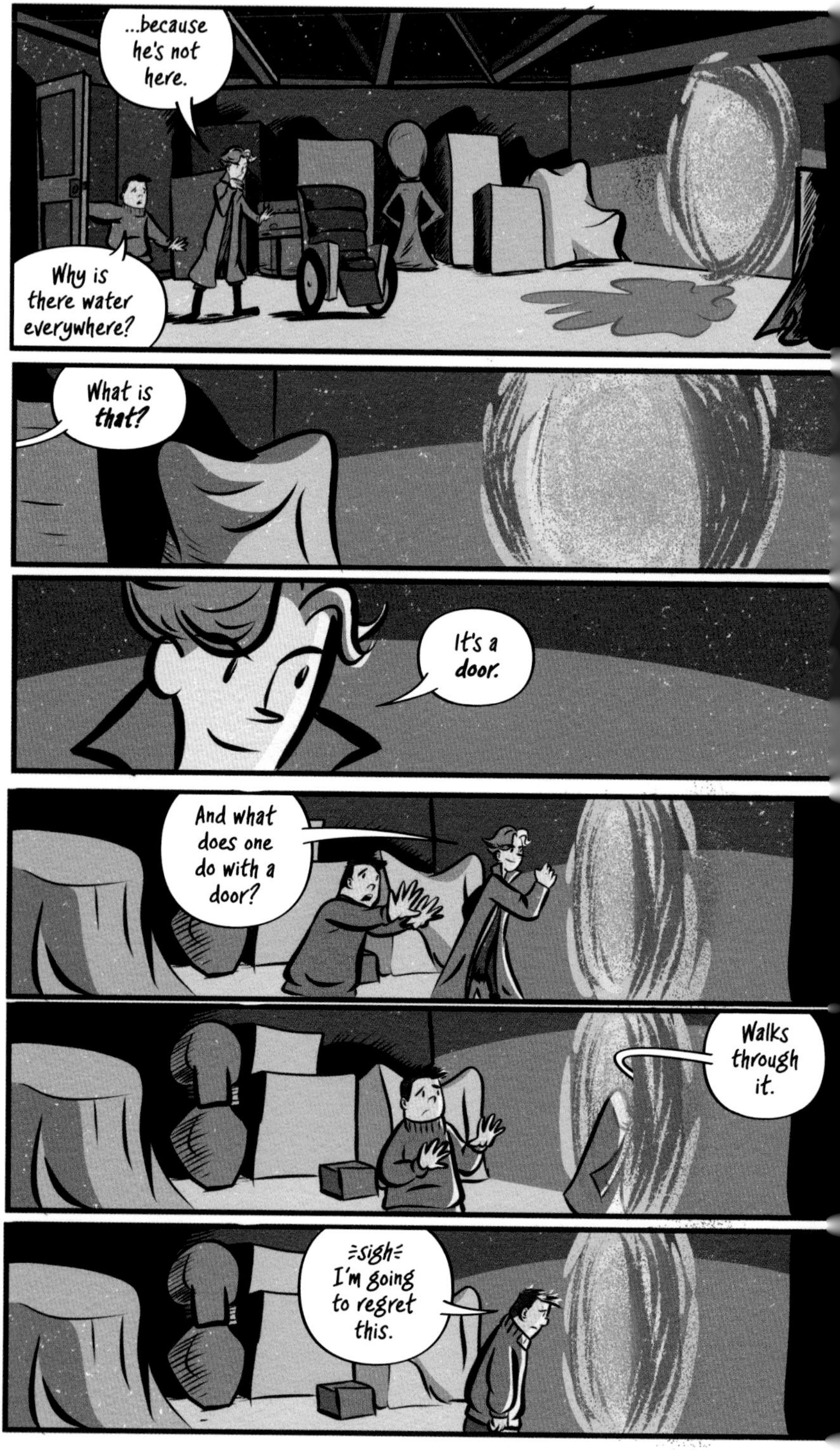
...because he's not here.
Why is there water everywhere?
What is *that?*
It's a door.
And what does one do with a door?
Walks through it.
=sigh= I'm going to regret this.

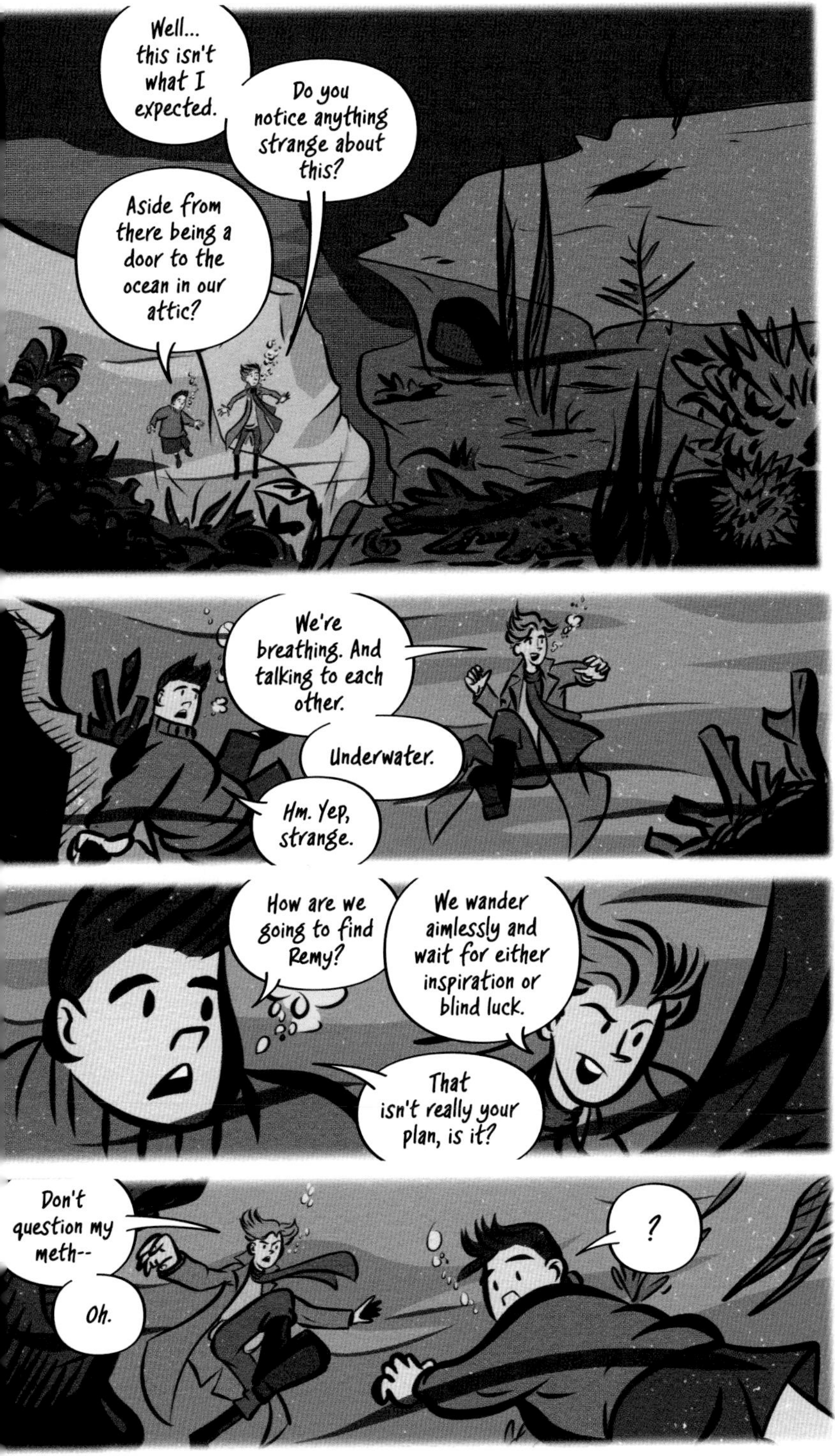

Well... this isn't what I expected.
Do you notice anything strange about this?
Aside from there being a door to the ocean in our attic?
We're breathing. And talking to each other.
Underwater.
Hm. Yep, strange.
How are we going to find Remy?
We wander aimlessly and wait for either inspiration or blind luck.
That isn't really your plan, is it?
Don't question my meth--
Oh.
?

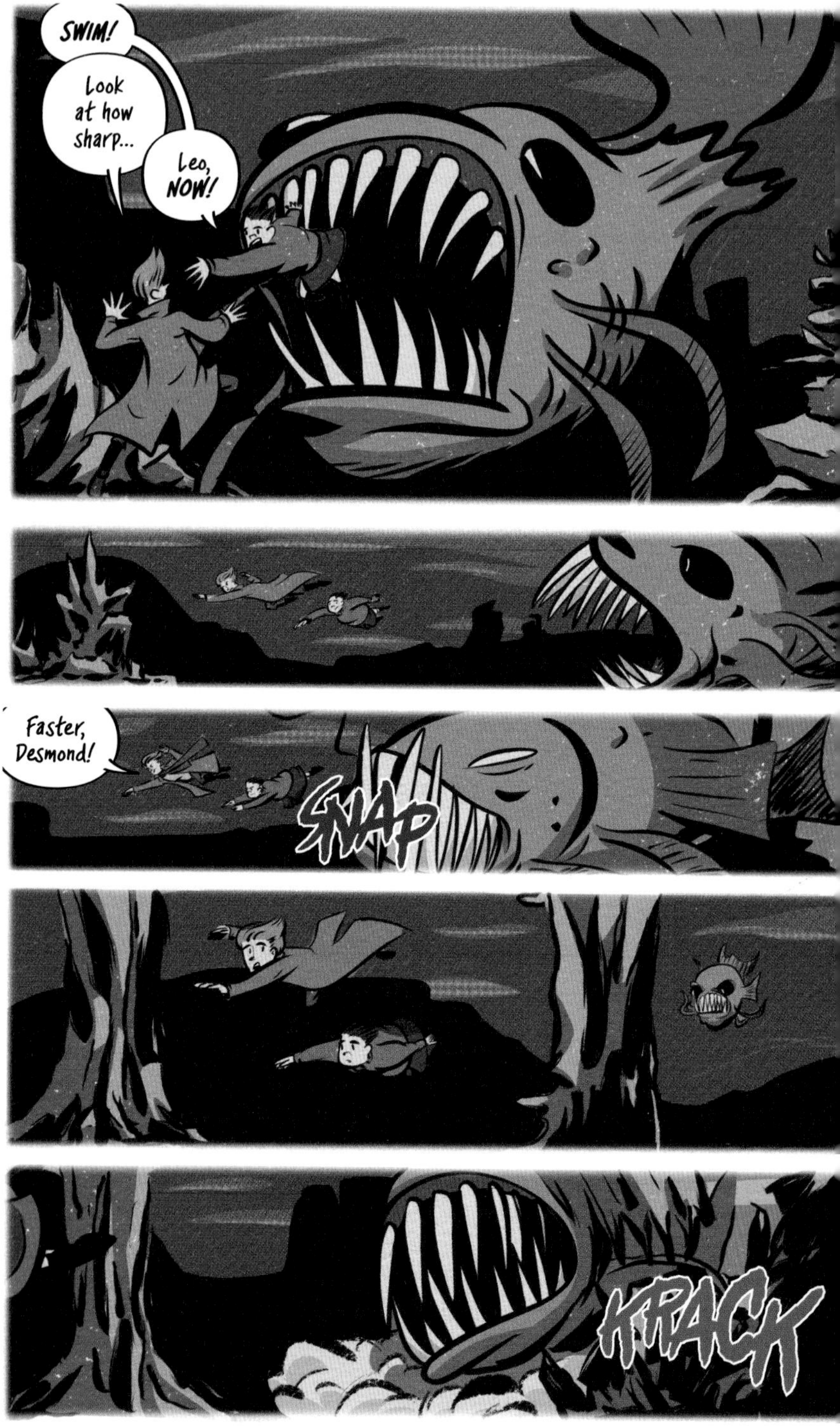
SWIM!
Look at how sharp...
Leo, NOW!
Faster, Desmond!
SNAP
KRACK

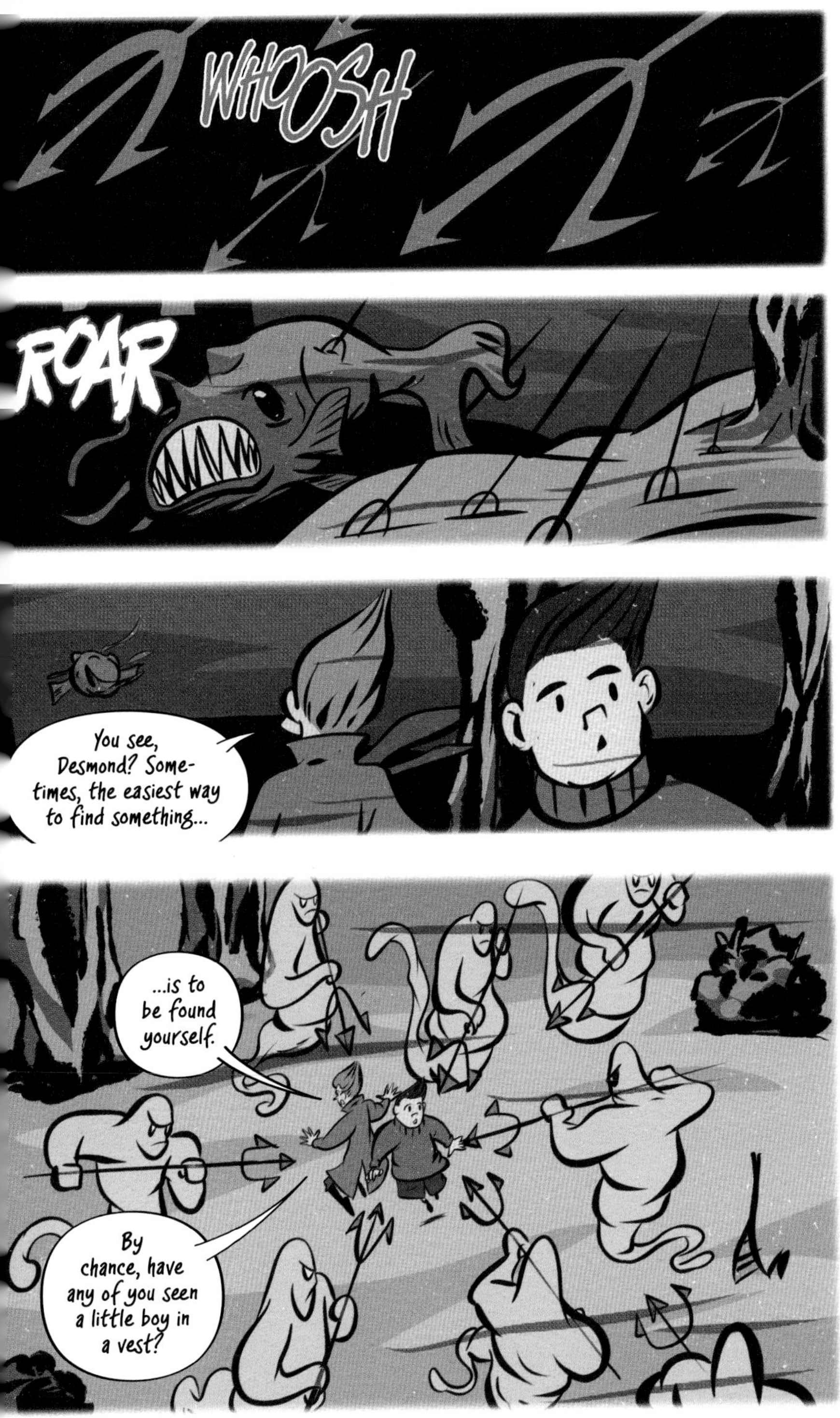
WHOOSH
ROAR
You see, Desmond? Sometimes, the easiest way to find something...
...is to be found yourself.
By chance, have any of you seen a little boy in a vest?

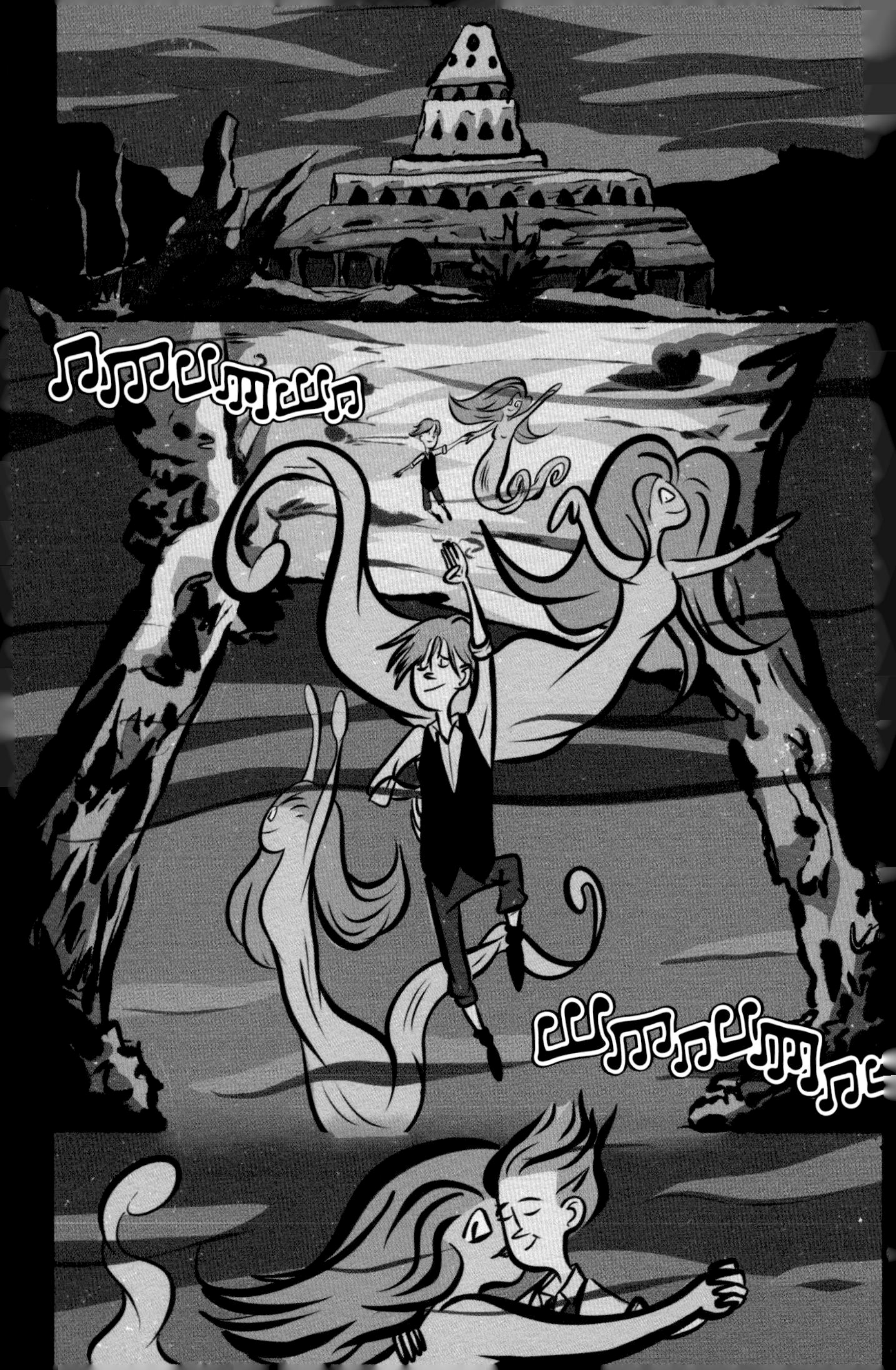

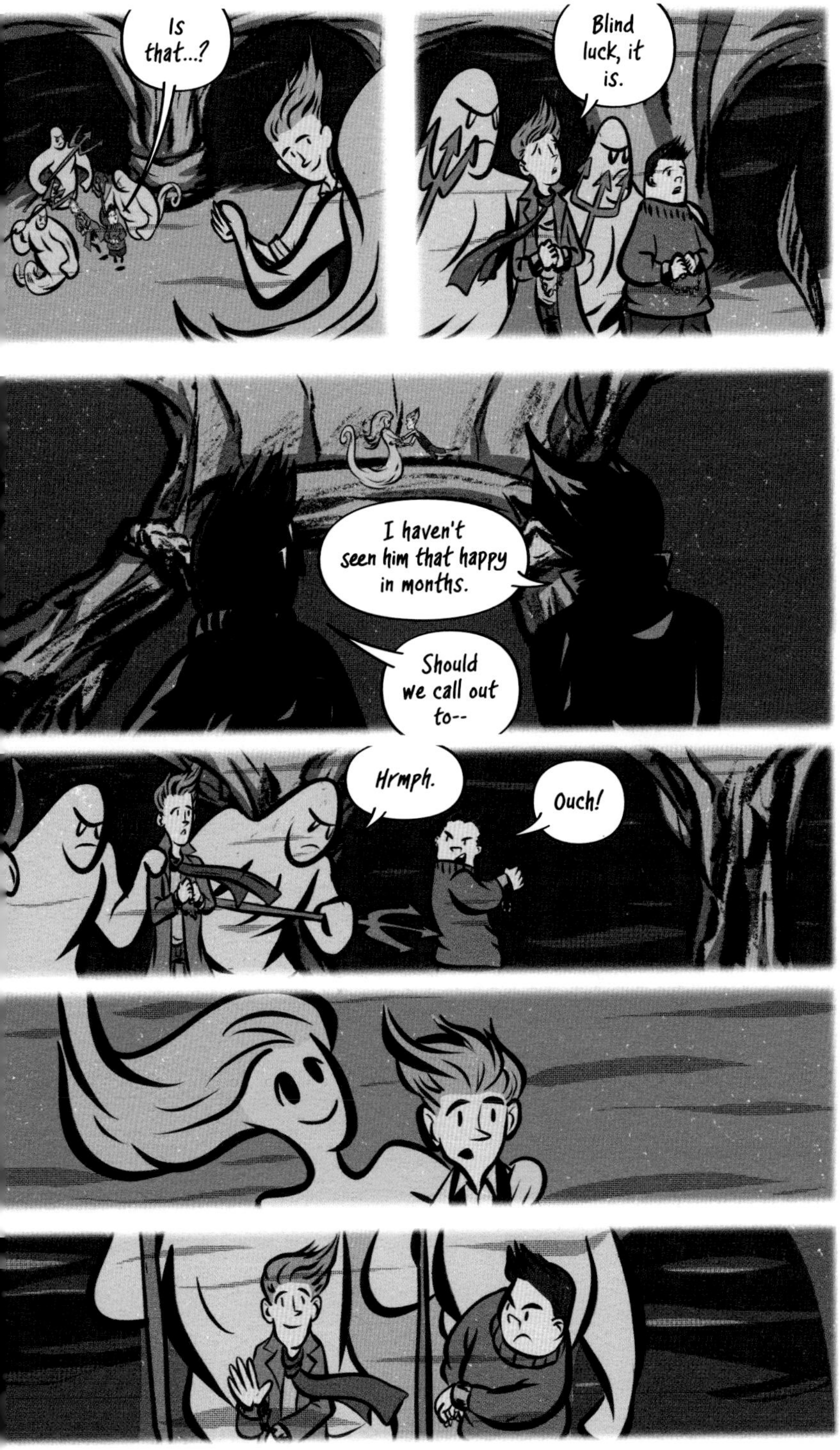

Is that...?
Blind luck, it is.
I haven't seen him that happy in months.
Should we call out to--
Hrmph.
Ouch!

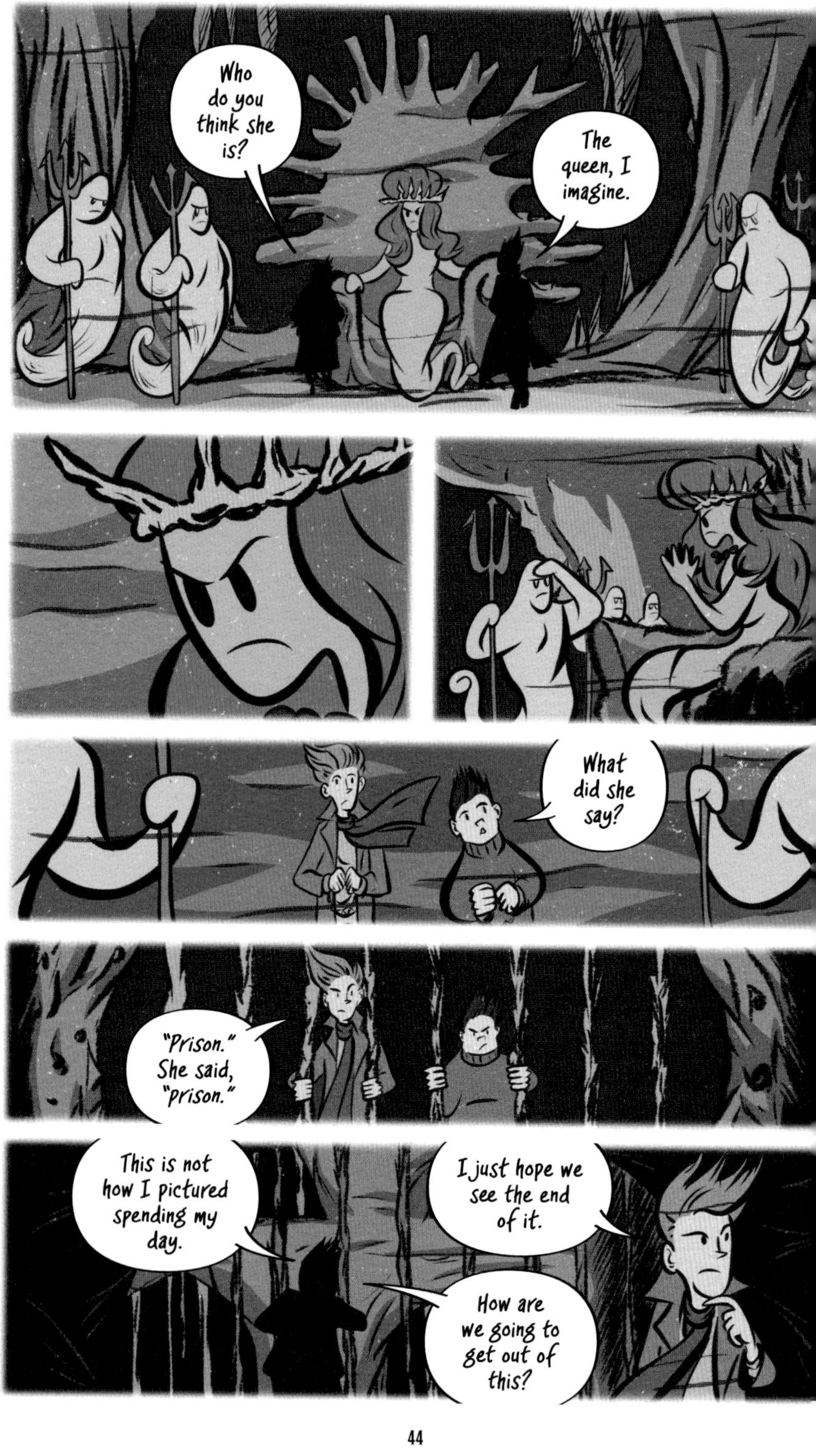

Who do you think she is?
The queen, I imagine.
What did she say?
"Prison." She said, "prison."
This is not how I pictured spending my day.
I just hope we see the end of it.
How are we going to get out of this?

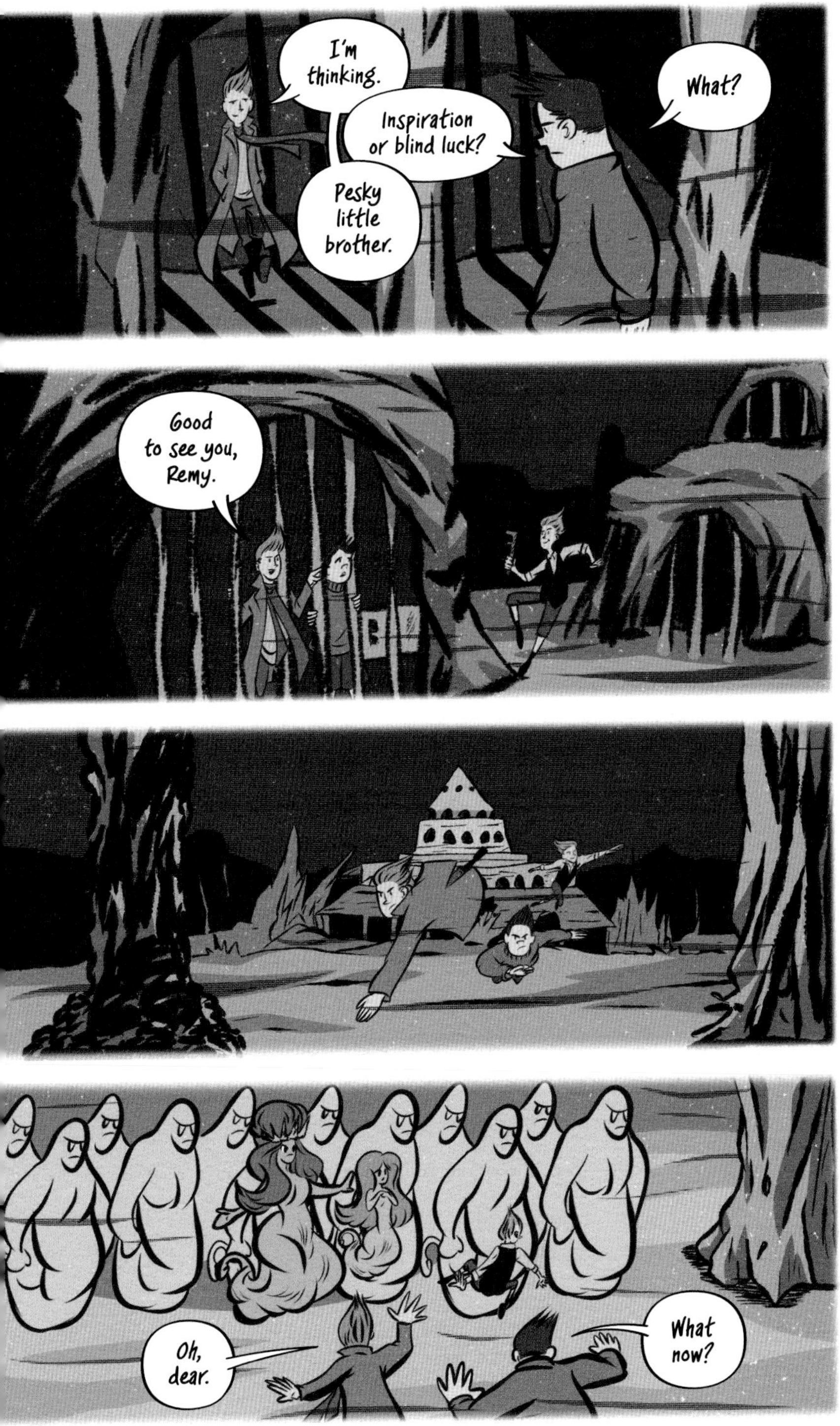
I'm thinking.
Inspiration or blind luck?
Pesky little brother.
What?
Good to see you, Remy.
Oh, dear.
What now?

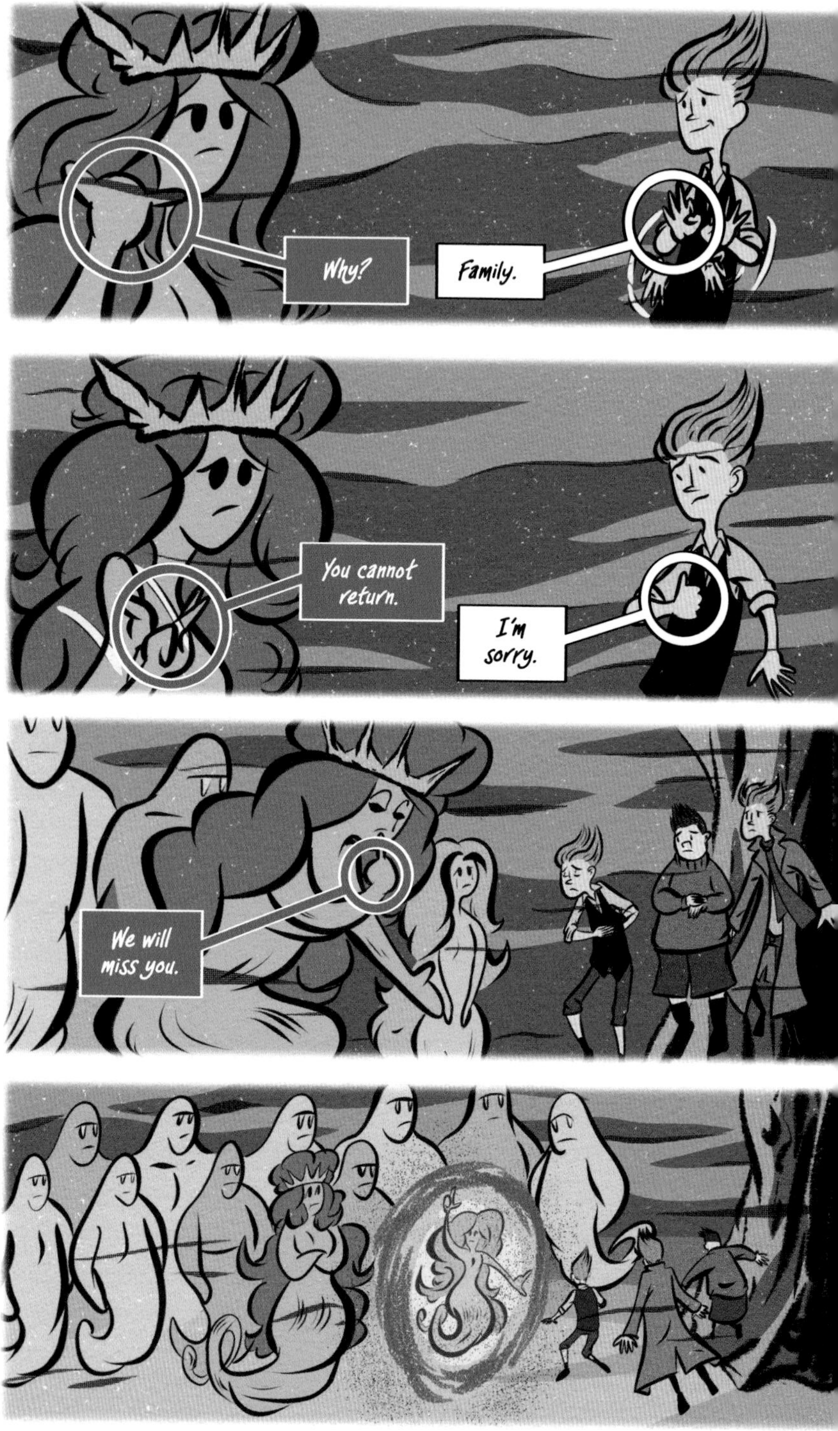
Why?
Family.
You cannot return.
I'm sorry.
We will miss you.

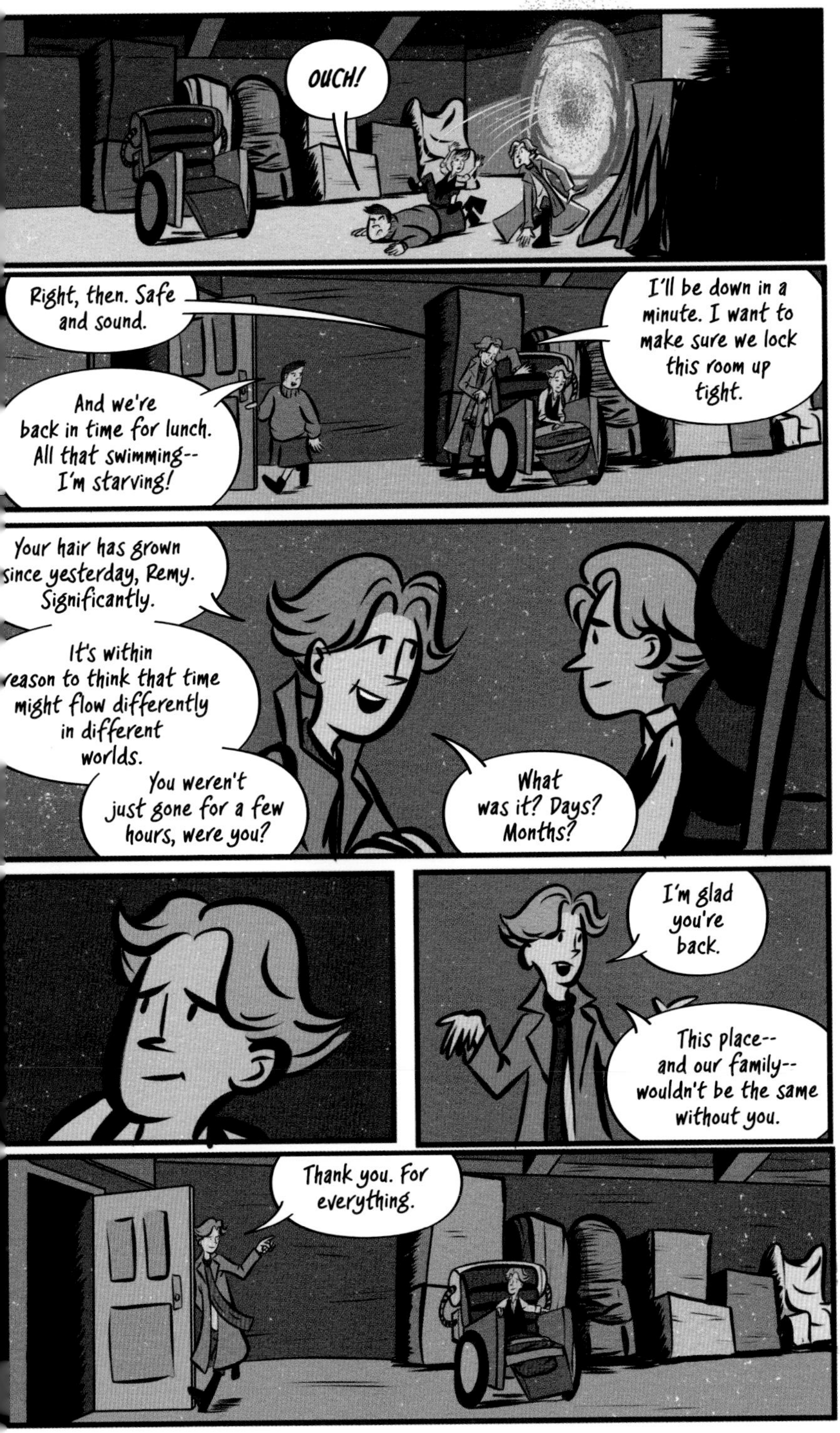
OUCH!
Right, then. Safe and sound.
I'll be down in a minute. I want to make sure we lock this room up tight.
And we're back in time for lunch. All that swimming-- I'm starving!
Your hair has grown since yesterday, Remy. Significantly.
It's within reason to think that time might flow differently in different worlds.
You weren't just gone for a few hours, were you?
What was it? Days? Months?
I'm glad you're back.
This place-- and our family-- wouldn't be the same without you.
Thank you. For everything.

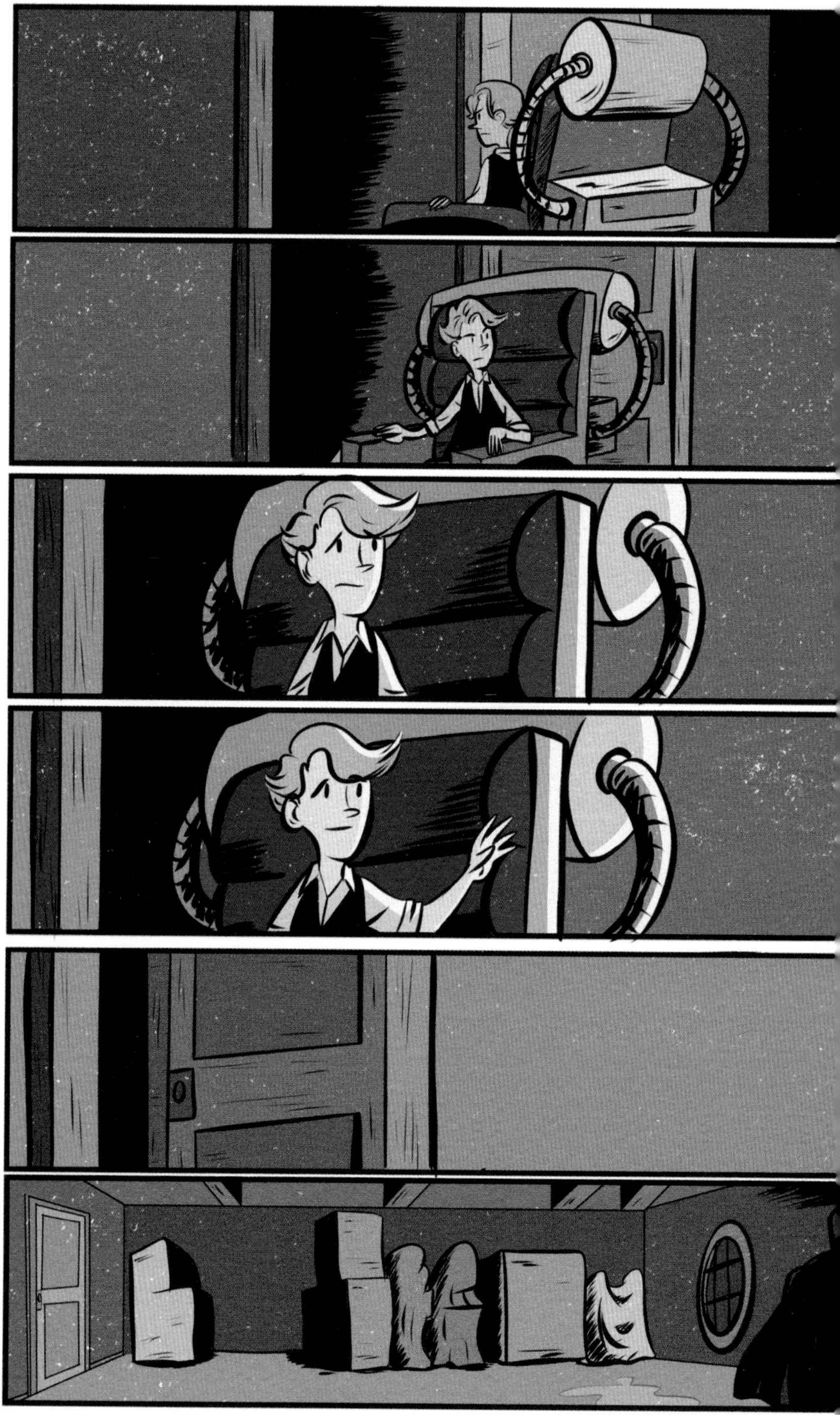

CHAPTER
3

HE OGRE WHO WAS TWO SIZES TOO LARGE

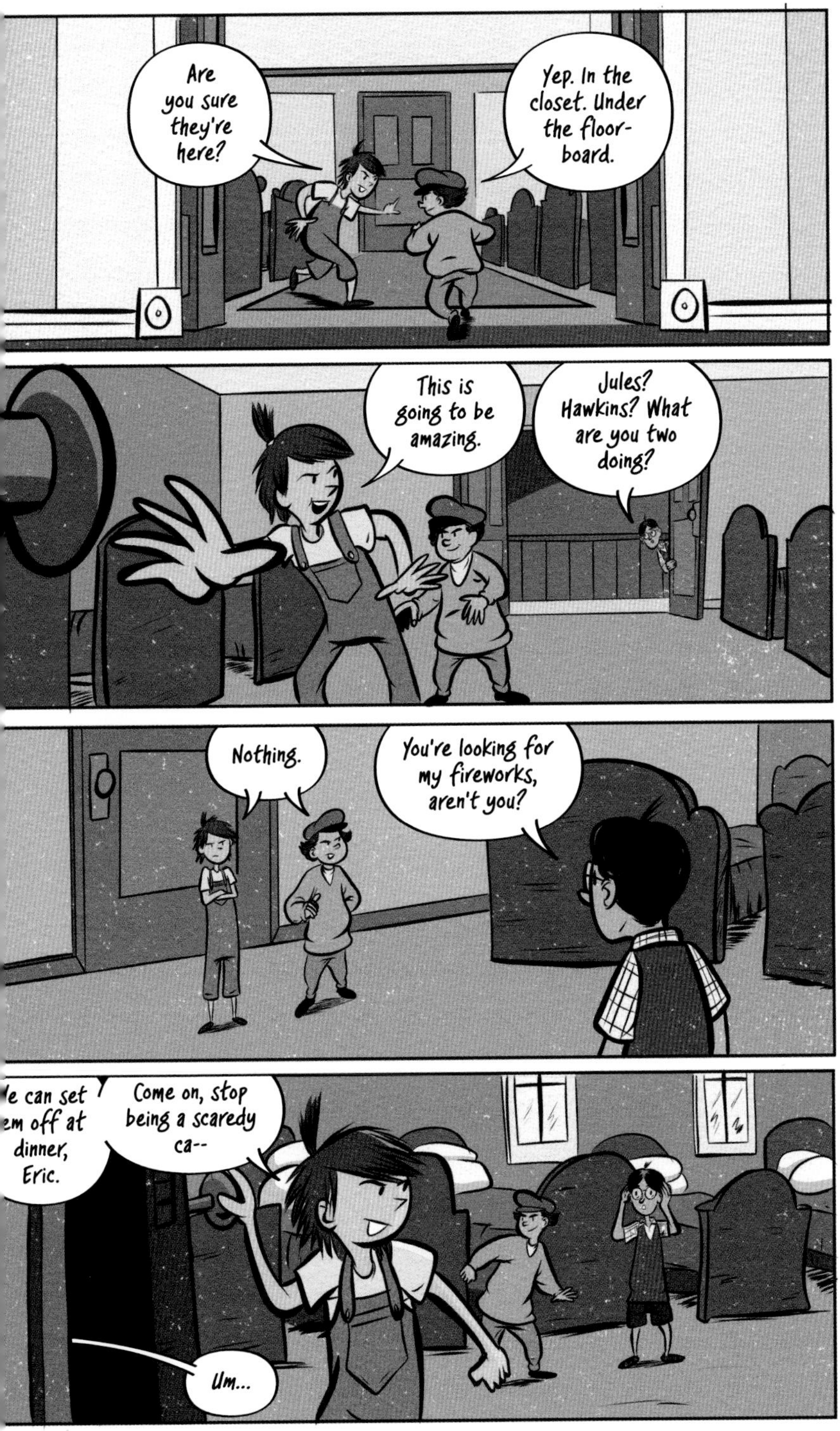
Are you sure they're here?
Yep. In the closet. Under the floor-board.
This is going to be amazing.
Jules? Hawkins? What are you two doing?
Nothing.
You're looking for my fireworks, aren't you?
e can set em off at dinner, Eric.
Come on, stop being a scaredy ca--
Um...

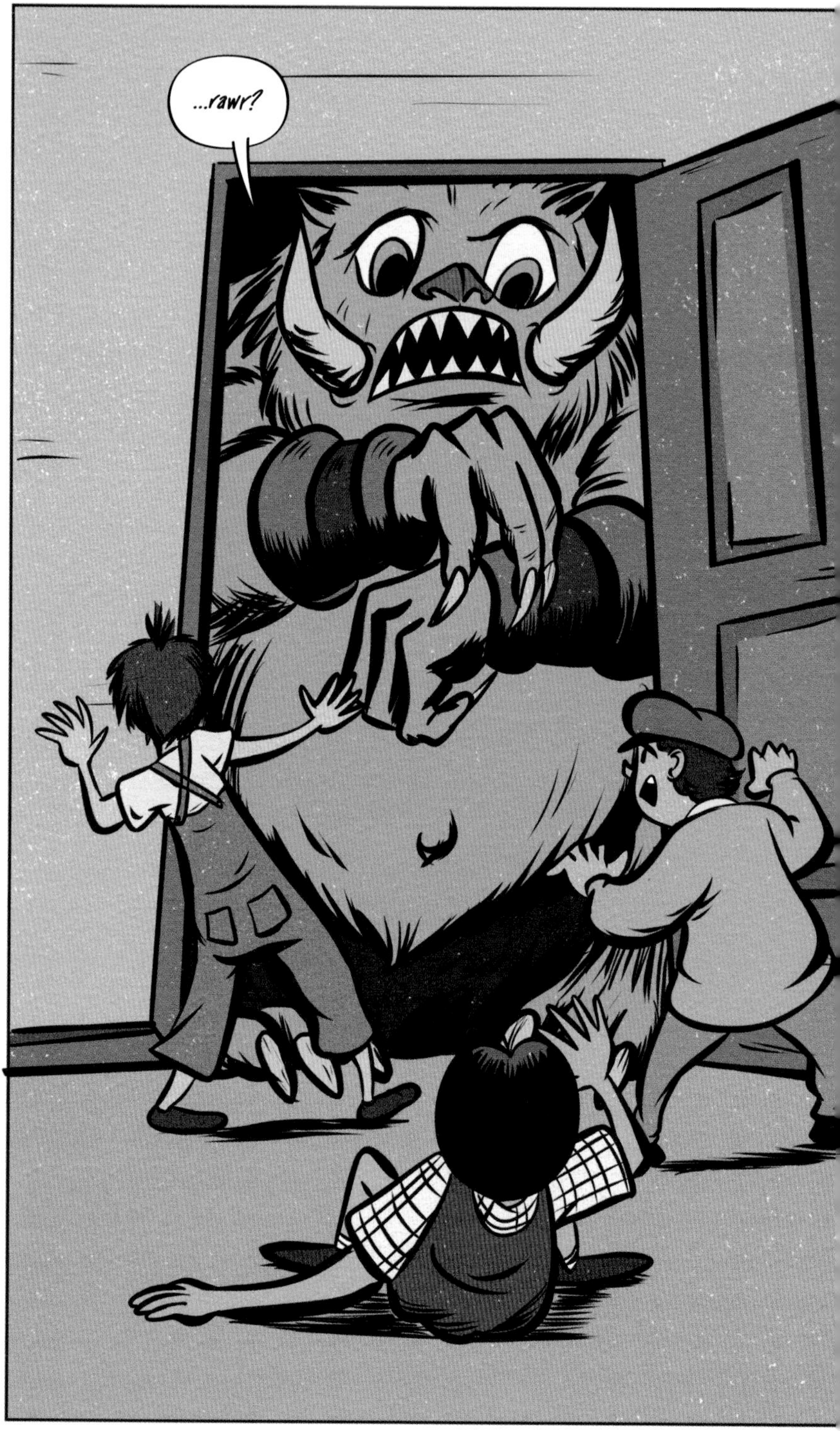
...rawr?

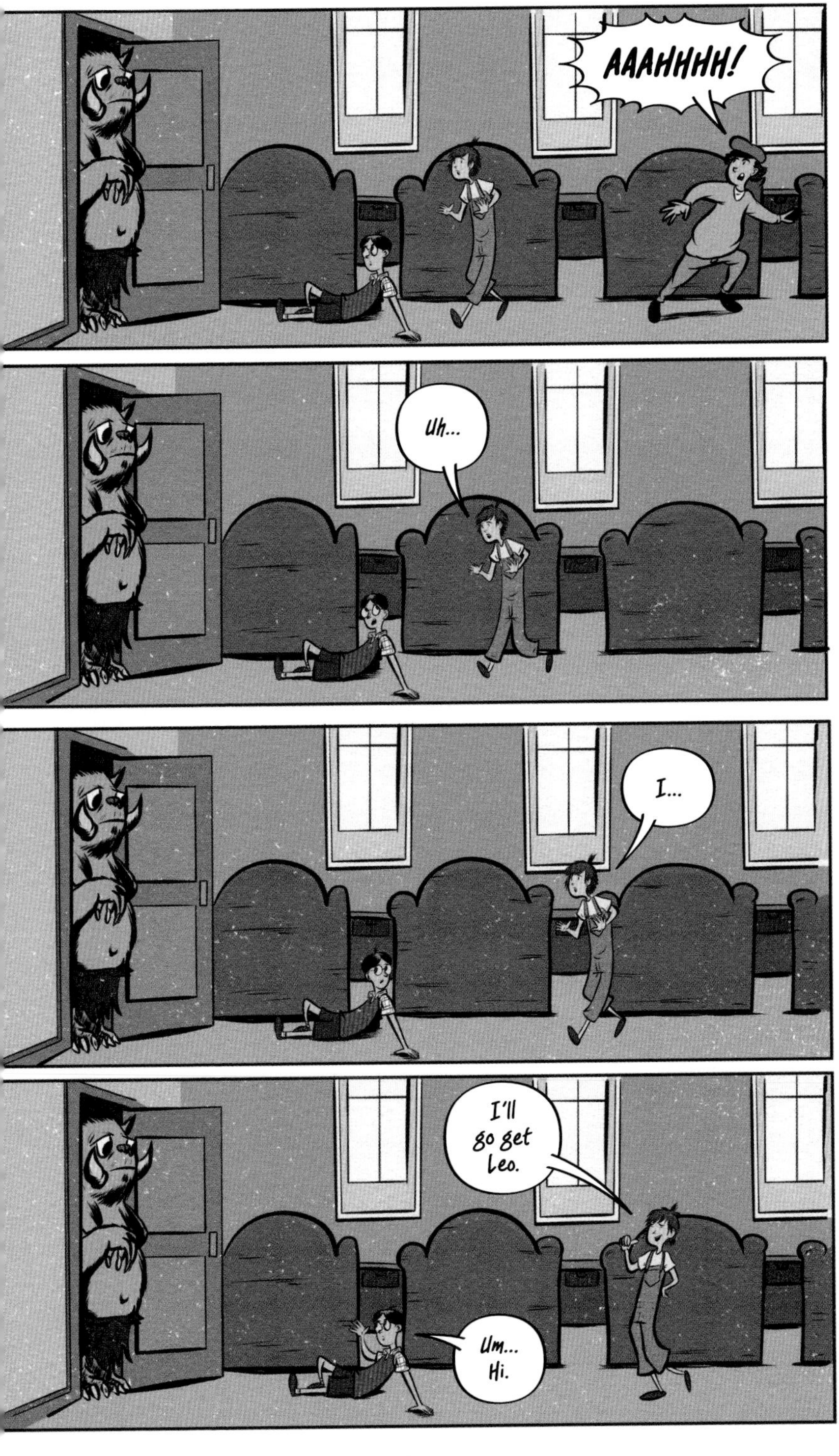
AAAHHHH!
Uh...
I...
I'll go get Leo.
Um... Hi.

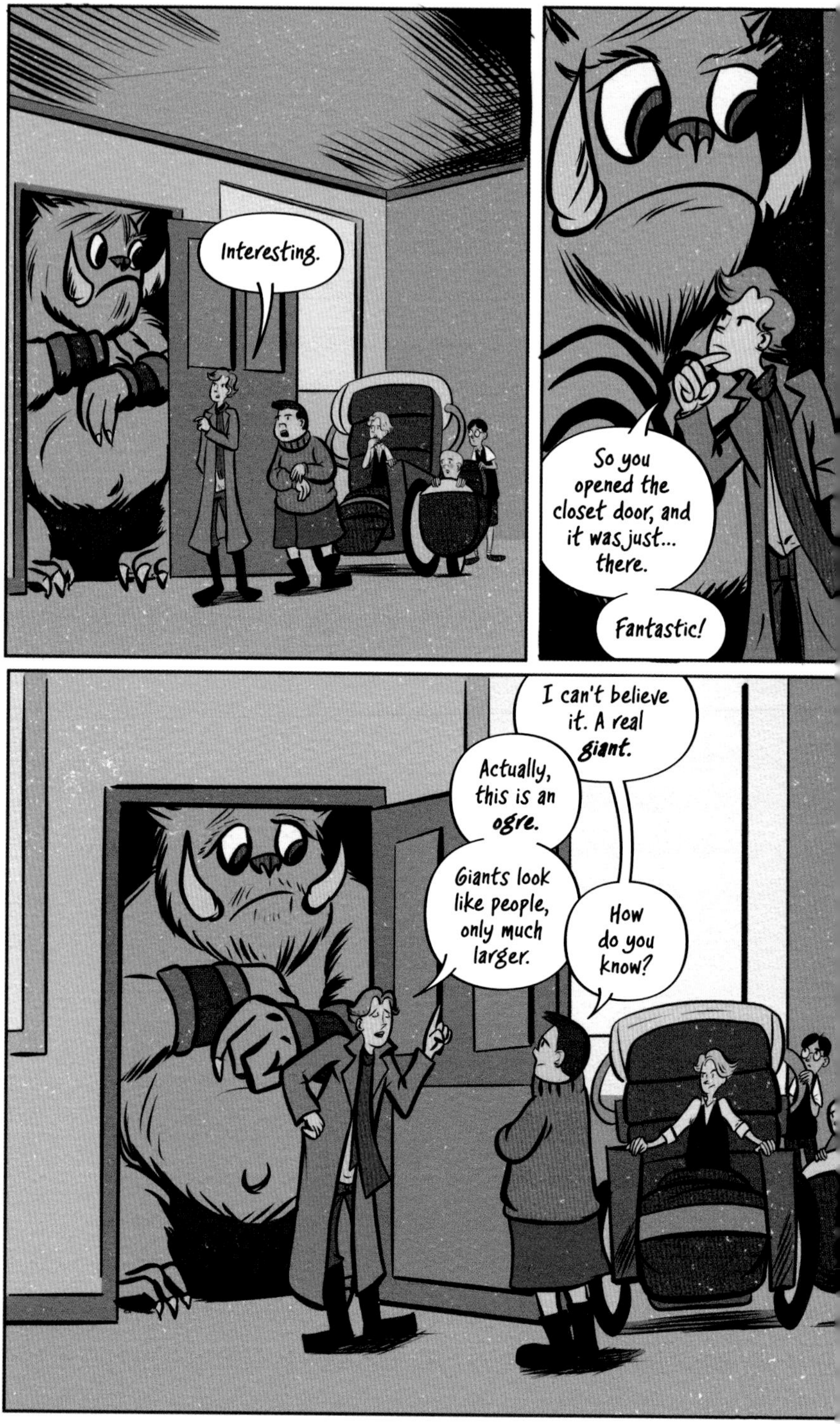

Interesting.
So you opened the closet door, and it was just... there.
Fantastic!
I can't believe it. A real giant.
Actually, this is an ogre.
Giants look like people, only much larger.
How do you know?

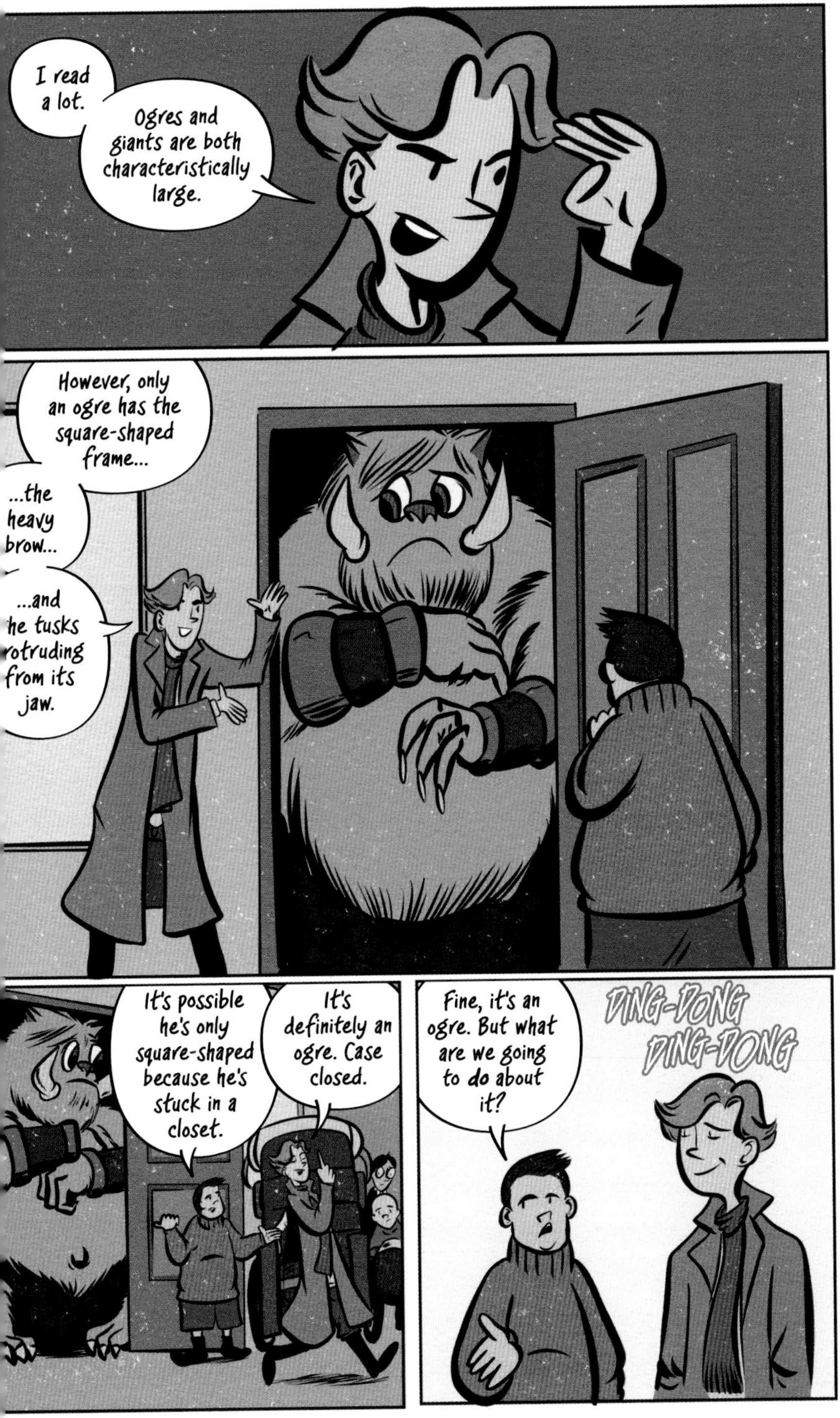

I read a lot.
Ogres and giants are both characteristically large.
However, only an ogre has the square-shaped frame...
...the heavy brow...
...and he tusks rotruding from its jaw.
It's possible he's only square-shaped because he's stuck in a closet.
It's definitely an ogre. Case closed.
Fine, it's an ogre. But what are we going to do about it?
DING-DONG DING-DONG

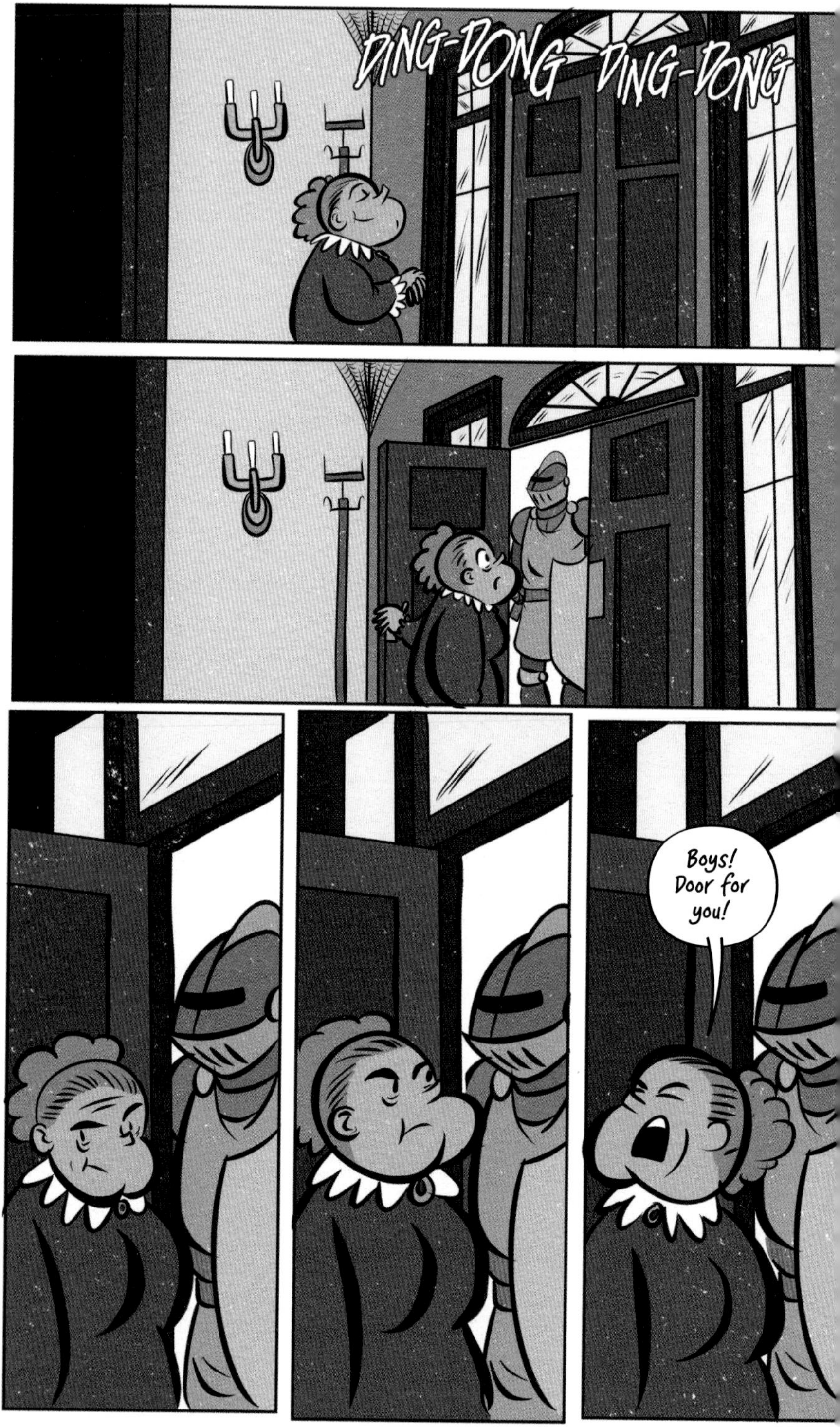
DING-DONG DING-DONG
Boys! Door for you!

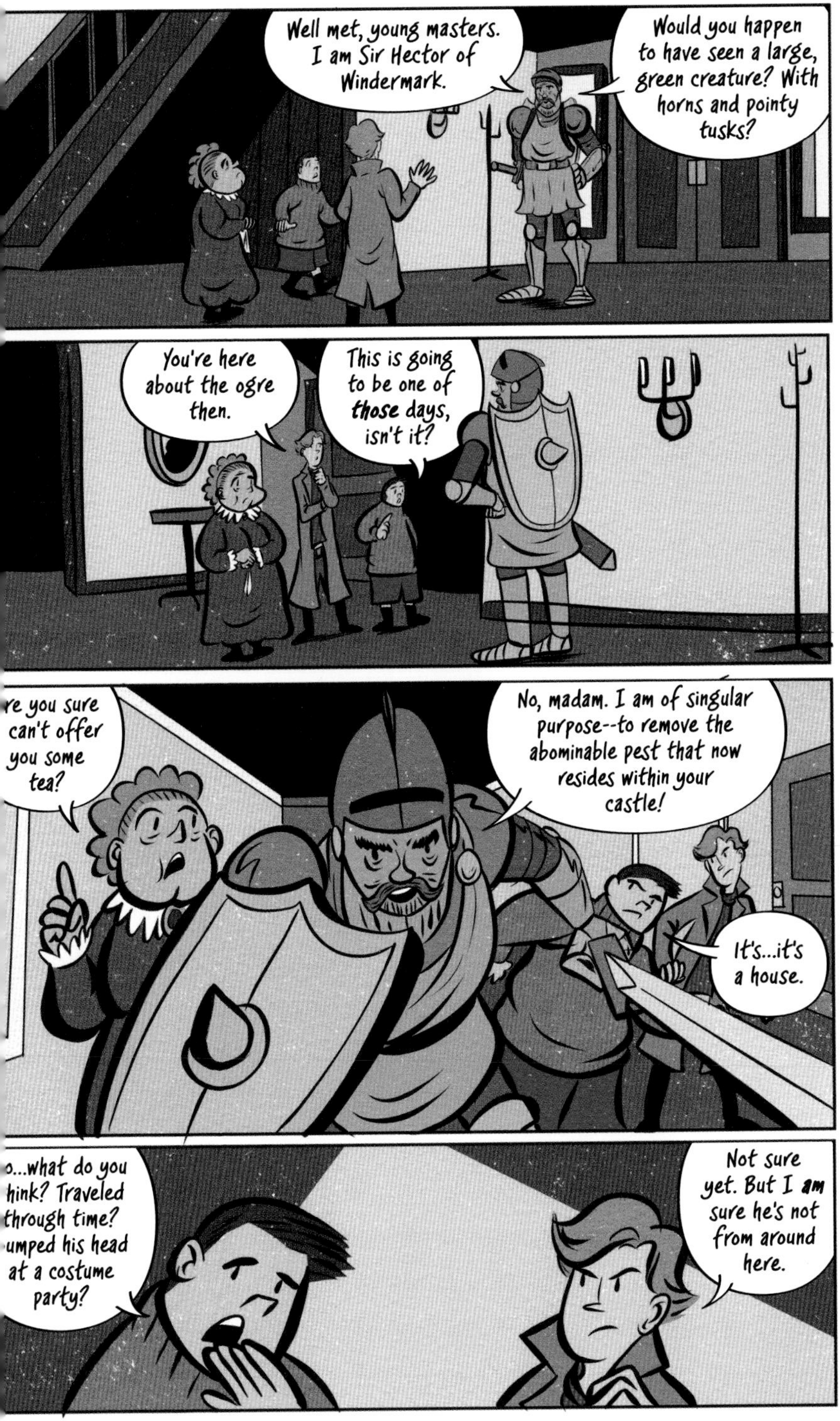
Well met, young masters. I am Sir Hector of Windermark.
Would you happen to have seen a large, green creature? With horns and pointy tusks?
You're here about the ogre then.
This is going to be one of *those* days, isn't it?
re you sure can't offer you some tea?
No, madam. I am of singular purpose--to remove the abominable pest that now resides within your castle!
It's...it's a house.
o...what do you hink? Traveled through time? umped his head at a costume party?
Not sure yet. But I **am** sure he's not from around here.

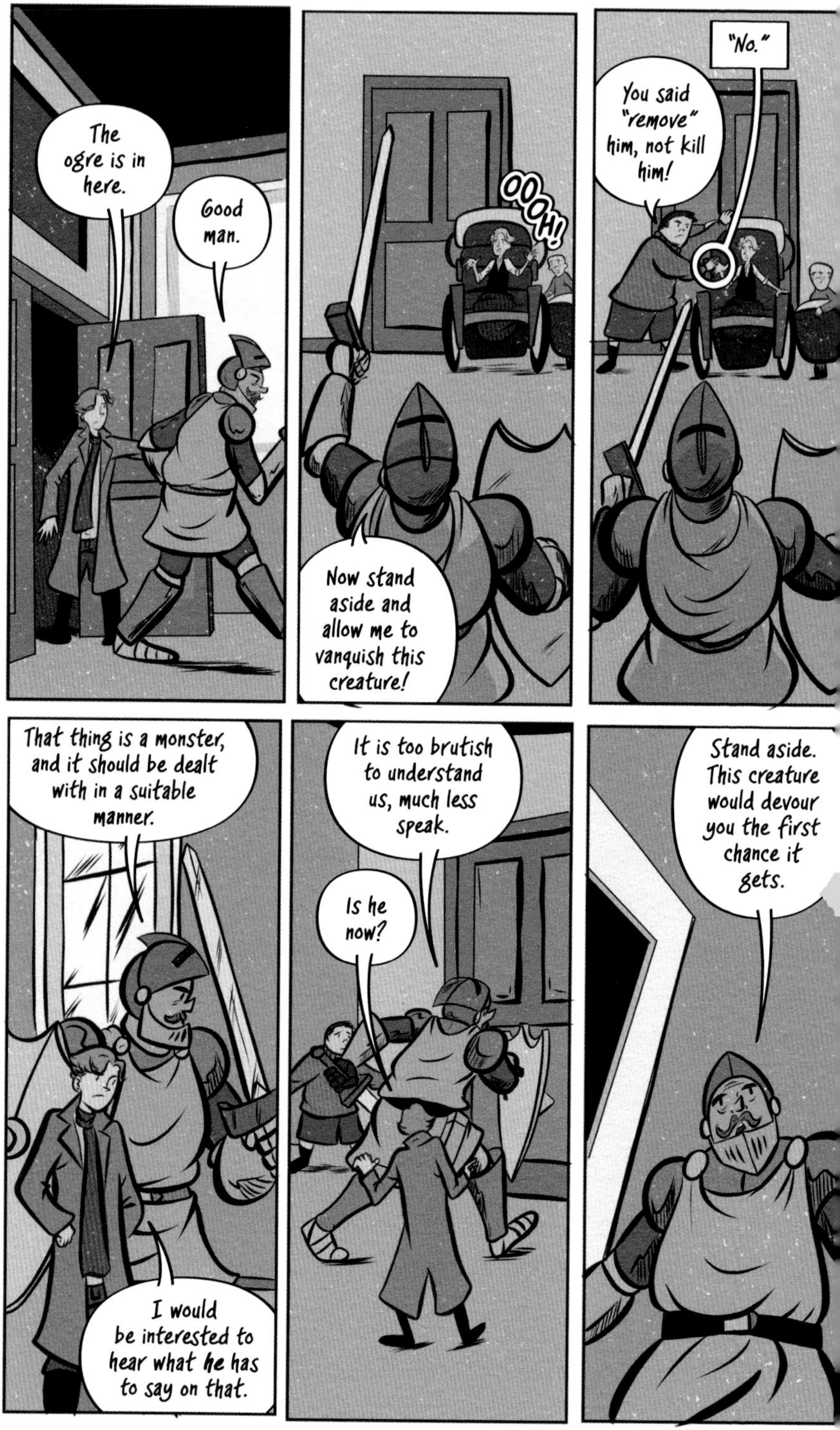

The ogre is in here.
Good man.
OOOH!
Now stand aside and allow me to vanquish this creature!
"No."
You said "remove" him, not kill him!
That thing is a monster, and it should be dealt with in a suitable manner.
I would be interested to hear what he has to say on that.
It is too brutish to understand us, much less speak.
Is he now?
Stand aside. This creature would devour you the first chance it gets.

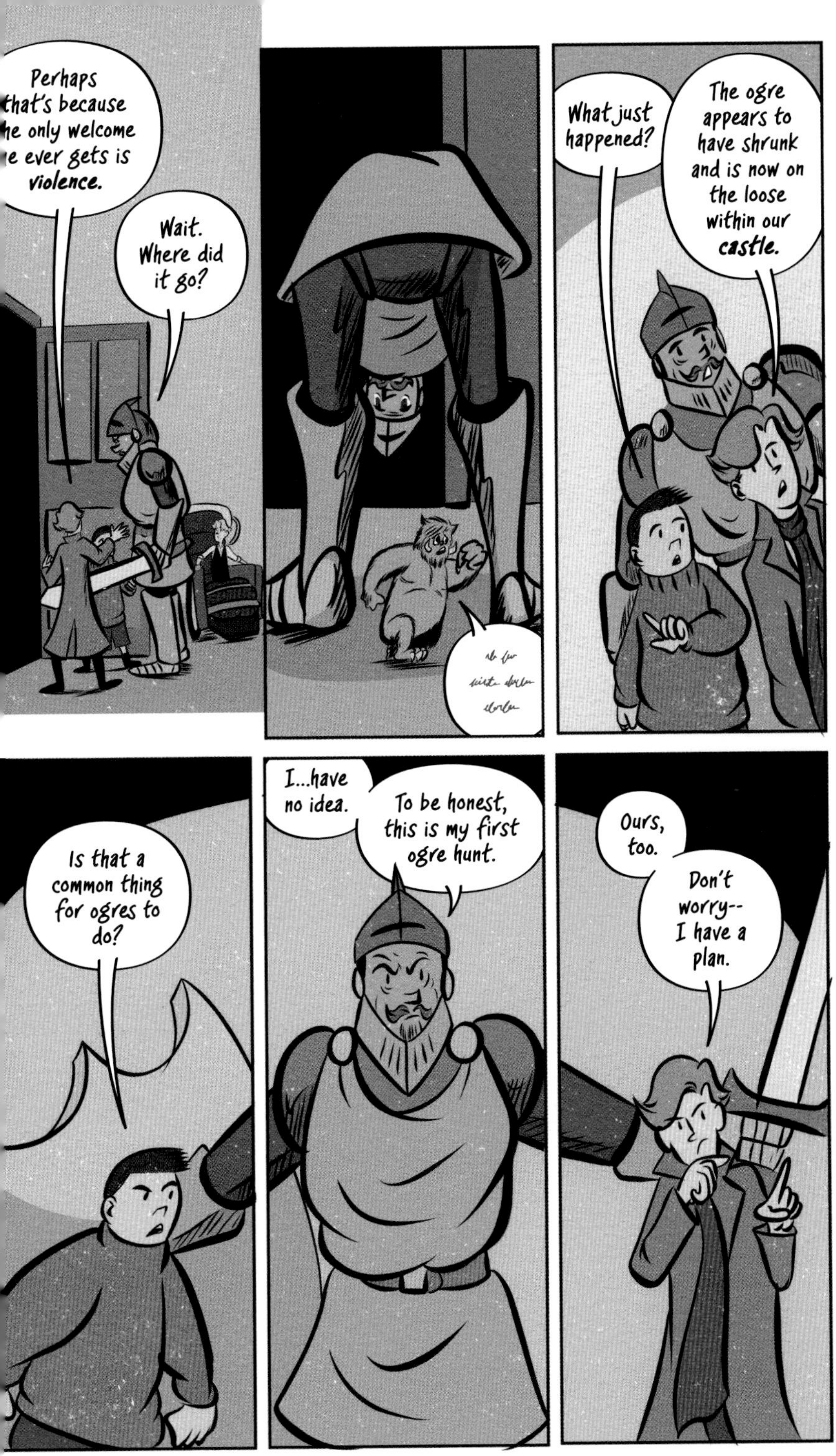

Perhaps that's because he only welcome e ever gets is **violence.**
Wait. Where did it go?
What just happened?
The ogre appears to have shrunk and is now on the loose within our **castle.**
Is that a common thing for ogres to do?
I...have no idea.
To be honest, this is my first ogre hunt.
Ours, too.
Don't worry-- I have a plan.

What are you looking for again?

Something that got away from us. Something small.

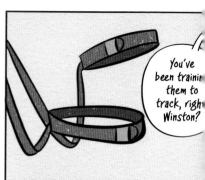

You've been traini them to track, righ Winston?

Here and there. They've been keeping the rabbits out of Mr. Morrow's garden.

Why is--

No questions about the knight, please. All in due time.

What we're looking for was in here.

Let's see if the invisi-dogs can pick up a scent.

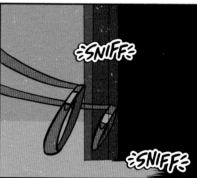

≈SNIFF≈

≈SNIFF≈

AAAHHH! NOT AGAIN!

RRRWOOF!

RRRWOOF!

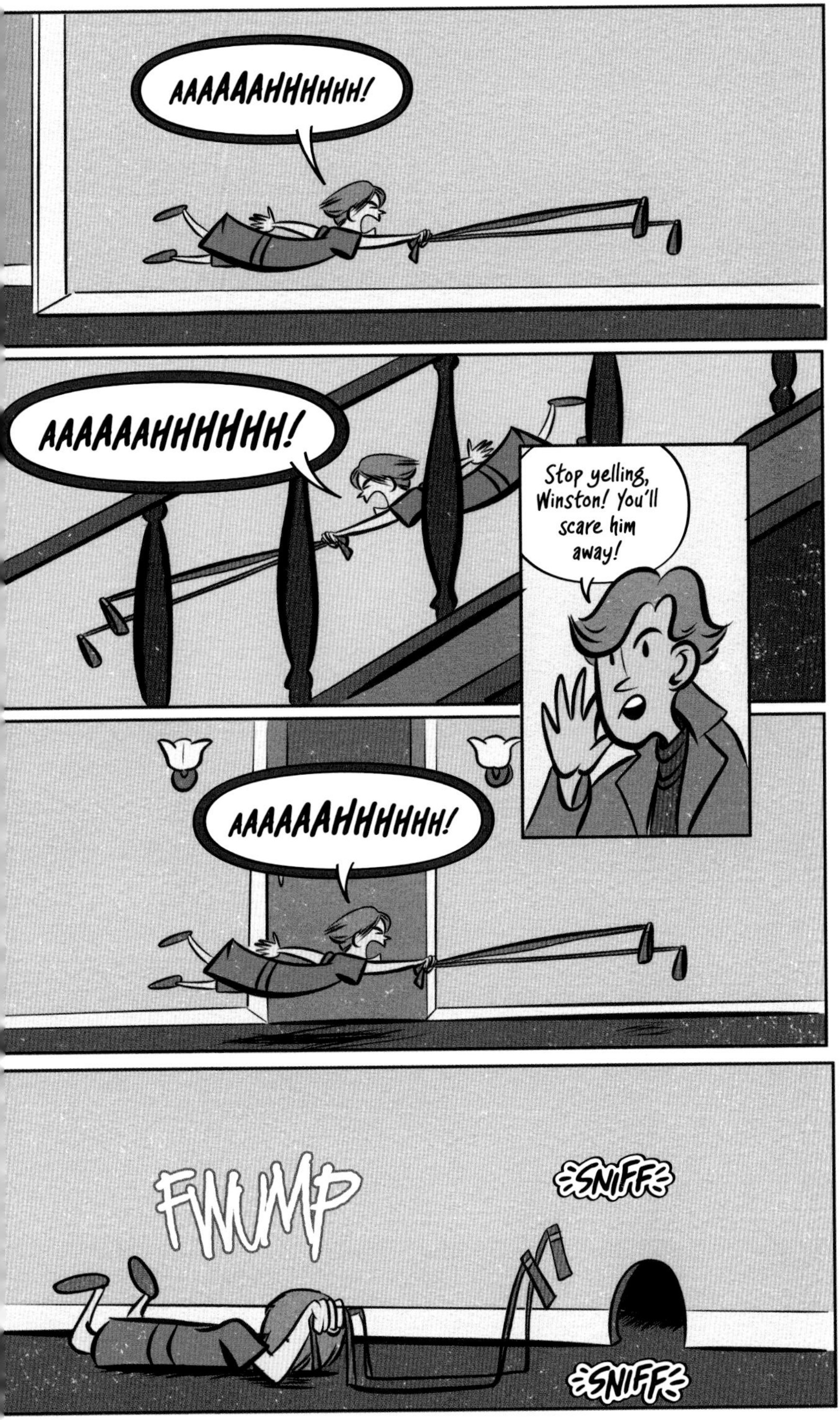
AAAAAAHHHHHH!
AAAAAAHHHHHH!
Stop yelling, Winston! You'll scare him away!
AAAAAAHHHHHH!
FWUMP
SNIFF
SNIFF

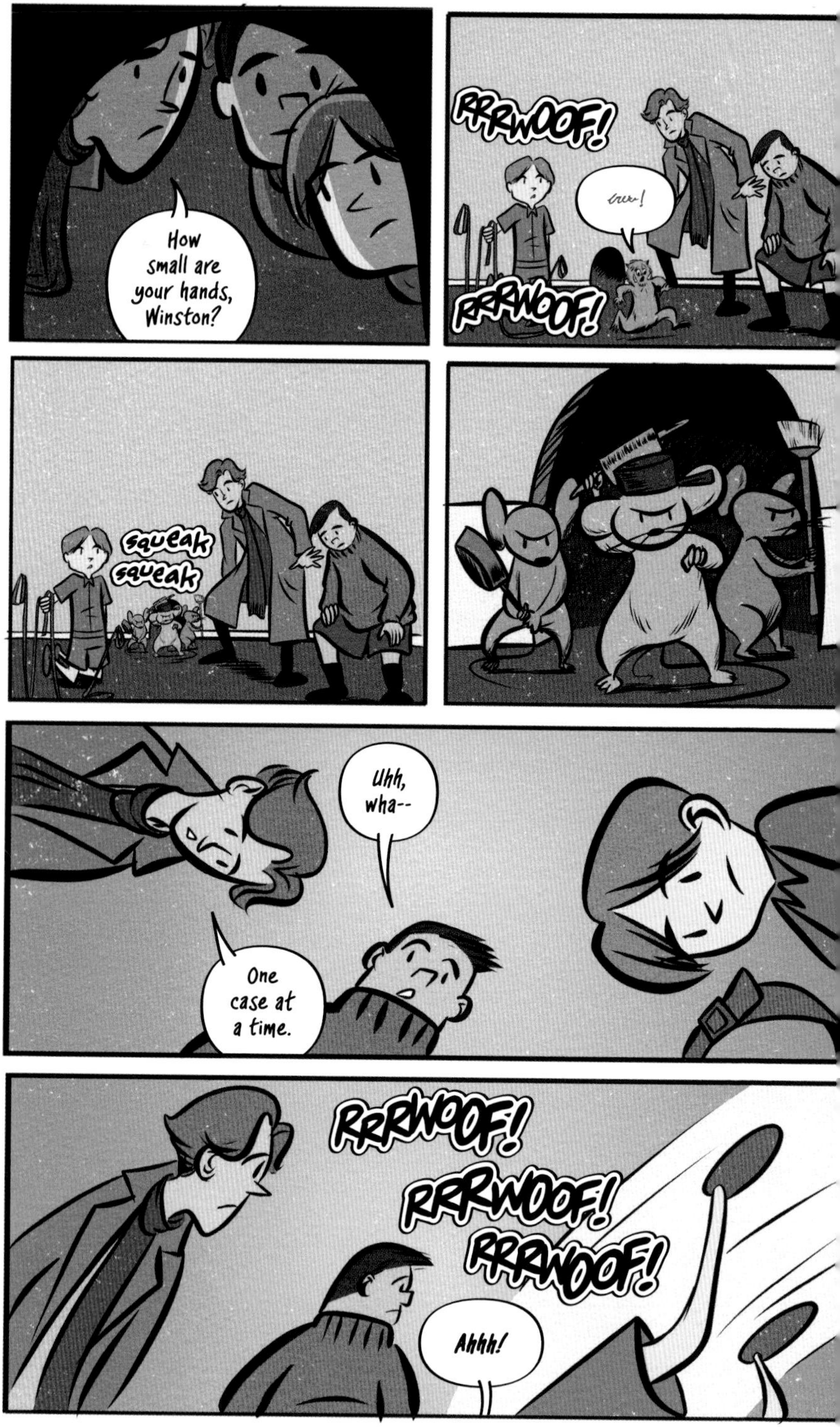

How small are your hands, Winston?
RRRWOOF!
RRRWOOF!
squeak squeak
Uhh, wha--
One case at a time.
RRRWOOF!
RRRWOOF!
RRRWOOF!
Ahhh!

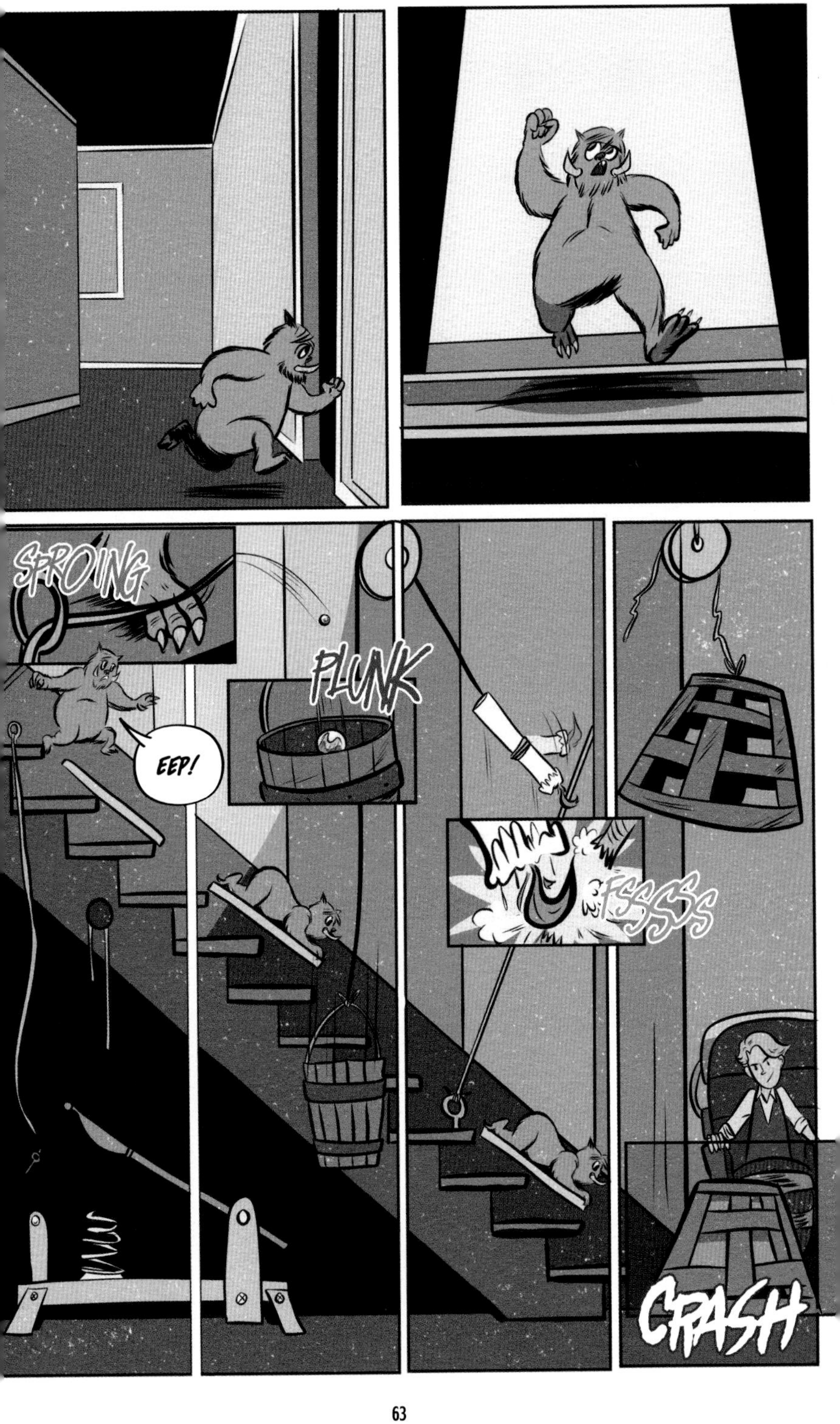
SPROING
EEP!
PLUNK
FSSSSS
CRASH

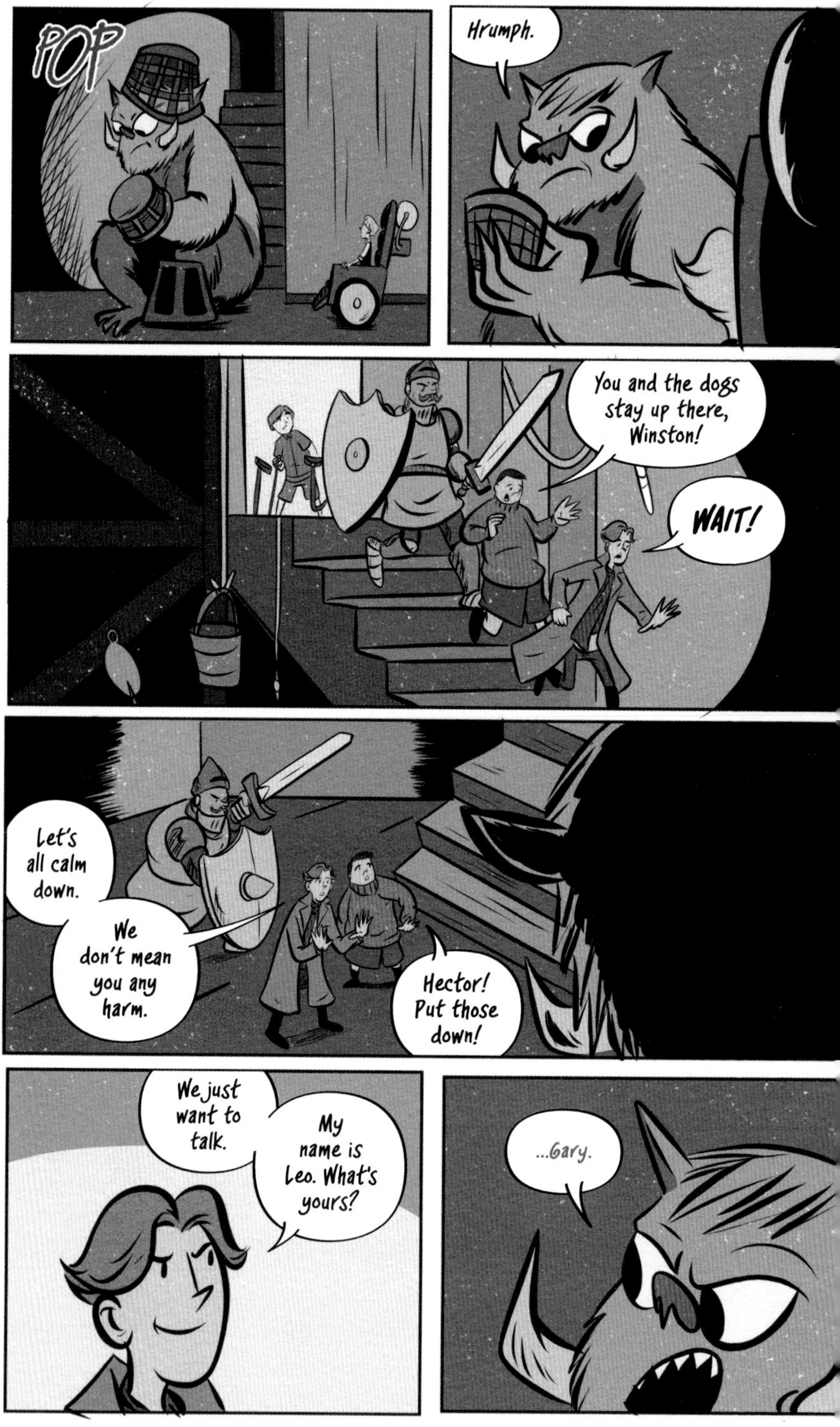
POP
Hrumph.
You and the dogs stay up there, Winston!
WAIT!
Let's all calm down.
We don't mean you any harm.
Hector! Put those down!
We just want to talk.
My name is Leo. What's yours?
...Gary.

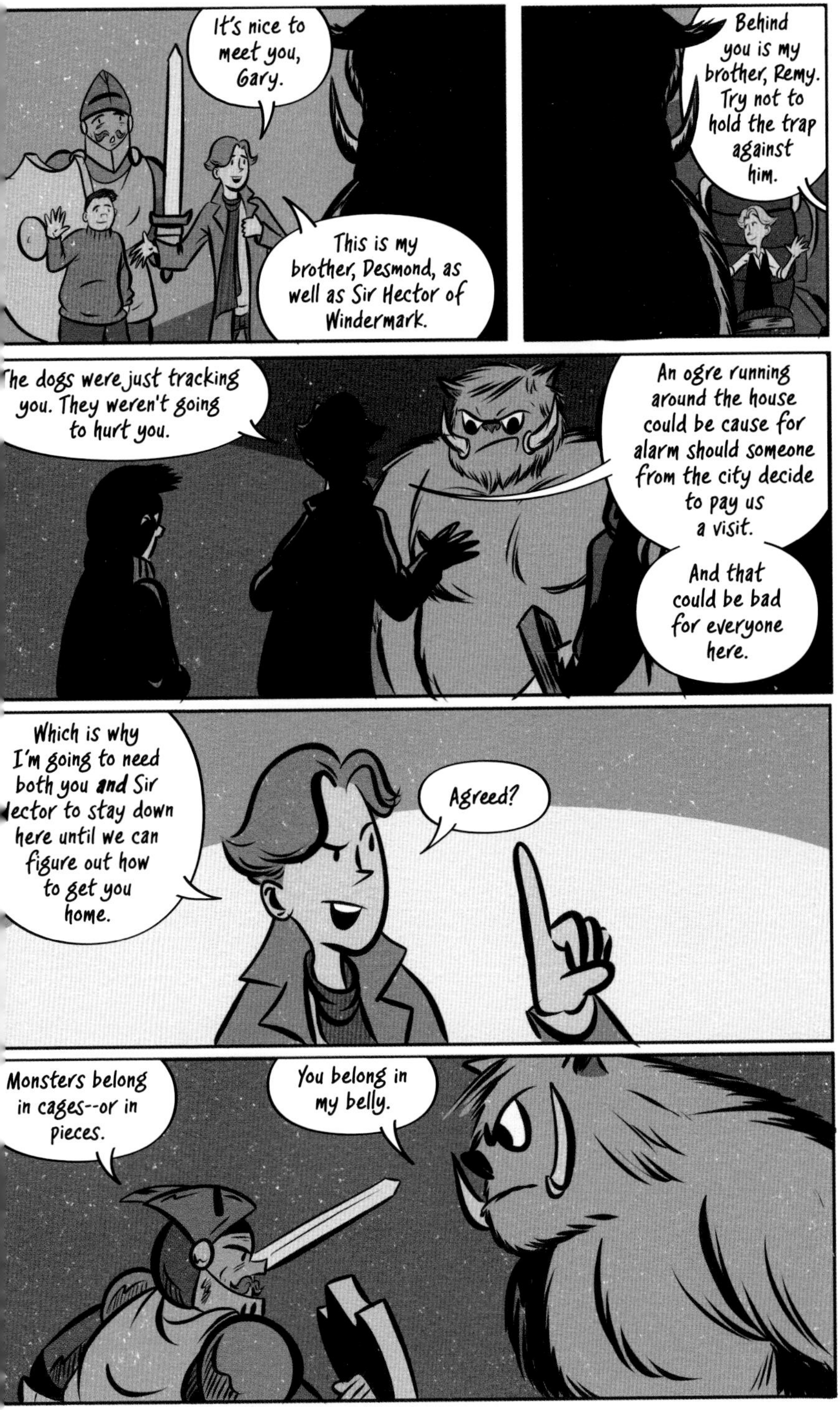
It's nice to meet you, Gary.
This is my brother, Desmond, as well as Sir Hector of Windermark.
Behind you is my brother, Remy. Try not to hold the trap against him.
The dogs were just tracking you. They weren't going to hurt you.
An ogre running around the house could be cause for alarm should someone from the city decide to pay us a visit.
And that could be bad for everyone here.
Which is why I'm going to need both you **and** Sir Hector to stay down here until we can figure out how to get you home.
Agreed?
Monsters belong in cages--or in pieces.
You belong in my belly.

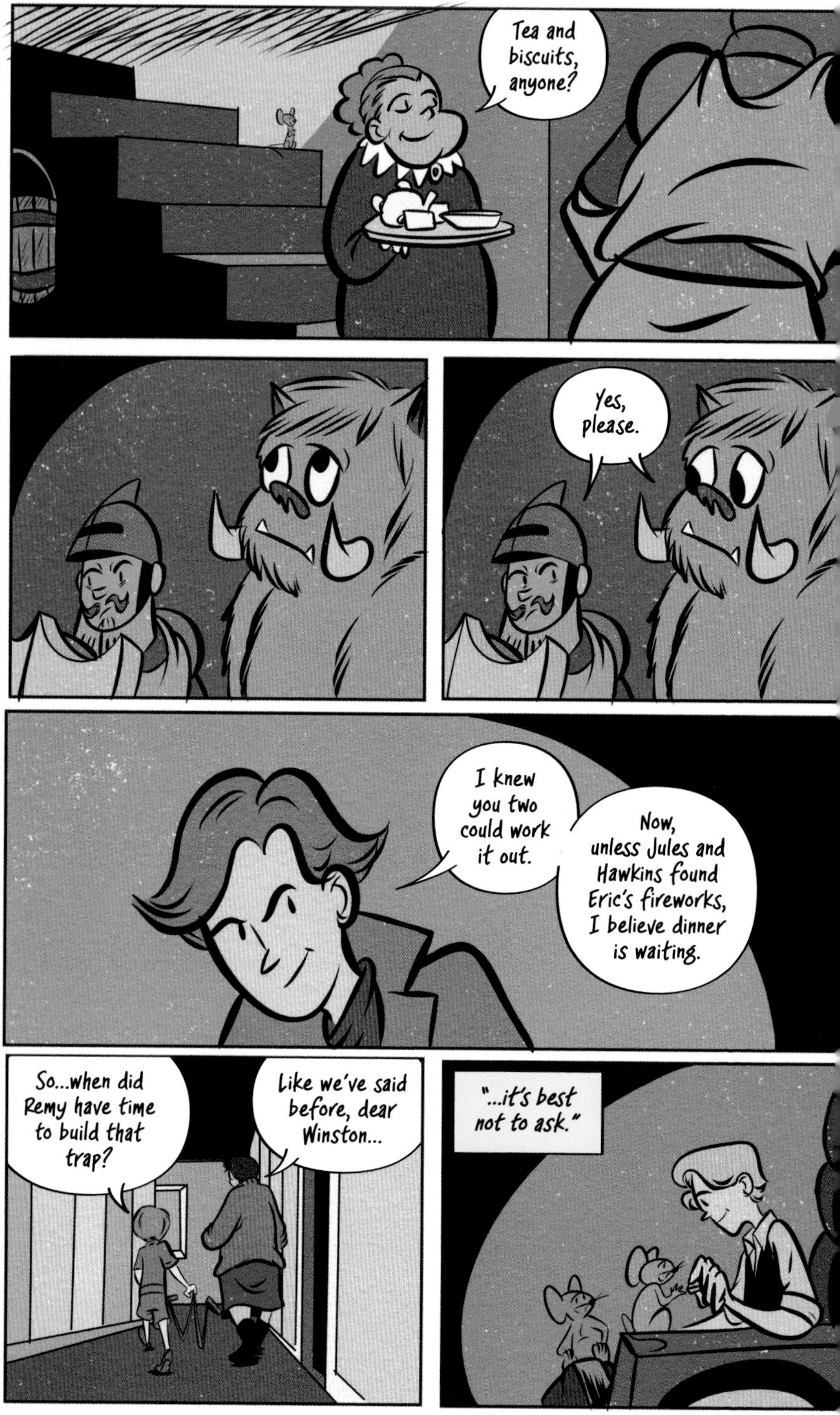
Tea and biscuits, anyone?
Yes, please.
I knew you two could work it out.
Now, unless Jules and Hawkins found Eric's fireworks, I believe dinner is waiting.
So...when did Remy have time to build that trap?
Like we've said before, dear Winston...
"...it's best not to ask."

CHAPTER
4

THE LIVING DARK

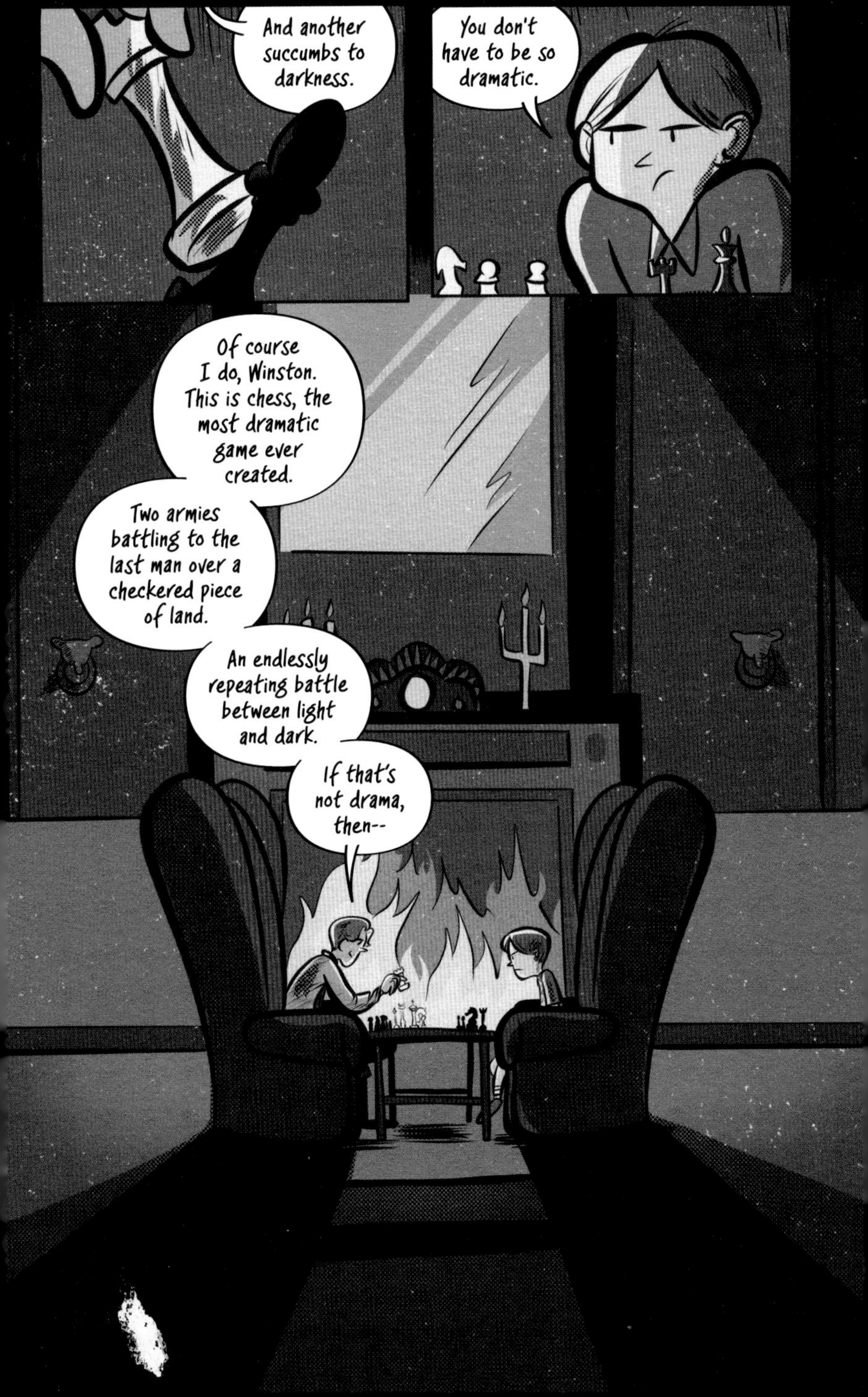
And another succumbs to darkness.
You don't have to be so dramatic.
Of course I do, Winston. This is chess, the most dramatic game ever created.
Two armies battling to the last man over a checkered piece of land.
An endlessly repeating battle between light and dark.
If that's not drama, then--

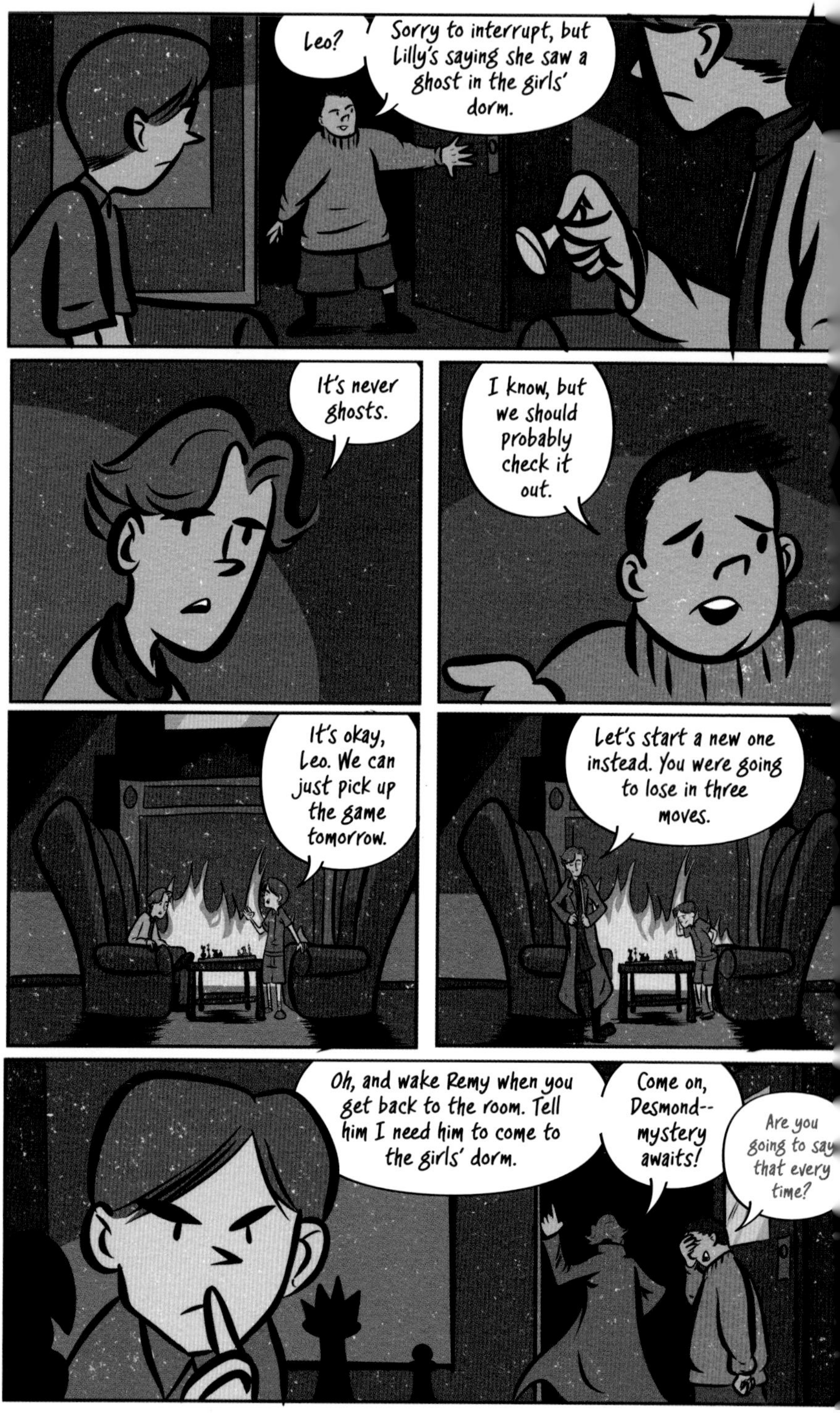
Leo?
Sorry to interrupt, but Lilly's saying she saw a ghost in the girls' dorm.
It's never ghosts.
I know, but we should probably check it out.
It's okay, Leo. We can just pick up the game tomorrow.
Let's start a new one instead. You were going to lose in three moves.
Oh, and wake Remy when you get back to the room. Tell him I need him to come to the girls' dorm.
Come on, Desmond--mystery awaits!
Are you going to say that every time?

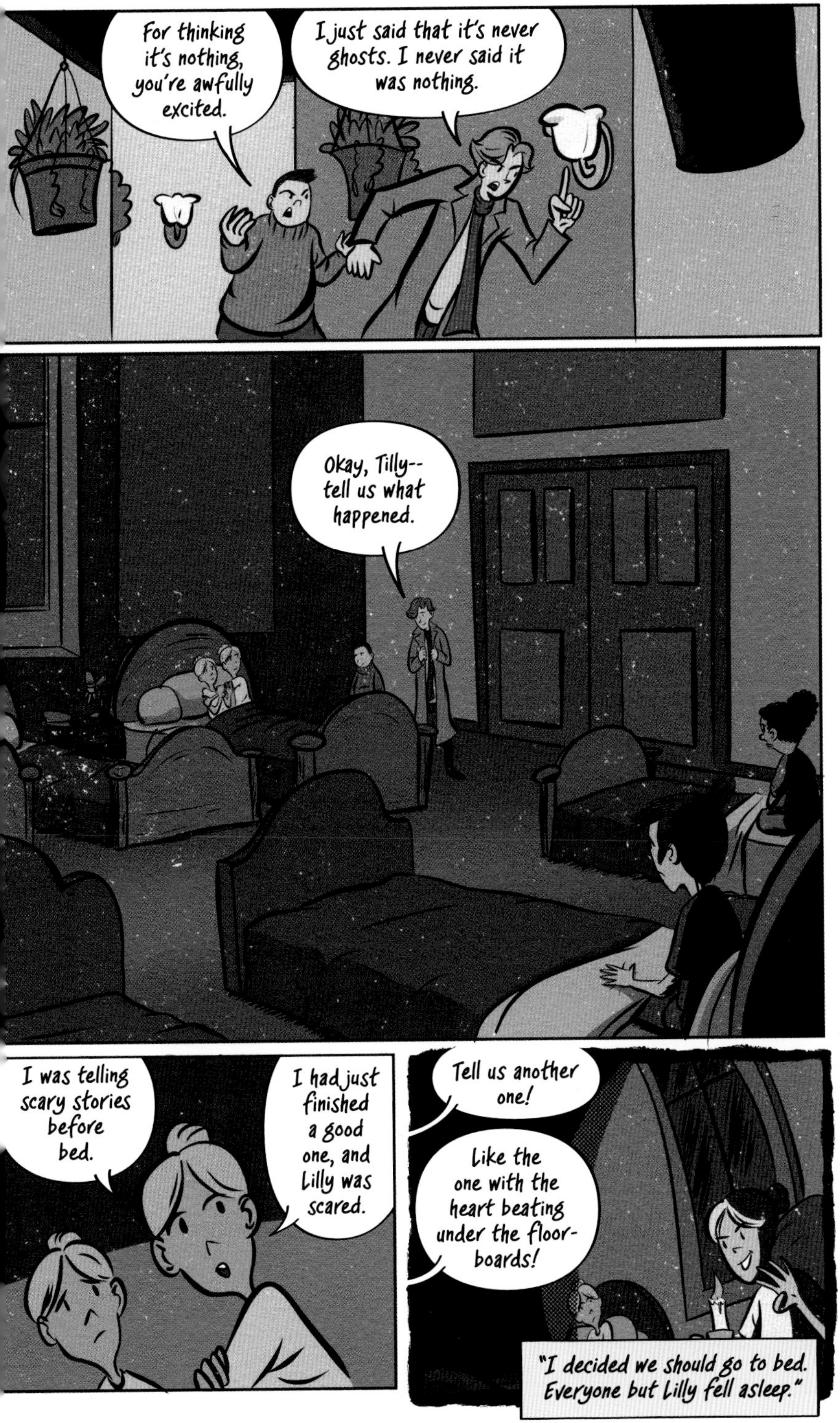

For thinking it's nothing, you're awfully excited.
I just said that it's never ghosts. I never said it was nothing.
Okay, Tilly-- tell us what happened.
I was telling scary stories before bed.
I had just finished a good one, and Lilly was scared.
Tell us another one!
Like the one with the heart beating under the floor-boards!
"I decided we should go to bed. Everyone but Lilly fell asleep."

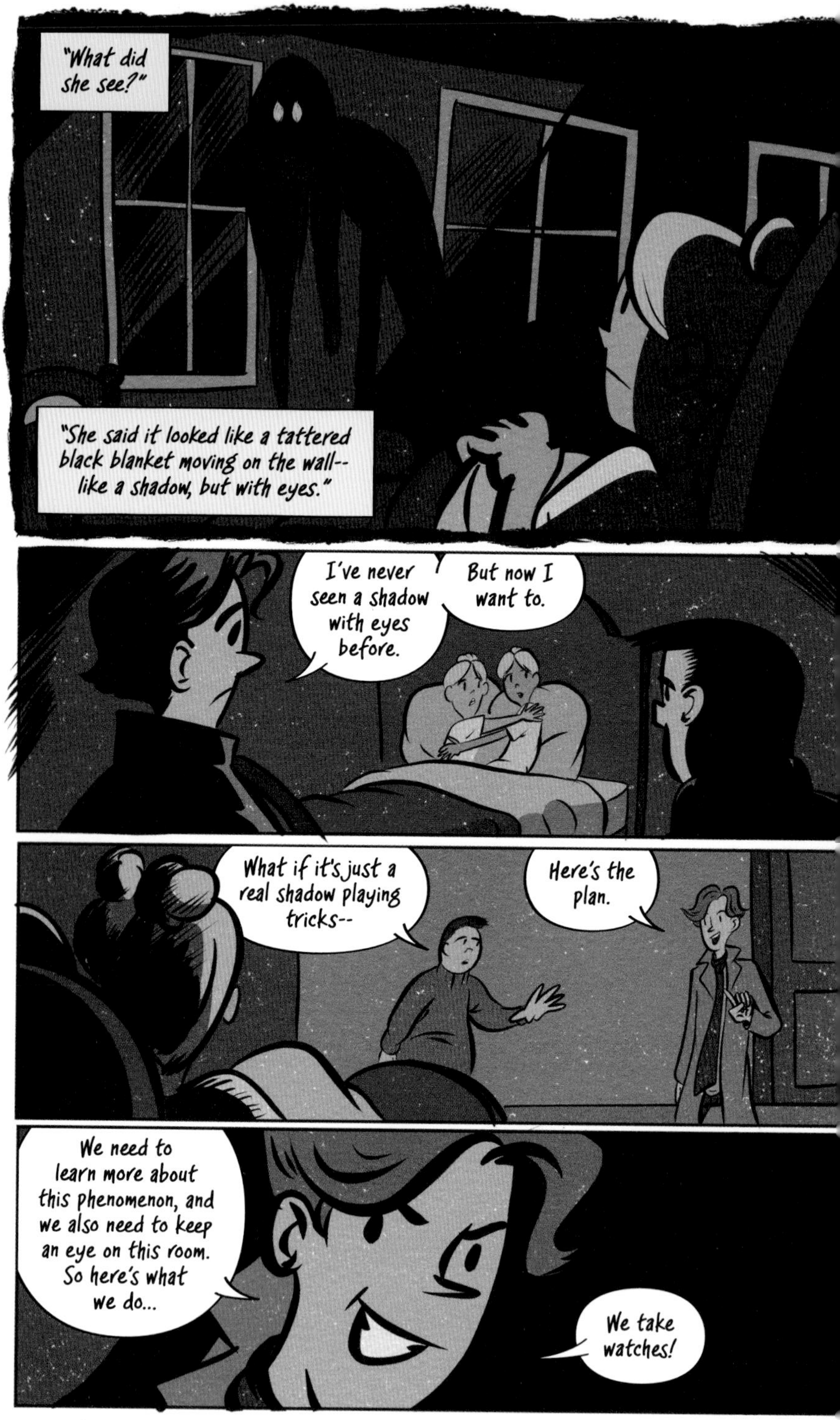
"What did she see?"
"She said it looked like a tattered black blanket moving on the wall-- like a shadow, but with eyes."
I've never seen a shadow with eyes before.
But now I want to.
What if it's just a real shadow playing tricks--
Here's the plan.
We need to learn more about this phenomenon, and we also need to keep an eye on this room. So here's what we do...
We take watches!

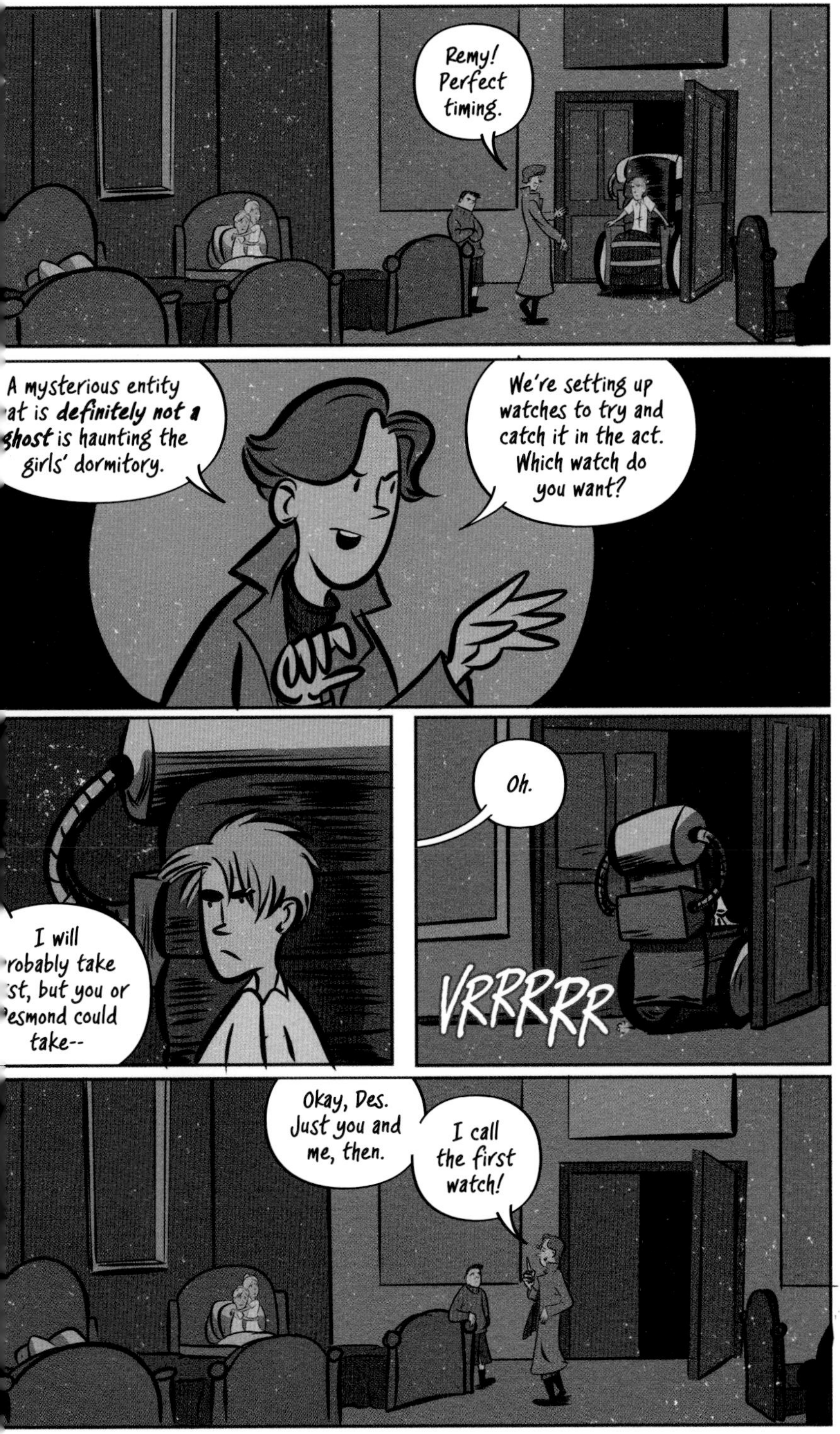

Remy! Perfect timing.
A mysterious entity at is definitely not a ghost is haunting the girls' dormitory.
We're setting up watches to try and catch it in the act. Which watch do you want?
I will robably take st, but you or esmond could take--
Oh.
VRRRRR
Okay, Des. Just you and me, then.
I call the first watch!

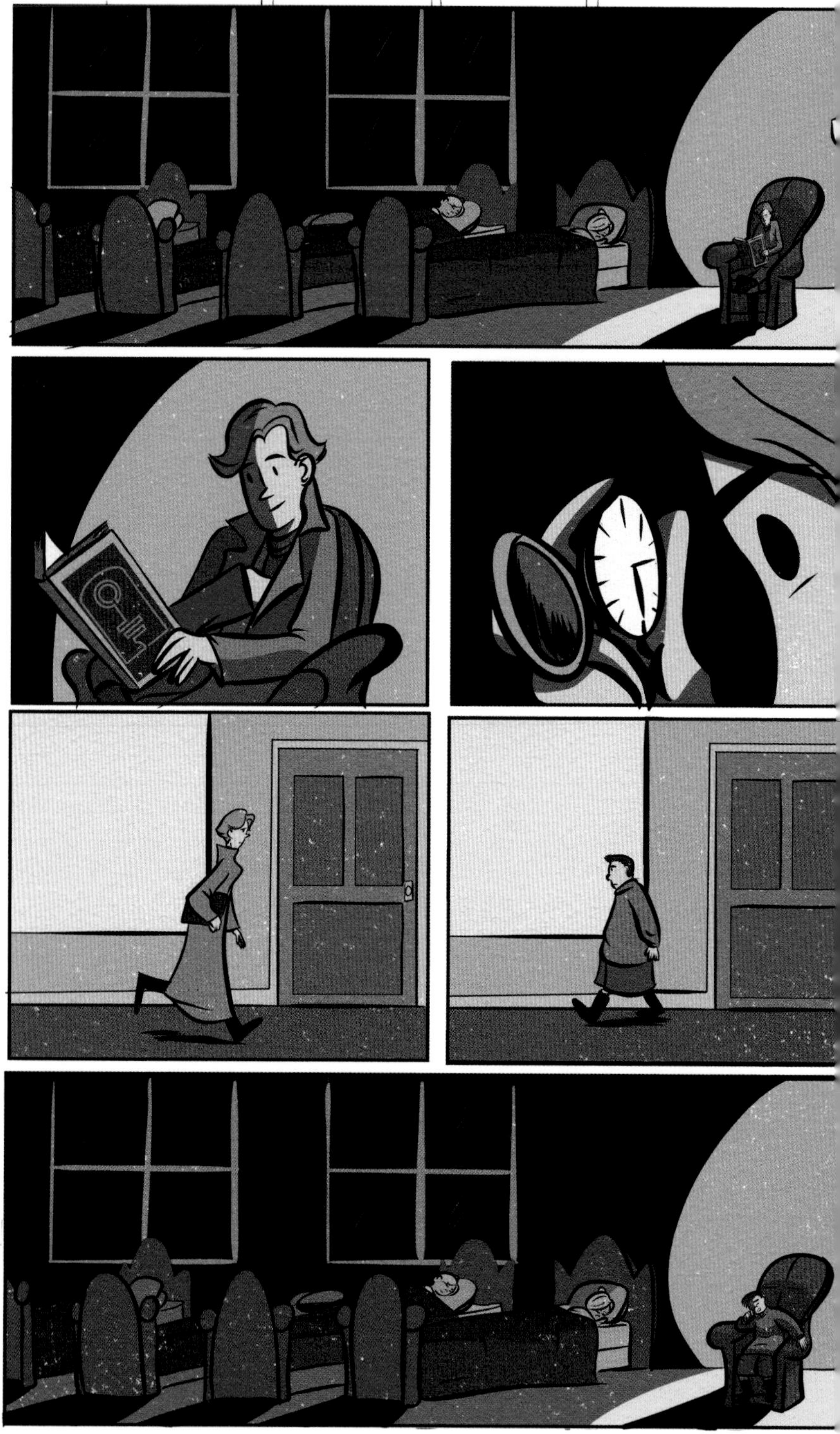

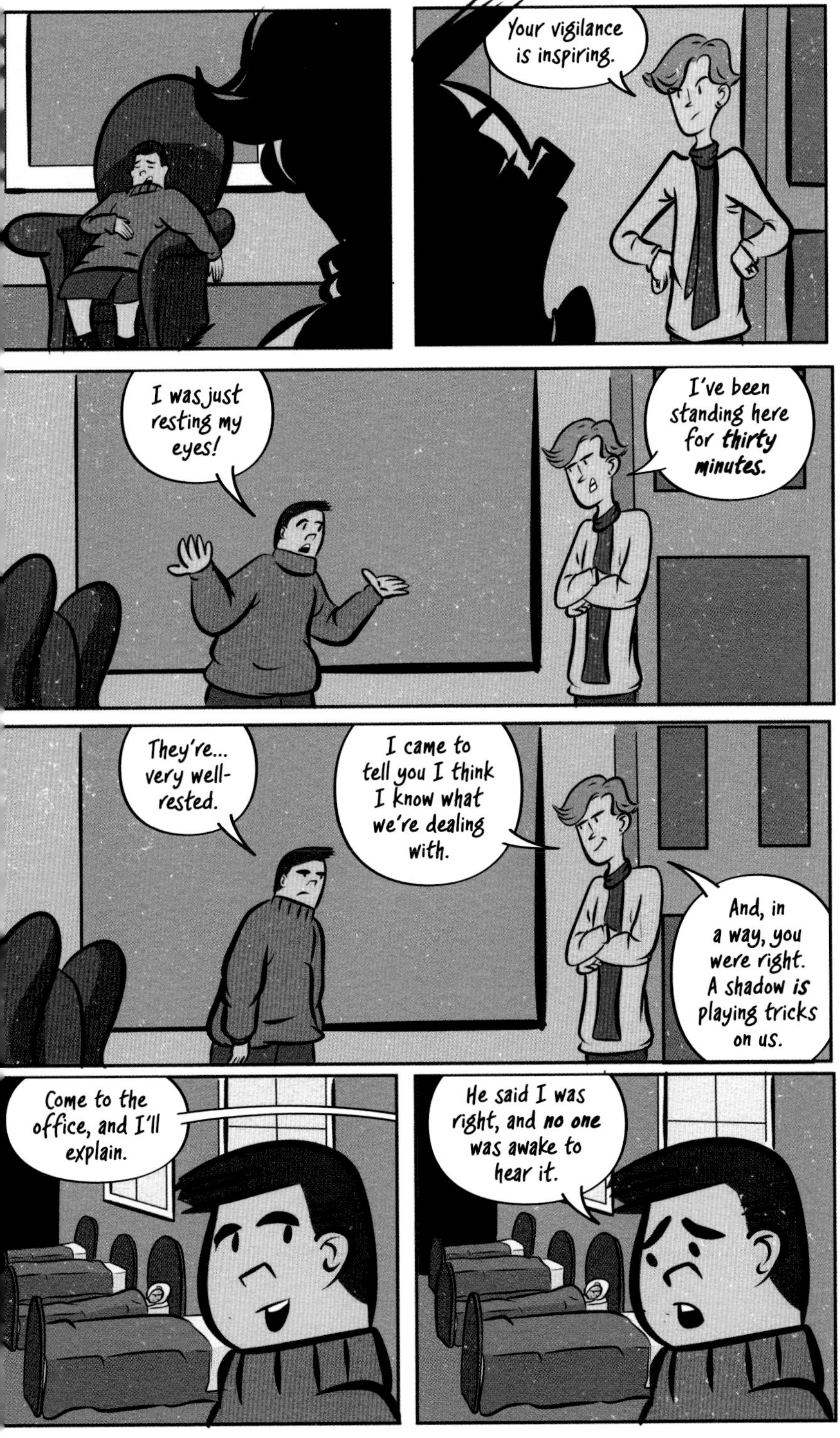
Your vigilance is inspiring.
I was just resting my eyes!
I've been standing here for *thirty minutes.*
They're... very well-rested.
I came to tell you I think I know what we're dealing with.
And, in a way, you were right. A shadow *is* playing tricks on us.
Come to the office, and I'll explain.
He said I was right, and *no one* was awake to hear it.

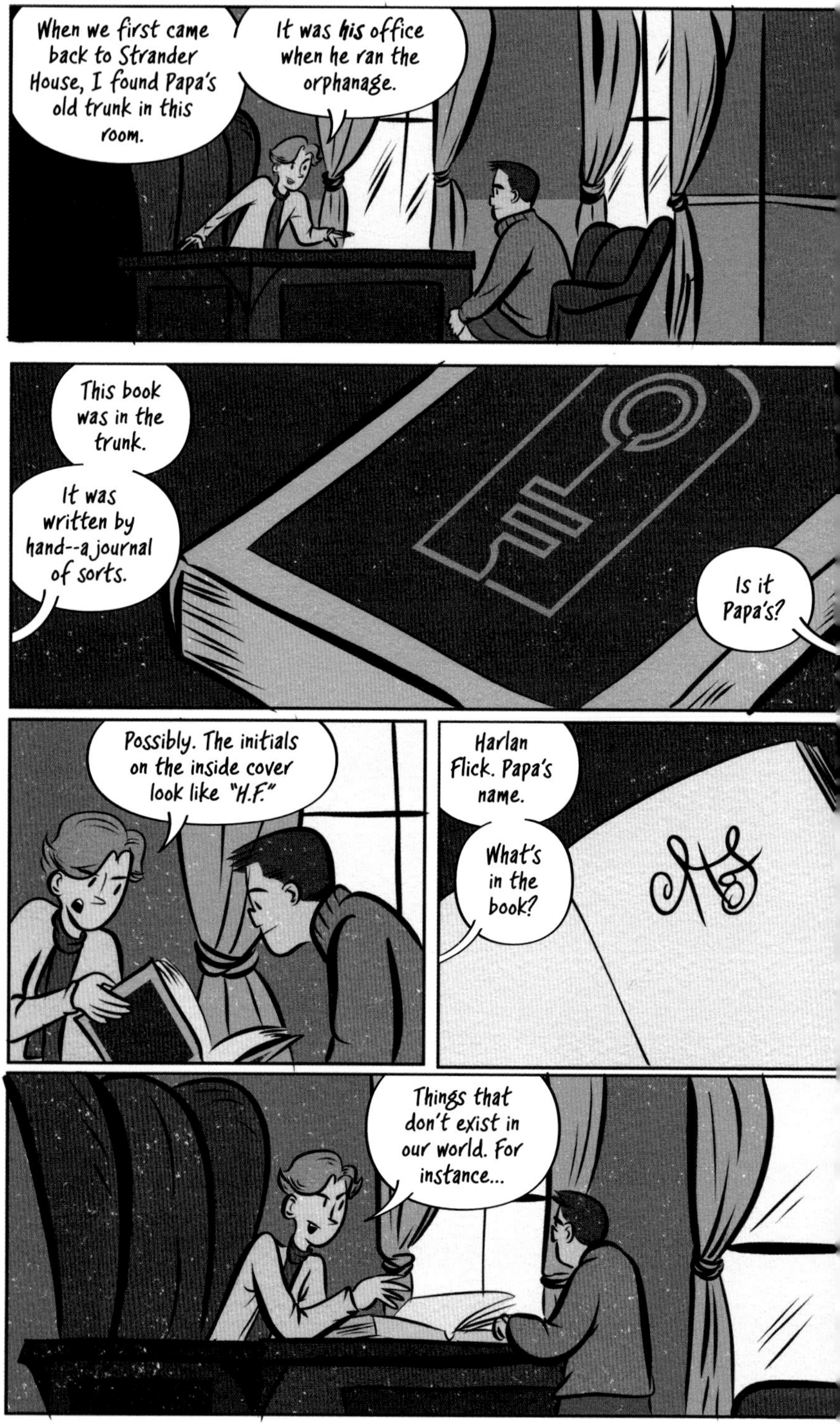
When we first came back to Strander House, I found Papa's old trunk in this room.
It was his office when he ran the orphanage.
This book was in the trunk.
It was written by hand--a journal of sorts.
Is it Papa's?
Possibly. The initials on the inside cover look like "H.F."
Harlan Flick. Papa's name.
What's in the book?
Things that don't exist in our world. For instance...

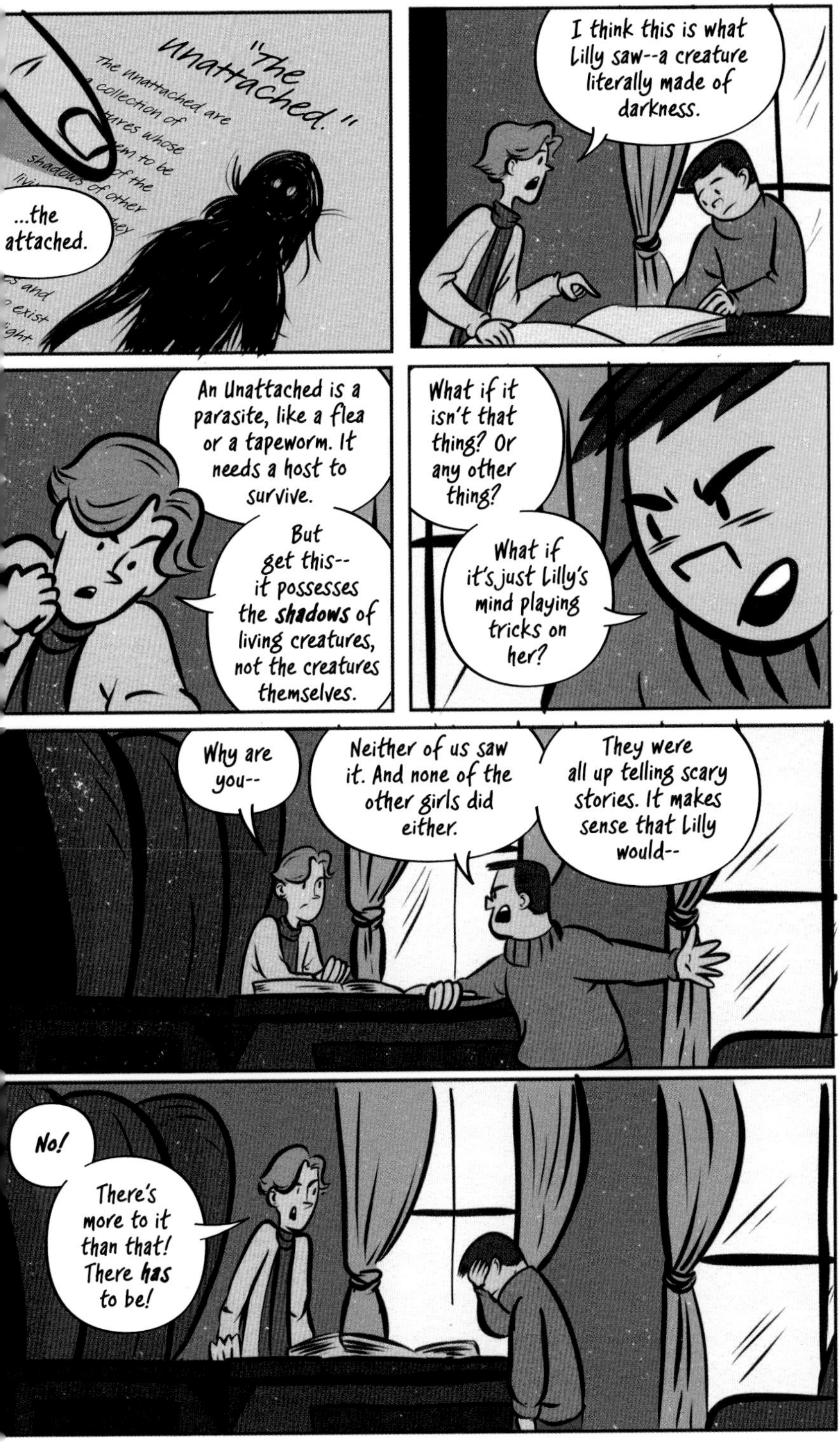
"The Unattached."
...the attached.
I think this is what Lilly saw--a creature literally made of darkness.
An Unattached is a parasite, like a flea or a tapeworm. It needs a host to survive.
But get this-- it possesses the **shadows** of living creatures, not the creatures themselves.
What if it isn't that thing? Or any other thing?
What if it's just Lilly's mind playing tricks on her?
Why are you--
Neither of us saw it. And none of the other girls did either.
They were all up telling scary stories. It makes sense that Lilly would--
No!
There's more to it than that! There **has** to be!

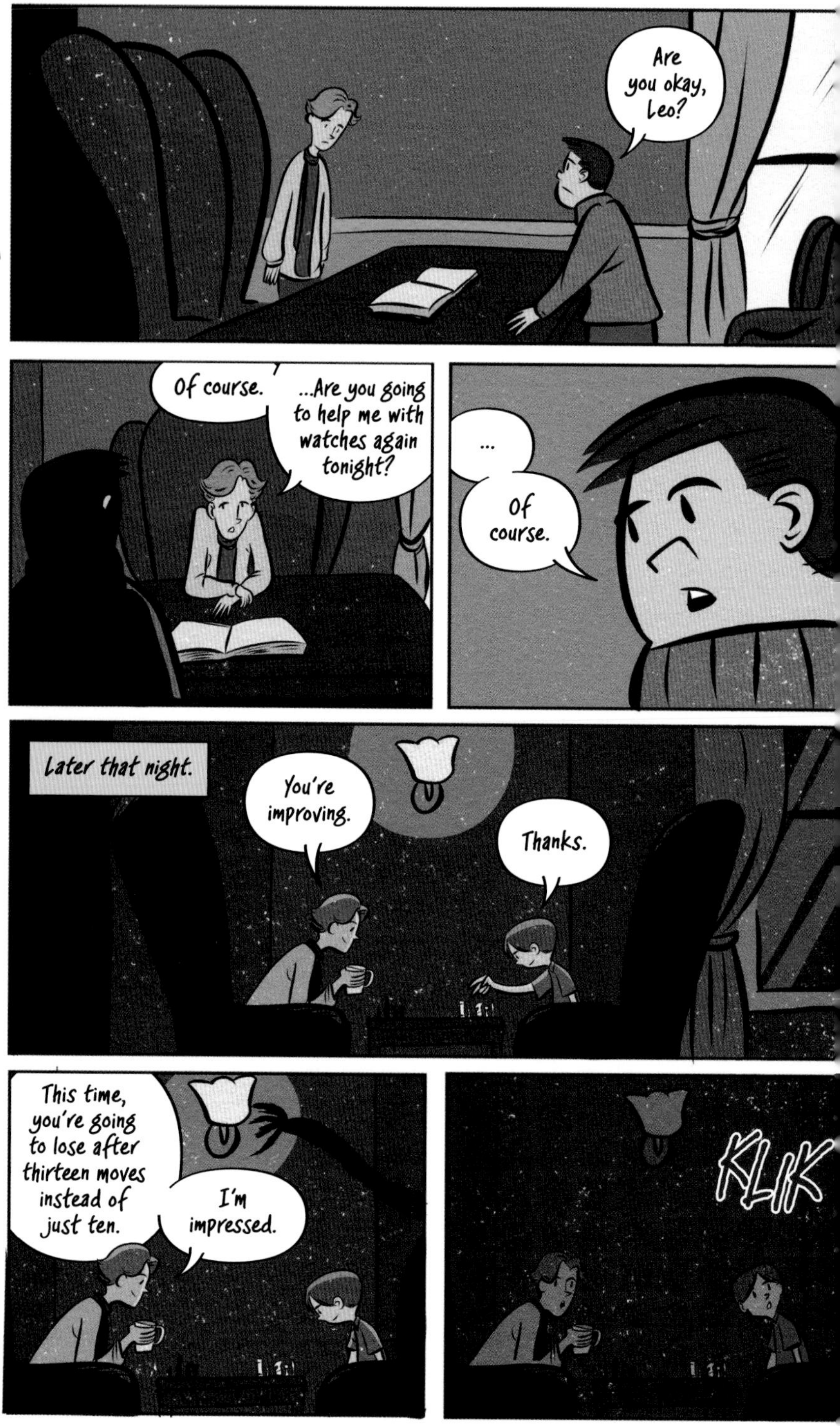
Are you okay, Leo?
Of course.
...Are you going to help me with watches again tonight?
...
Of course.
Later that night.
You're improving.
Thanks.
This time, you're going to lose after thirteen moves instead of just ten.
I'm impressed.
KLIK

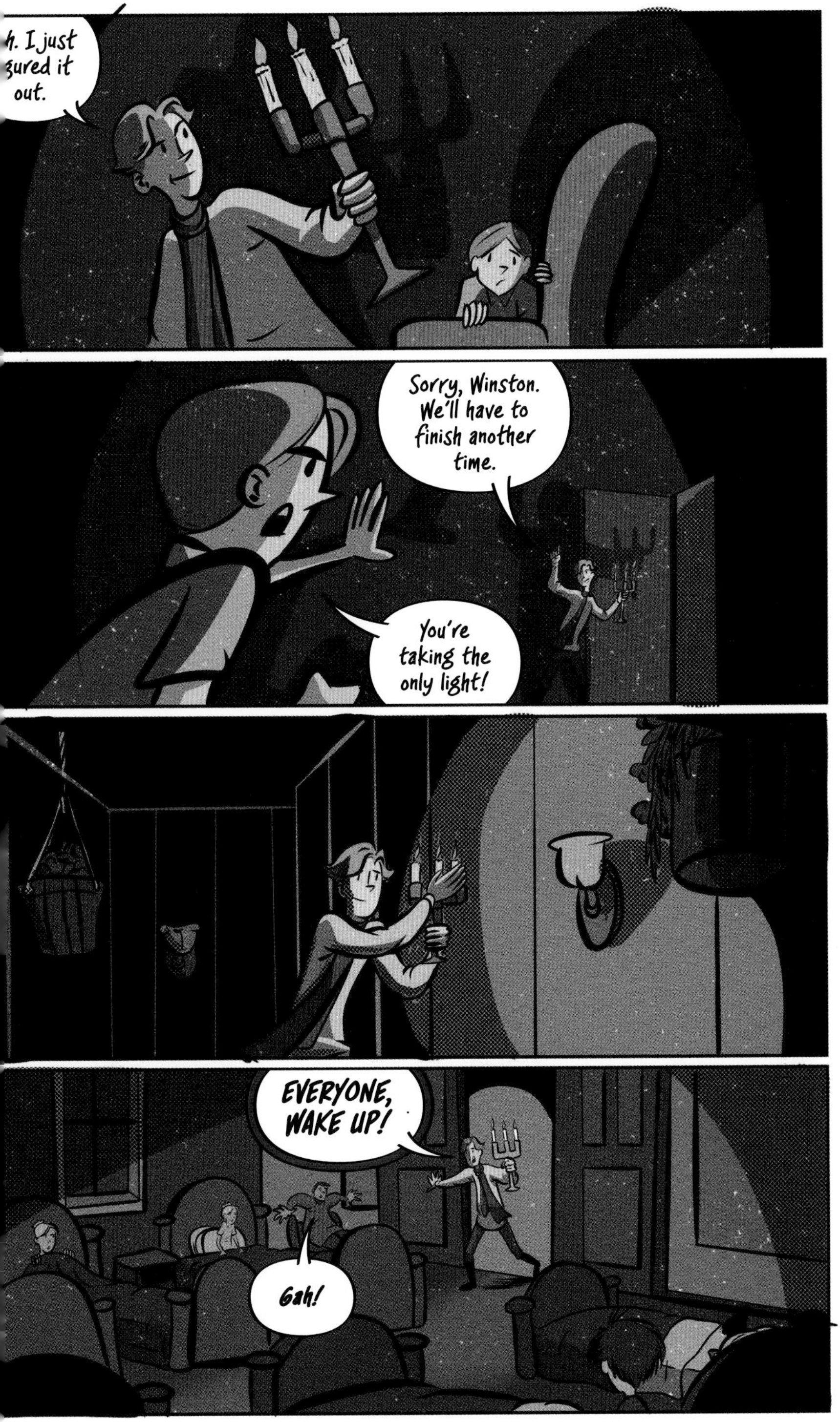
h. I just
gured it
out.
Sorry, Winston. We'll have to finish another time.
You're taking the only light!
EVERYONE, WAKE UP!
Gah!

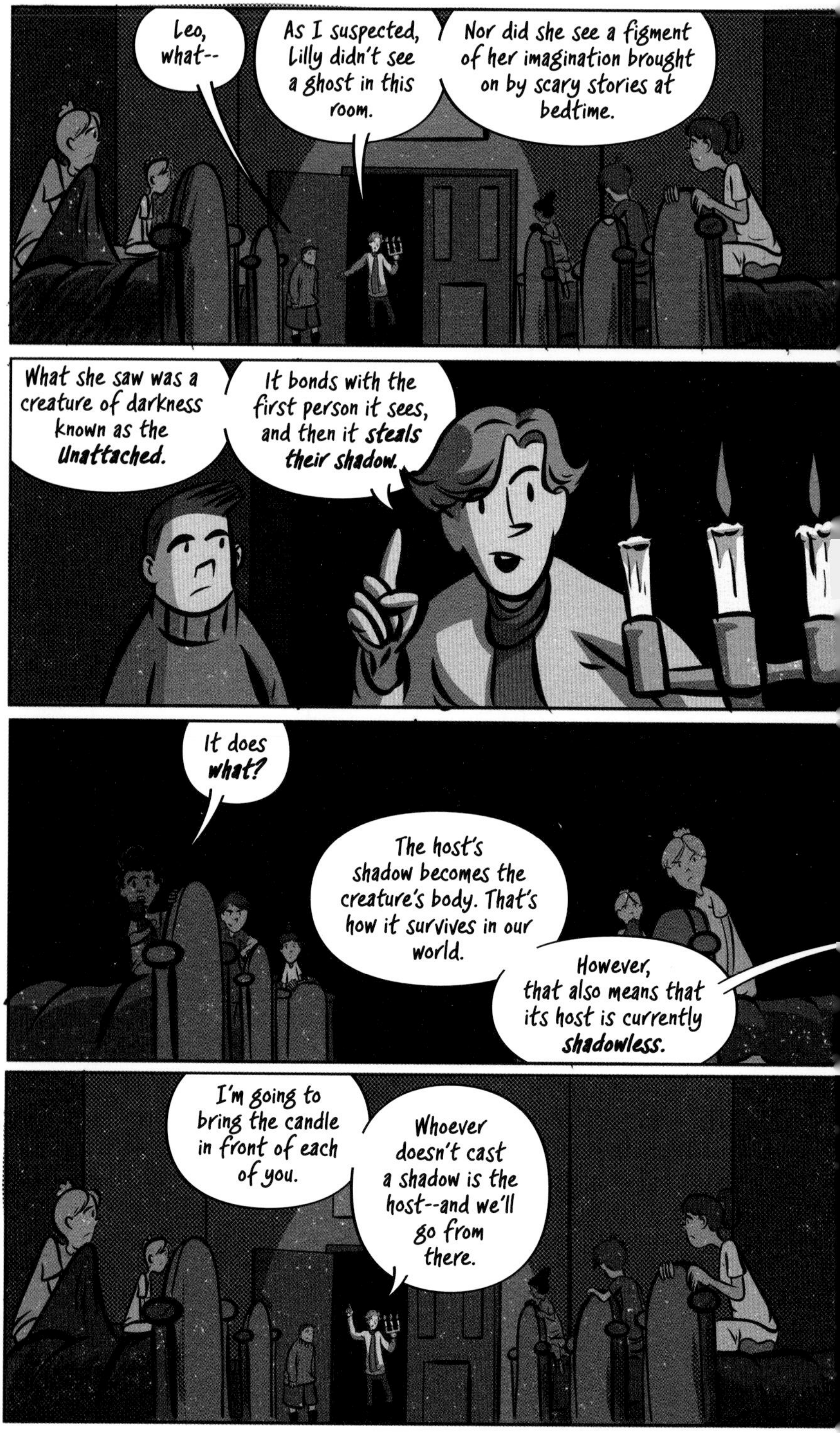
Leo, what--
As I suspected, Lilly didn't see a ghost in this room.
Nor did she see a figment of her imagination brought on by scary stories at bedtime.
What she saw was a creature of darkness known as the *Unattached.*
It bonds with the first person it sees, and then it *steals their shadow.*
It does *what?*
The host's shadow becomes the creature's body. That's how it survives in our world.
However, that also means that its host is currently *shadowless.*
I'm going to bring the candle in front of each of you.
Whoever doesn't cast a shadow is the host--and we'll go from there.

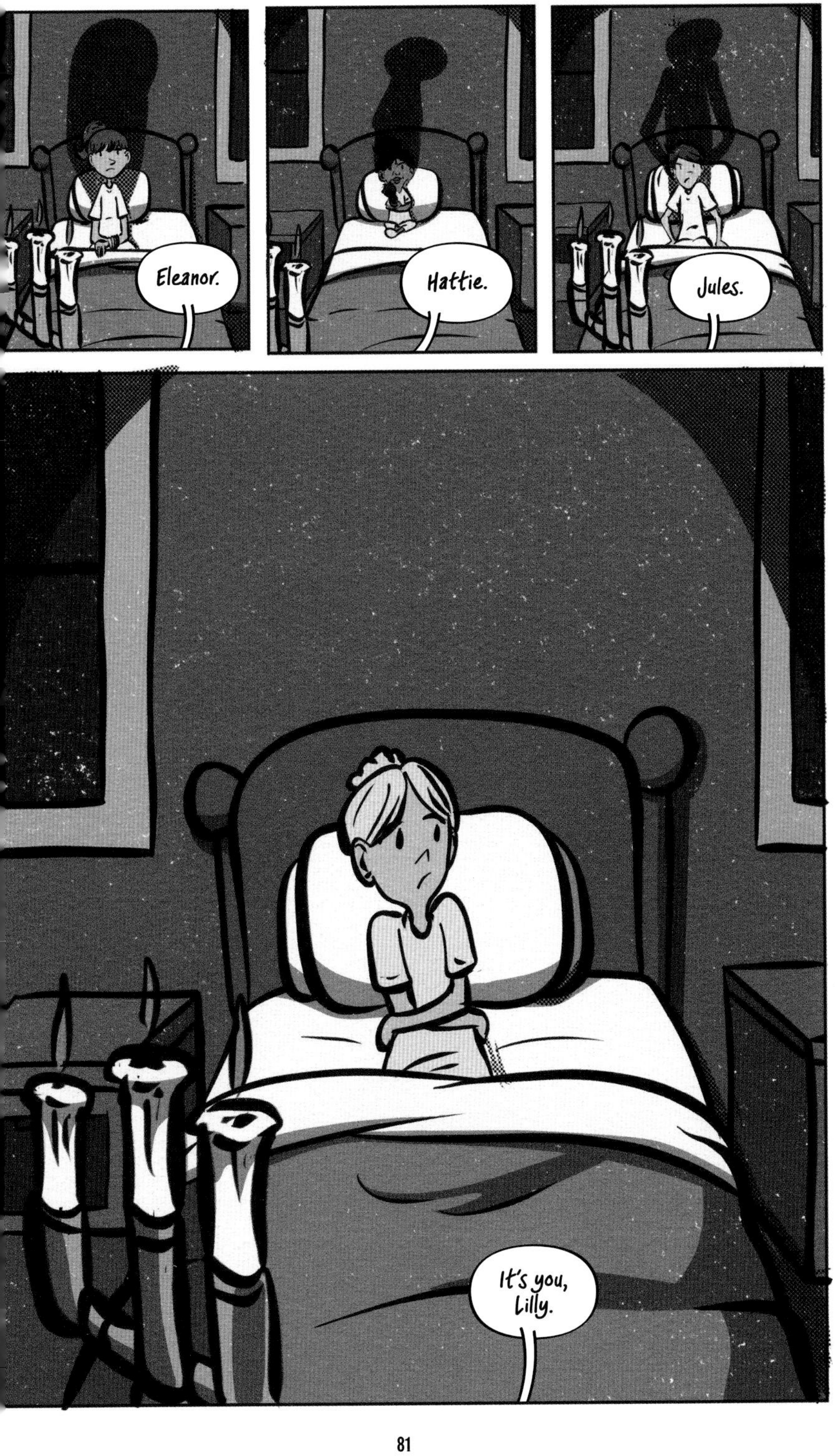
Eleanor.
Hattie.
Jules.
It's you, Lilly.

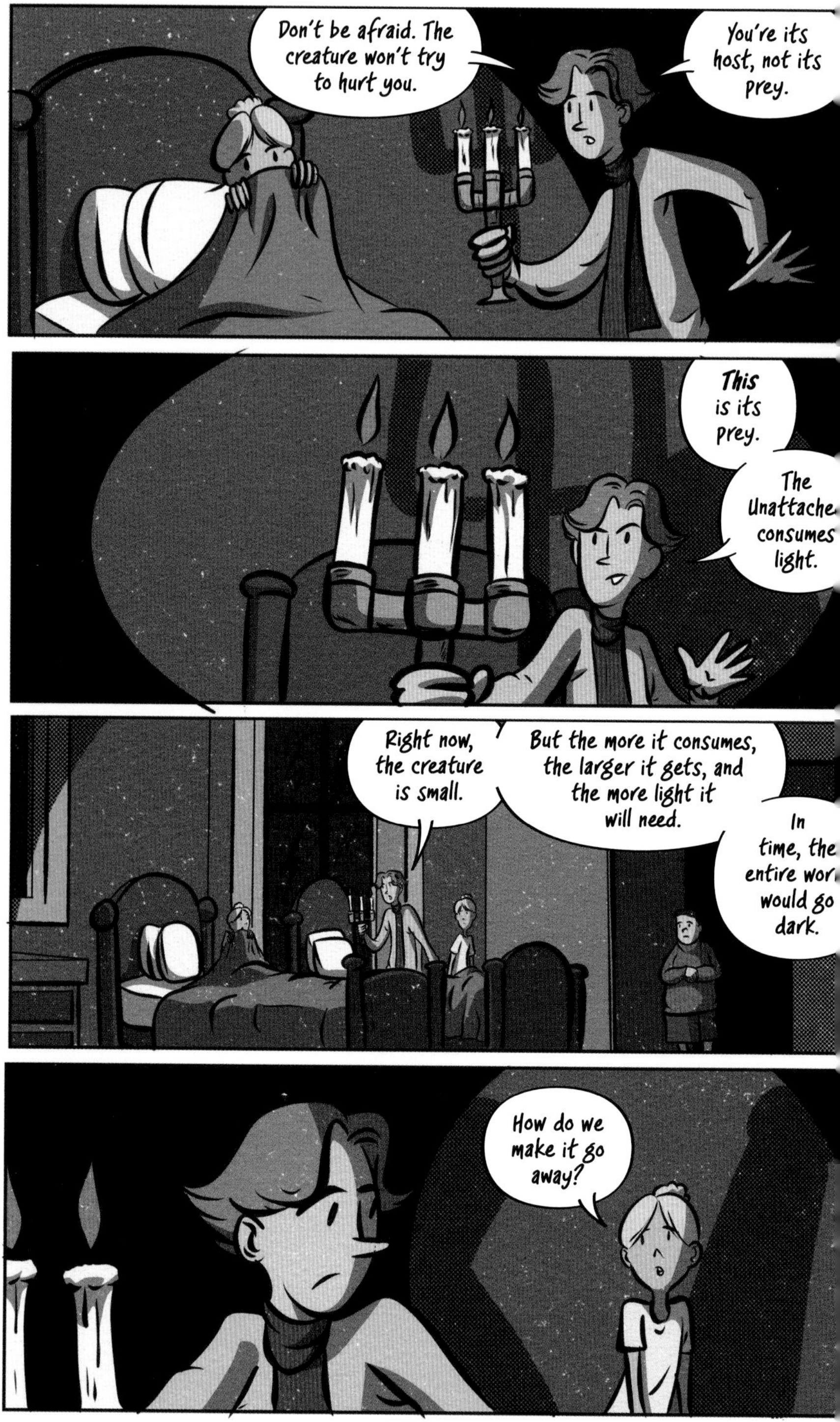
Don't be afraid. The creature won't try to hurt you.
You're its host, not its prey.
This is its prey.
The Unattache consumes light.
Right now, the creature is small.
But the more it consumes, the larger it gets, and the more light it will need.
In time, the entire wor would go dark.
How do we make it go away?

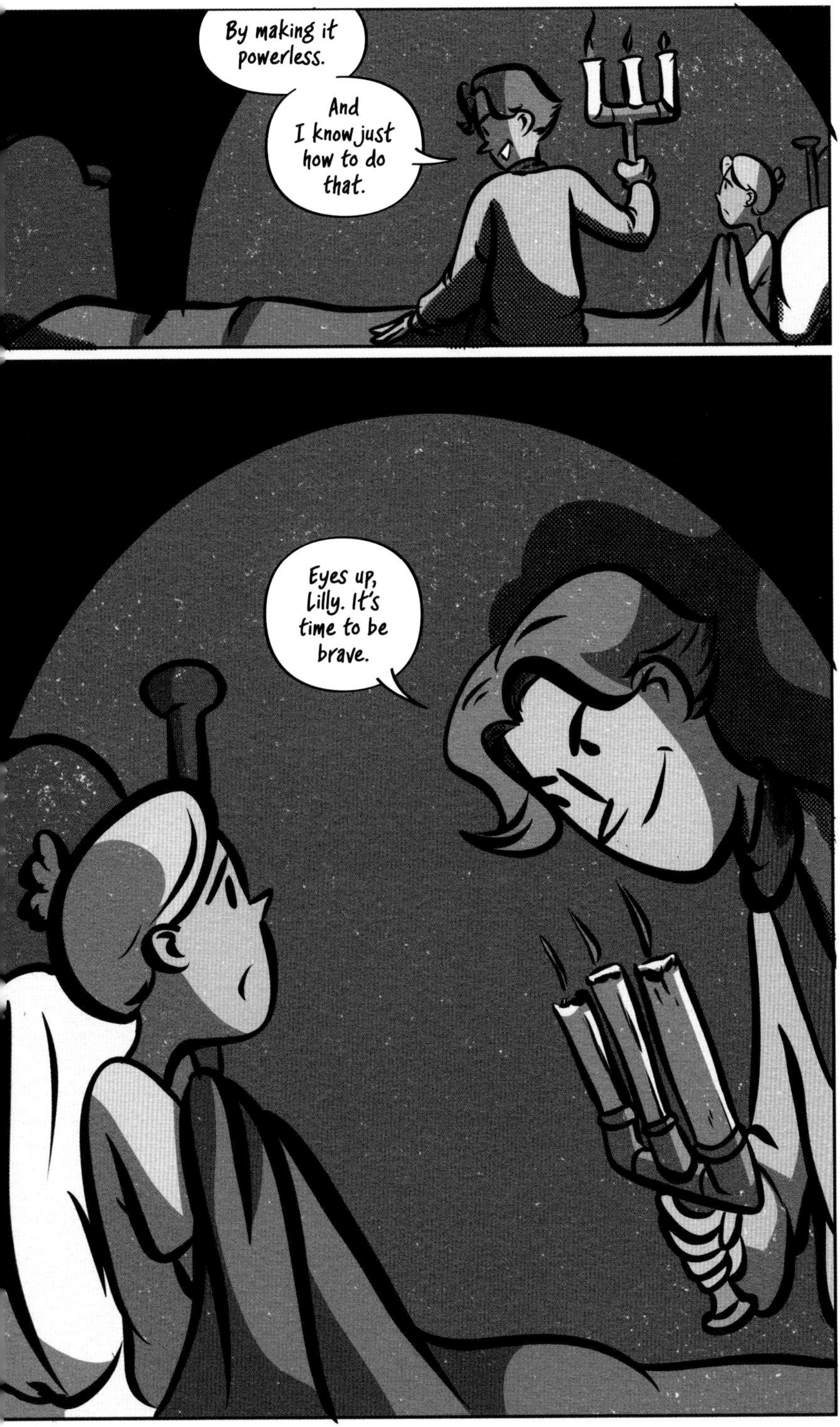
By making it powerless.
And I know just how to do that.
Eyes up, Lilly. It's time to be brave.

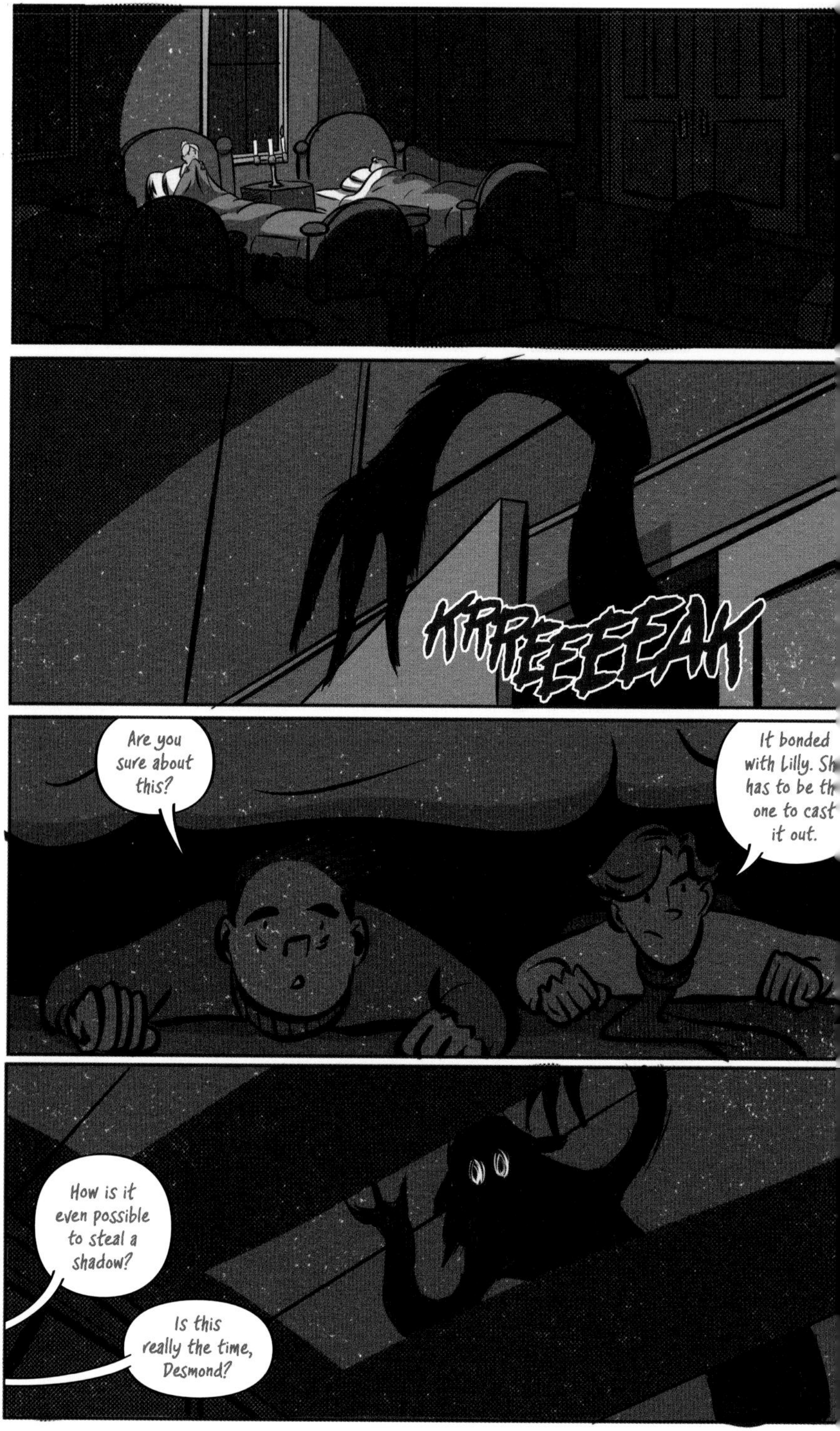
KRREEEEAK
Are you sure about this?
It bonded with Lilly. Sh has to be th one to cast it out.
How is it even possible to steal a shadow?
Is this really the time, Desmond?

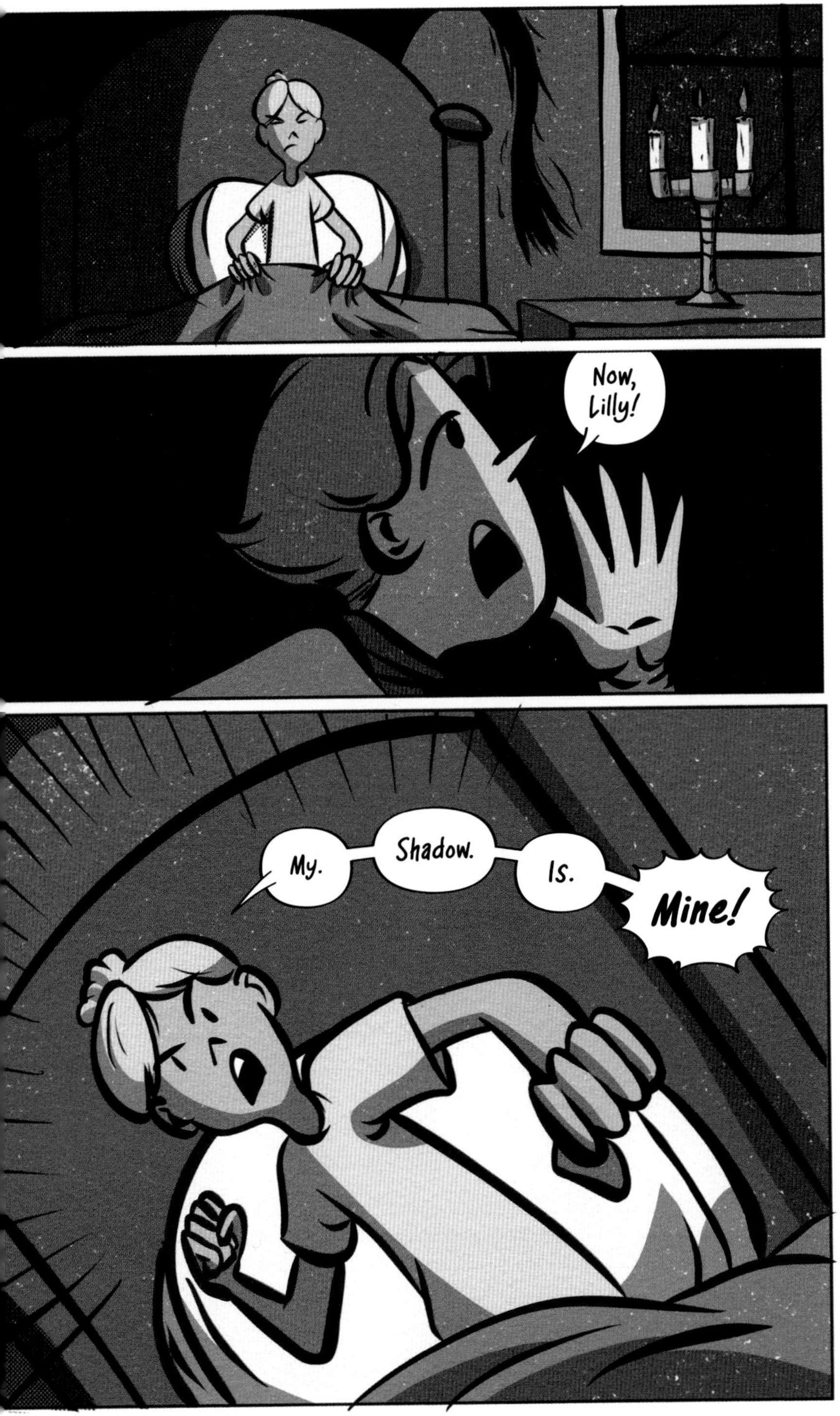
Now, Lilly!
My.
Shadow.
Is.
Mine!

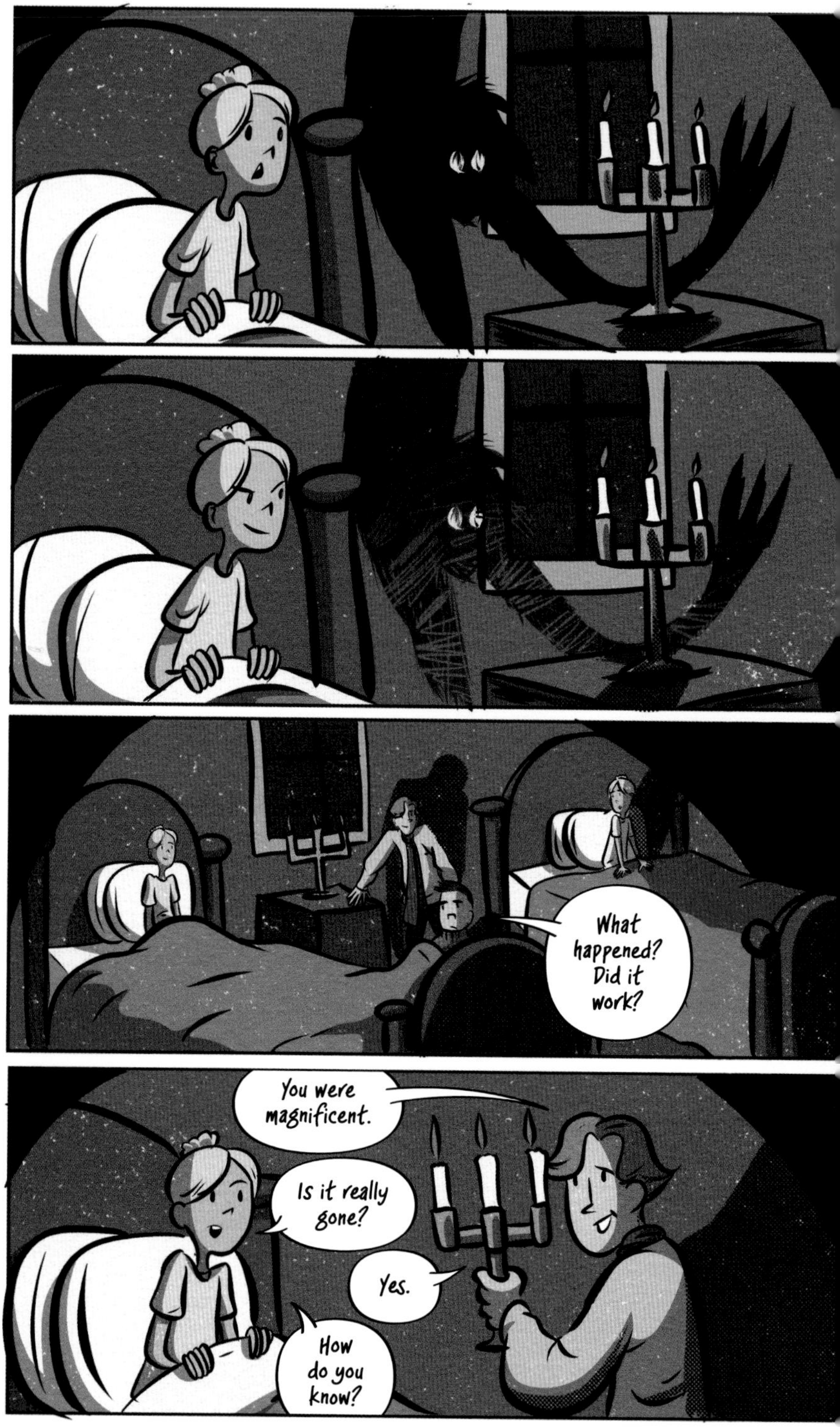
What happened? Did it work?
You were magnificent.
Is it really gone?
Yes.
How do you know?

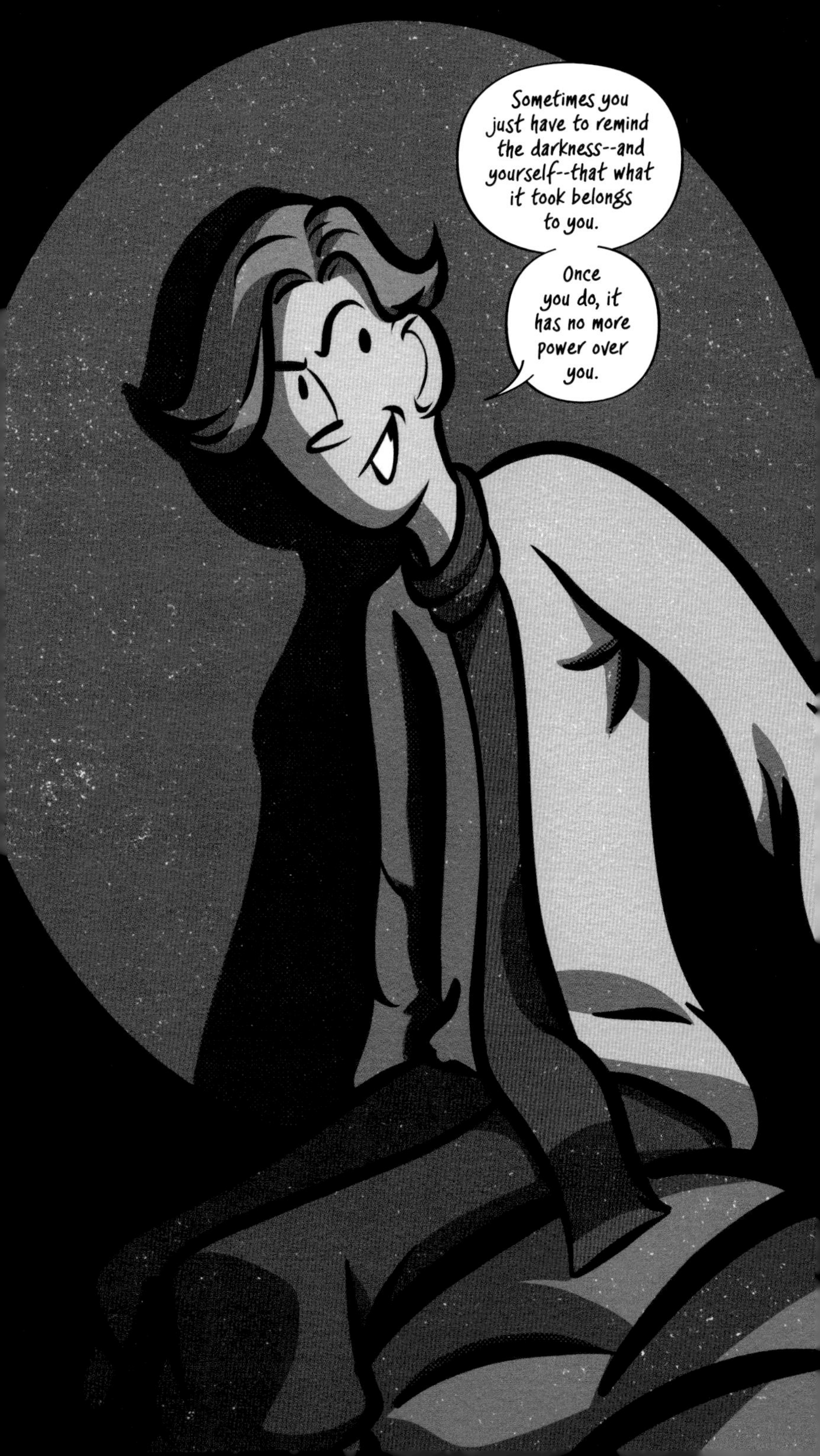
Sometimes you just have to remind the darkness--and yourself--that what it took belongs to you.
Once you do, it has no more power over you.

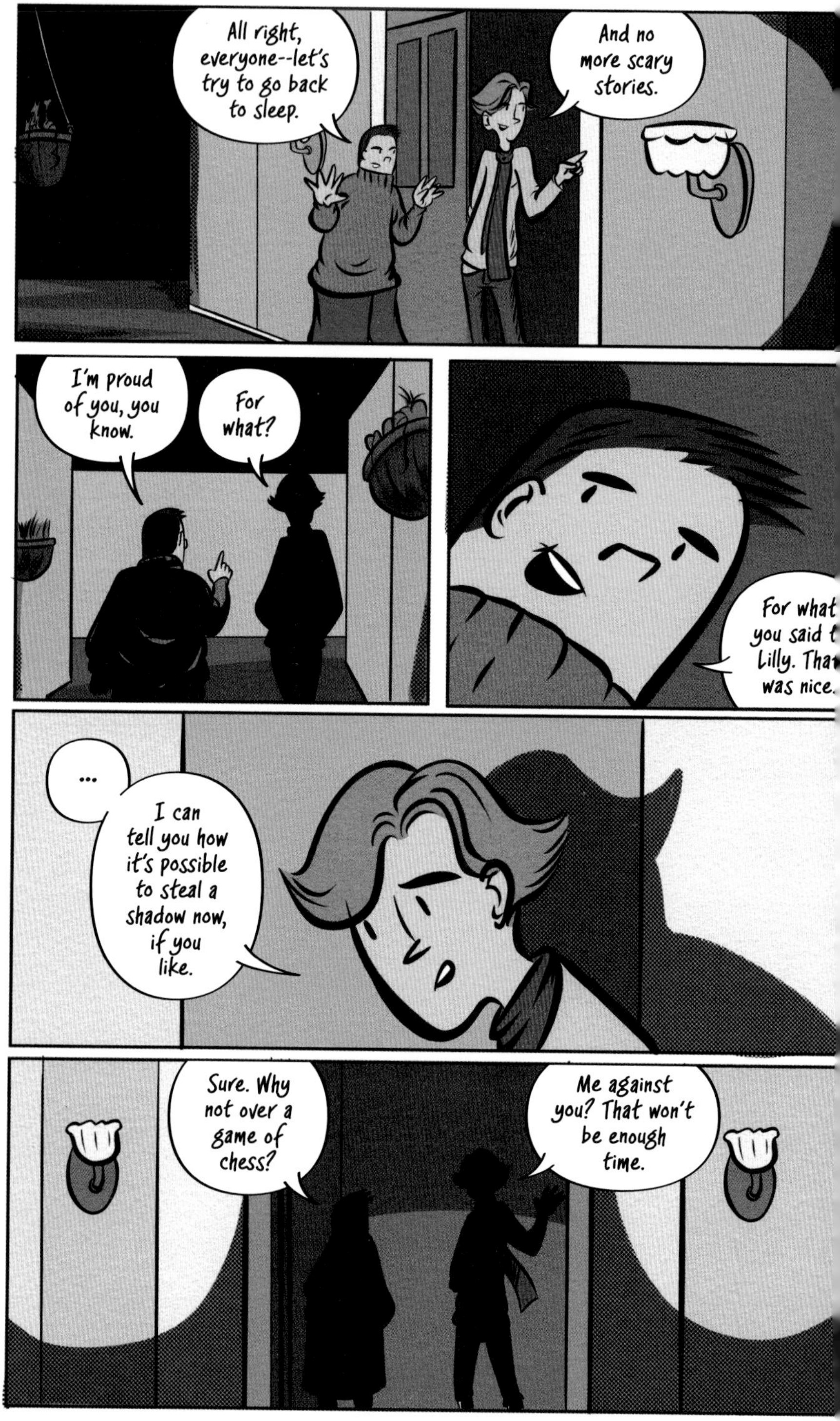
All right, everyone--let's try to go back to sleep.
And no more scary stories.
I'm proud of you, you know.
For what?
For what you said t Lilly. That was nice.
...
I can tell you how it's possible to steal a shadow now, if you like.
Sure. Why not over a game of chess?
Me against you? That won't be enough time.

CHAPTER

5

THE PALACE IN THE PANTRY

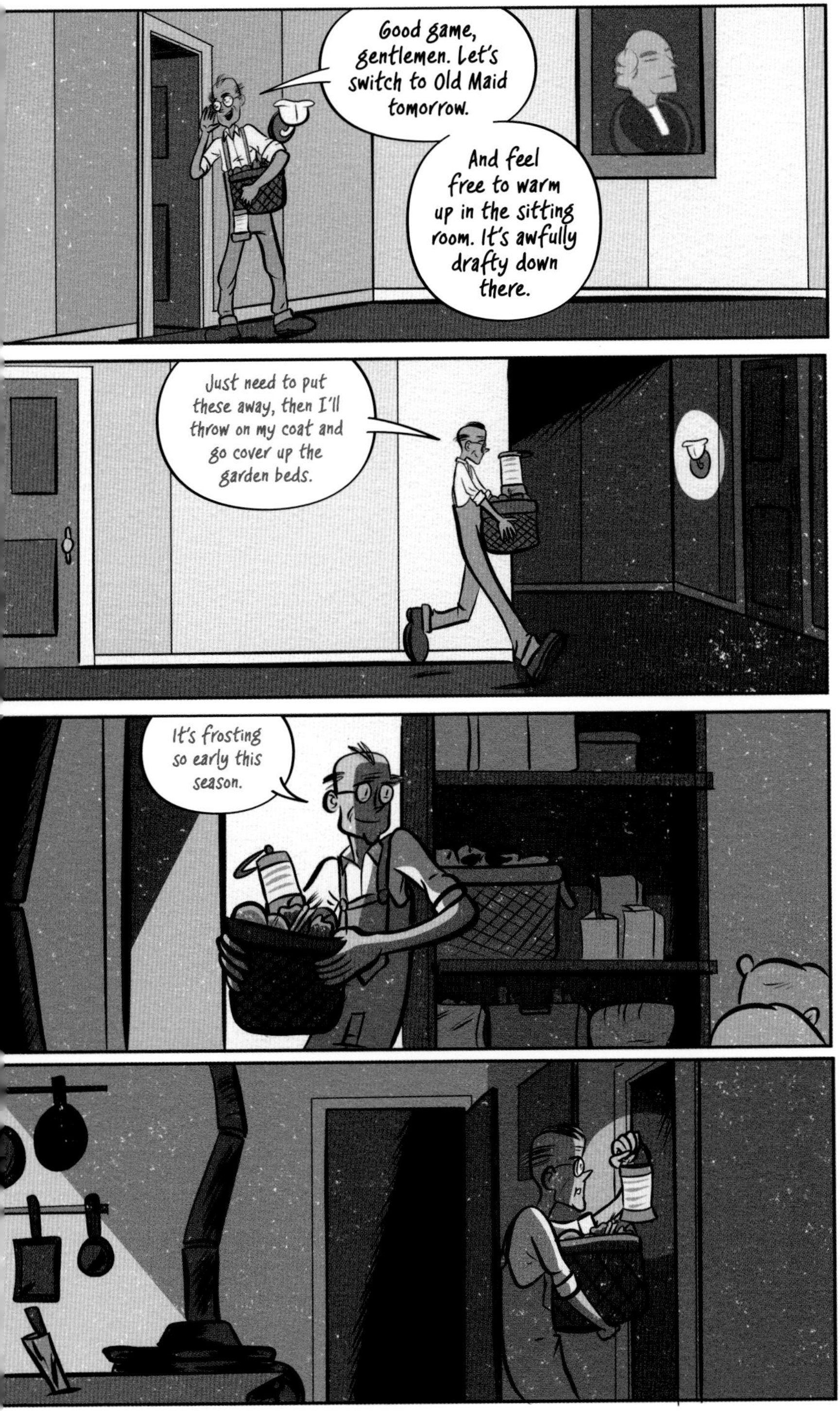

Good game, gentlemen. Let's switch to Old Maid tomorrow.
And feel free to warm up in the sitting room. It's awfully drafty down there.
Just need to put these away, then I'll throw on my coat and go cover up the garden beds.
It's frosting so early this season.

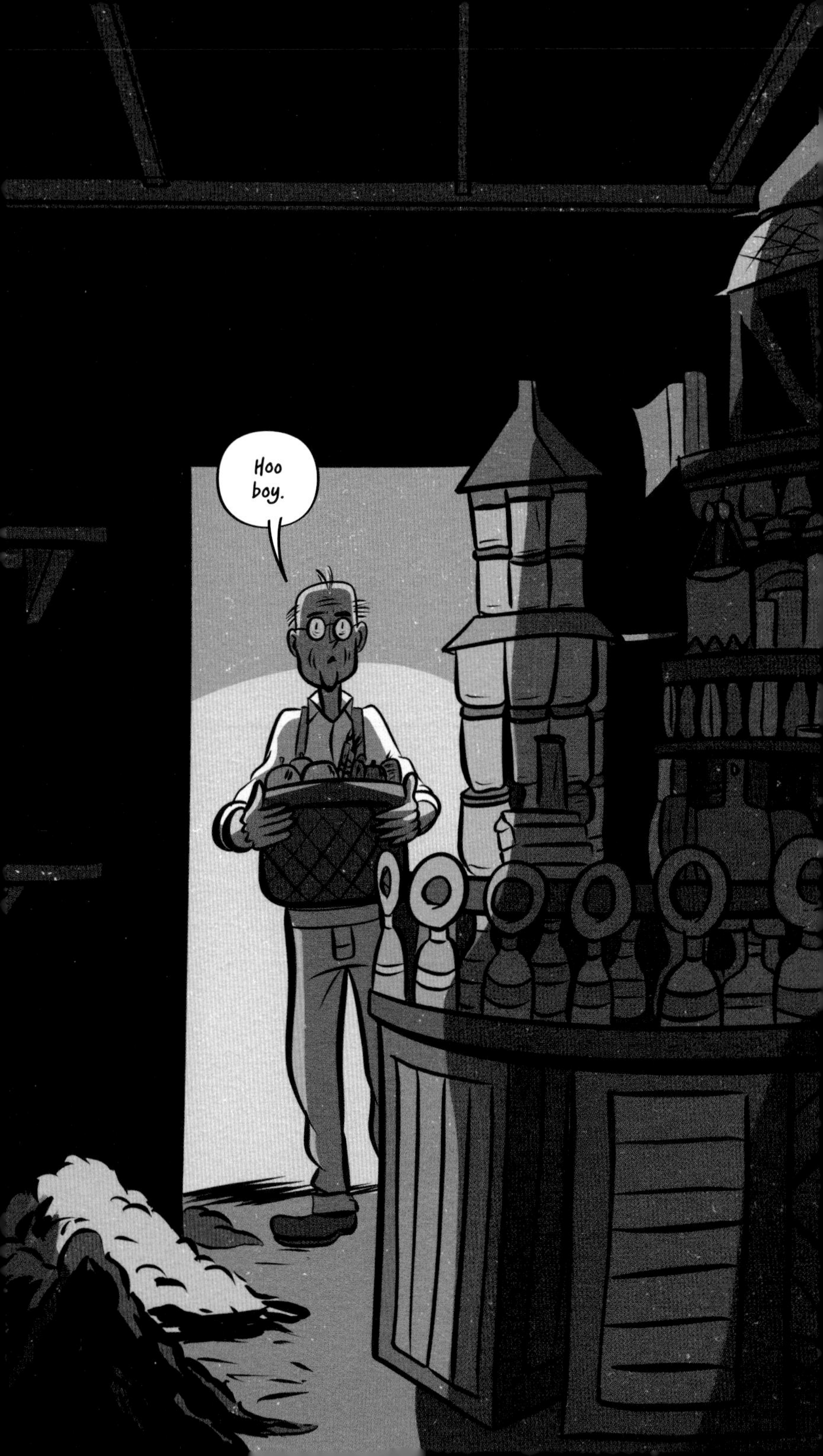
Hoo boy.

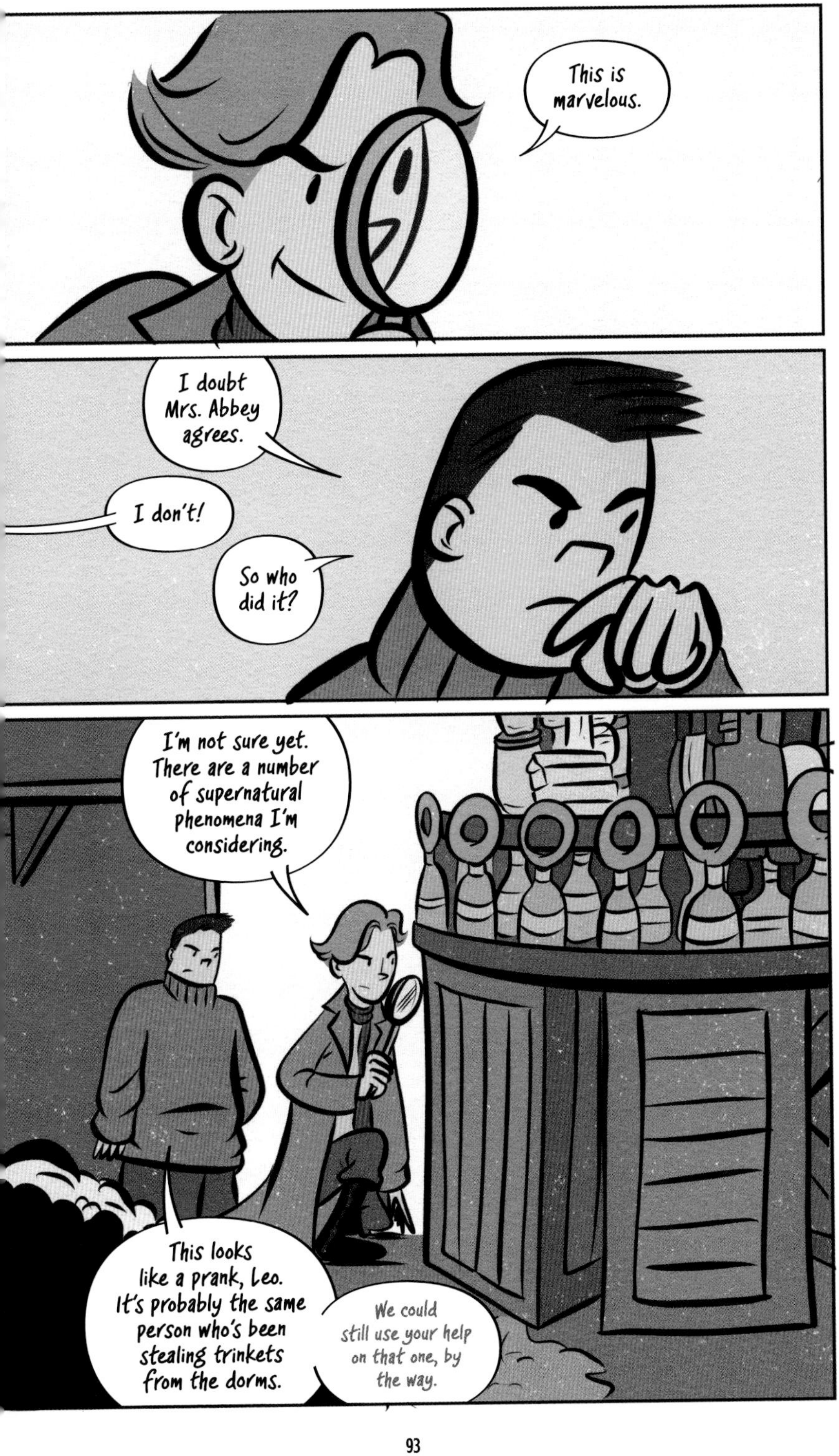
This is marvelous.
I doubt Mrs. Abbey agrees.
I don't!
So who did it?
I'm not sure yet. There are a number of supernatural phenomena I'm considering.
This looks like a prank, Leo. It's probably the same person who's been stealing trinkets from the dorms.
We could still use your help on that one, by the way.

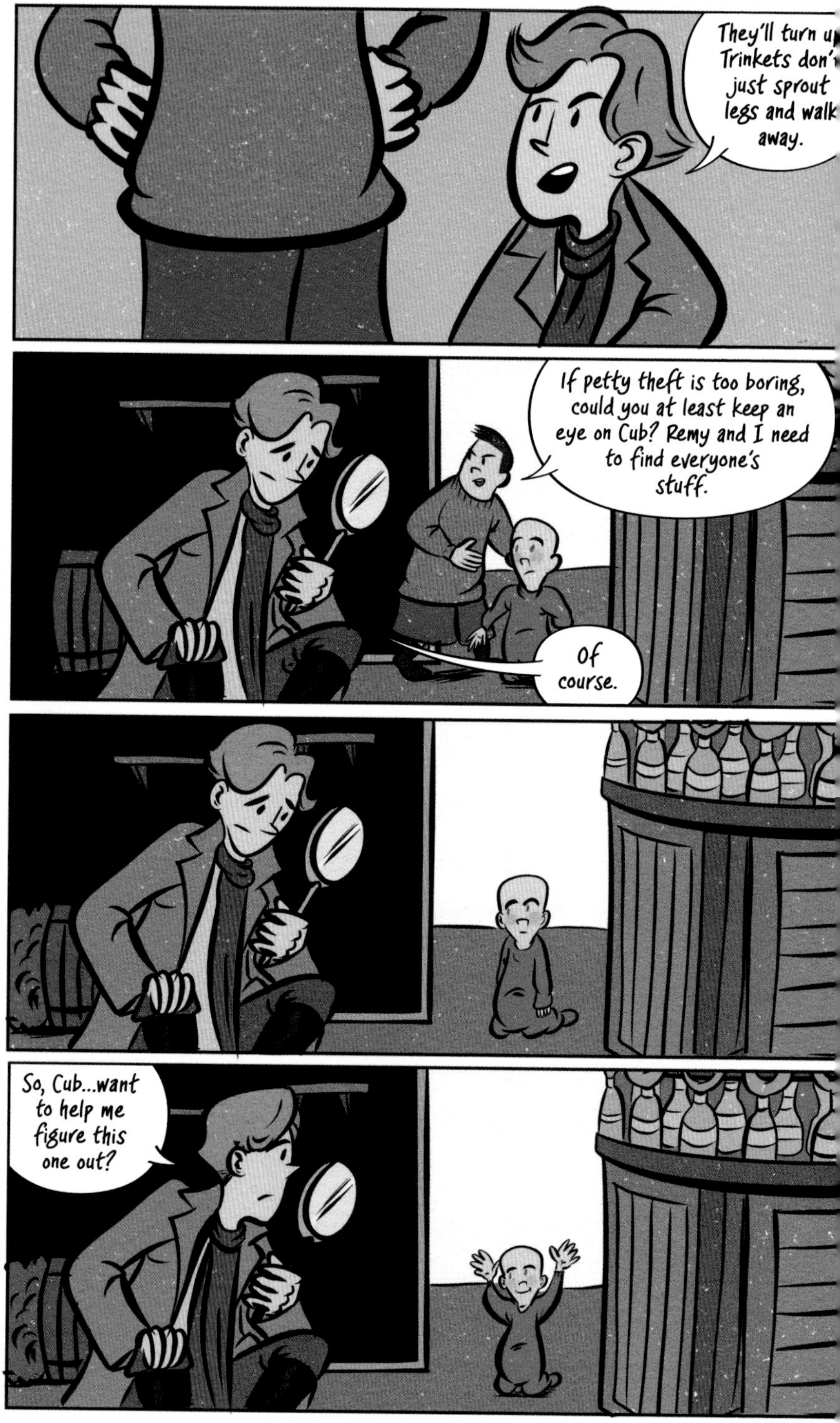
They'll turn up. Trinkets don't just sprout legs and walk away.
If petty theft is too boring, could you at least keep an eye on Cub? Remy and I need to find everyone's stuff.
Of course.
So, Cub...want to help me figure this one out?

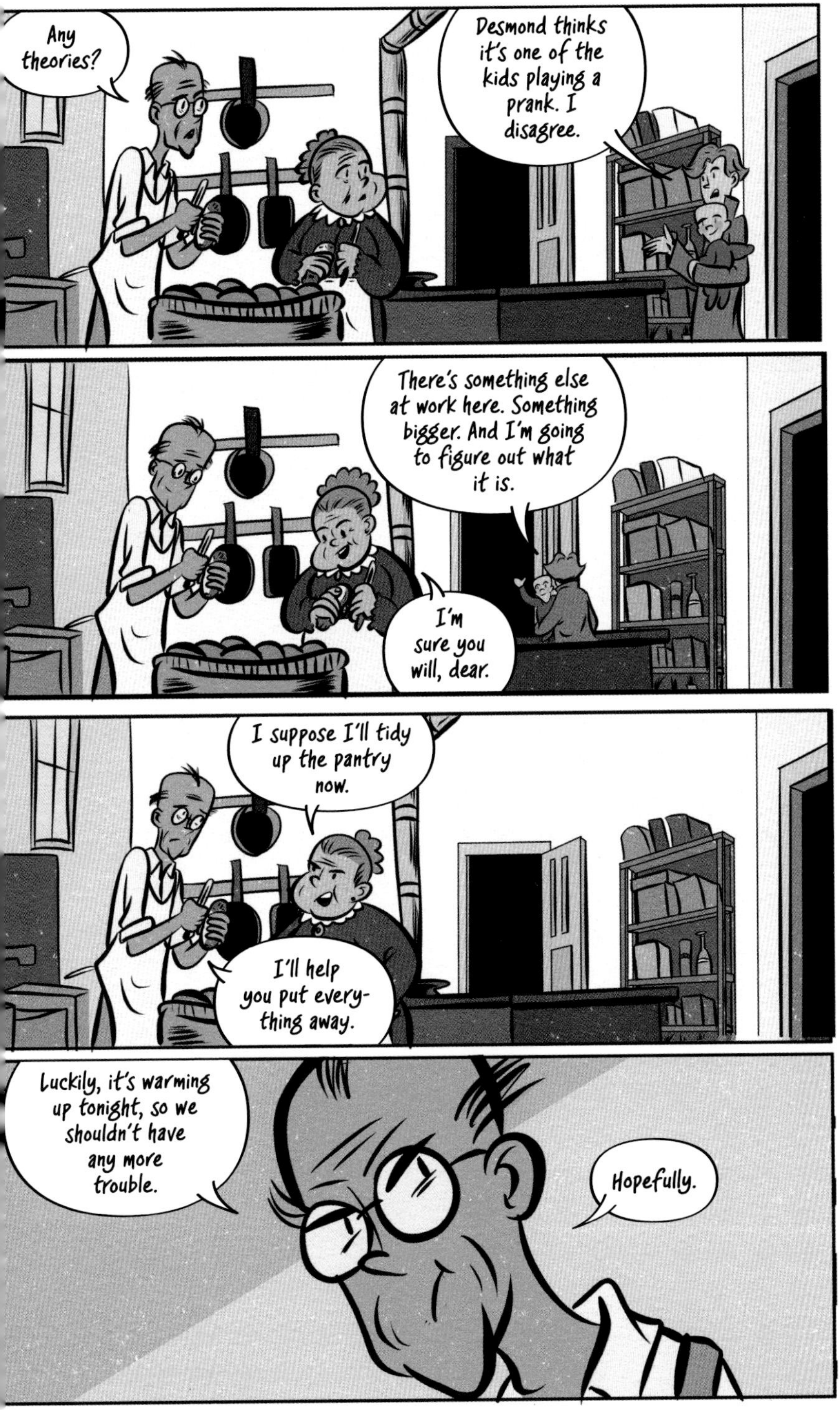
Any theories?
Desmond thinks it's one of the kids playing a prank. I disagree.
There's something else at work here. Something bigger. And I'm going to figure out what it is.
I'm sure you will, dear.
I suppose I'll tidy up the pantry now.
I'll help you put every-thing away.
Luckily, it's warming up tonight, so we shouldn't have any more trouble.
Hopefully.

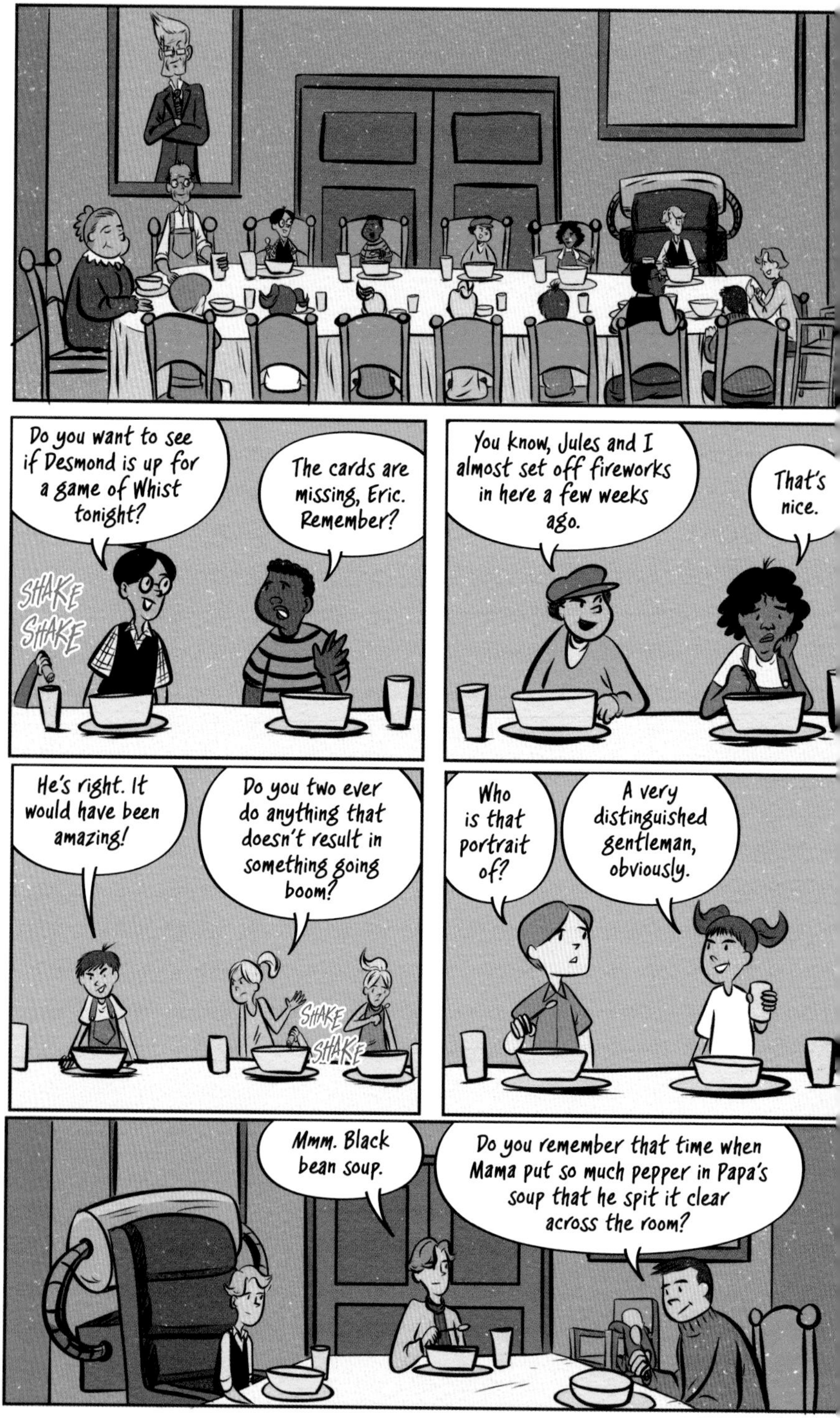
Do you want to see if Desmond is up for a game of Whist tonight?
SHAKE SHAKE
The cards are missing, Eric. Remember?
You know, Jules and I almost set off fireworks in here a few weeks ago.
That's nice.
He's right. It would have been amazing!
Do you two ever do anything that doesn't result in something going boom?
SHAKE SHAKE
Who is that portrait of?
A very distinguished gentleman, obviously.
Mmm. Black bean soup.
Do you remember that time when Mama put so much pepper in Papa's soup that he spit it clear across the room?

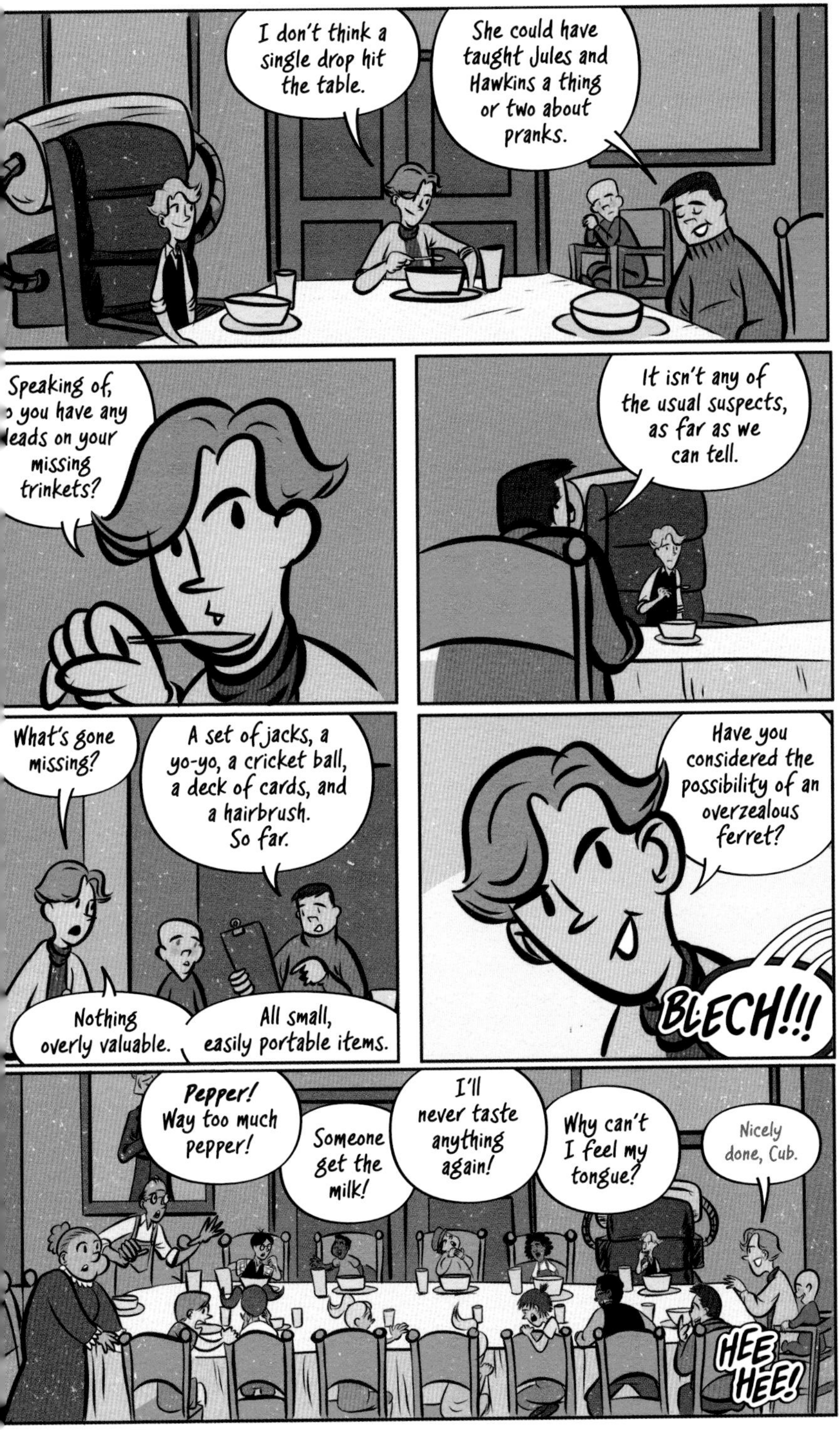

I don't think a single drop hit the table.
She could have taught Jules and Hawkins a thing or two about pranks.
Speaking of, o you have any leads on your missing trinkets?
It isn't any of the usual suspects, as far as we can tell.
What's gone missing?
A set of jacks, a yo-yo, a cricket ball, a deck of cards, and a hairbrush. So far.
Nothing overly valuable.
All small, easily portable items.
Have you considered the possibility of an overzealous ferret?
BLECH!!!
Pepper! Way too much pepper!
Someone get the milk!
I'll never taste anything again!
Why can't I feel my tongue?
Nicely done, Cub.
HEE HEE!

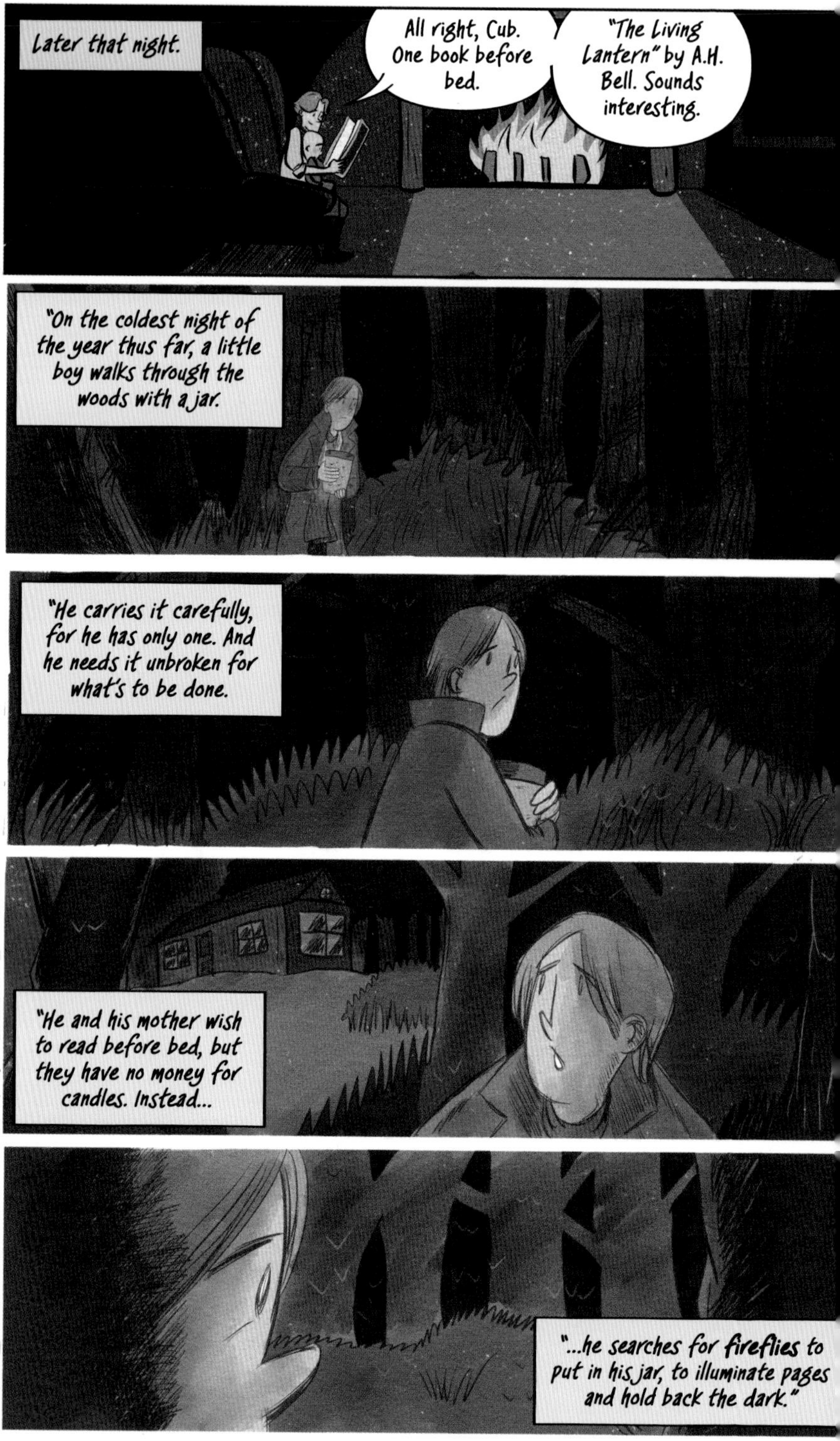
Later that night.
All right, Cub. One book before bed.
"The Living Lantern" by A.H. Bell. Sounds interesting.
"On the coldest night of the year thus far, a little boy walks through the woods with a jar.
"He carries it carefully, for he has only one. And he needs it unbroken for what's to be done.
"He and his mother wish to read before bed, but they have no money for candles. Instead...
"...he searches for fireflies to put in his jar, to illuminate pages and hold back the dark."

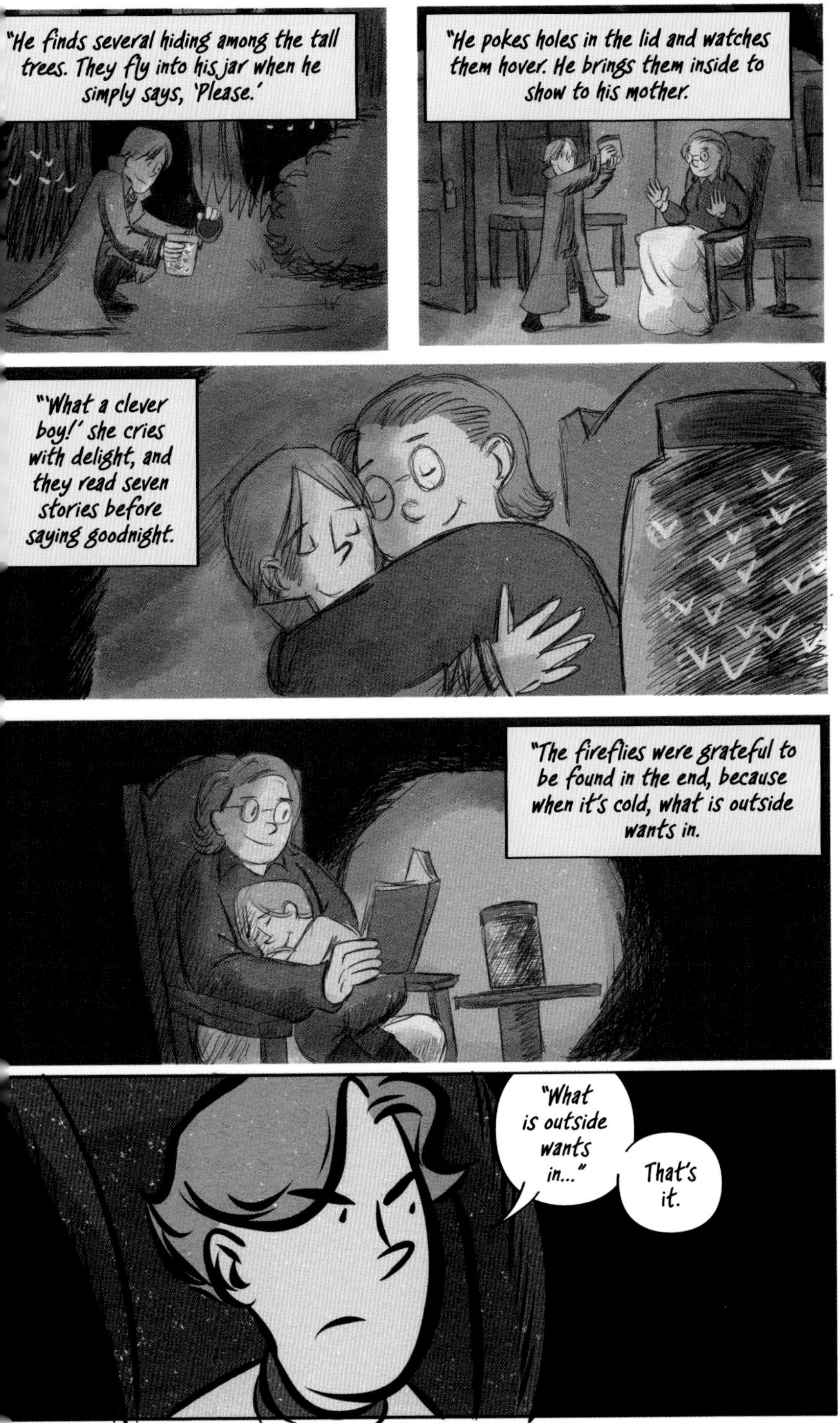
"He finds several hiding among the tall trees. They fly into his jar when he simply says, 'Please.'
"He pokes holes in the lid and watches them hover. He brings them inside to show to his mother.
"'What a clever boy!' she cries with delight, and they read seven stories before saying goodnight.
"The fireflies were grateful to be found in the end, because when it's cold, what is outside wants in.
"What is outside wants in..."
That's it.

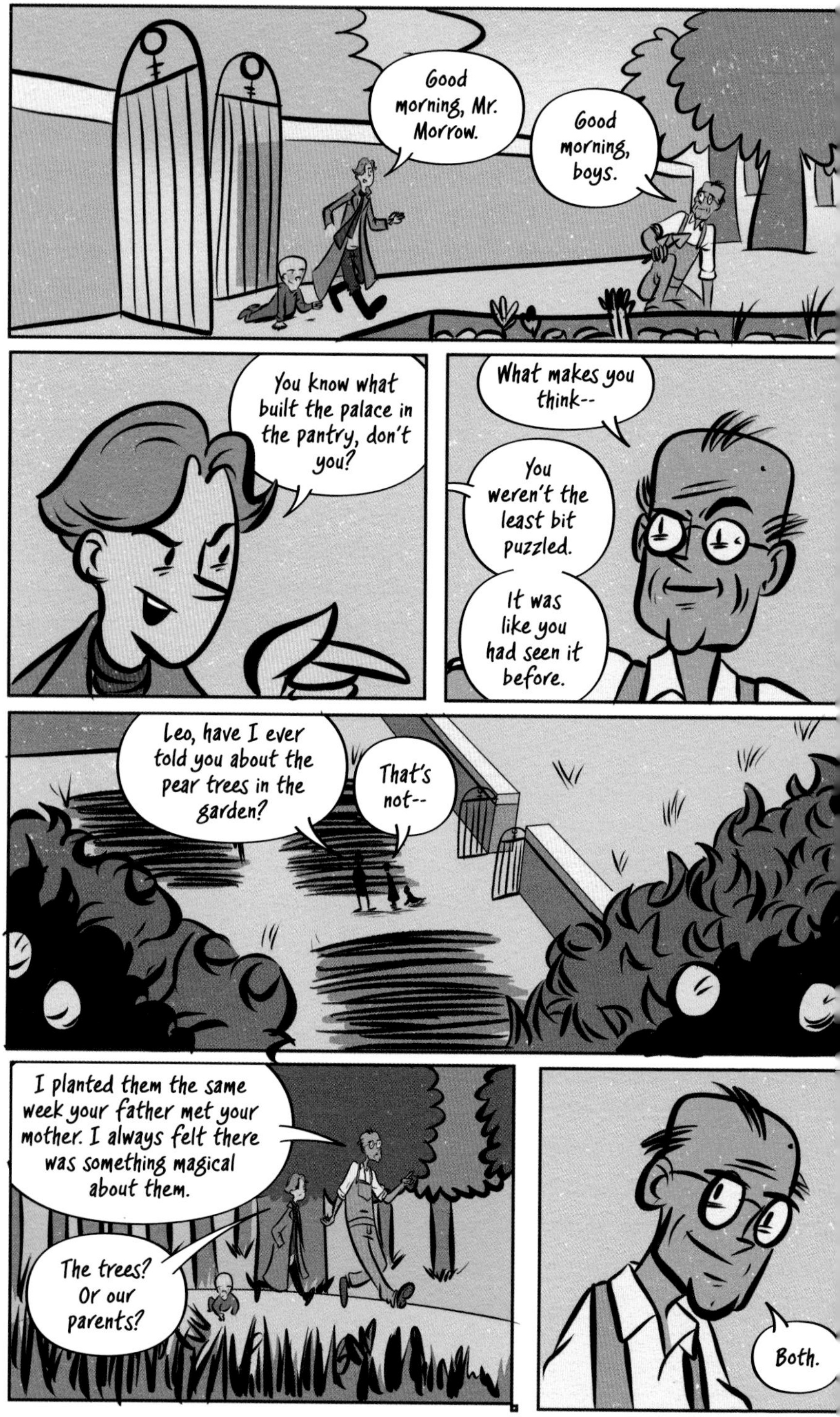

Good morning, Mr. Morrow.
Good morning, boys.
You know what built the palace in the pantry, don't you?
What makes you think--
You weren't the least bit puzzled.
It was like you had seen it before.
Leo, have I ever told you about the pear trees in the garden?
That's not--
I planted them the same week your father met your mother. I always felt there was something magical about them.
The trees? Or our parents?
Both.

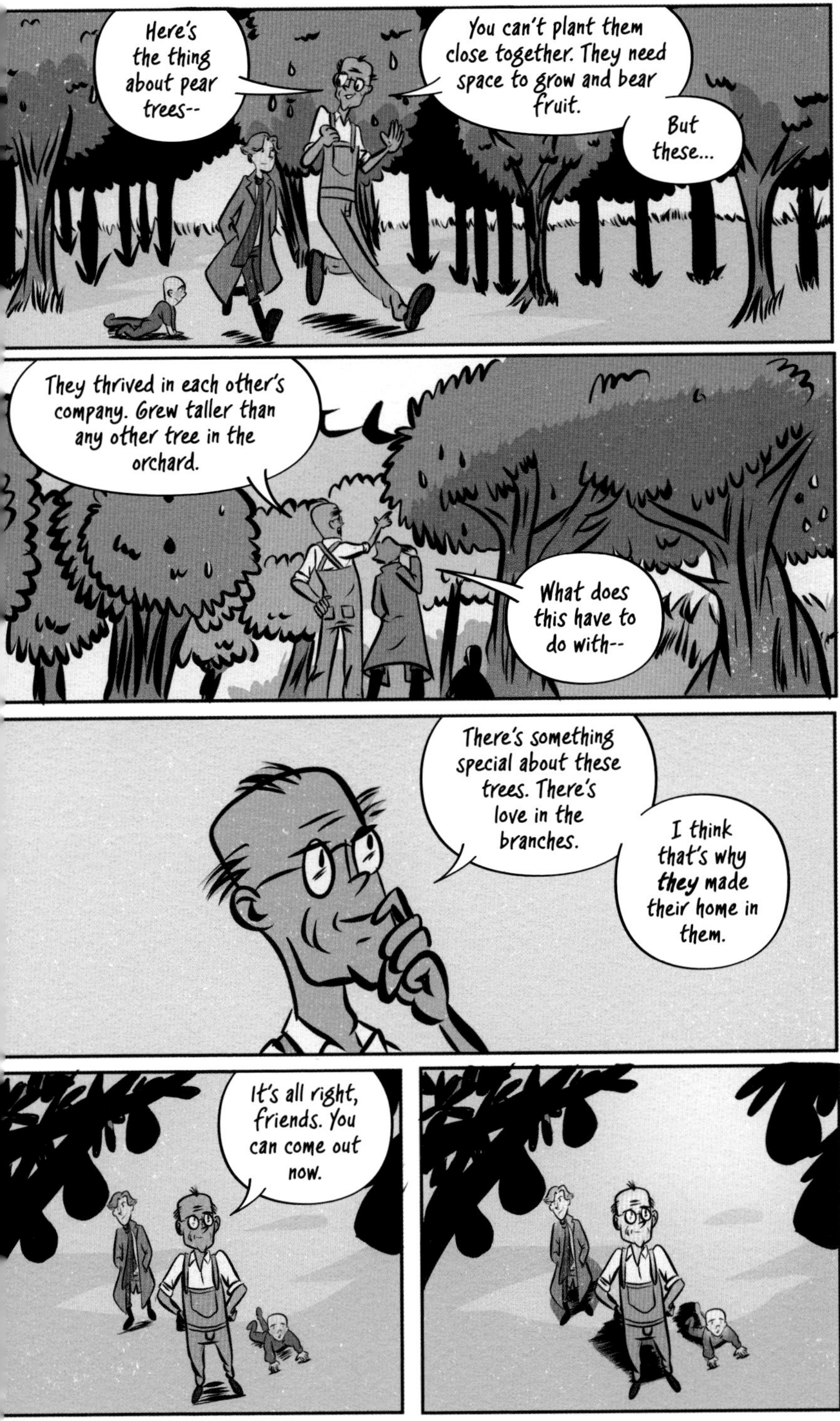
Here's the thing about pear trees--
You can't plant them close together. They need space to grow and bear fruit.
But these...
They thrived in each other's company. Grew taller than any other tree in the orchard.
What does this have to do with--
There's something special about these trees. There's love in the branches.
I think that's why *they* made their home in them.
It's all right, friends. You can come out now.

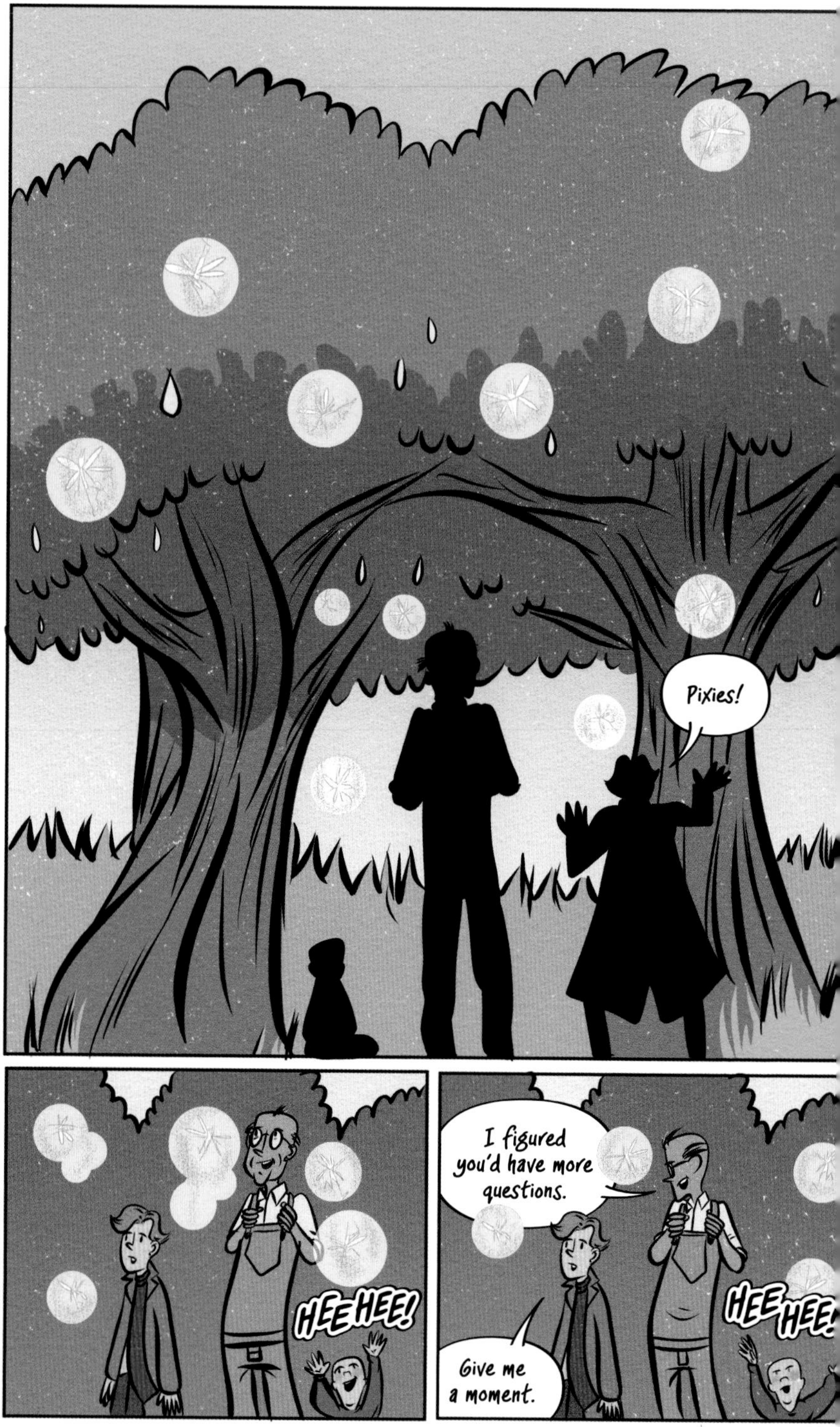
Pixies!
HEE HEE!
I figured you'd have more questions.
Give me a moment.
HEE HEE!

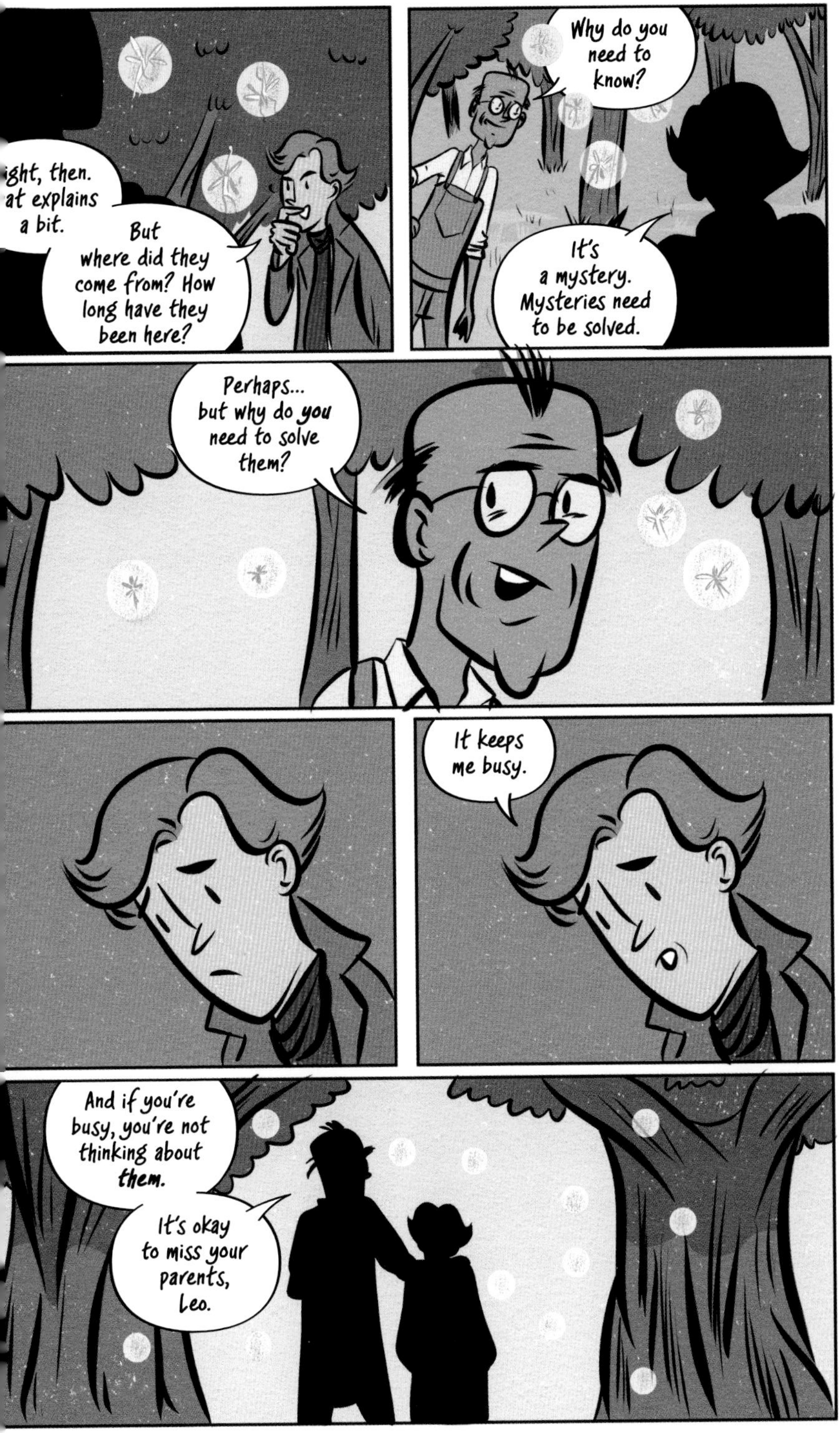

ight, then.
at explains
a bit.
But where did they come from? How long have they been here?
Why do you need to know?
It's a mystery. Mysteries need to be solved.
Perhaps... but why do *you* need to solve them?
It keeps me busy.
And if you're busy, you're not thinking about *them.*
It's okay to miss your parents, Leo.

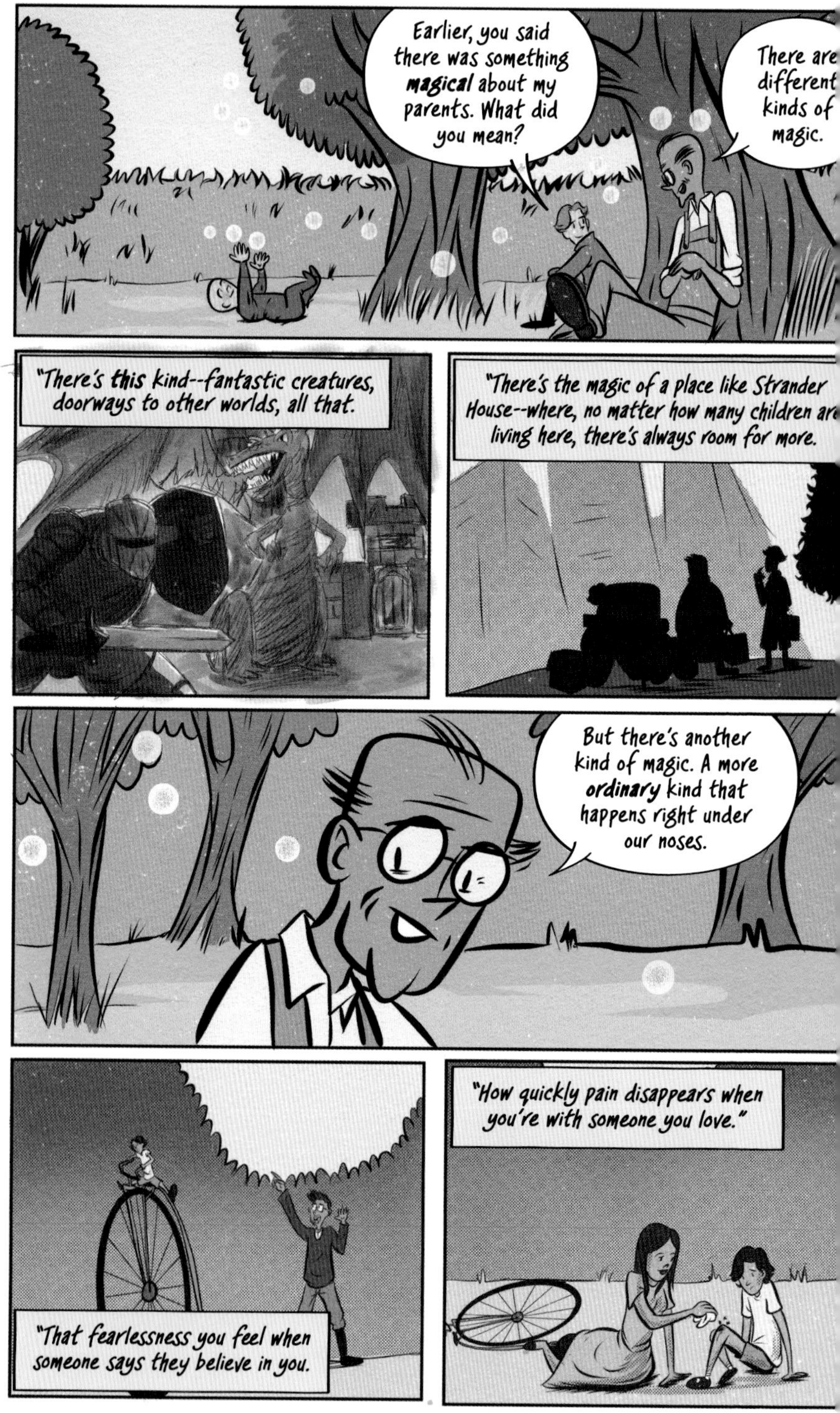

Earlier, you said there was something **magical** about my parents. What did you mean?
There are different kinds of magic.
"There's **this** kind--fantastic creatures, doorways to other worlds, all that.
"There's the magic of a place like Strander House--where, no matter how many children are living here, there's always room for more.
But there's another kind of magic. A more **ordinary** kind that happens right under our noses.
"That fearlessness you feel when someone says they believe in you.
"How quickly pain disappears when you're with someone you love."

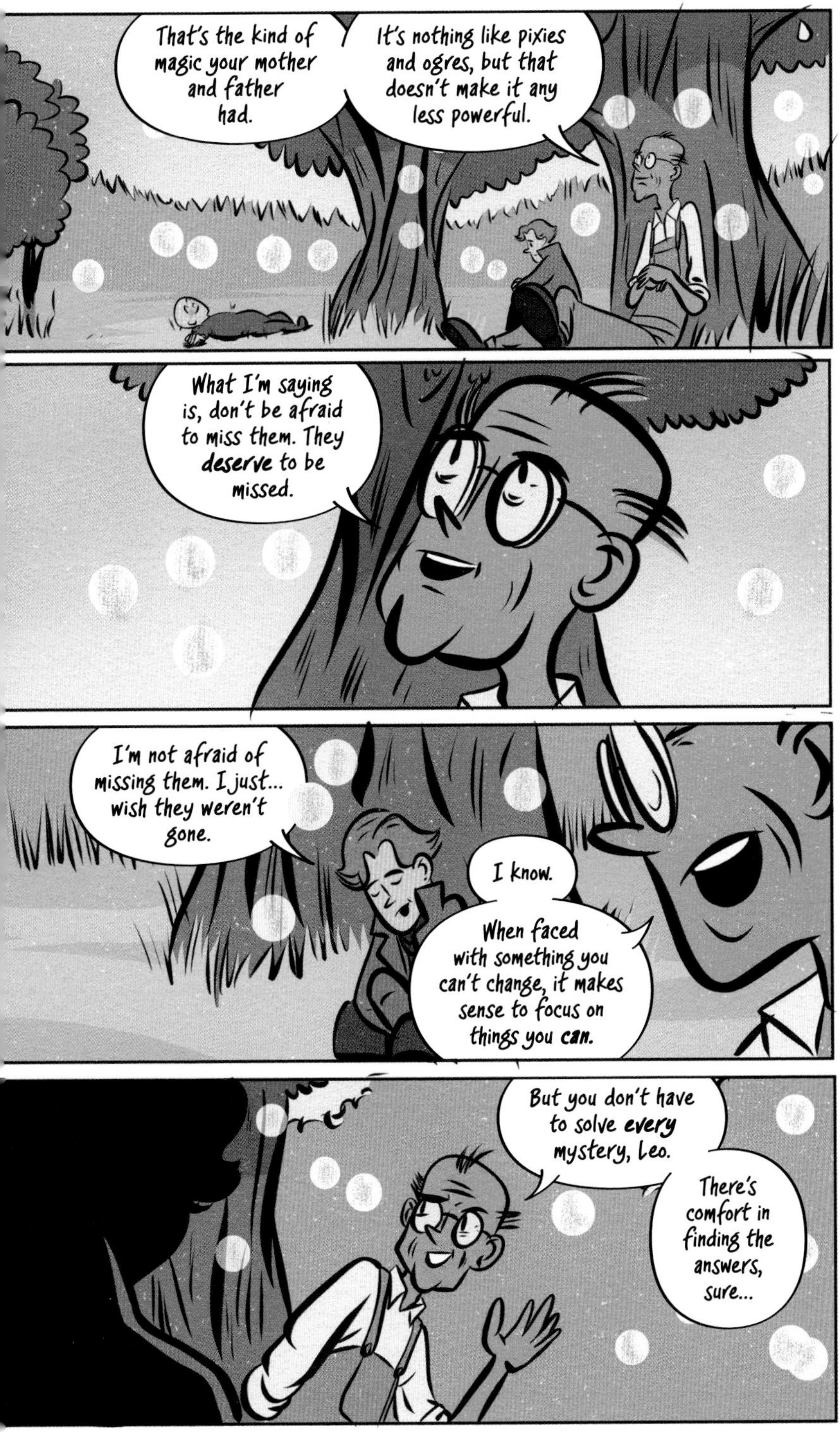
That's the kind of magic your mother and father had.
It's nothing like pixies and ogres, but that doesn't make it any less powerful.
What I'm saying is, don't be afraid to miss them. They *deserve* to be missed.
I'm not afraid of missing them. I just... wish they weren't gone.
I know.
When faced with something you can't change, it makes sense to focus on things you *can*.
But you don't have to solve *every* mystery, Leo.
There's comfort in finding the answers, sure...

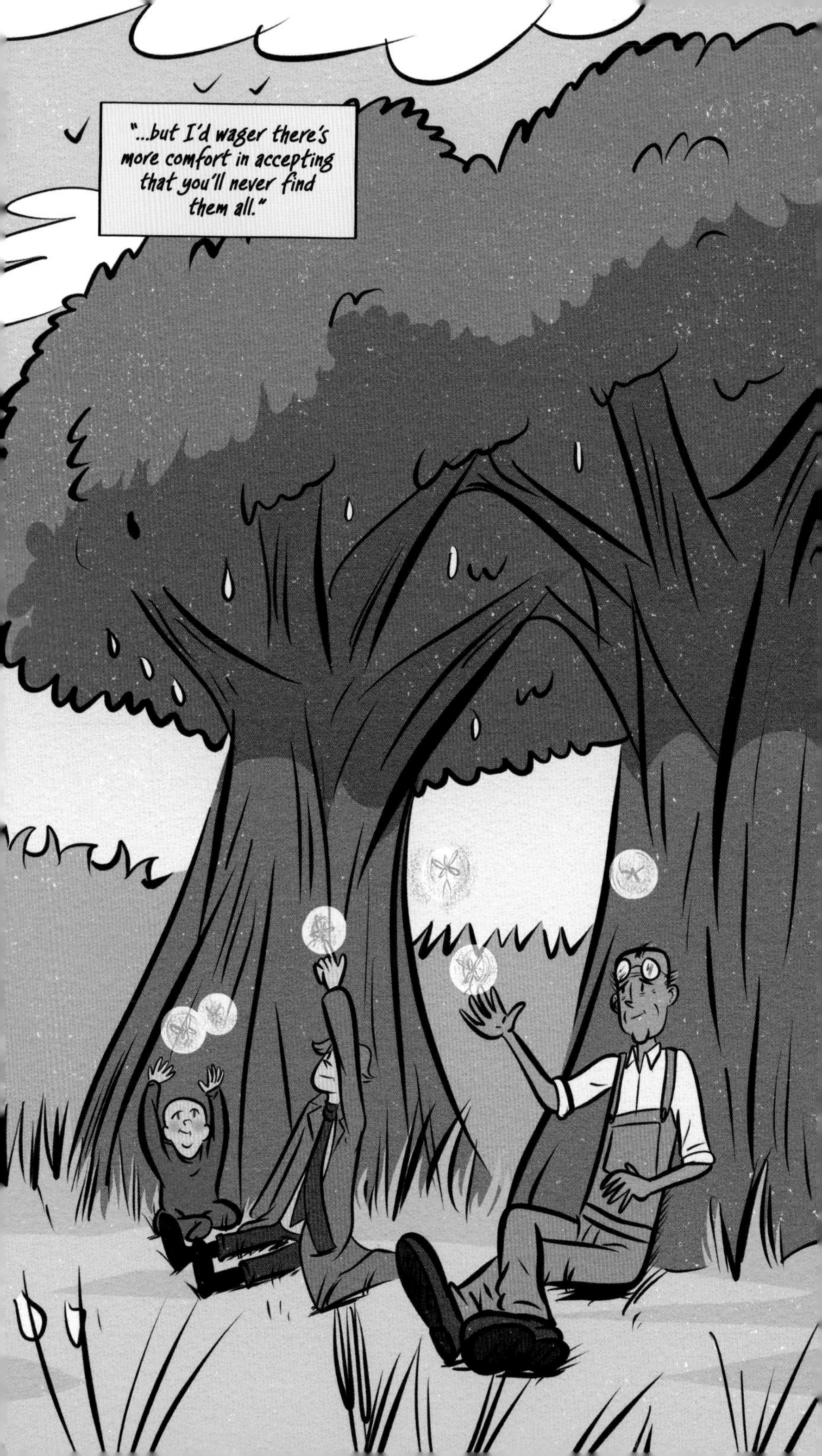
"...but I'd wager there's more comfort in accepting that you'll never find them all."

CHAPTER

6

THE UNEXPECTED LABYRINTH

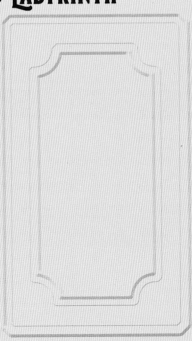

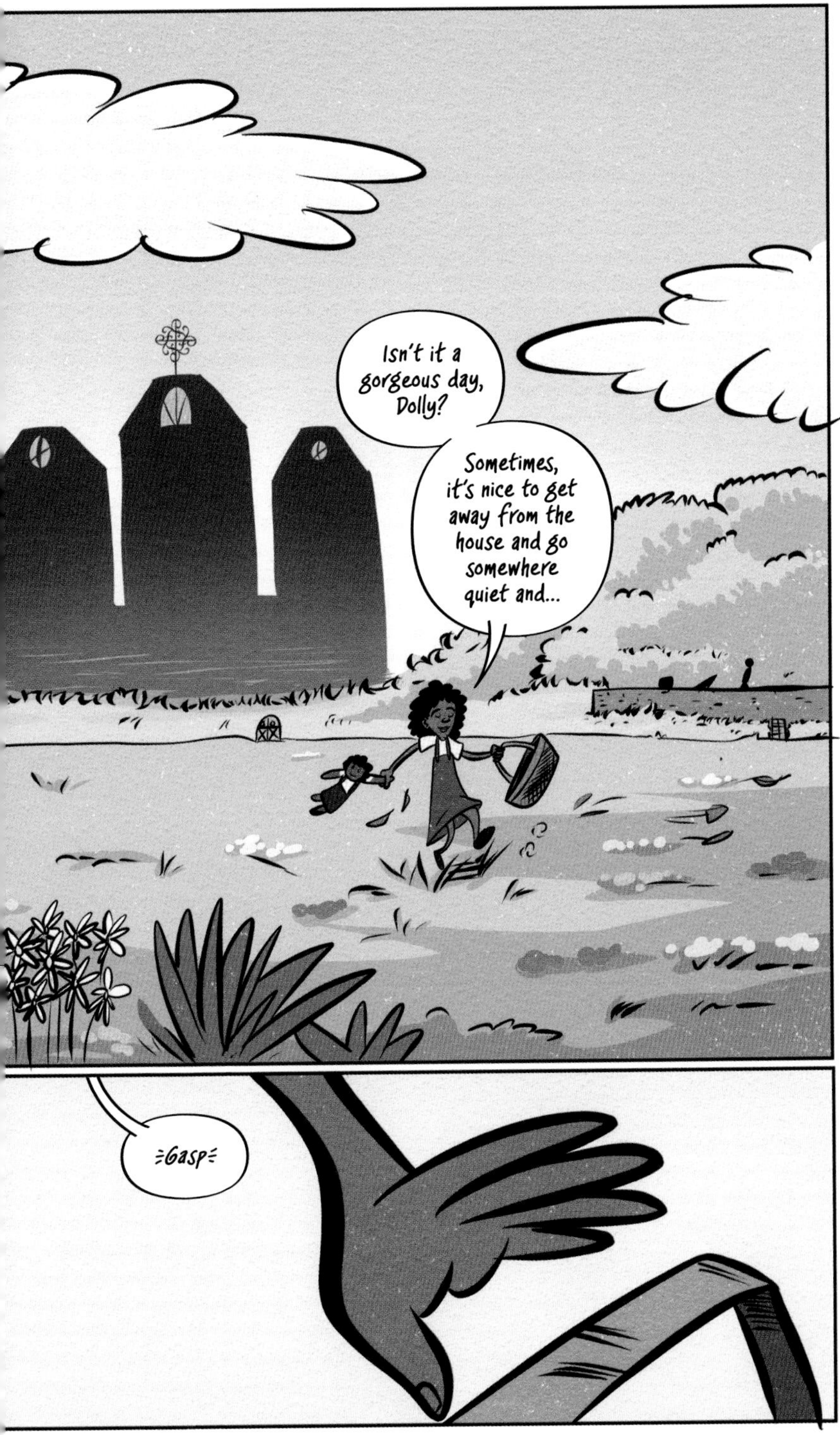
Isn't it a gorgeous day, Dolly?
Sometimes, it's nice to get away from the house and go somewhere quiet and...
Gasp

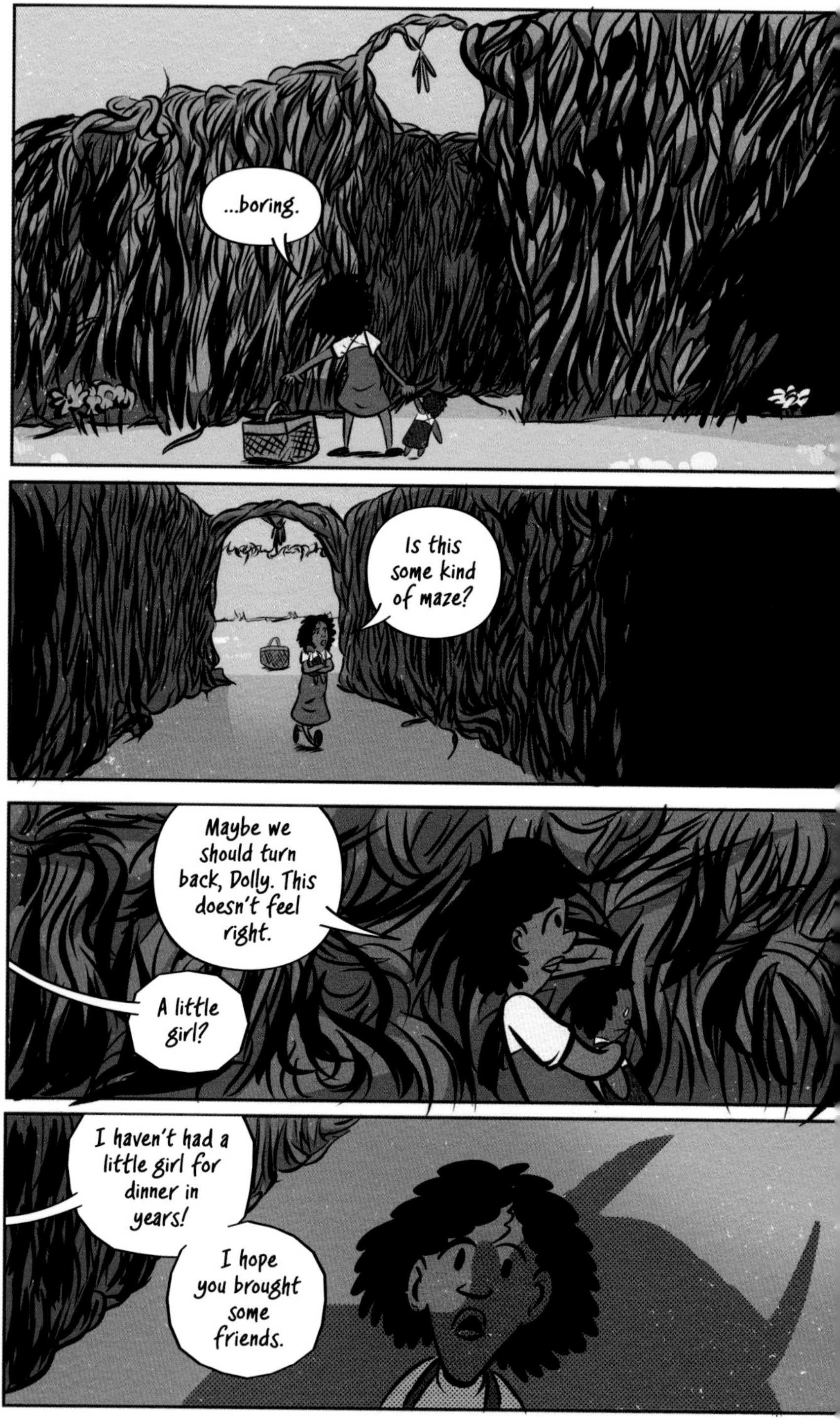
...boring.
Is this some kind of maze?
Maybe we should turn back, Dolly. This doesn't feel right.
A little girl?
I haven't had a little girl for dinner in years!
I hope you brought some friends.

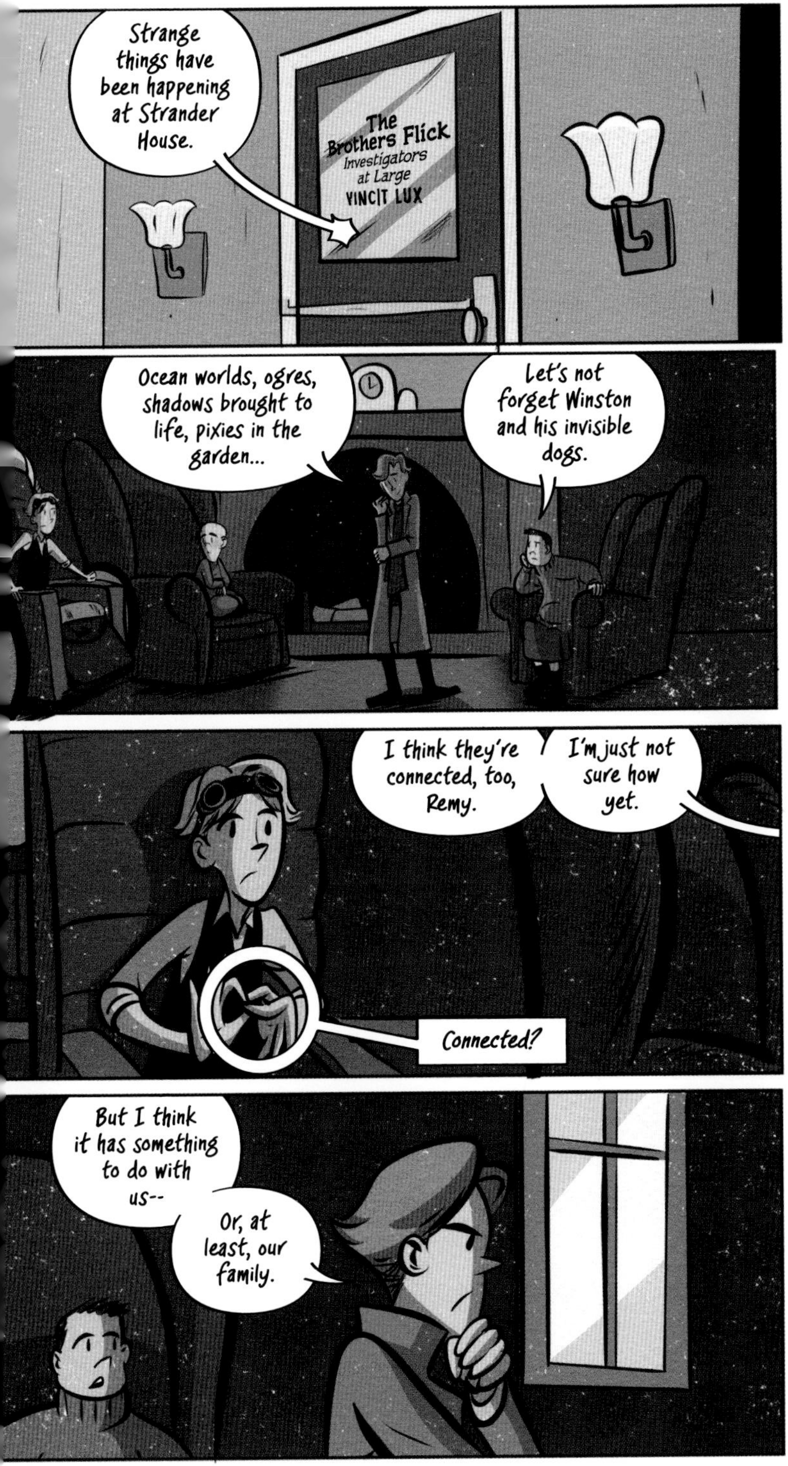
Strange things have been happening at Strander House.
The Brothers Flick Investigators at Large VINCIT LUX
Ocean worlds, ogres, shadows brought to life, pixies in the garden...
Let's not forget Winston and his invisible dogs.
I think they're connected, too, Remy.
I'm just not sure how yet.
Connected?
But I think it has something to do with us--
Or, at least, our family.

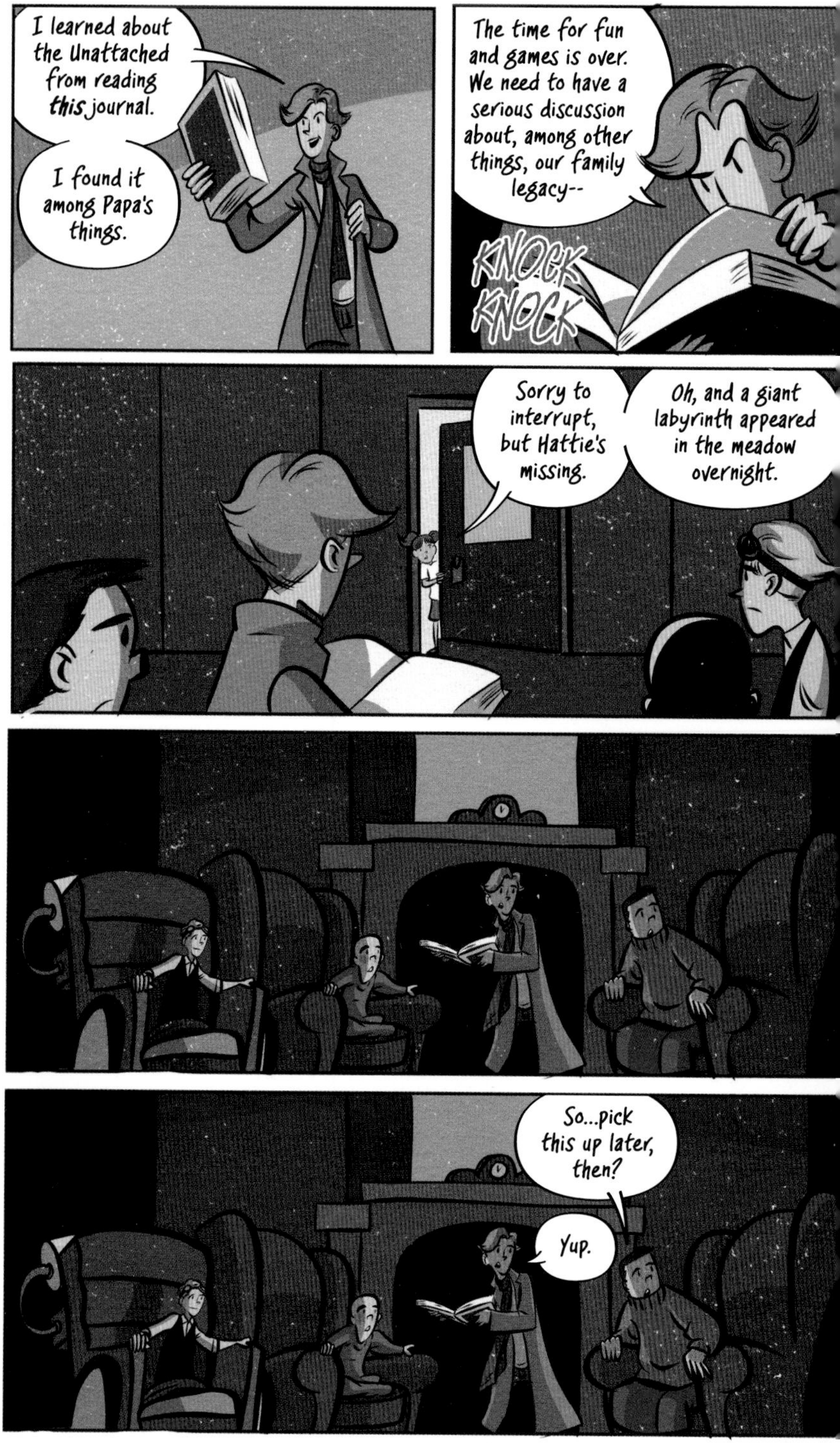
I learned about the Unattached from reading *this* journal.
I found it among Papa's things.
The time for fun and games is over. We need to have a serious discussion about, among other things, our family legacy--
KNOCK KNOCK
Sorry to interrupt, but Hattie's missing.
Oh, and a giant labyrinth appeared in the meadow overnight.
So...pick this up later, then?
Yup.

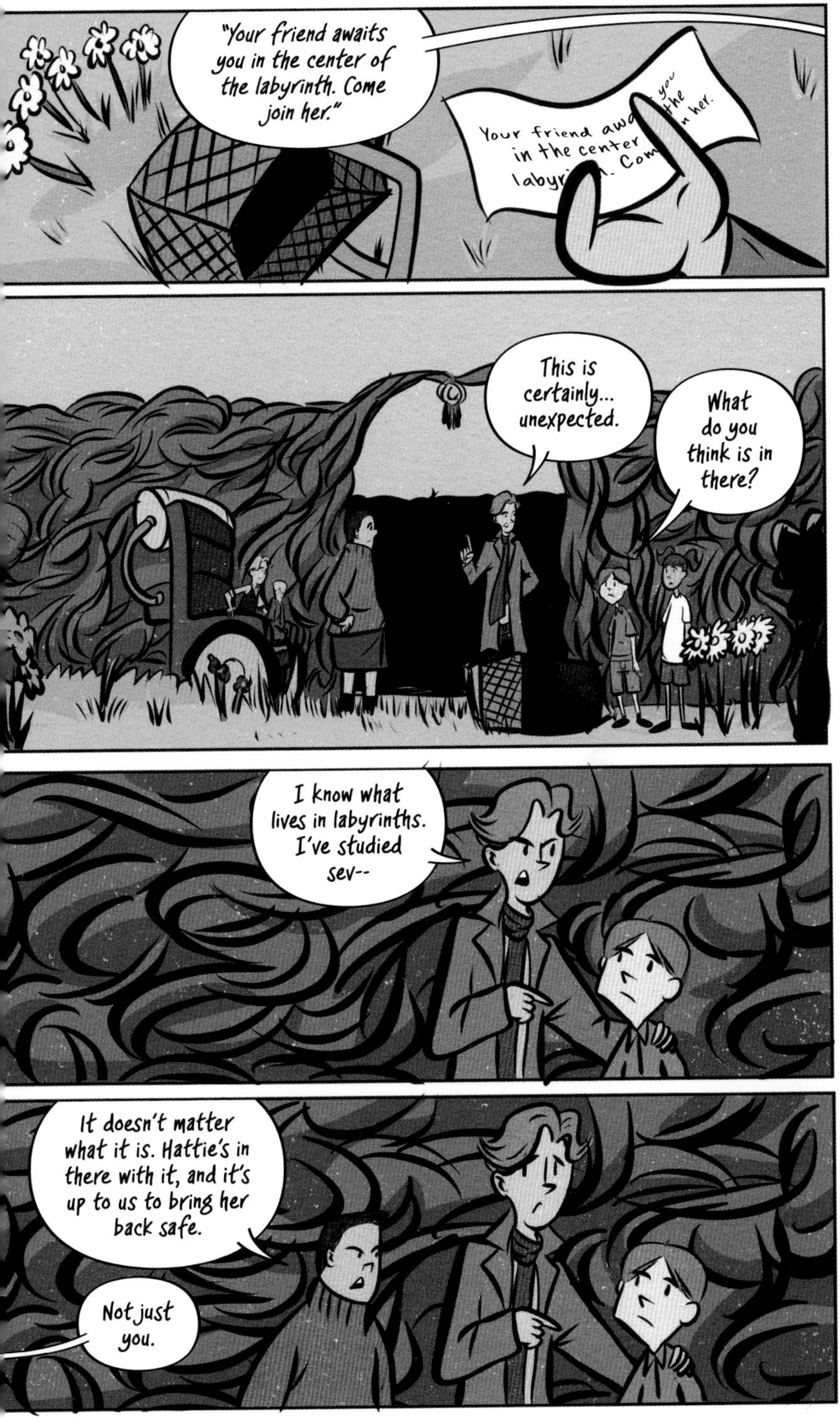
"Your friend awaits you in the center of the labyrinth. Come join her."
This is certainly... unexpected.
What do you think is in there?
I know what lives in labyrinths. I've studied sev--
It doesn't matter what it is. Hattie's in there with it, and it's up to us to bring her back safe.
Not just you.

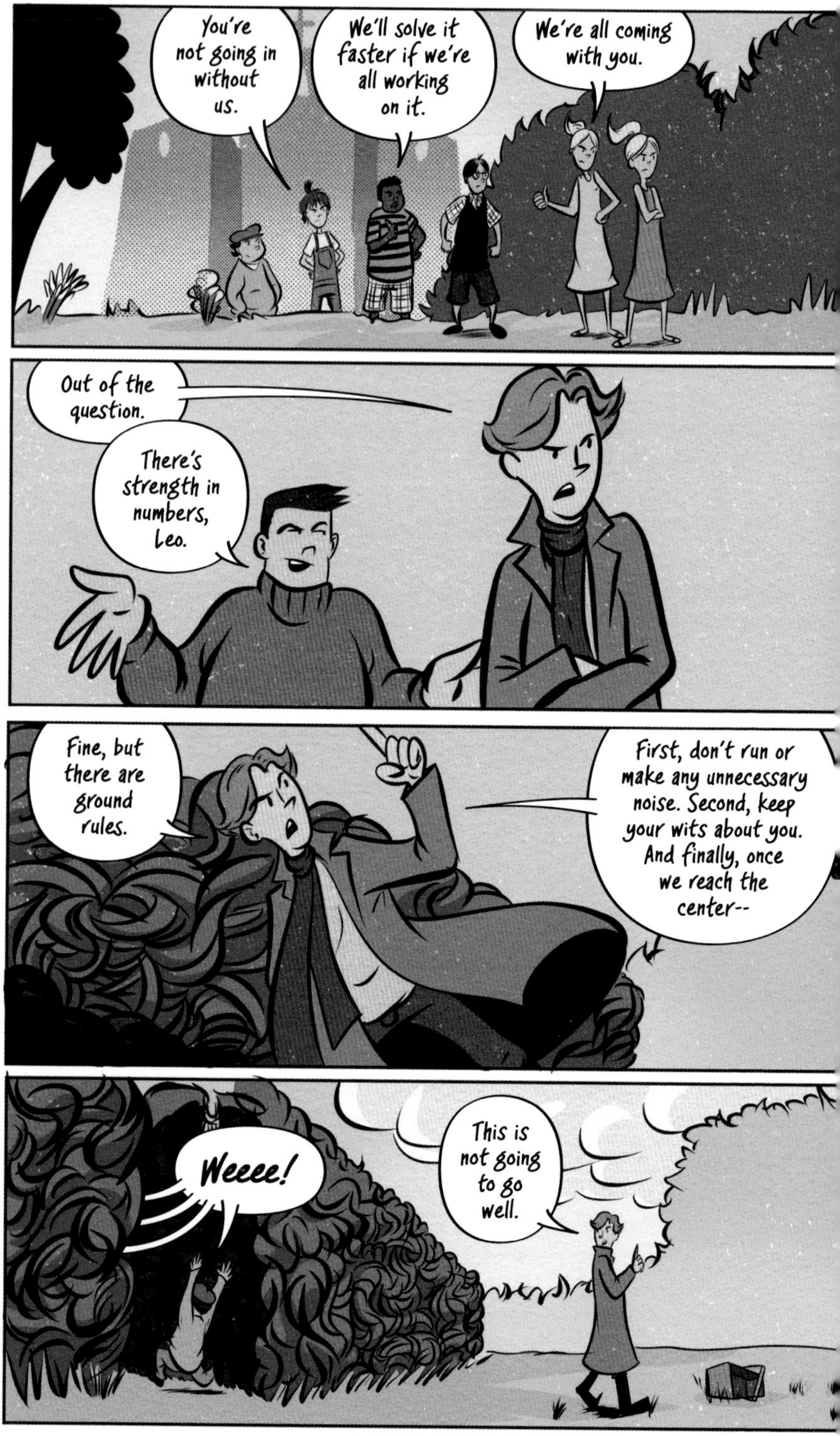

You're not going in without us.
We'll solve it faster if we're all working on it.
We're all coming with you.
Out of the question.
There's strength in numbers, Leo.
Fine, but there are ground rules.
First, don't run or make any unnecessary noise. Second, keep your wits about you. And finally, once we reach the center--
Weeee!
This is not going to go well.

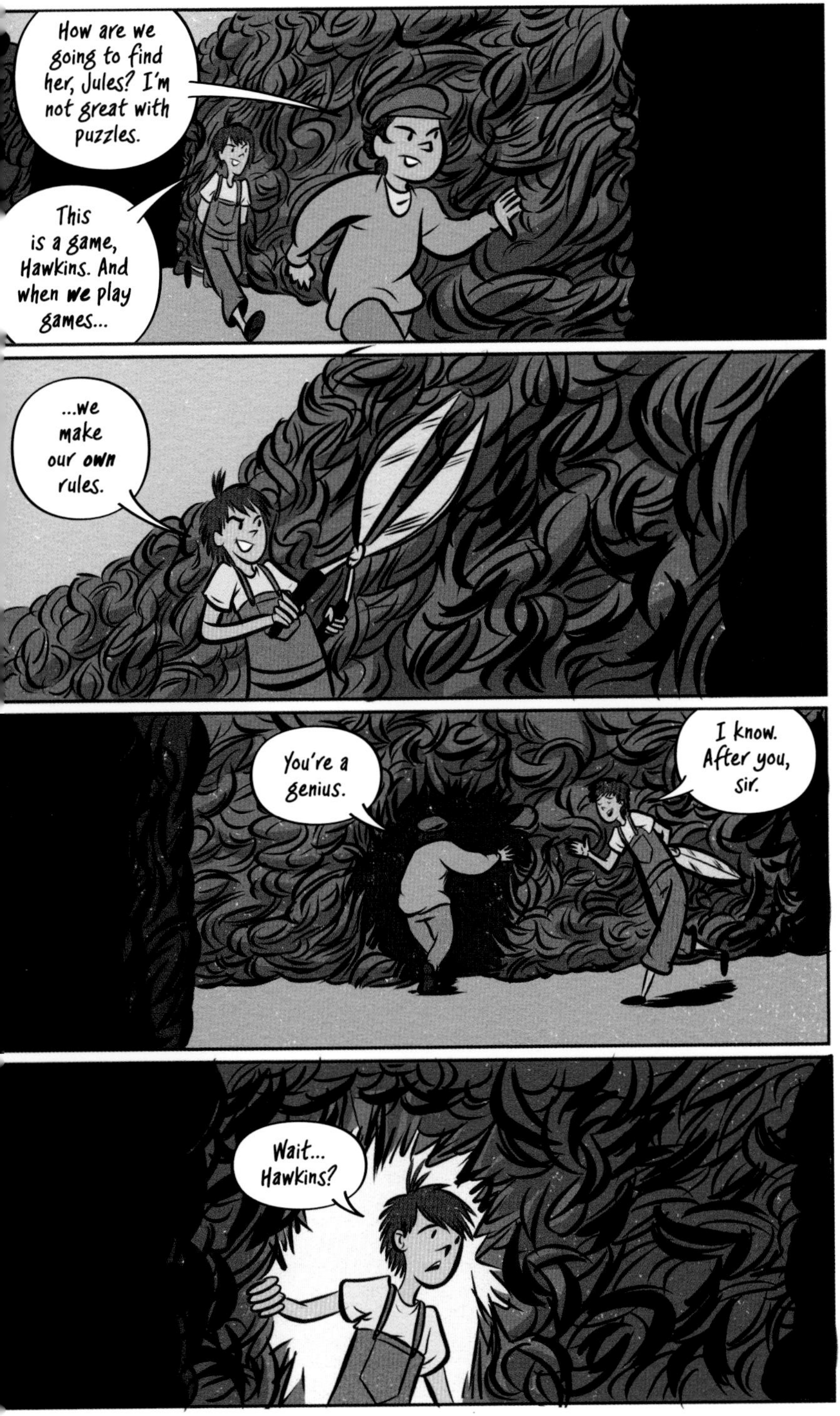
How are we going to find her, Jules? I'm not great with puzzles.
This is a game, Hawkins. And when we play games...
...we make our own rules.
You're a genius.
I know. After you, sir.
Wait... Hawkins?

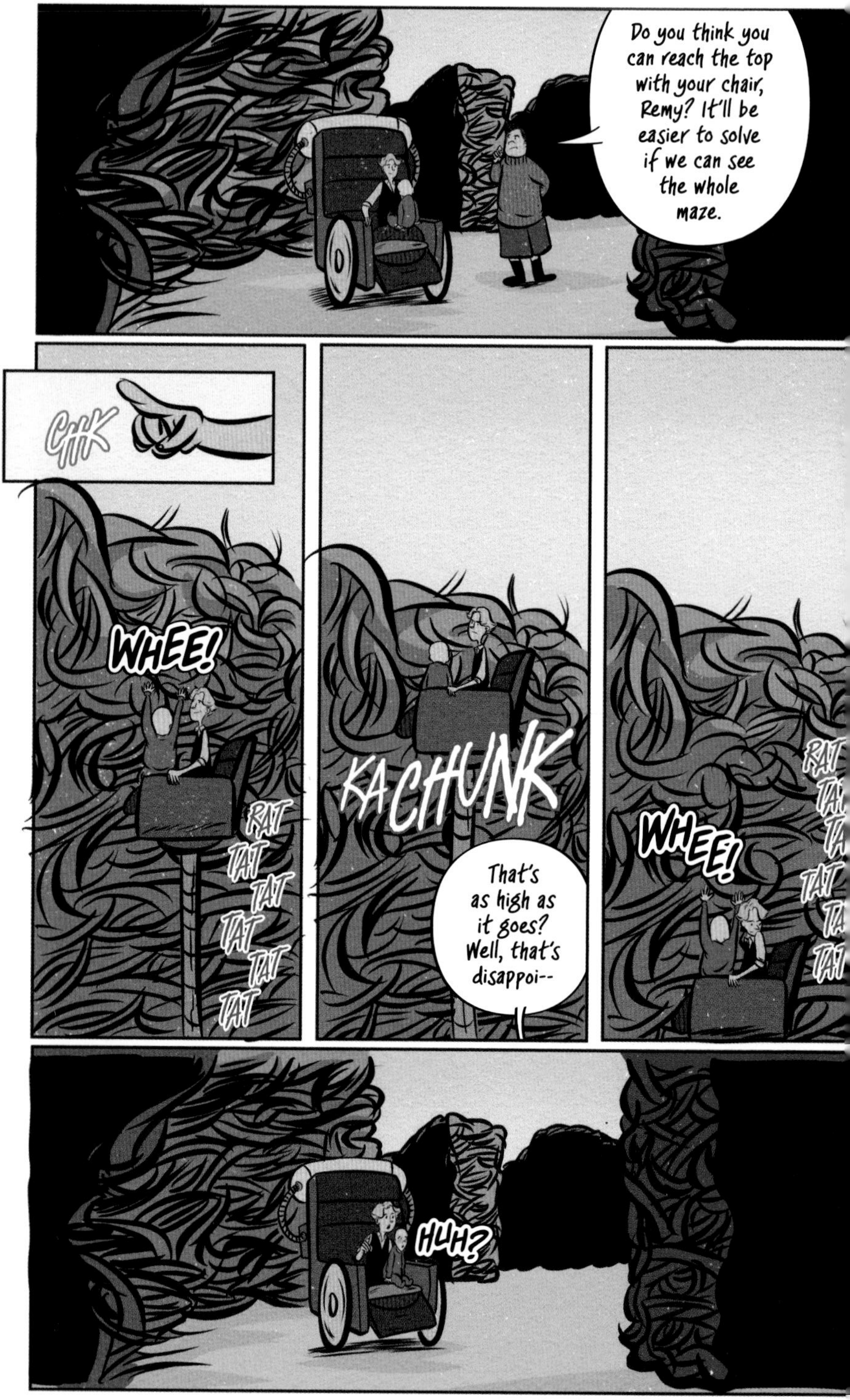
Do you think you can reach the top with your chair, Remy? It'll be easier to solve if we can see the whole maze.
CHK
WHEE!
RAT TAT TAT TAT TAT TAT
KA CHUNK
That's as high as it goes? Well, that's disappoi--
WHEE!
HUH?

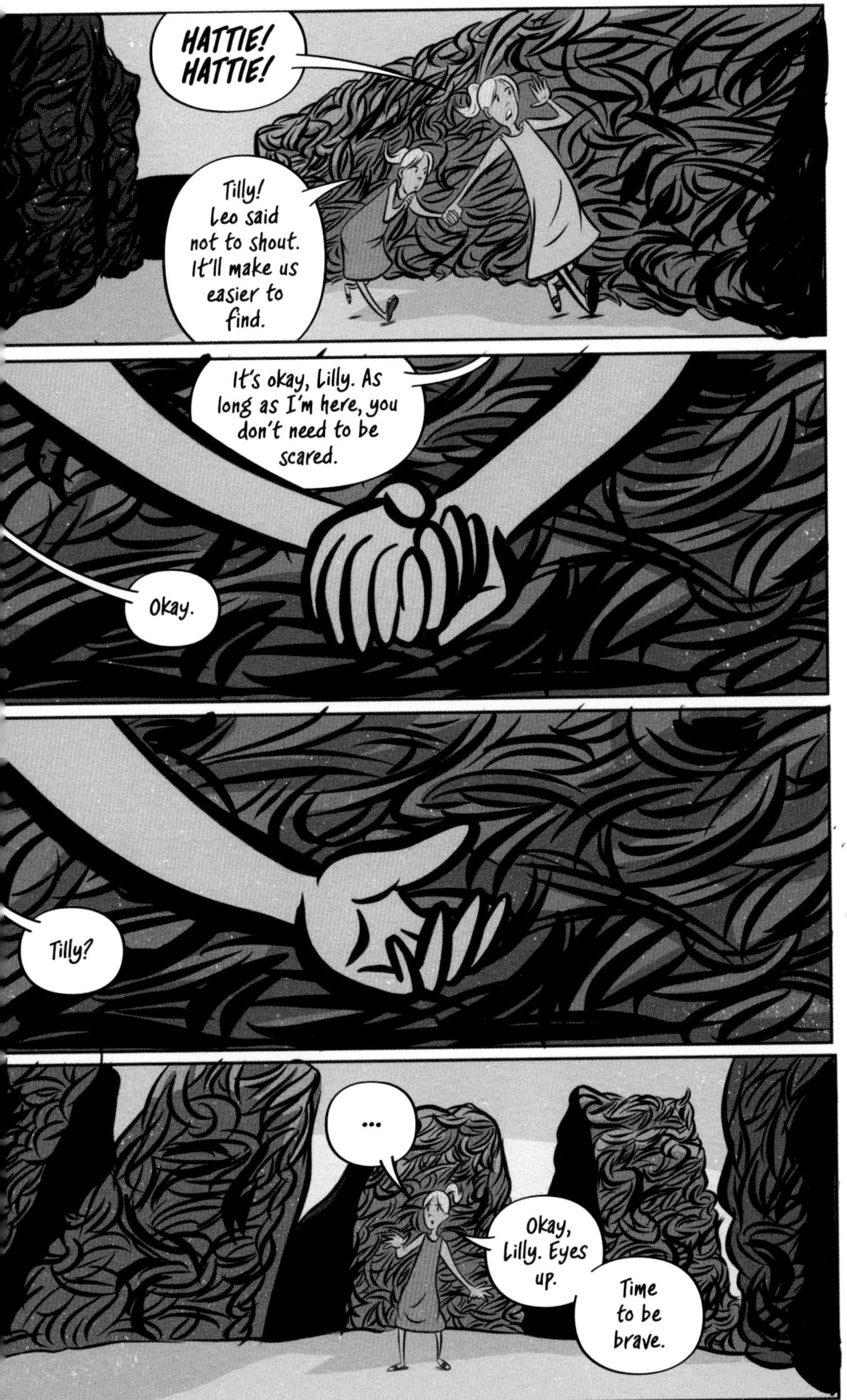
HATTIE!
HATTIE!
Tilly! Leo said not to shout. It'll make us easier to find.
It's okay, Lilly. As long as I'm here, you don't need to be scared.
Okay.
Tilly?
...
Okay, Lilly. Eyes up.
Time to be brave.

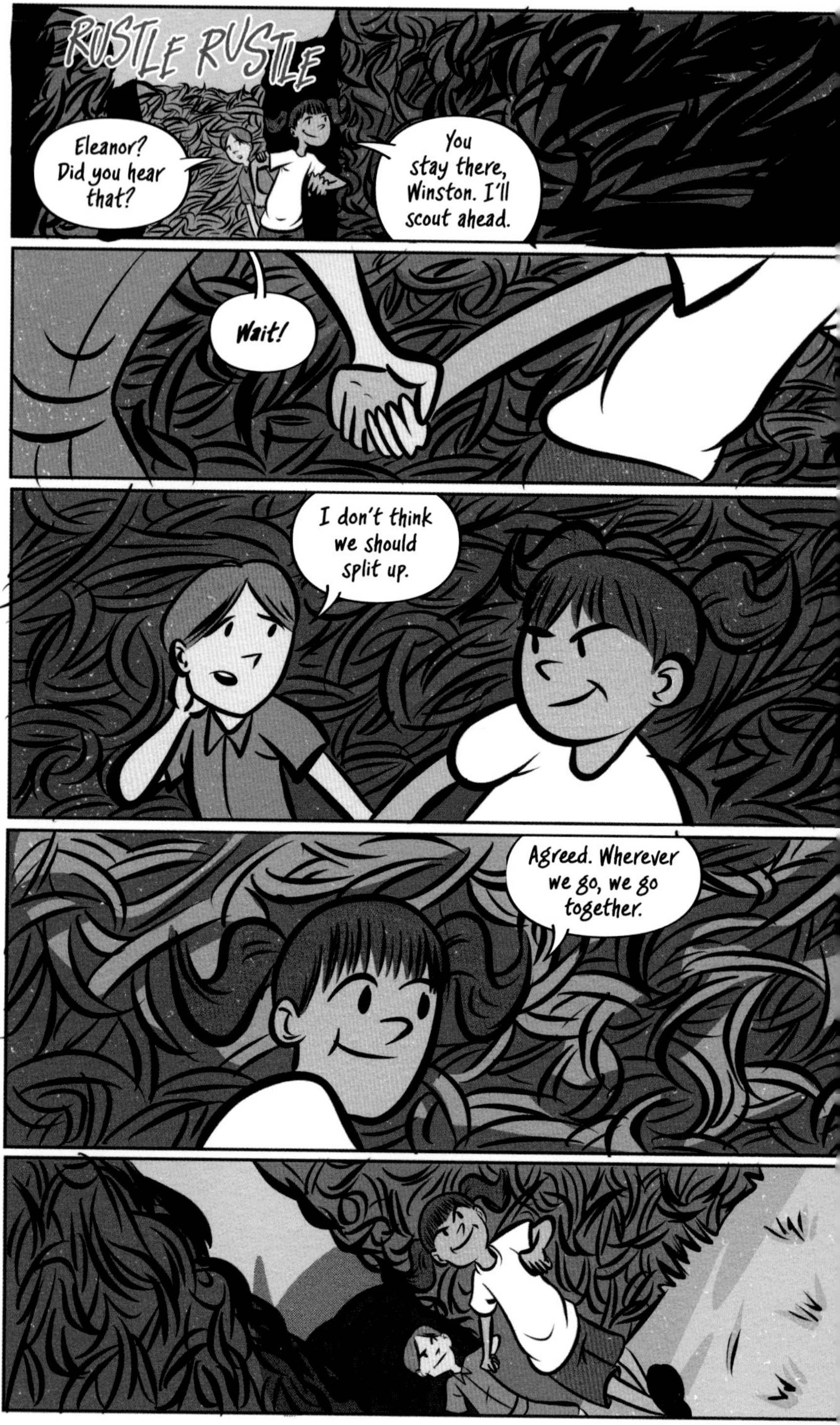
RUSTLE RUSTLE
Eleanor? Did you hear that?
You stay there, Winston. I'll scout ahead.
Wait!
I don't think we should split up.
Agreed. Wherever we go, we go together.

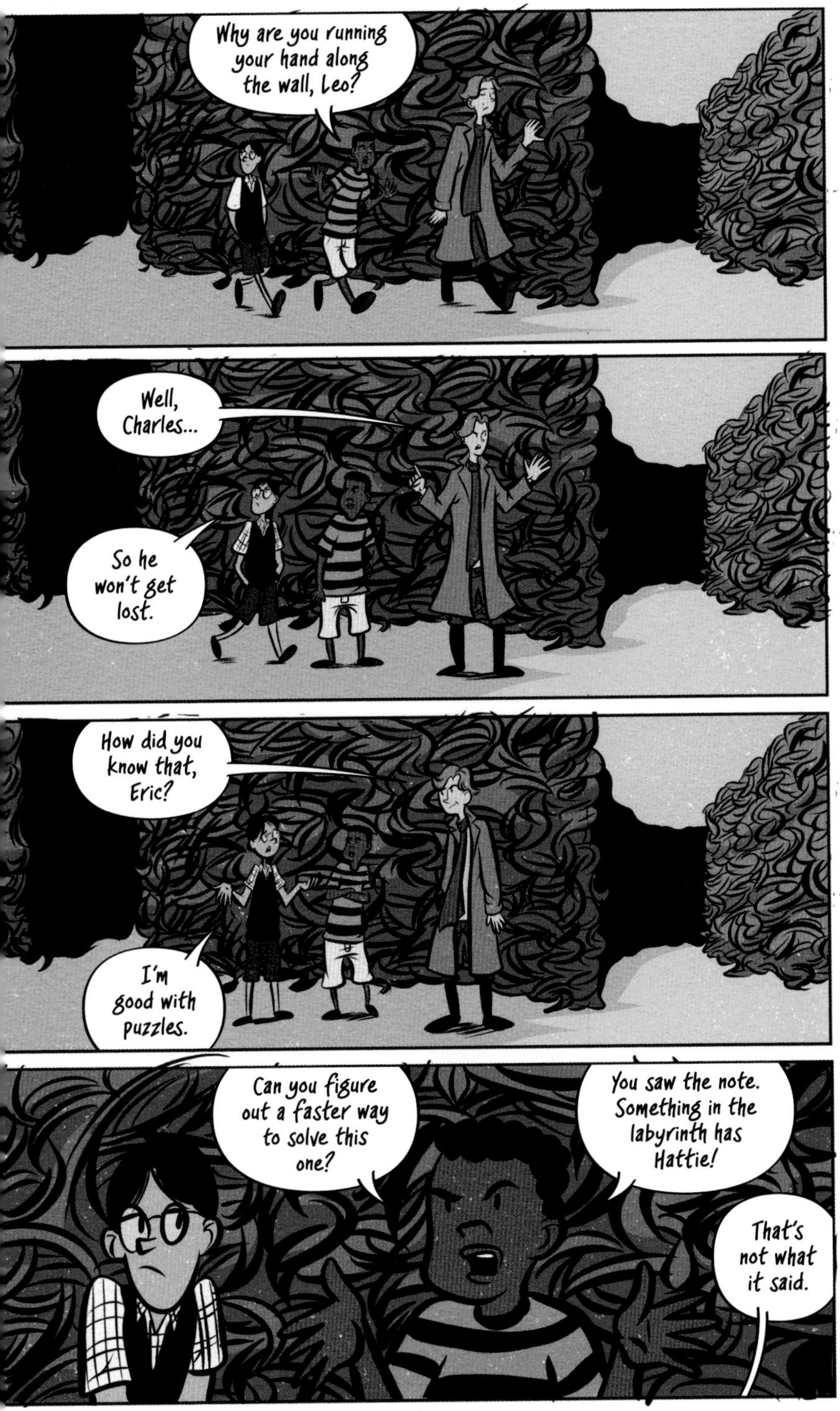

Why are you running your hand along the wall, Leo?
Well, Charles...
So he won't get lost.
How did you know that, Eric?
I'm good with puzzles.
Can you figure out a faster way to solve this one?
You saw the note. Something in the labyrinth has Hattie!
That's not what it said.

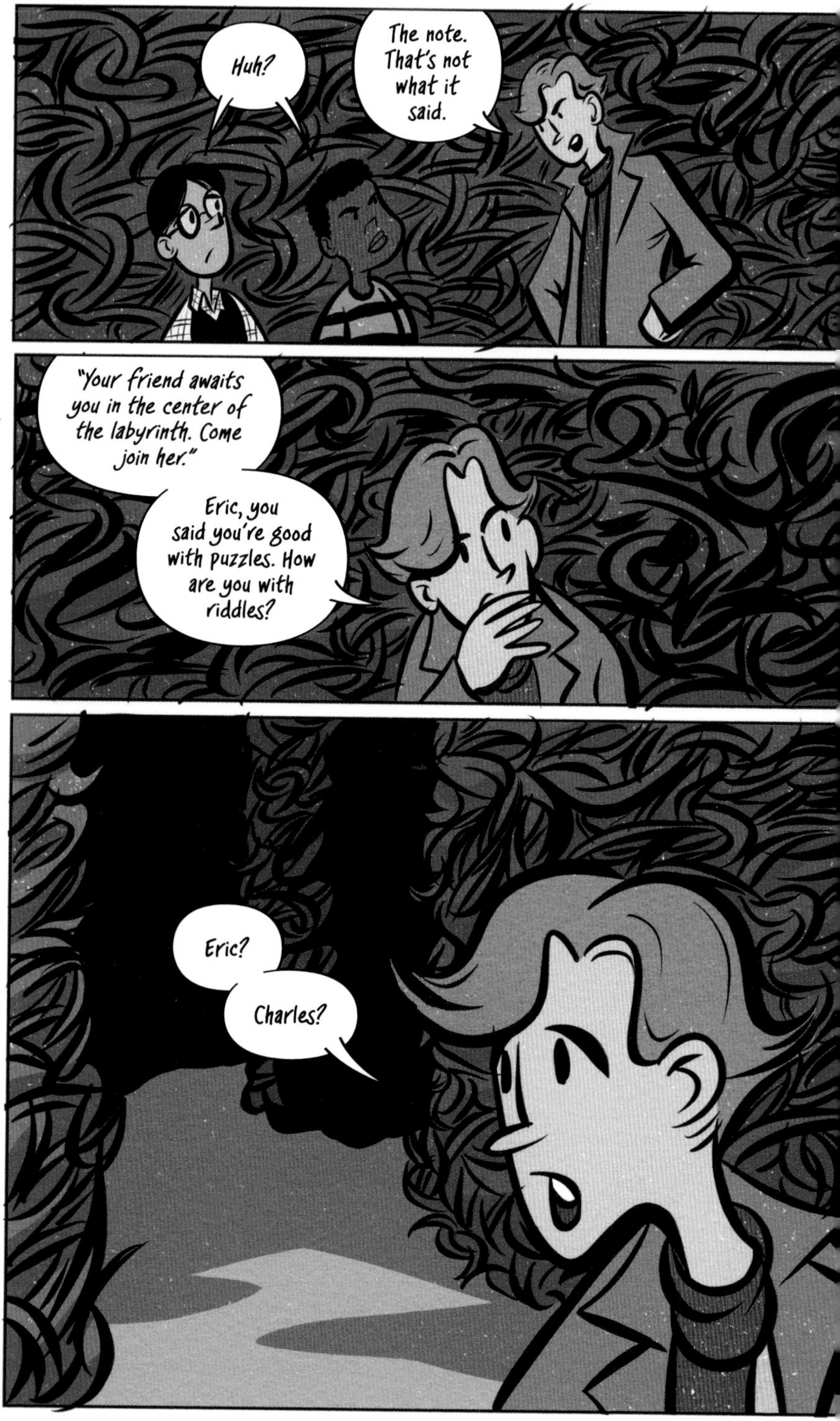
Huh?
The note. That's not what it said.
"Your friend awaits you in the center of the labyrinth. Come join her."
Eric, you said you're good with puzzles. How are you with riddles?
Eric?
Charles?

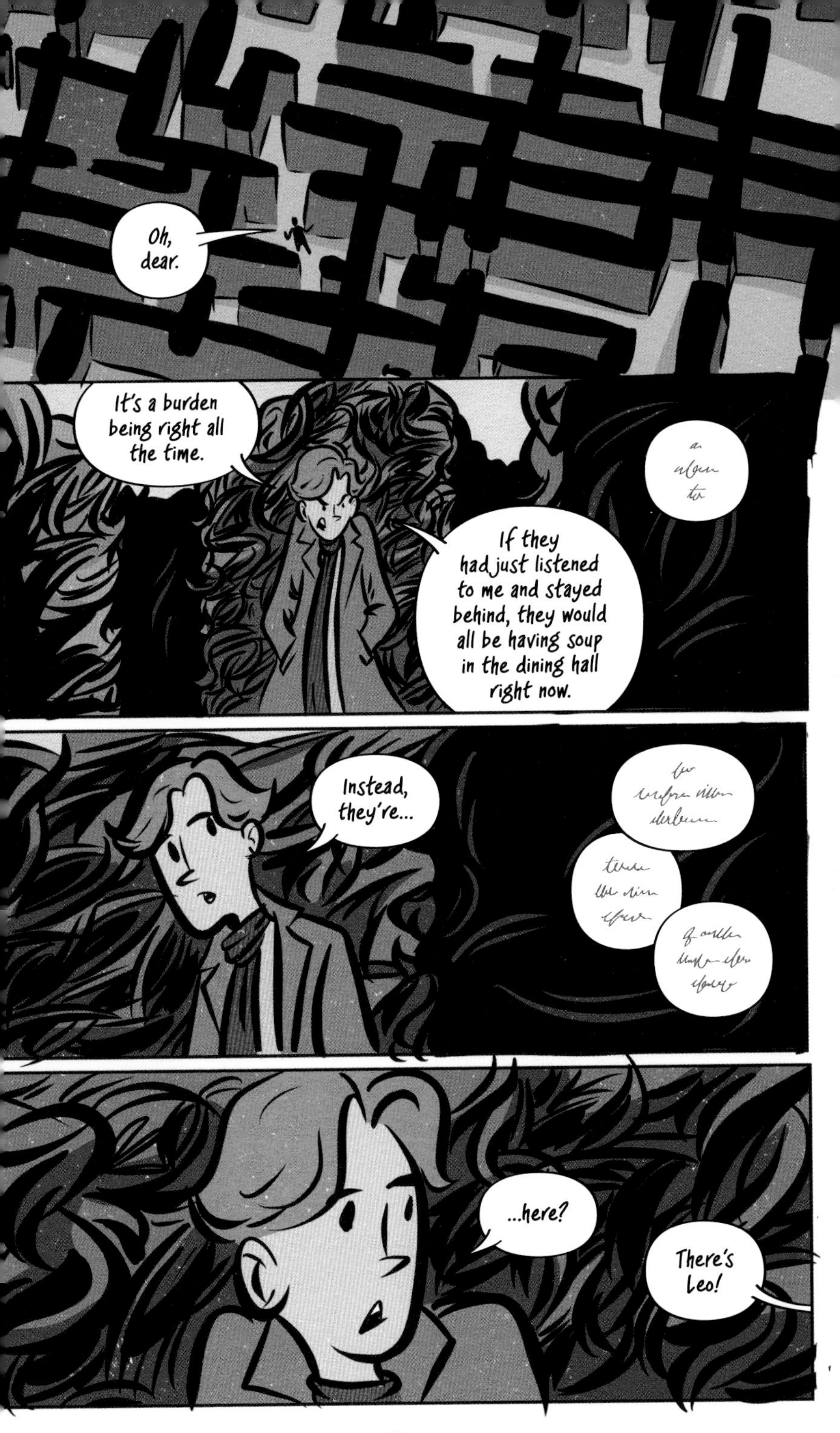

Oh, dear.
It's a burden being right all the time.
If they had just listened to me and stayed behind, they would all be having soup in the dining hall right now.
Instead, they're...
...here?
There's Leo!

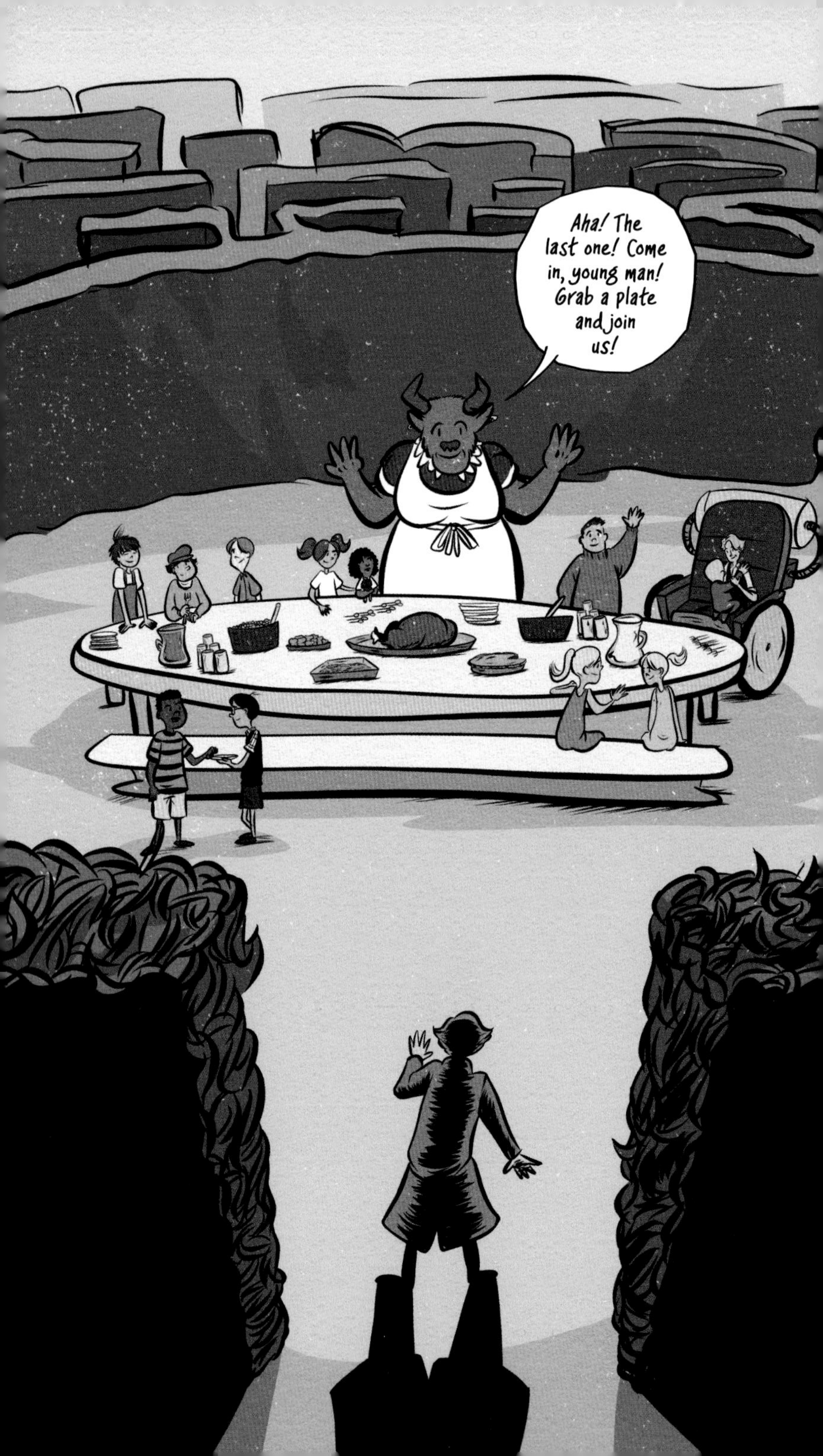
Aha! The last one! Come in, young man! Grab a plate and join us!

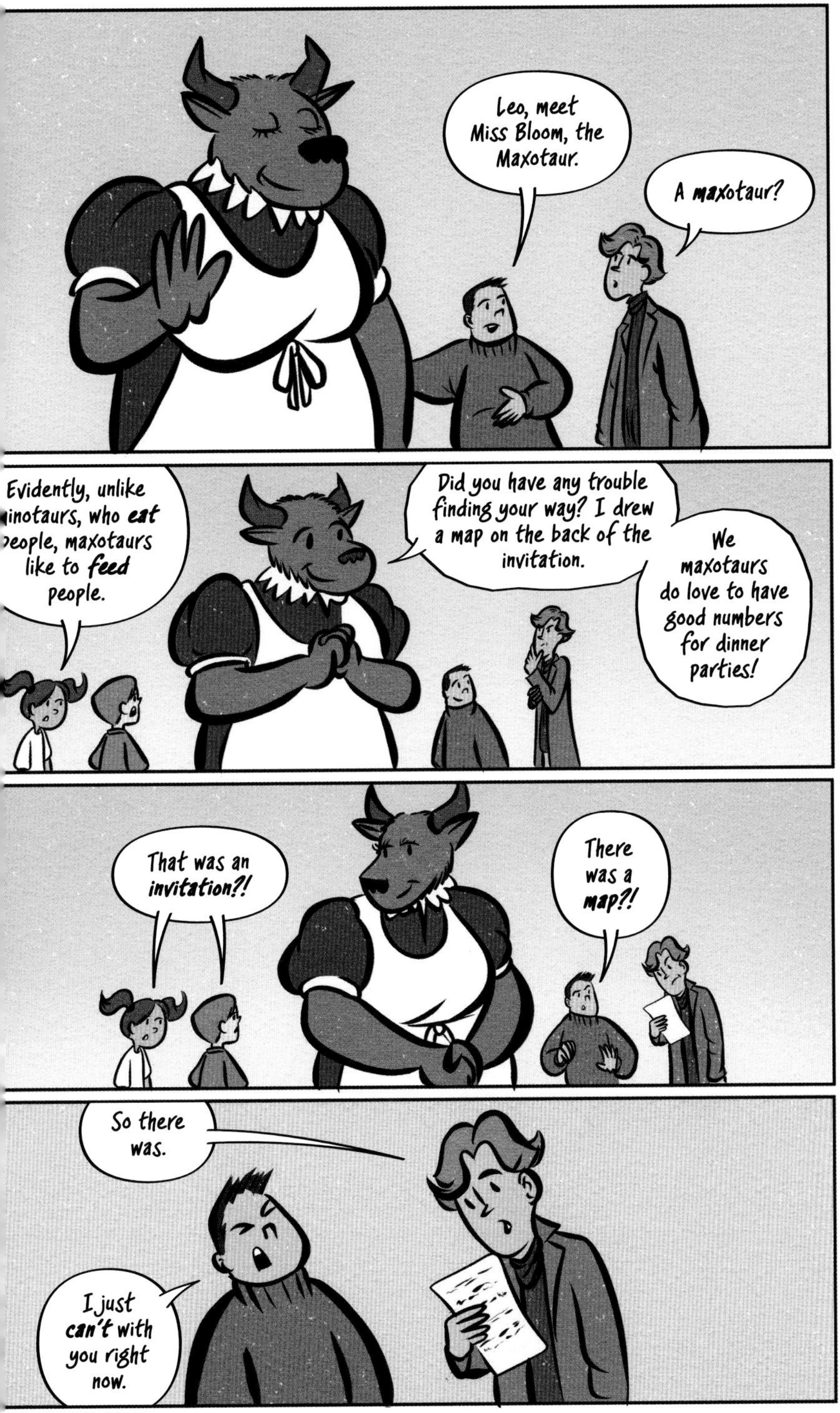
Leo, meet Miss Bloom, the Maxotaur.
A maxotaur?
Evidently, unlike minotaurs, who eat people, maxotaurs like to feed people.
Did you have any trouble finding your way? I drew a map on the back of the invitation.
We maxotaurs do love to have good numbers for dinner parties!
That was an invitation?!
There was a map?!
So there was.
I just can't with you right now.

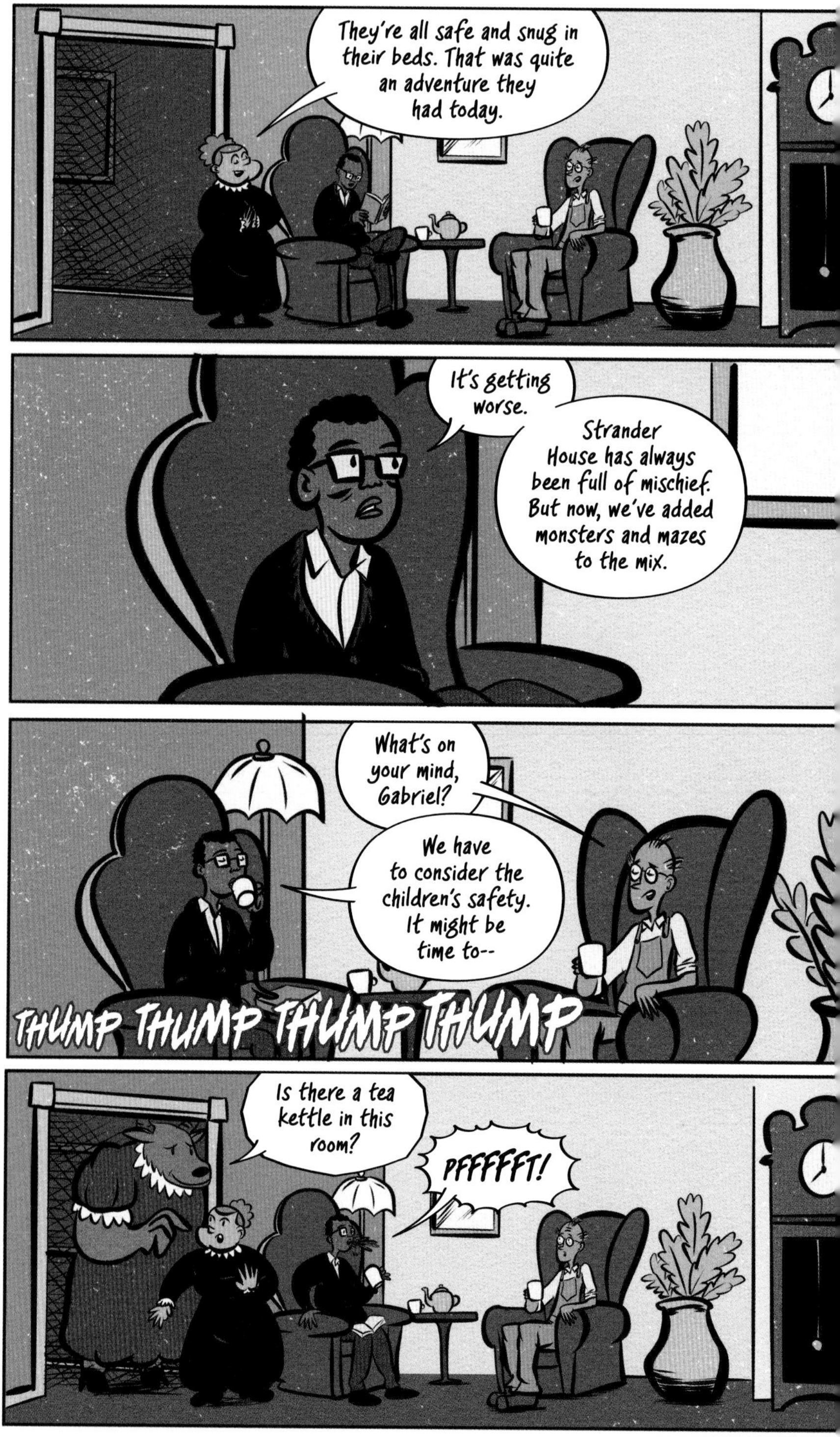
They're all safe and snug in their beds. That was quite an adventure they had today.
It's getting worse.
Strander House has always been full of mischief. But now, we've added monsters and mazes to the mix.
What's on your mind, Gabriel?
We have to consider the children's safety. It might be time to--
THUMP THUMP THUMP THUMP
Is there a tea kettle in this room?
PFFFFFT!

CHAPTER

7

THE WORLDS OUTSIDE THE CLASSROOM

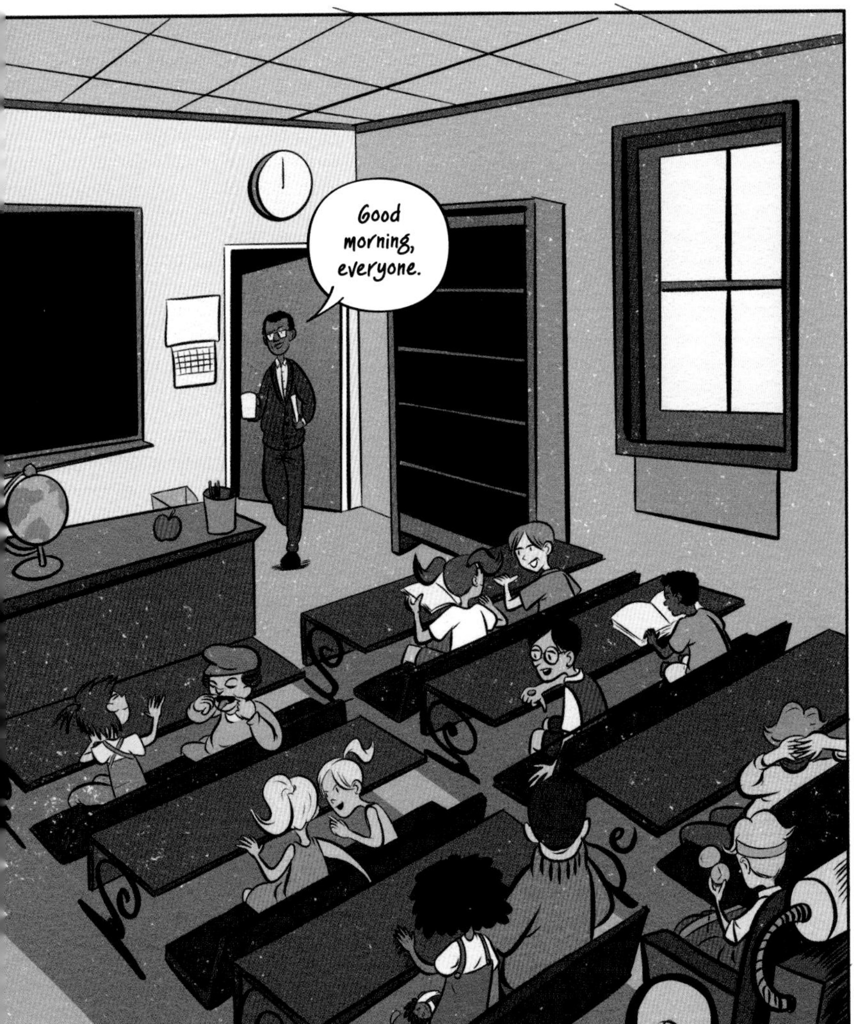
Good morning, everyone.

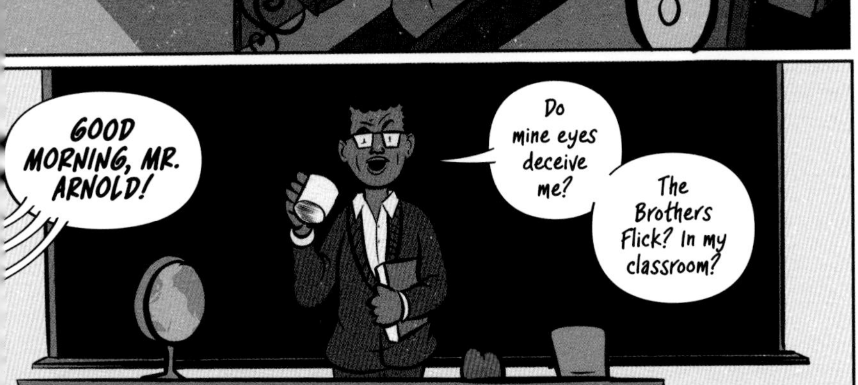
GOOD MORNING, MR. ARNOLD!
Do mine eyes deceive me?
The Brothers Flick? In my classroom?

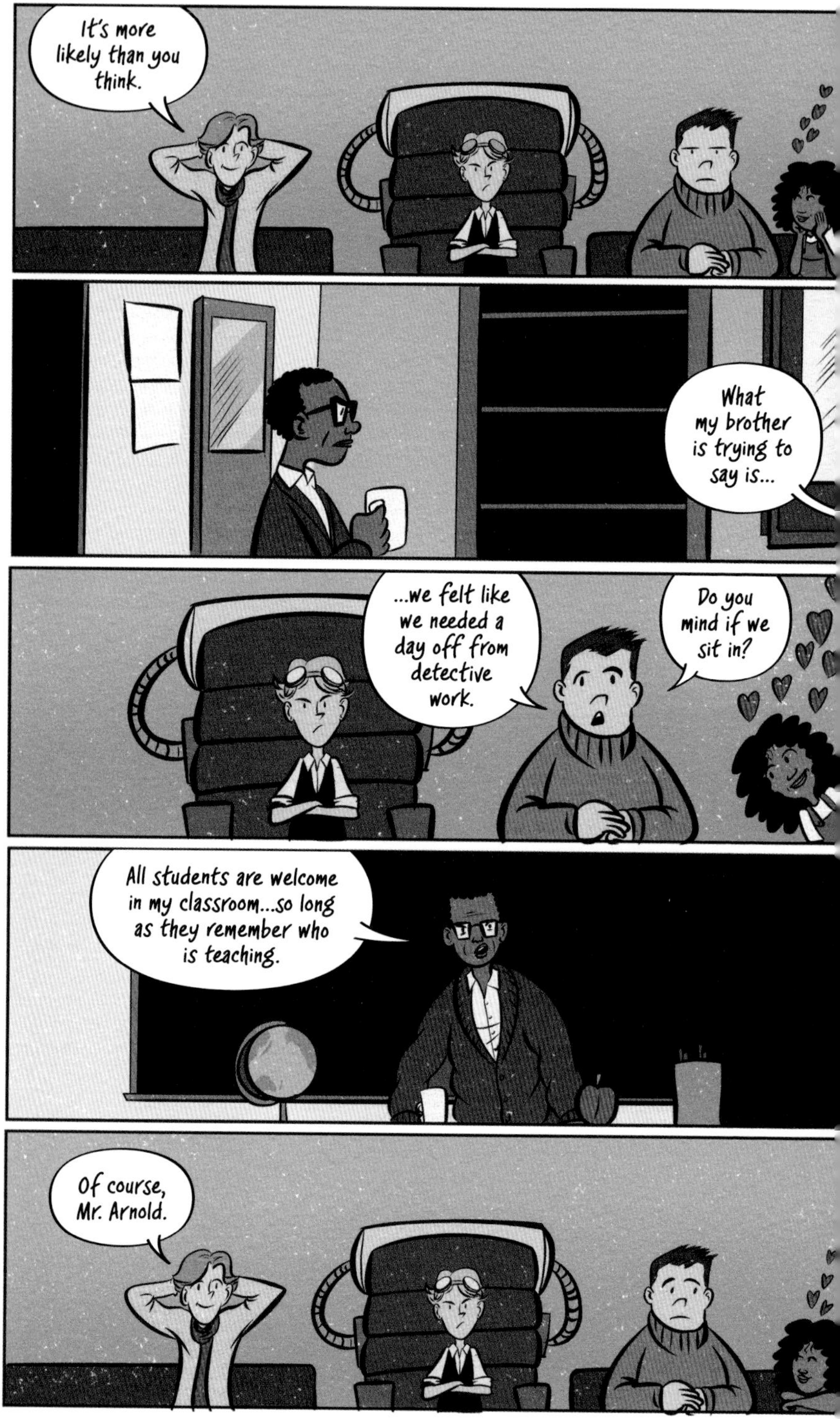
It's more likely than you think.
What my brother is trying to say is...
...we felt like we needed a day off from detective work.
Do you mind if we sit in?
All students are welcome in my classroom...so long as they remember who is teaching.
Of course, Mr. Arnold.

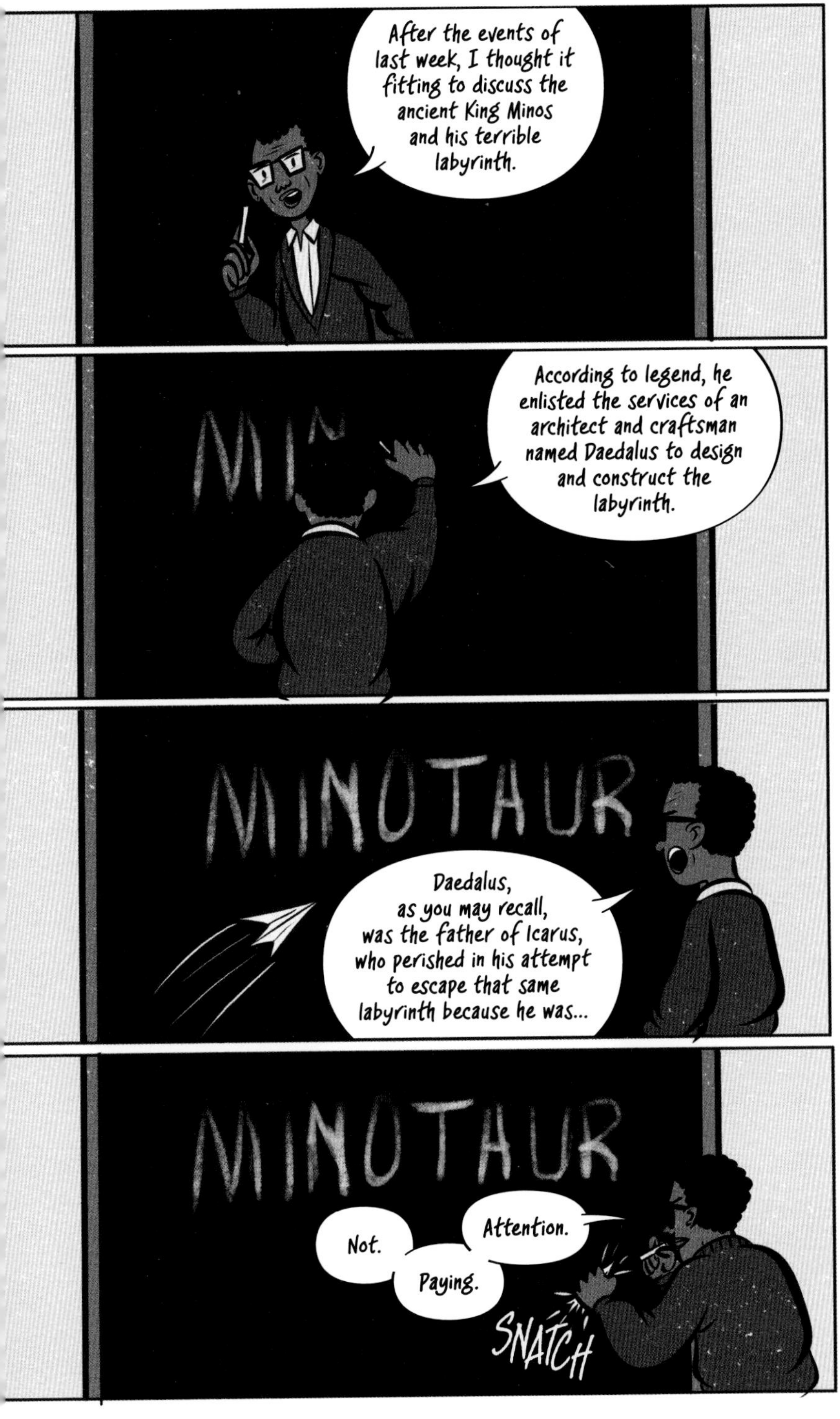
After the events of last week, I thought it fitting to discuss the ancient King Minos and his terrible labyrinth.
MIN
According to legend, he enlisted the services of an architect and craftsman named Daedalus to design and construct the labyrinth.
MINOTAUR
Daedalus, as you may recall, was the father of Icarus, who perished in his attempt to escape that same labyrinth because he was...
MINOTAUR
Not.
Paying.
Attention.
SNATCH

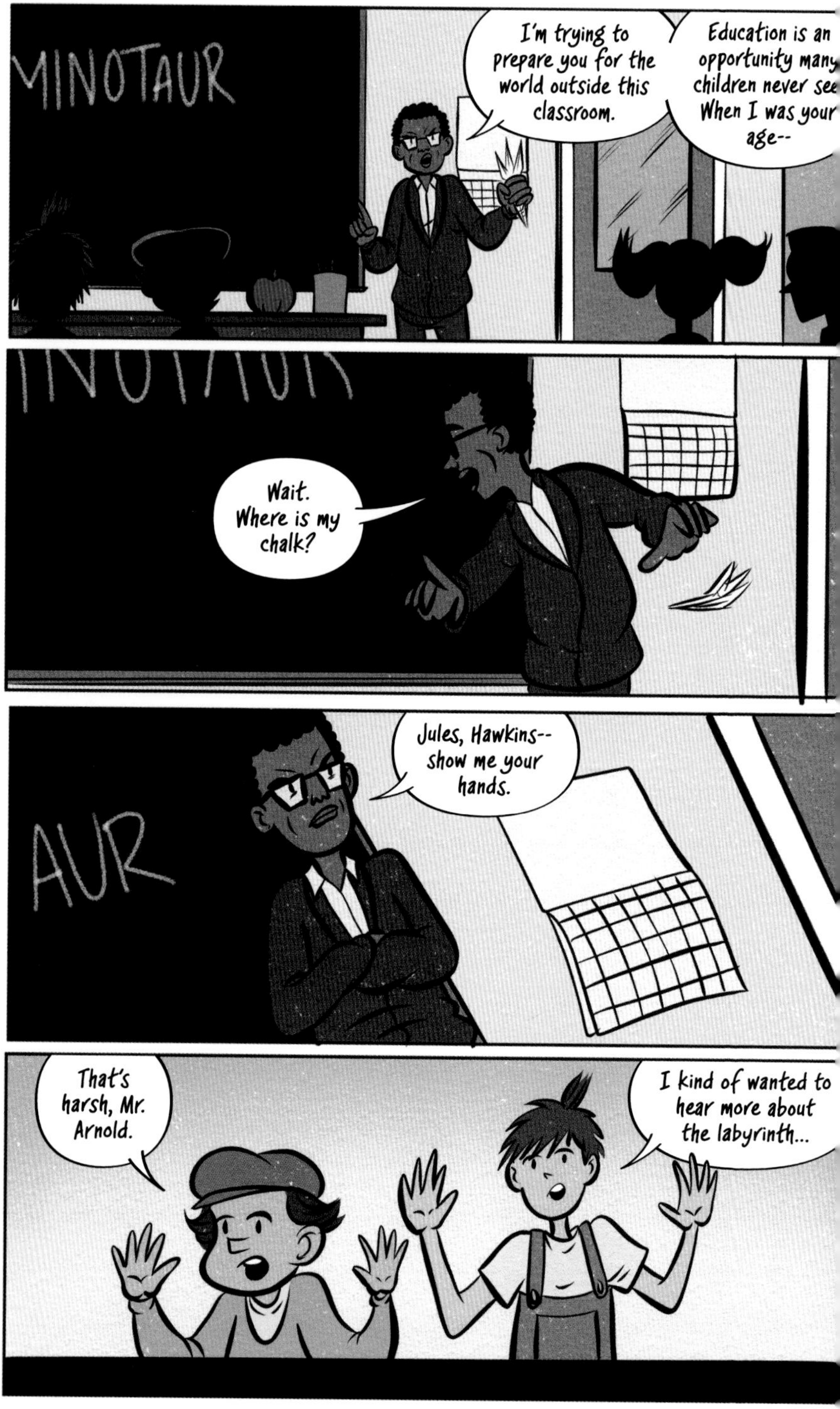
MINOTAUR
I'm trying to prepare you for the world outside this classroom.
Education is an opportunity many children never see. When I was your age--
Wait. Where is my chalk?
AUR
Jules, Hawkins-- show me your hands.
That's harsh, Mr. Arnold.
I kind of wanted to hear more about the labyrinth...

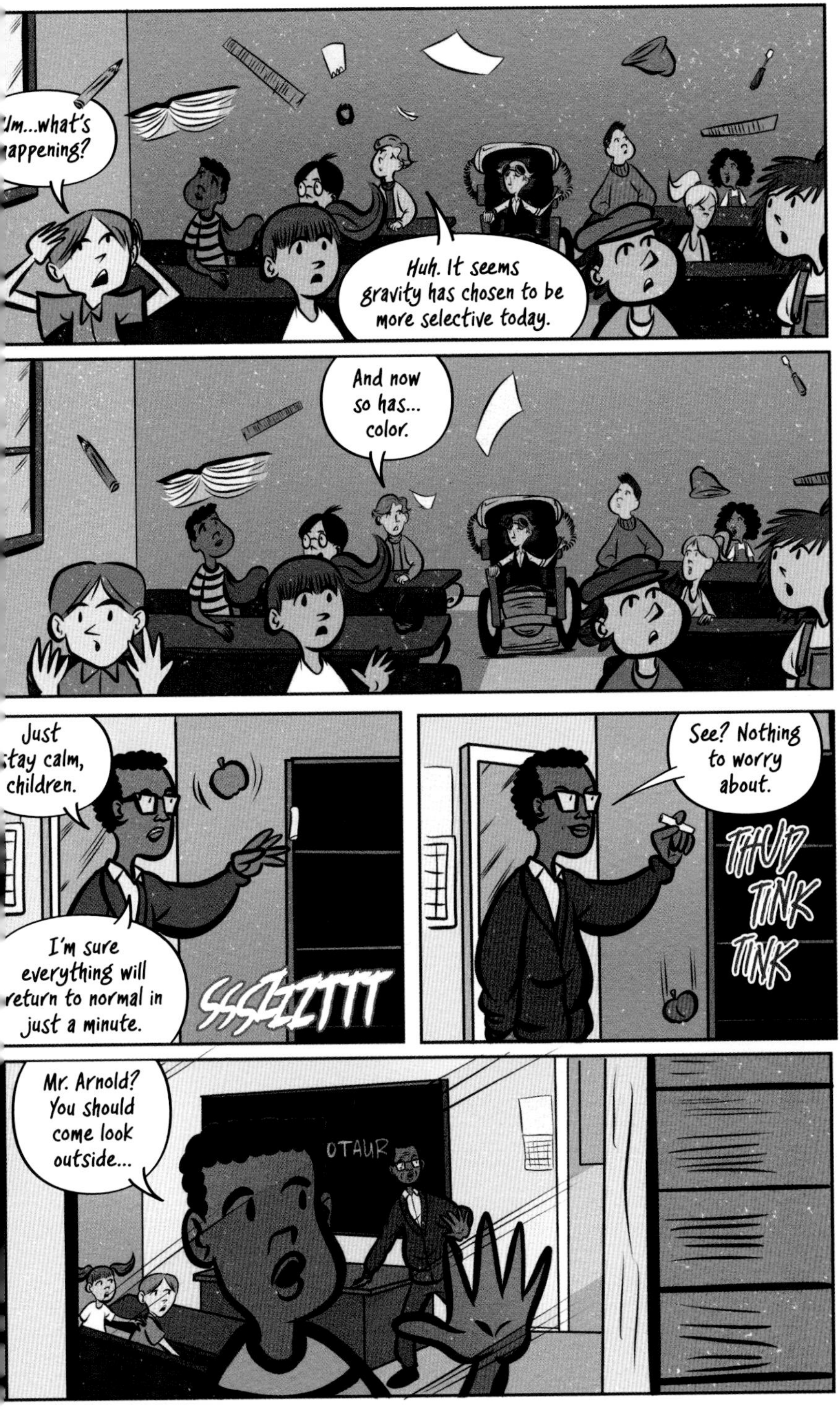
Um...what's happening?
Huh. It seems gravity has chosen to be more selective today.
And now so has... color.
Just stay calm, children.
I'm sure everything will return to normal in just a minute.
SSSLIIITTT
See? Nothing to worry about.
THUD
TINK
TINK
Mr. Arnold? You should come look outside...
OTAUR

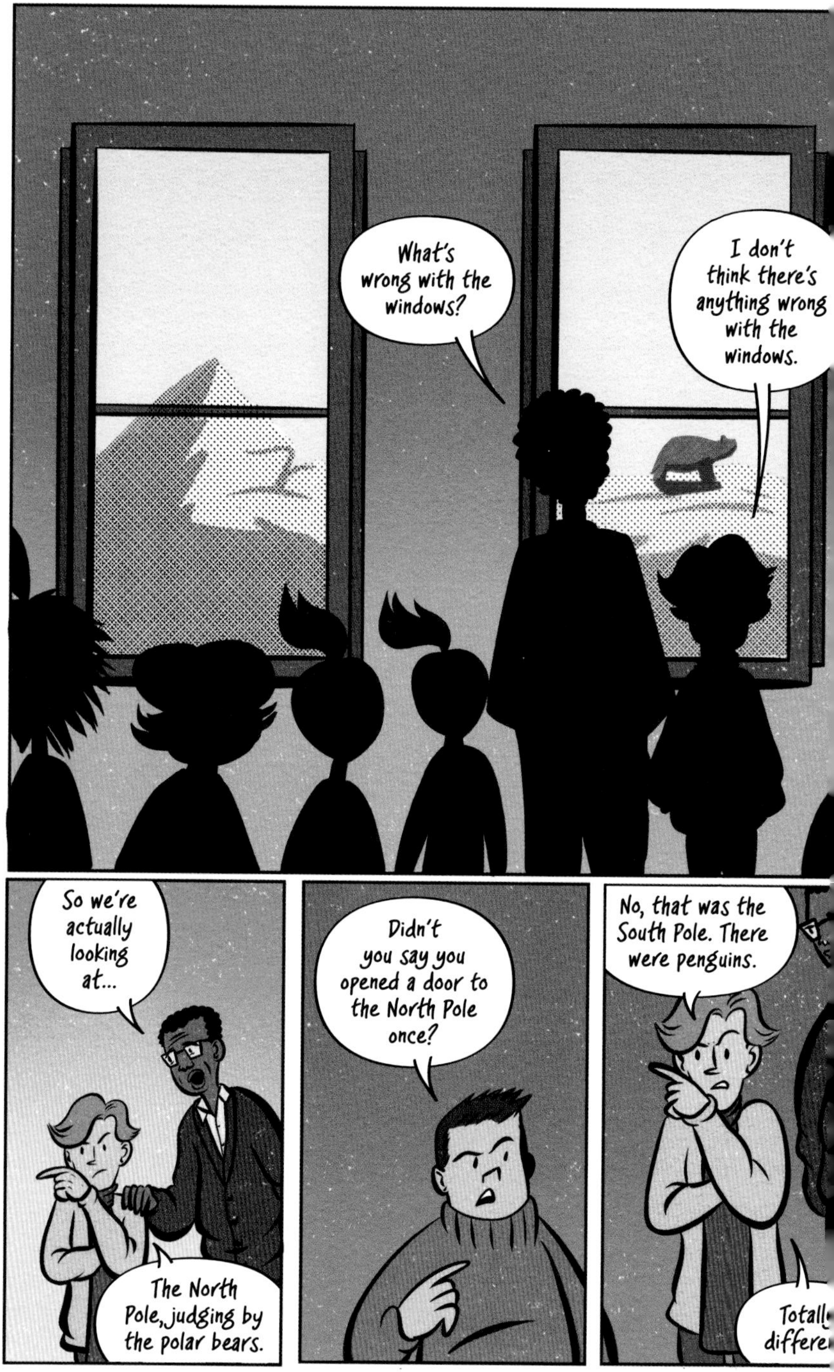
What's wrong with the windows?
I don't think there's anything wrong with the windows.
So we're actually looking at...
The North Pole, judging by the polar bears.
Didn't you say you opened a door to the North Pole once?
No, that was the South Pole. There were penguins.

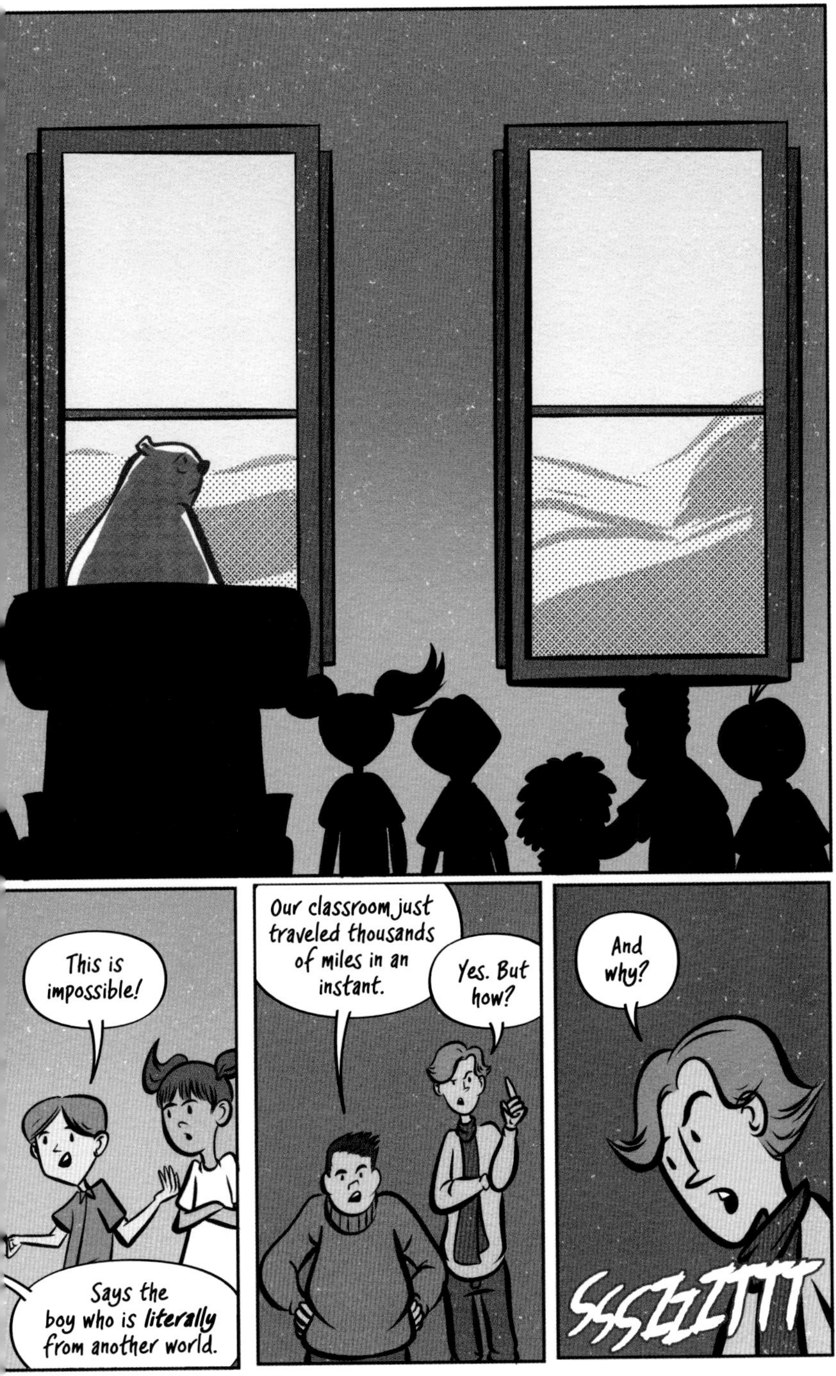
This is impossible!
Says the boy who is *literally* from another world.
Our classroom just traveled thousands of miles in an instant.
Yes. But how?
And why?
SSSZZZTTT

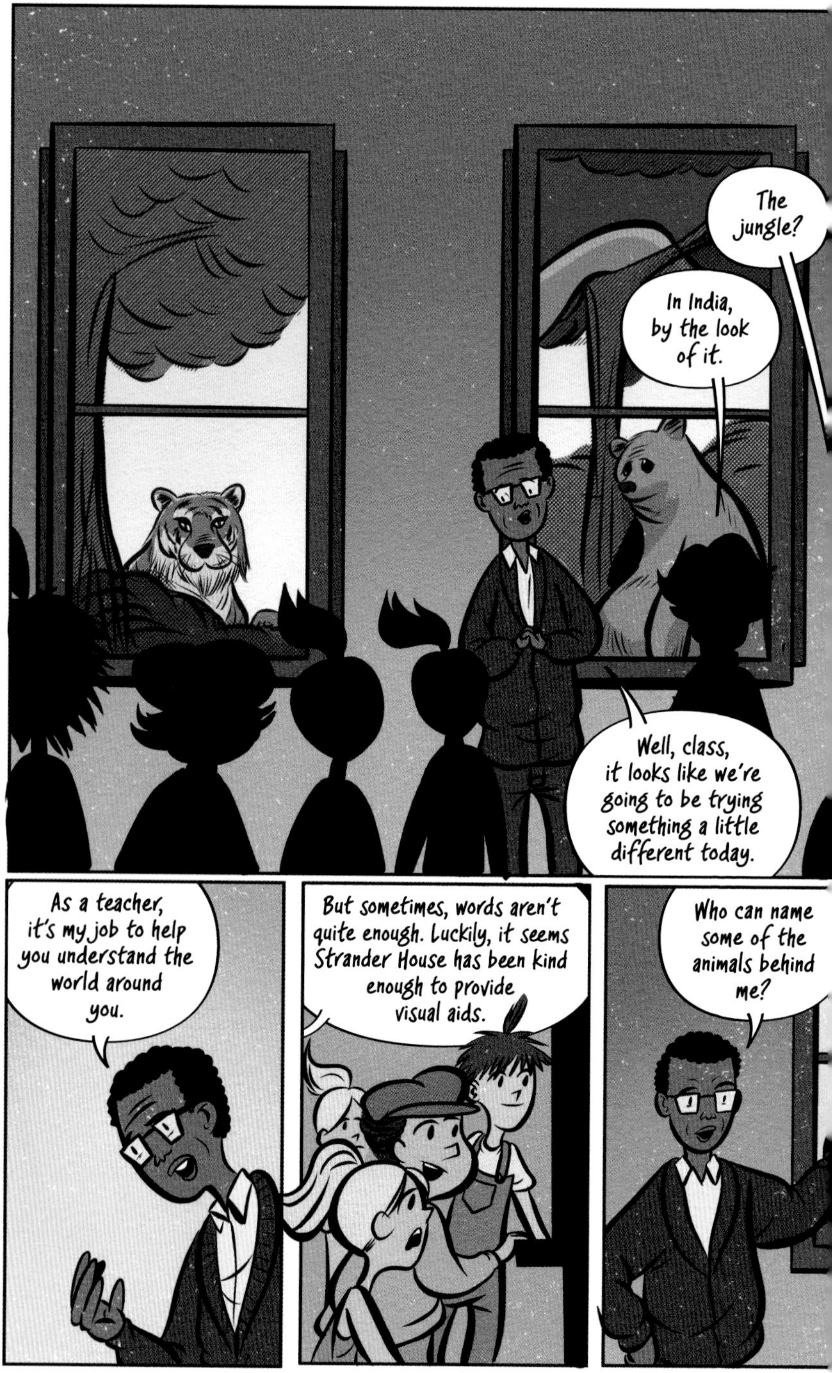
The jungle?
In India, by the look of it.
Well, class, it looks like we're going to be trying something a little different today.
As a teacher, it's my job to help you understand the world around you.
But sometimes, words aren't quite enough. Luckily, it seems Strander House has been kind enough to provide visual aids.
Who can name some of the animals behind me?

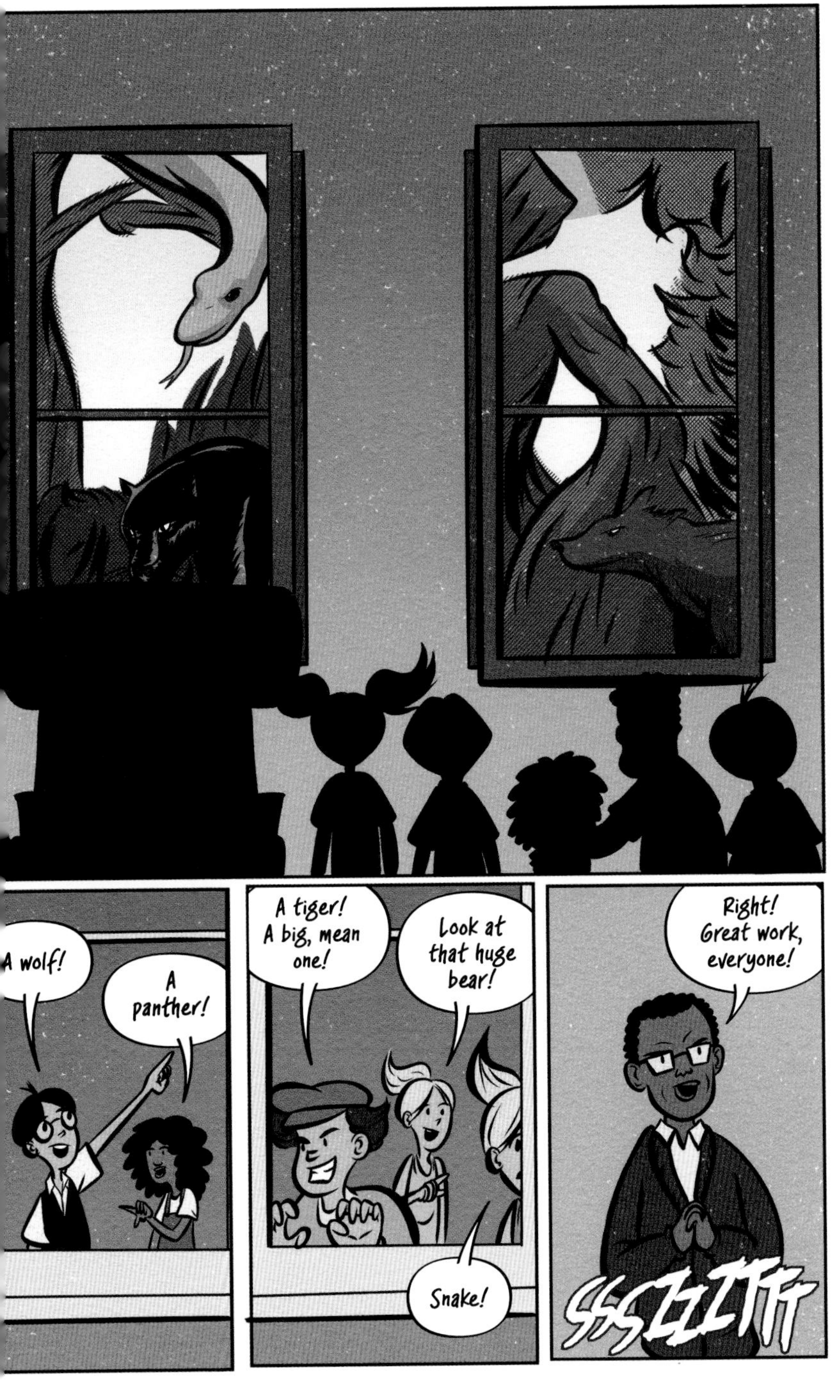
A wolf!
A panther!
A tiger! A big, mean one!
Look at that huge bear!
Snake!
Right! Great work, everyone!
SSSZZZTTT

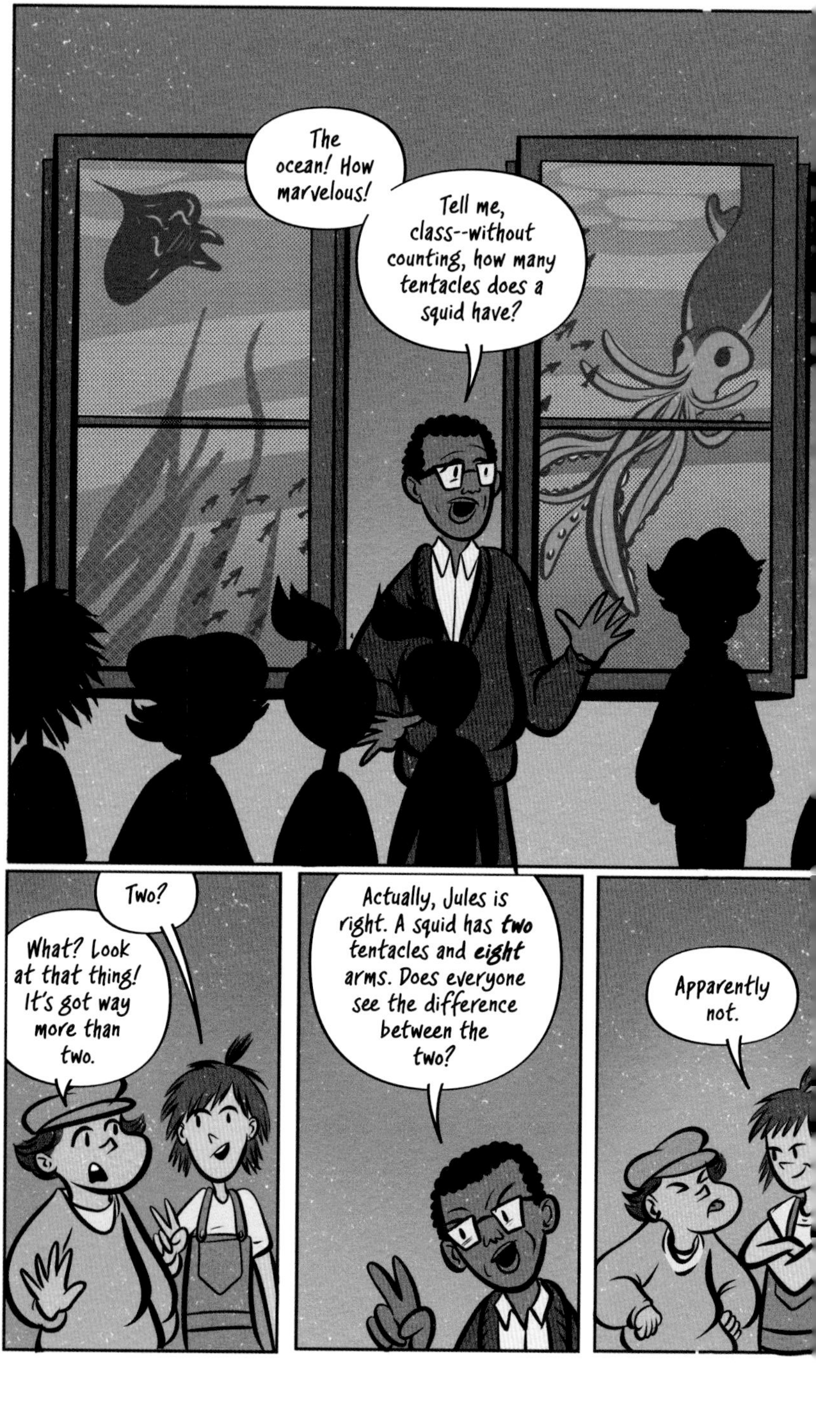
The ocean! How marvelous!
Tell me, class--without counting, how many tentacles does a squid have?
Two?
What? Look at that thing! It's got way more than two.
Actually, Jules is right. A squid has **two** tentacles and **eight** arms. Does everyone see the difference between the two?
Apparently not.

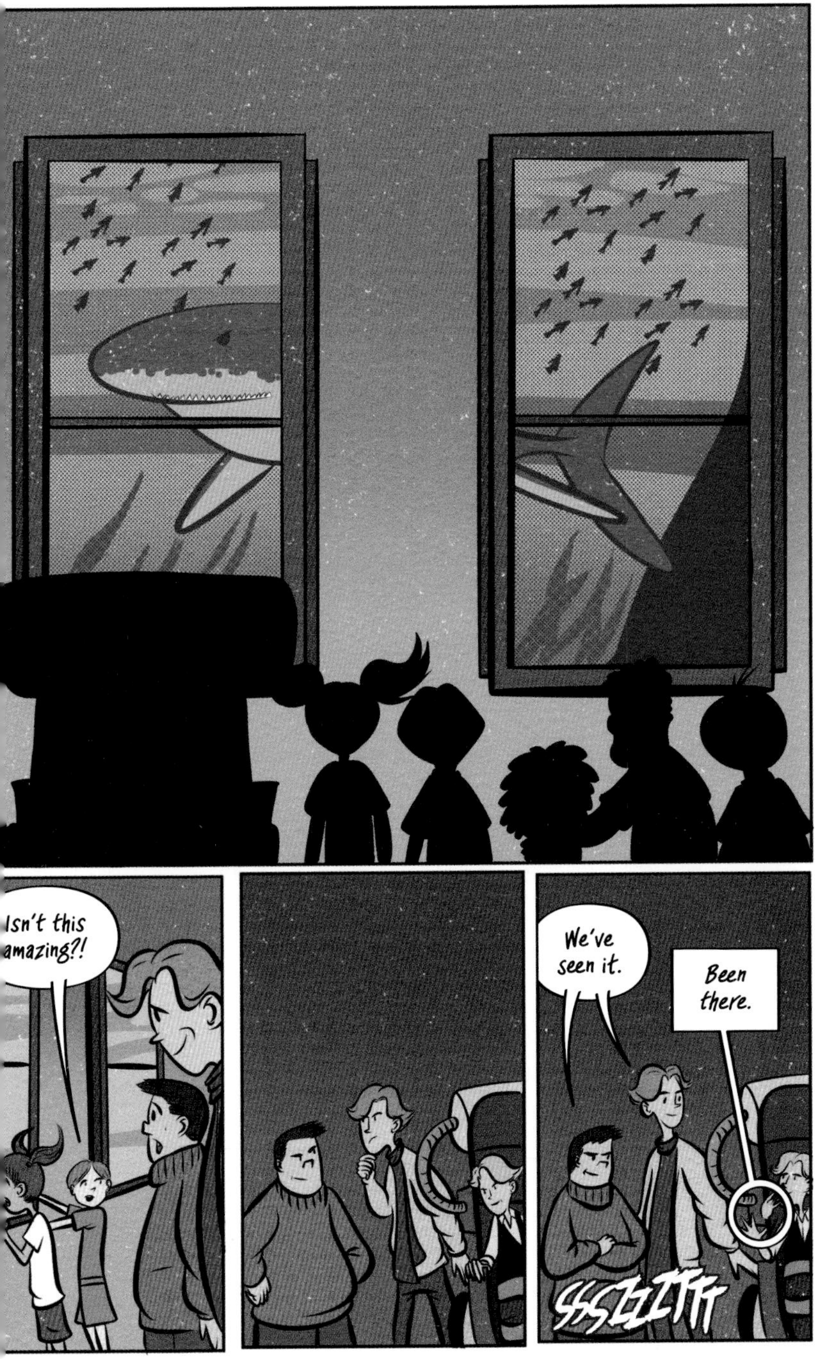
Isn't this amazing?!
We've seen it.
Been there.
SSSZZZTTT

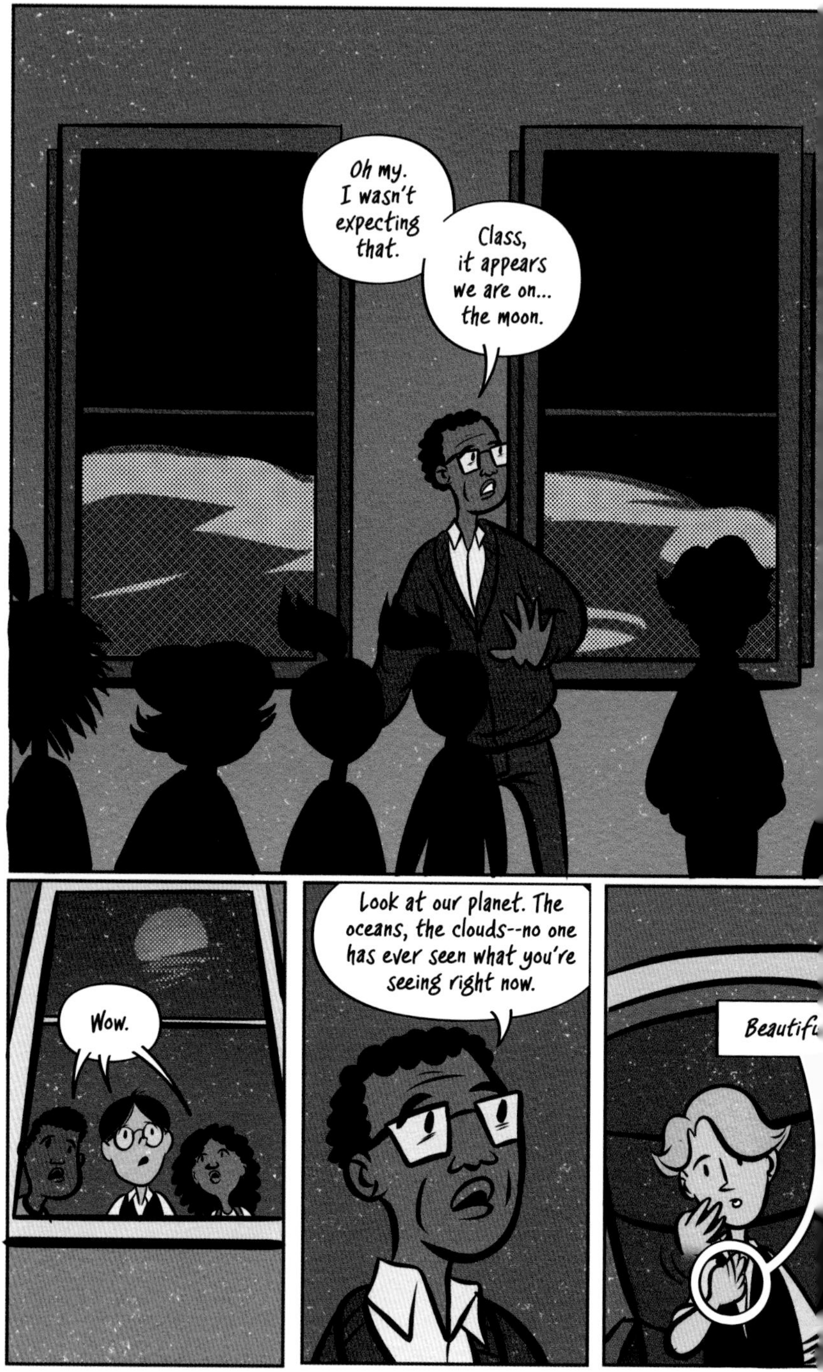
Oh my. I wasn't expecting that.
Class, it appears we are on... the moon.
Wow.
Look at our planet. The oceans, the clouds--no one has ever seen what you're seeing right now.
Beautifu

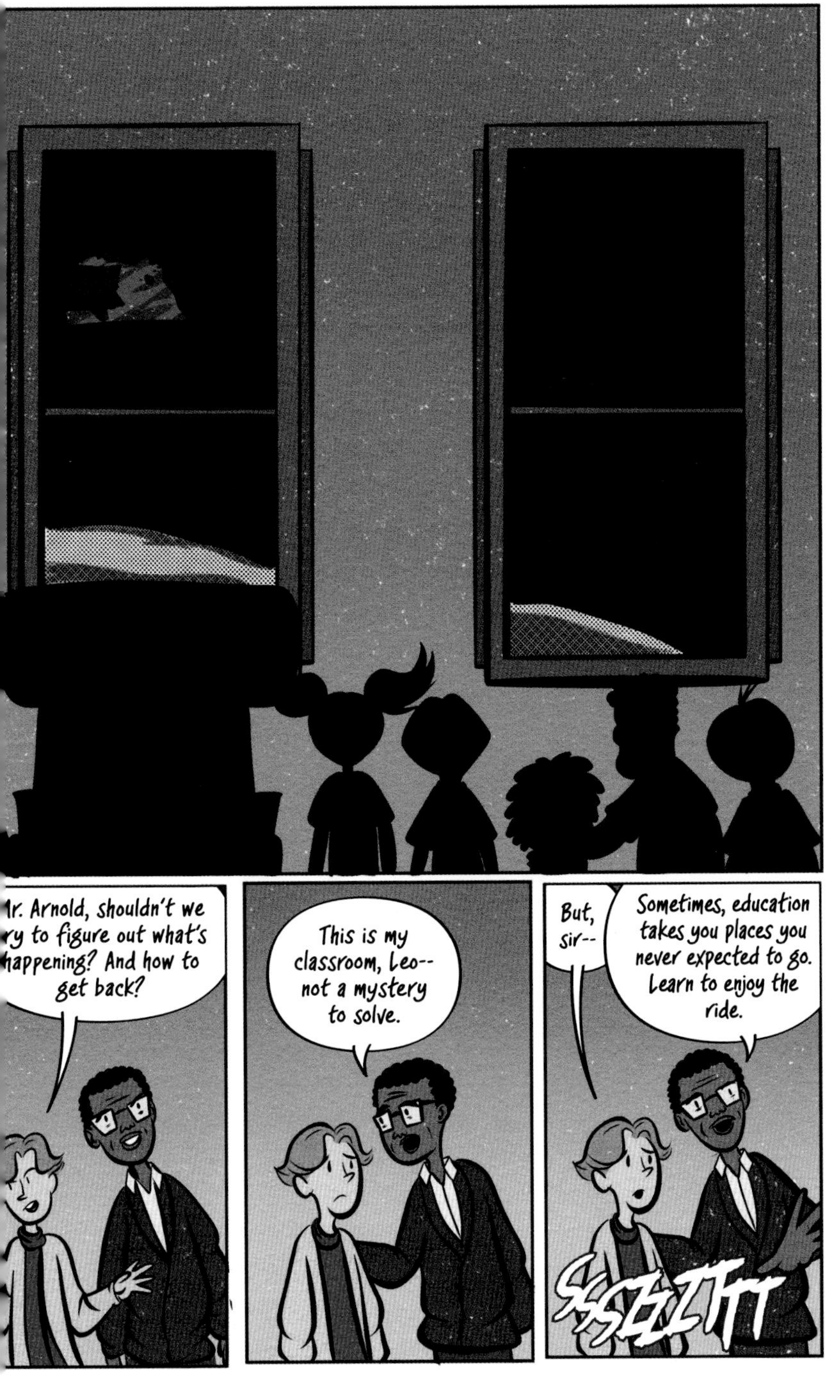

Mr. Arnold, shouldn't we try to figure out what's happening? And how to get back?
This is my classroom, Leo--not a mystery to solve.
But, sir--
Sometimes, education takes you places you never expected to go. Learn to enjoy the ride.
SSSZZZTTT

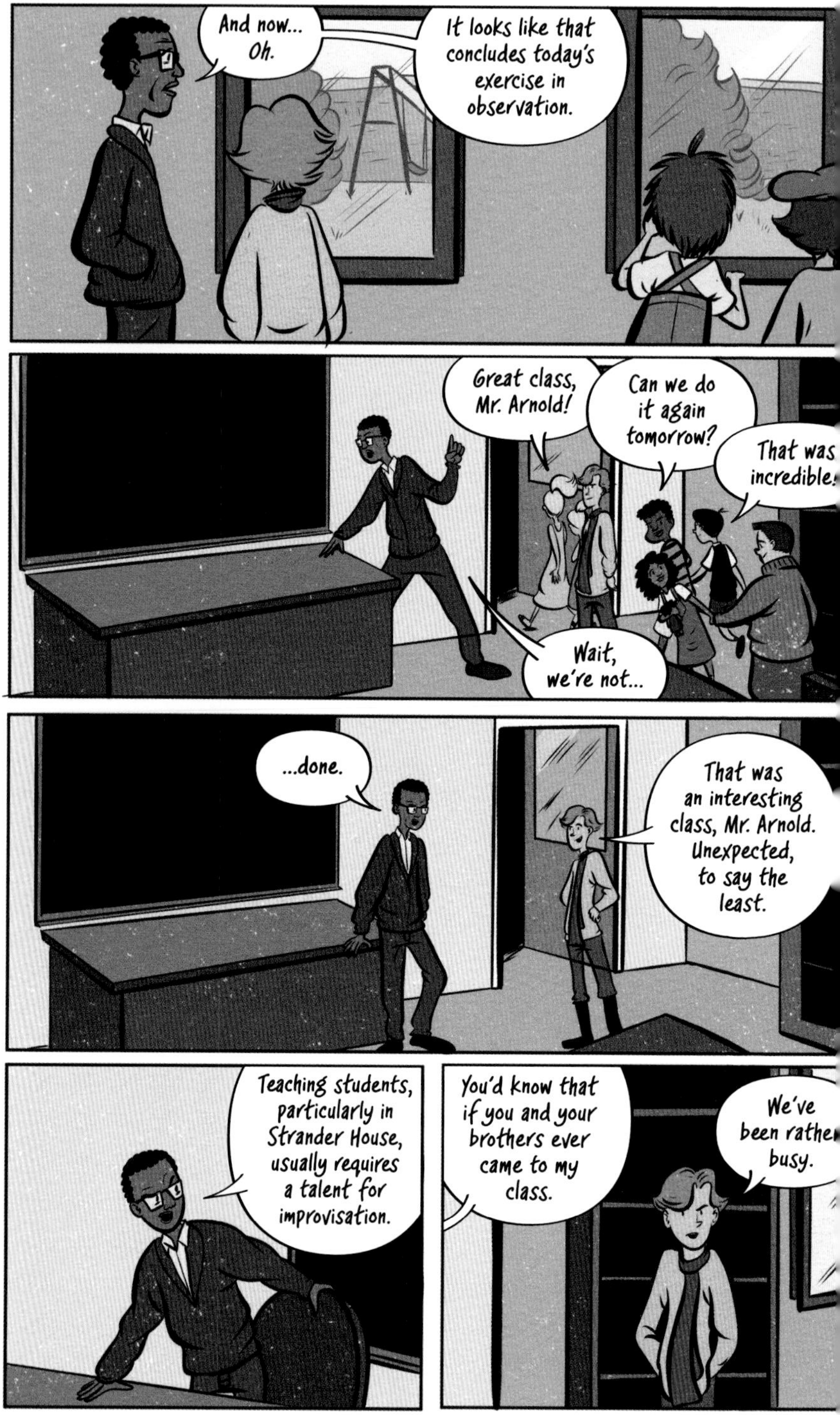
And now... Oh.
It looks like that concludes today's exercise in observation.
Great class, Mr. Arnold!
Can we do it again tomorrow?
That was incredible.
Wait, we're not...
...done.
That was an interesting class, Mr. Arnold. Unexpected, to say the least.
Teaching students, particularly in Strander House, usually requires a talent for improvisation.
You'd know that if you and your brothers ever came to my class.
We've been rathe busy.

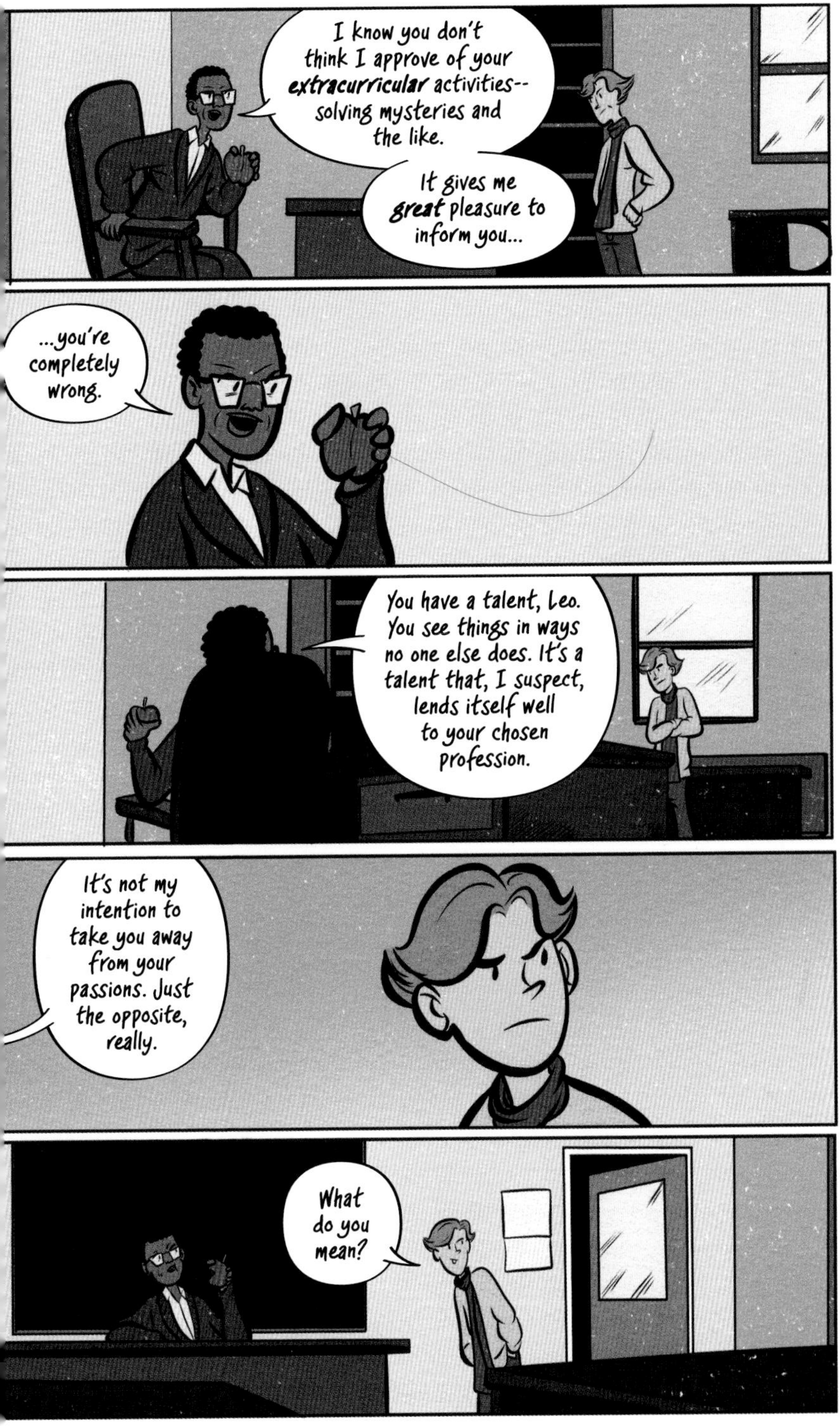
I know you don't think I approve of your extracurricular activities--solving mysteries and the like.
It gives me great pleasure to inform you...
...you're completely wrong.
You have a talent, Leo. You see things in ways no one else does. It's a talent that, I suspect, lends itself well to your chosen profession.
It's not my intention to take you away from your passions. Just the opposite, really.
What do you mean?

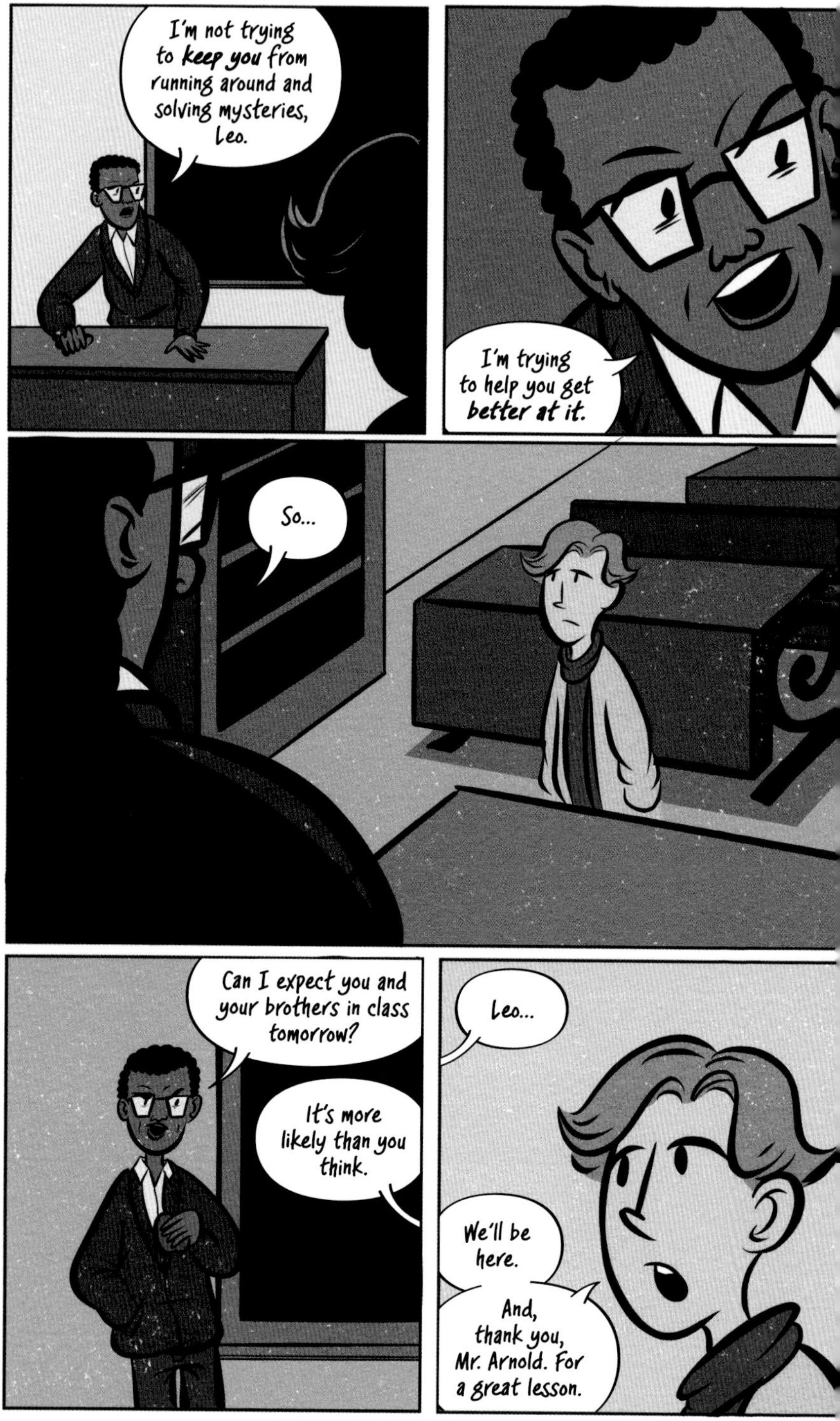
I'm not trying to **keep you** from running around and solving mysteries, Leo.
I'm trying to help you get **better at it.**
So...
Can I expect you and your brothers in class tomorrow?
It's more likely than you think.
Leo...
We'll be here.
And, thank you, Mr. Arnold. For a great lesson.

CHAPTER

8

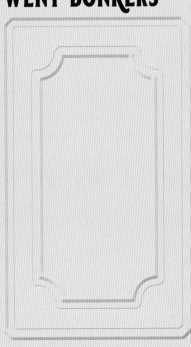

THE DAY THE HOUSE WENT BONKERS

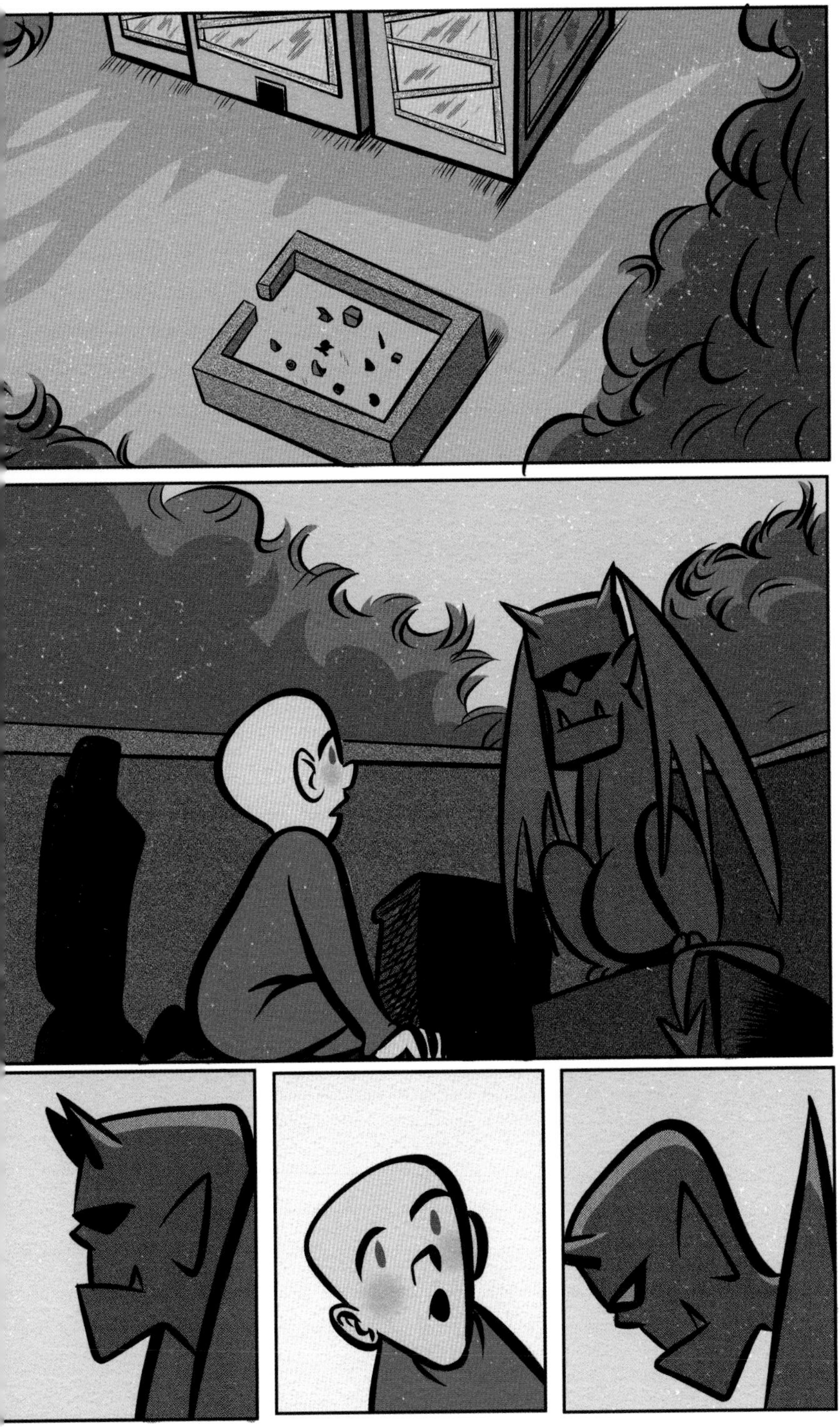

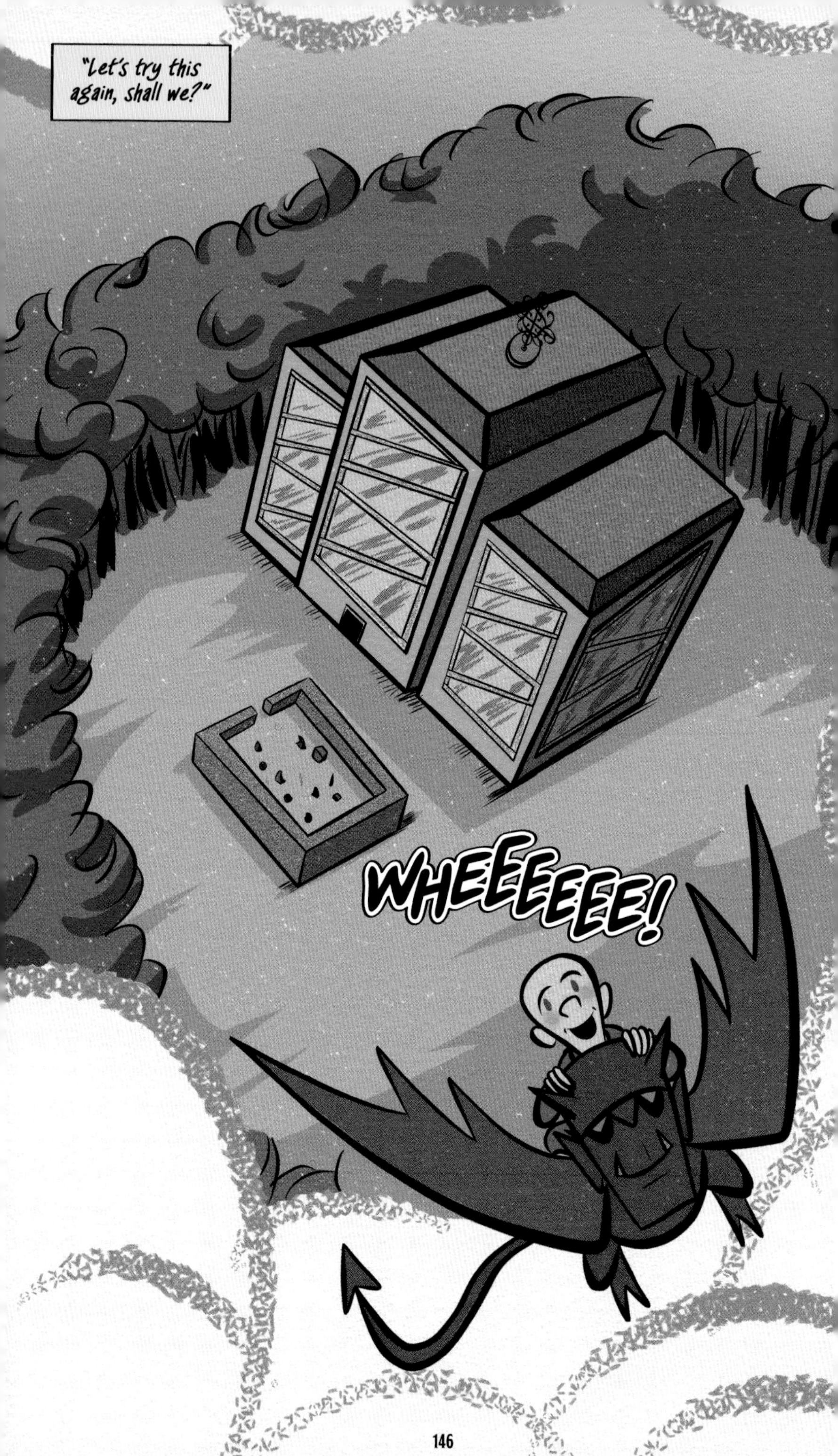
"Let's try this again, shall we?"
WHEEEEEEE!

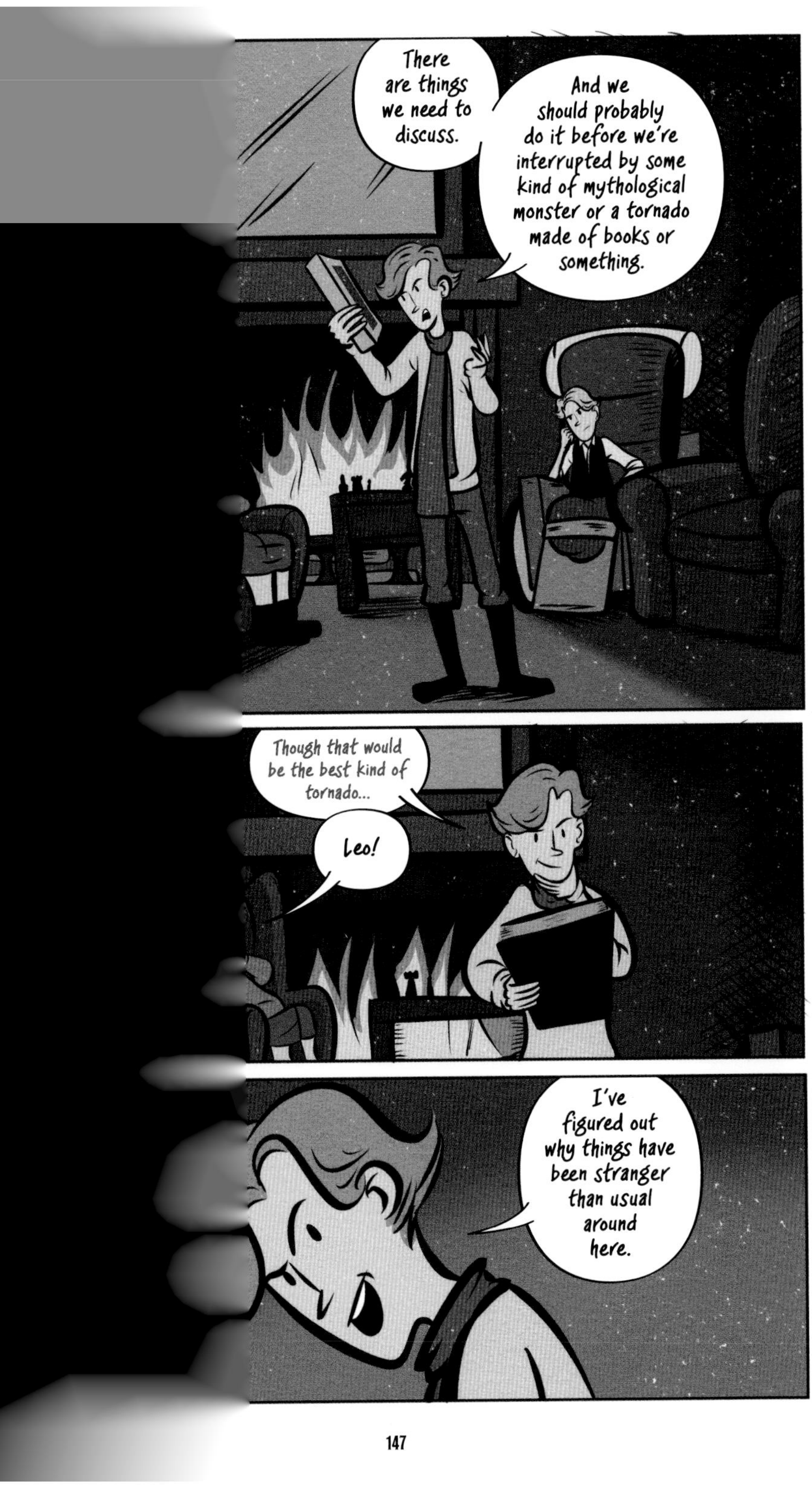
There are things we need to discuss.
And we should probably do it before we're interrupted by some kind of mythological monster or a tornado made of books or something.
Though that would be the best kind of tornado...
Leo!
I've figured out why things have been stranger than usual around here.

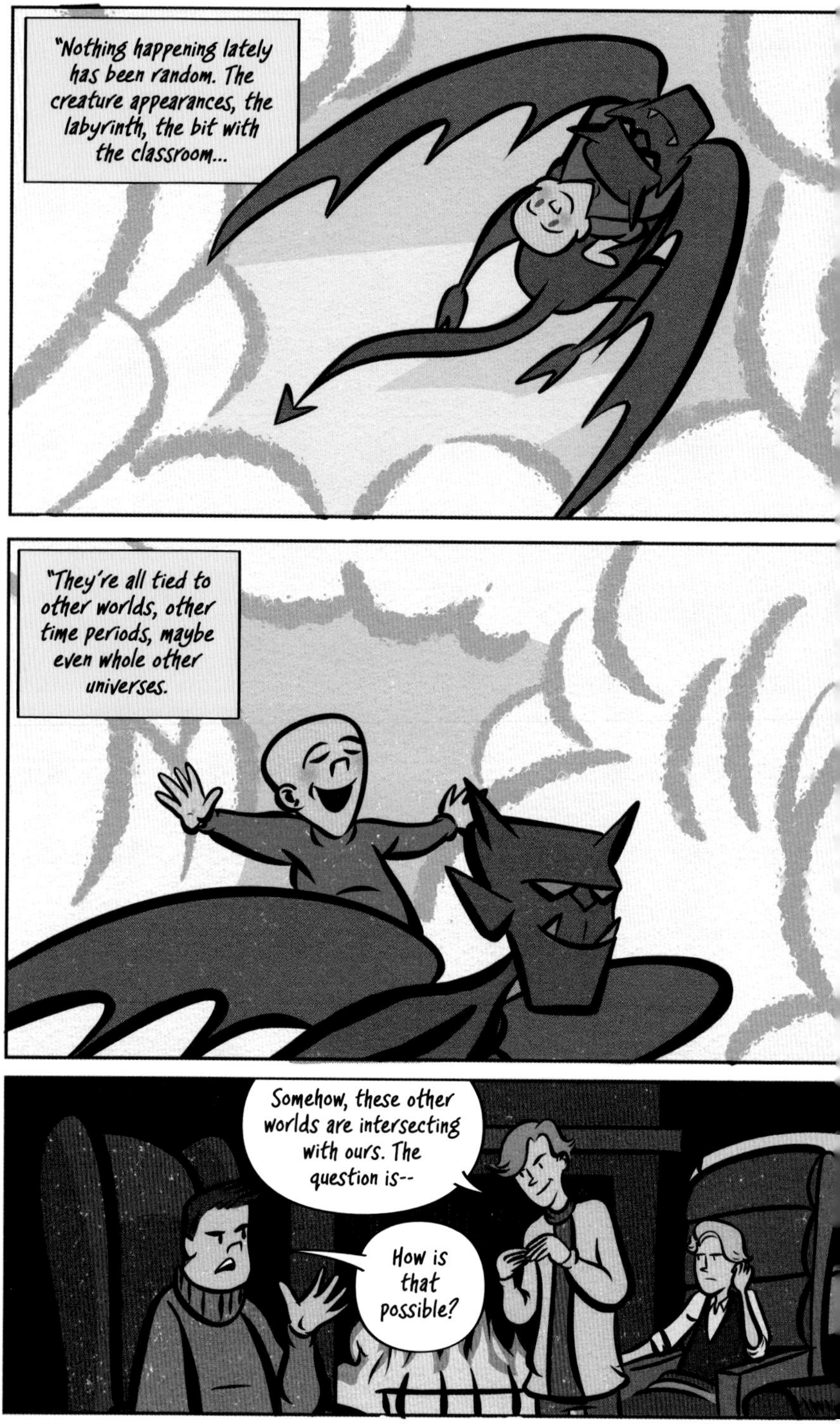
"Nothing happening lately has been random. The creature appearances, the labyrinth, the bit with the classroom...
"They're all tied to other worlds, other time periods, maybe even whole other universes.
Somehow, these other worlds are intersecting with ours. The question is--
How is that possible?

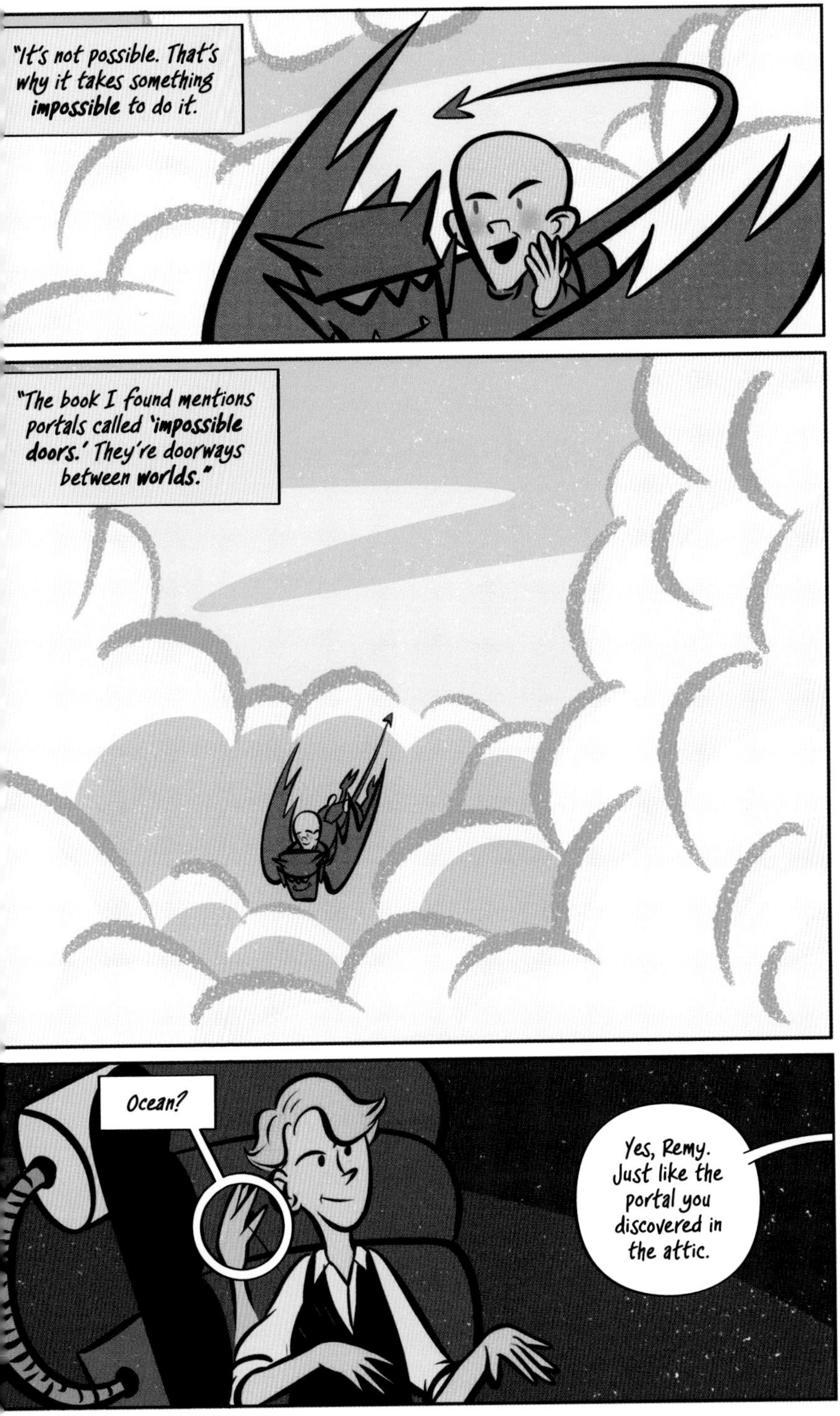
"It's not possible. That's why it takes something impossible to do it.
"The book I found mentions portals called 'impossible doors.' They're doorways between worlds."
Ocean?
Yes, Remy. Just like the portal you discovered in the attic.

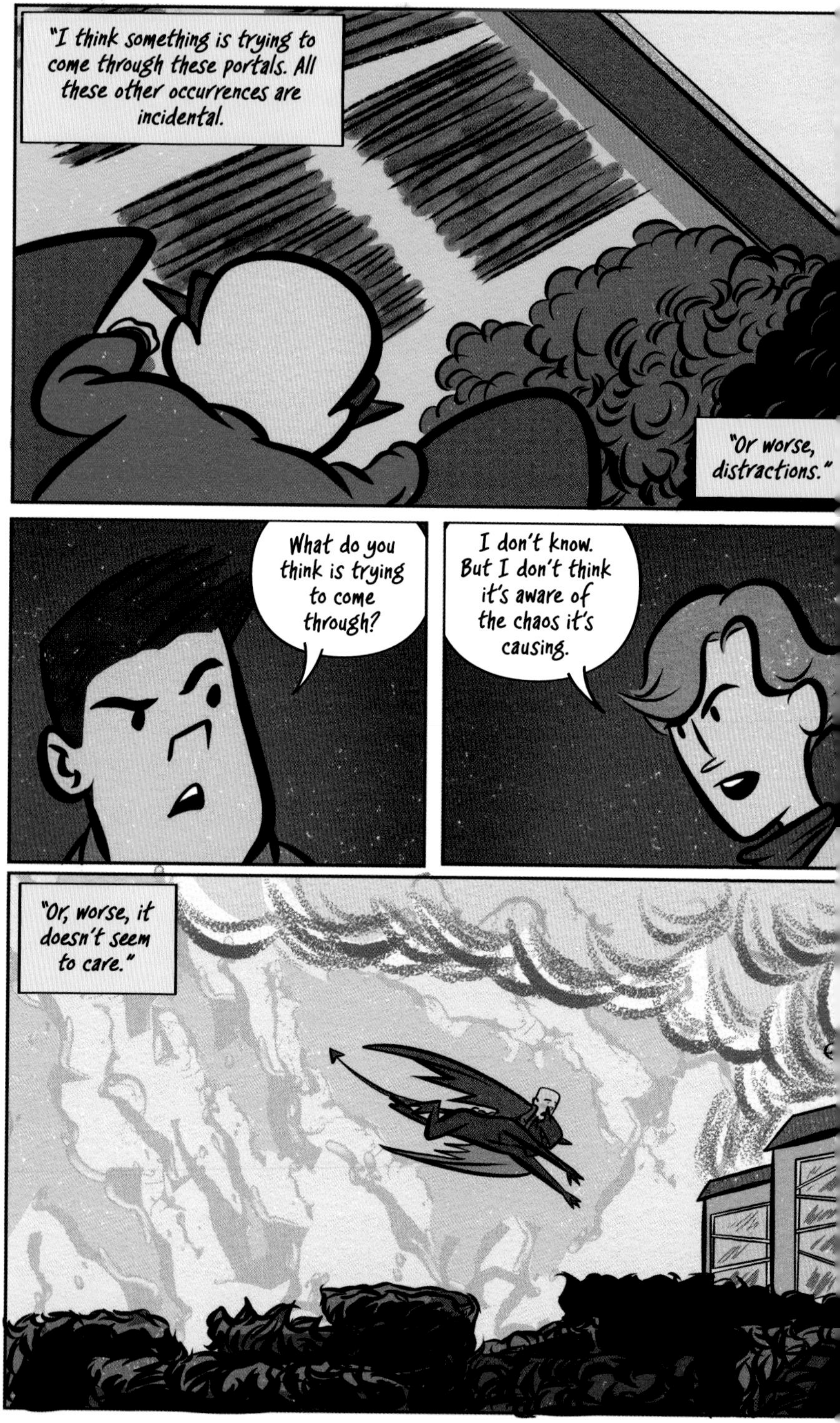
"I think something is trying to come through these portals. All these other occurrences are incidental.
"Or worse, distractions."
What do you think is trying to come through?
I don't know. But I don't think it's aware of the chaos it's causing.
"Or, worse, it doesn't seem to care."

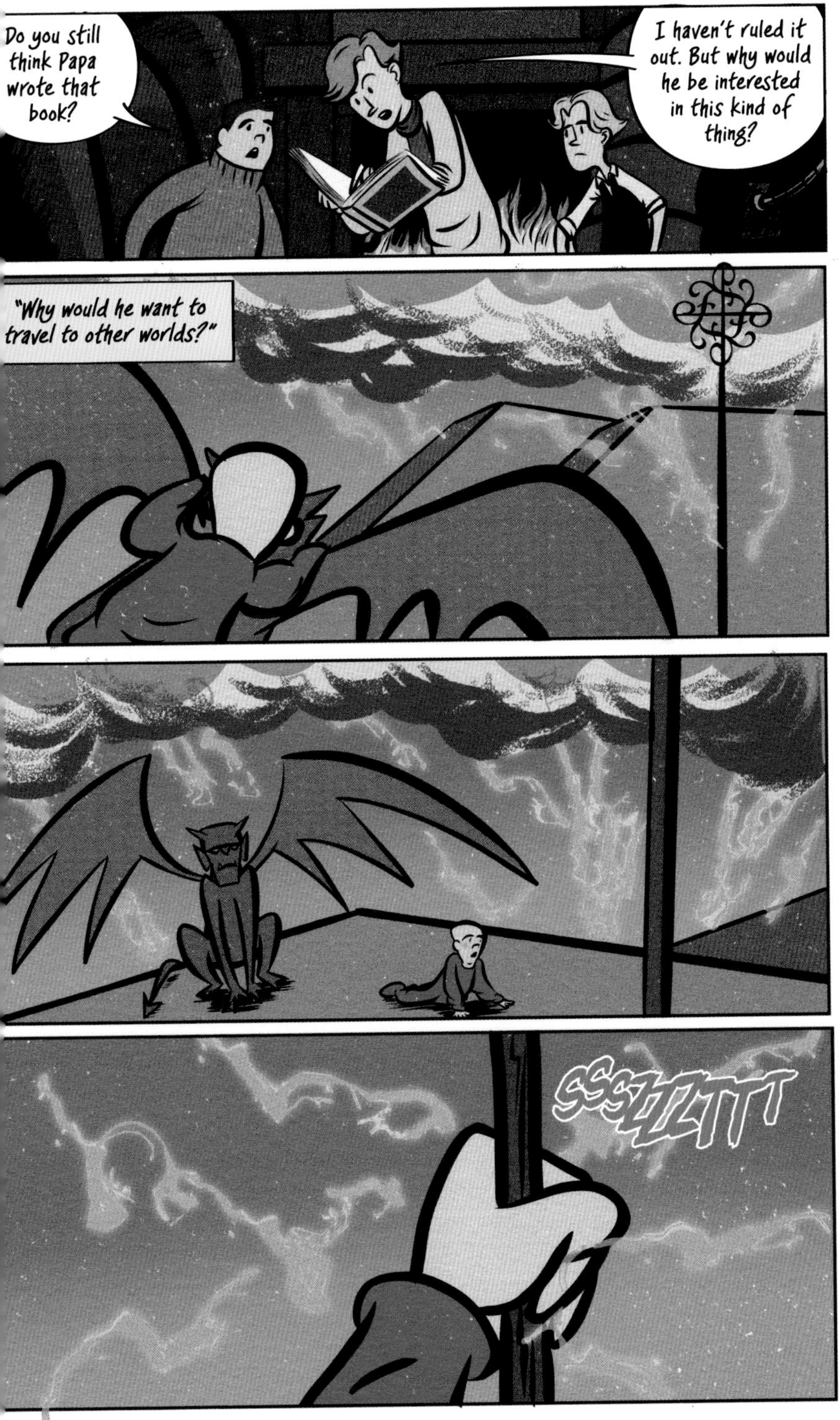
Do you still think Papa wrote that book?
I haven't ruled it out. But why would he be interested in this kind of thing?
"Why would he want to travel to other worlds?"
SSSZZZTTT

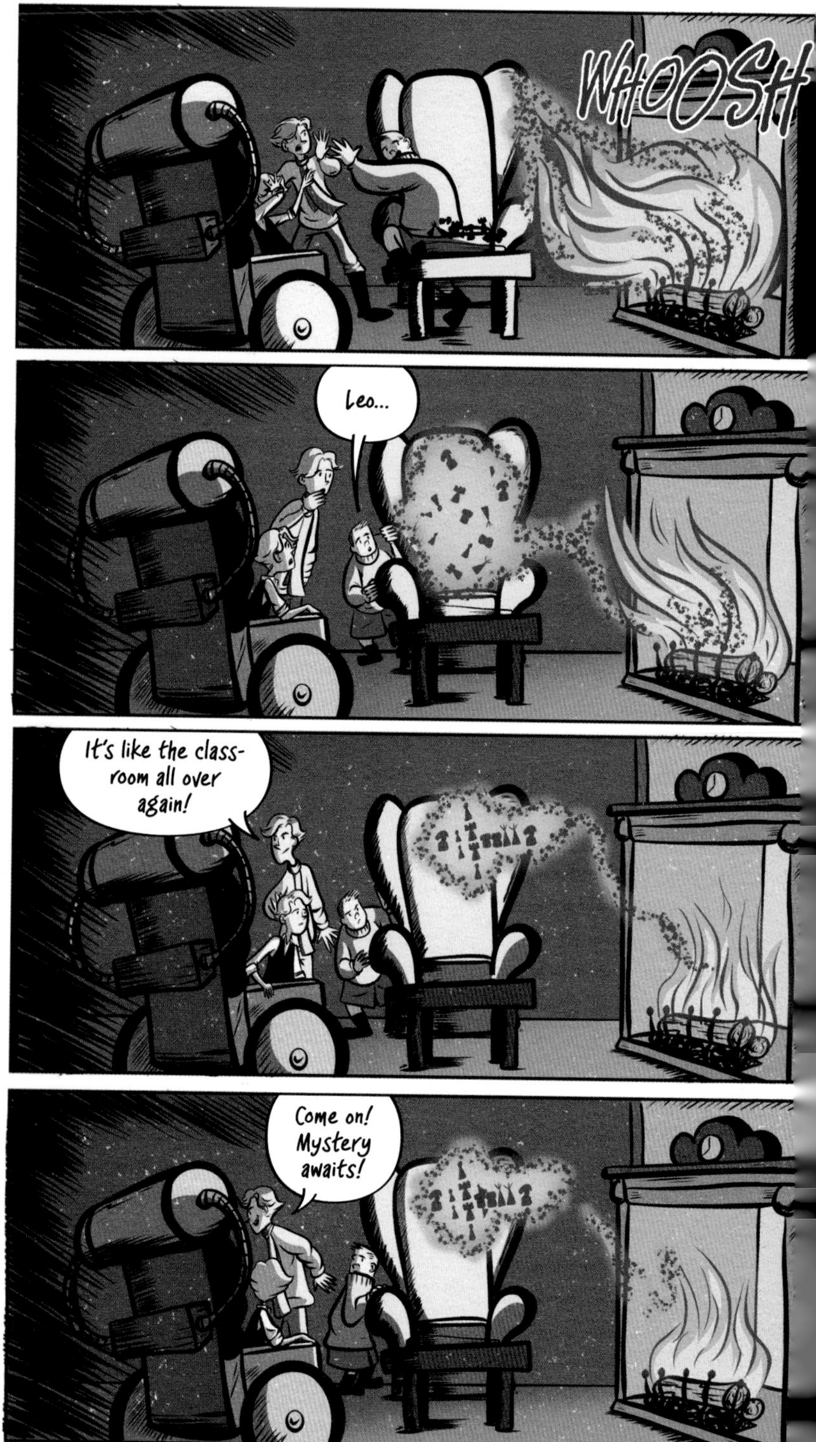
WHOOSH
Leo...
It's like the class-room all over again!
Come on! Mystery awaits!

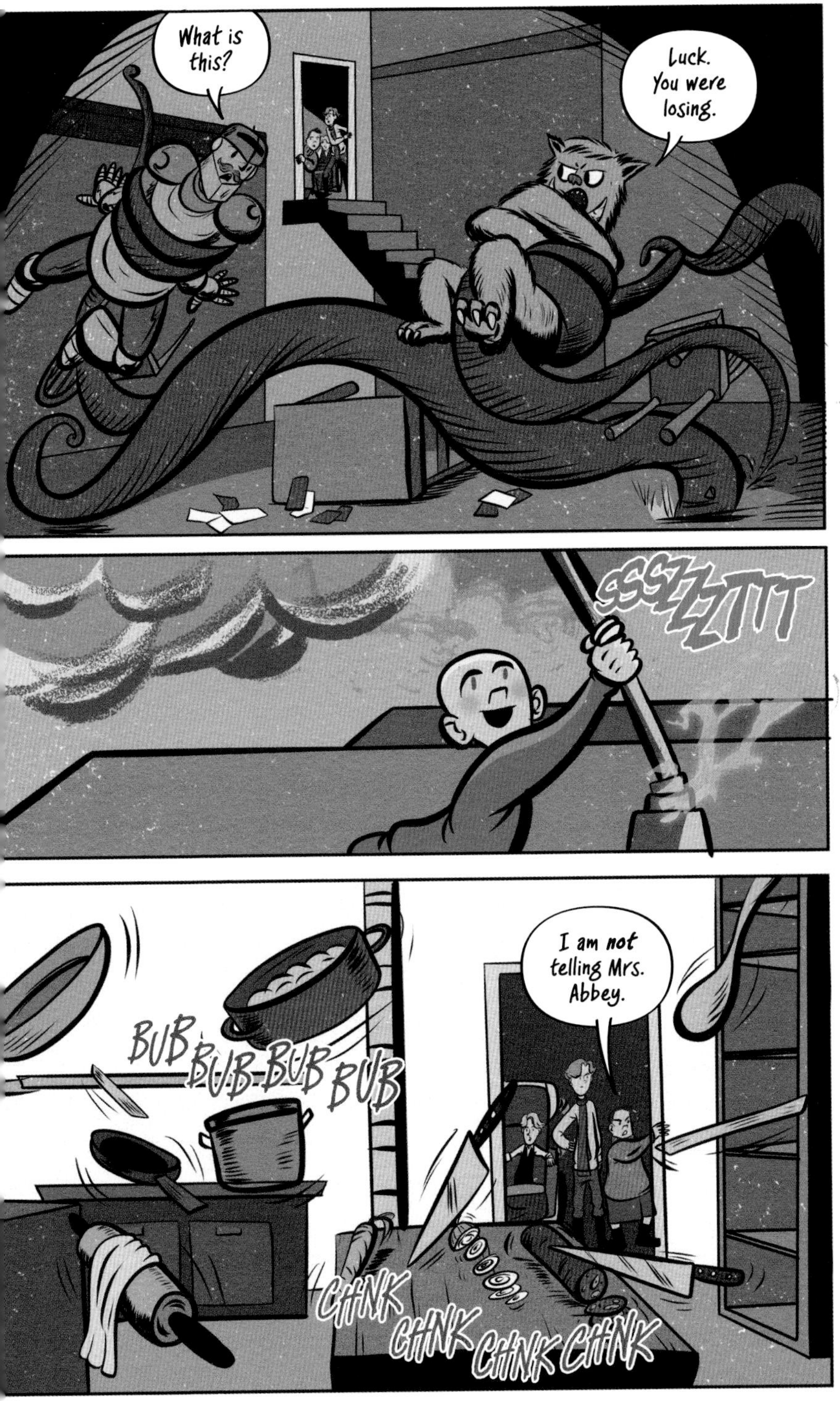
What is this?
Luck. You were losing.
SSSZZZTTT
BUB BUB BUB BUB BUB
I am *not* telling Mrs. Abbey.
CHNK CHNK CHNK CHNK

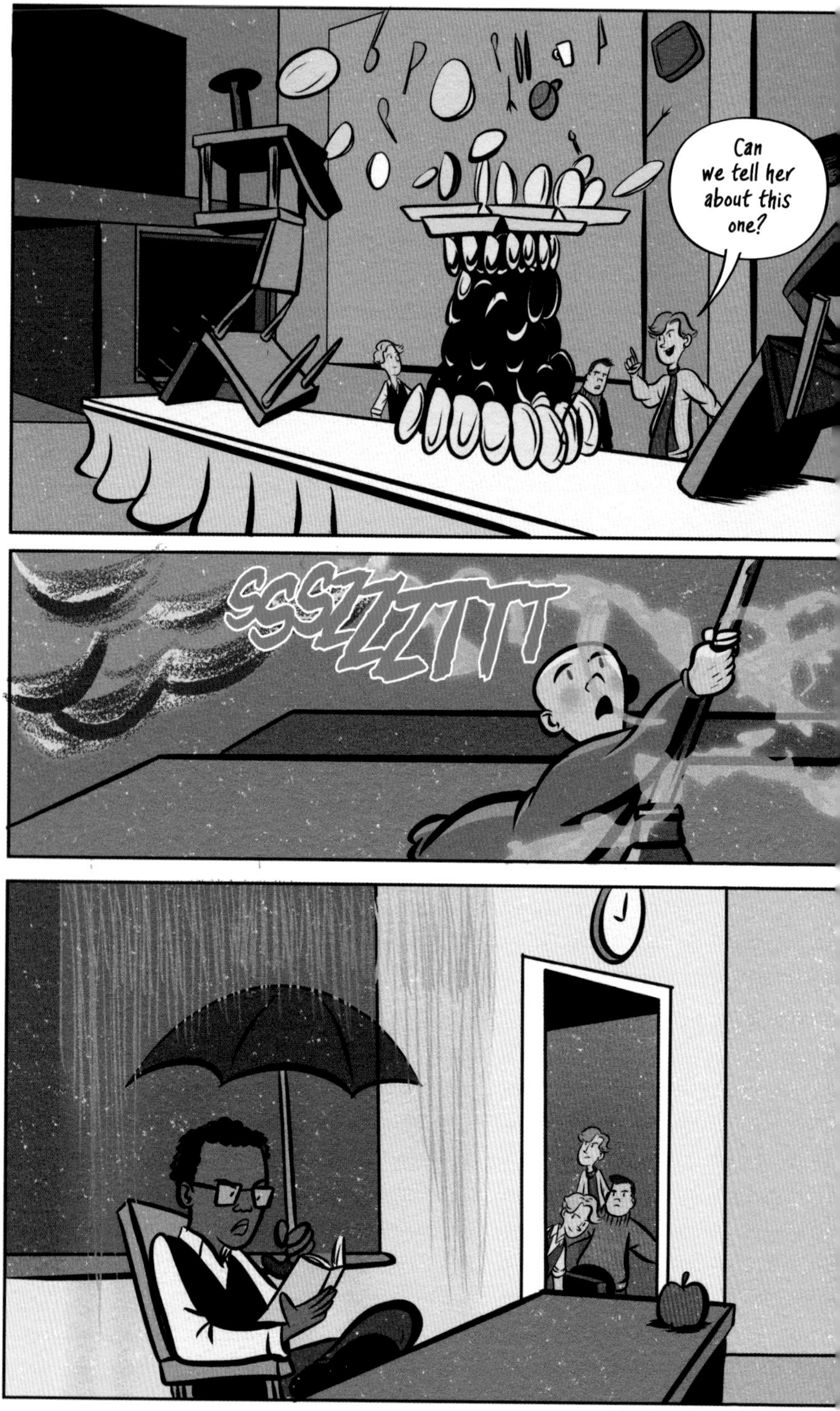
Can we tell her about this one?
SSSZZZTTTT

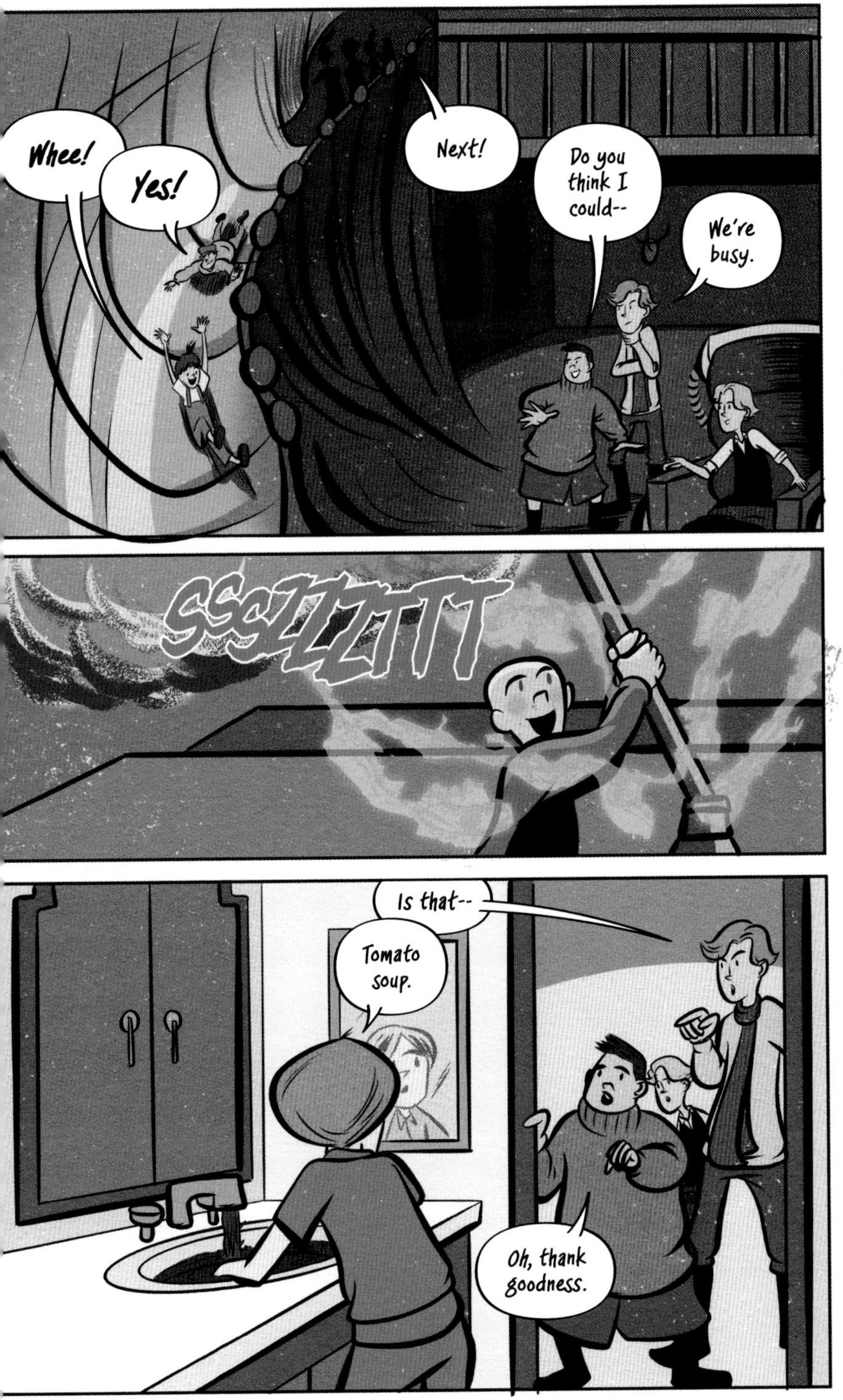
Whee!
Yes!
Next!
Do you think I could--
We're busy.
SSSZZZTTT
Is that--
Tomato soup.
Oh, thank goodness.

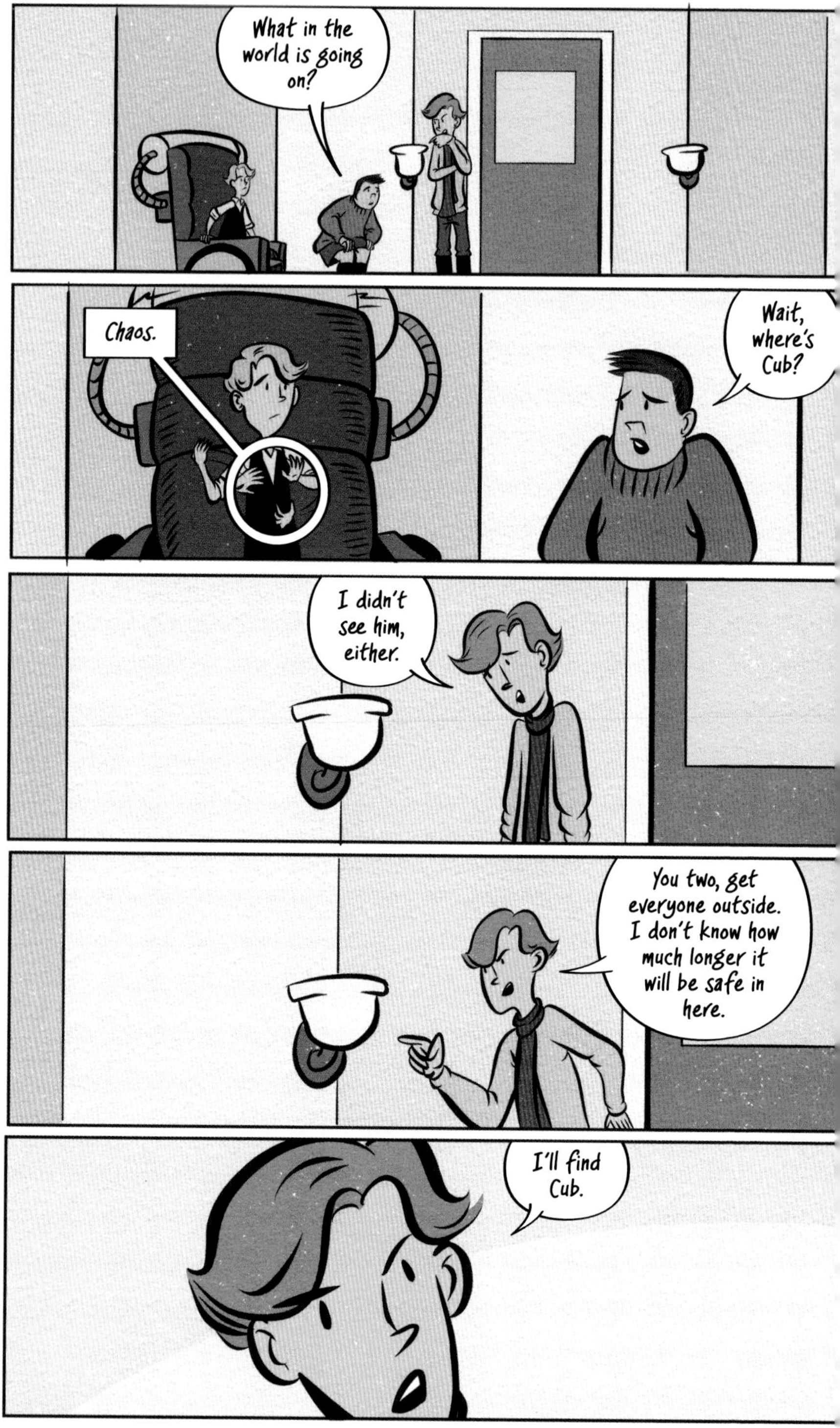
What in the world is going on?
Chaos.
Wait, where's Cub?
I didn't see him, either.
You two, get everyone outside. I don't know how much longer it will be safe in here.
I'll find Cub.

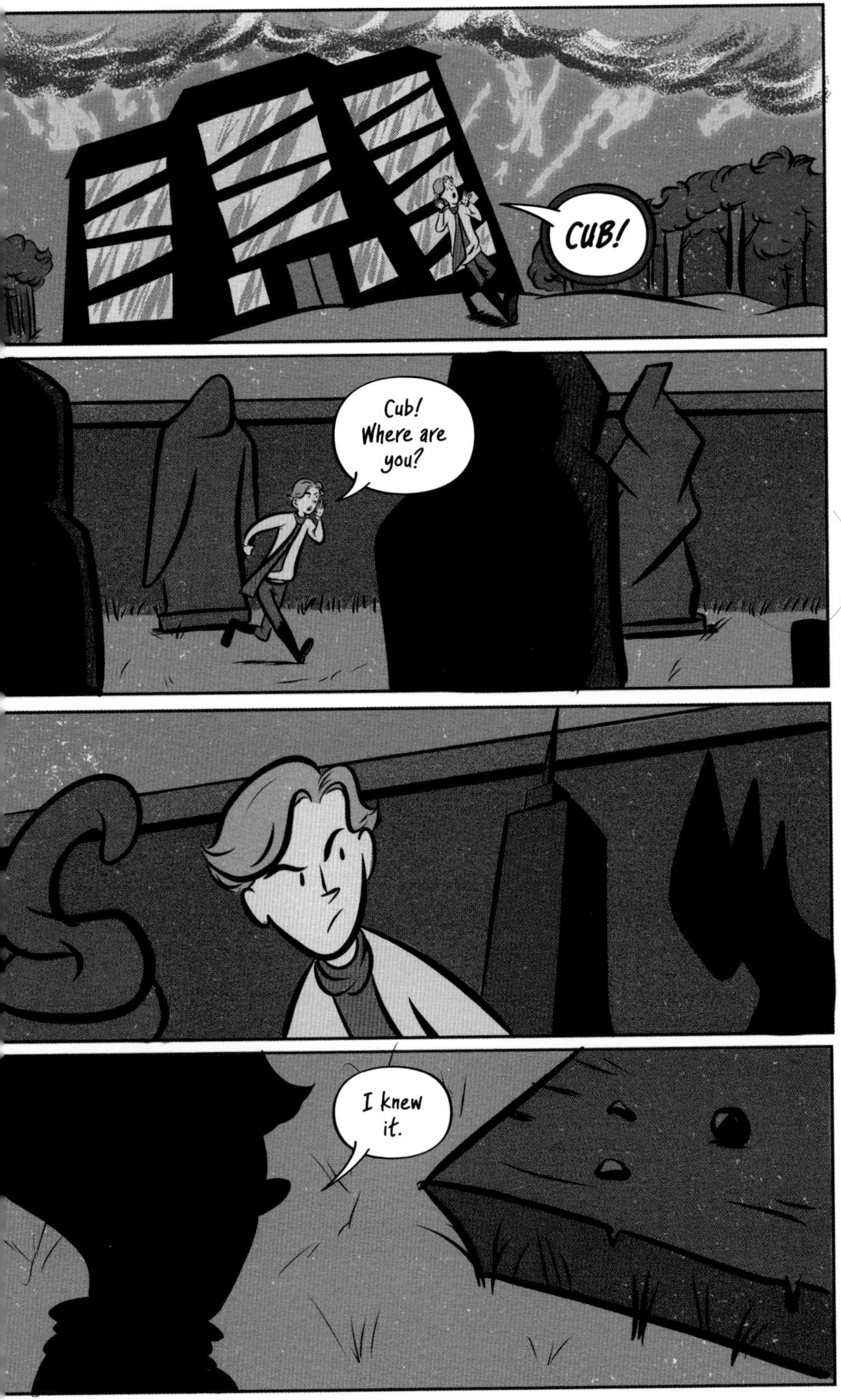
CUB!
Cub! Where are you?
I knew it.

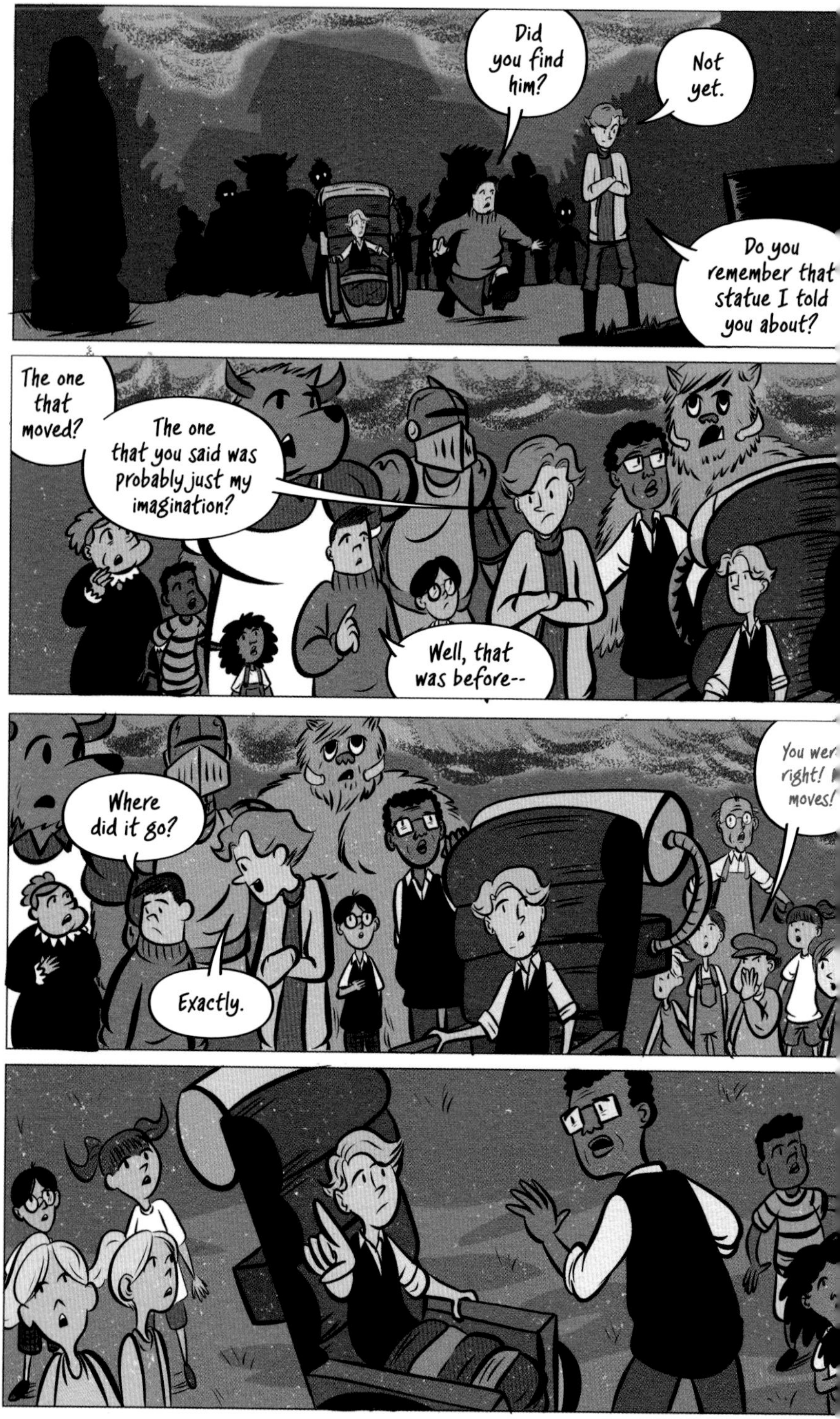
Did you find him?
Not yet.
Do you remember that statue I told you about?
The one that moved?
The one that you said was probably just my imagination?
Well, that was before--
Where did it go?
Exactly.
You wer right! moves!

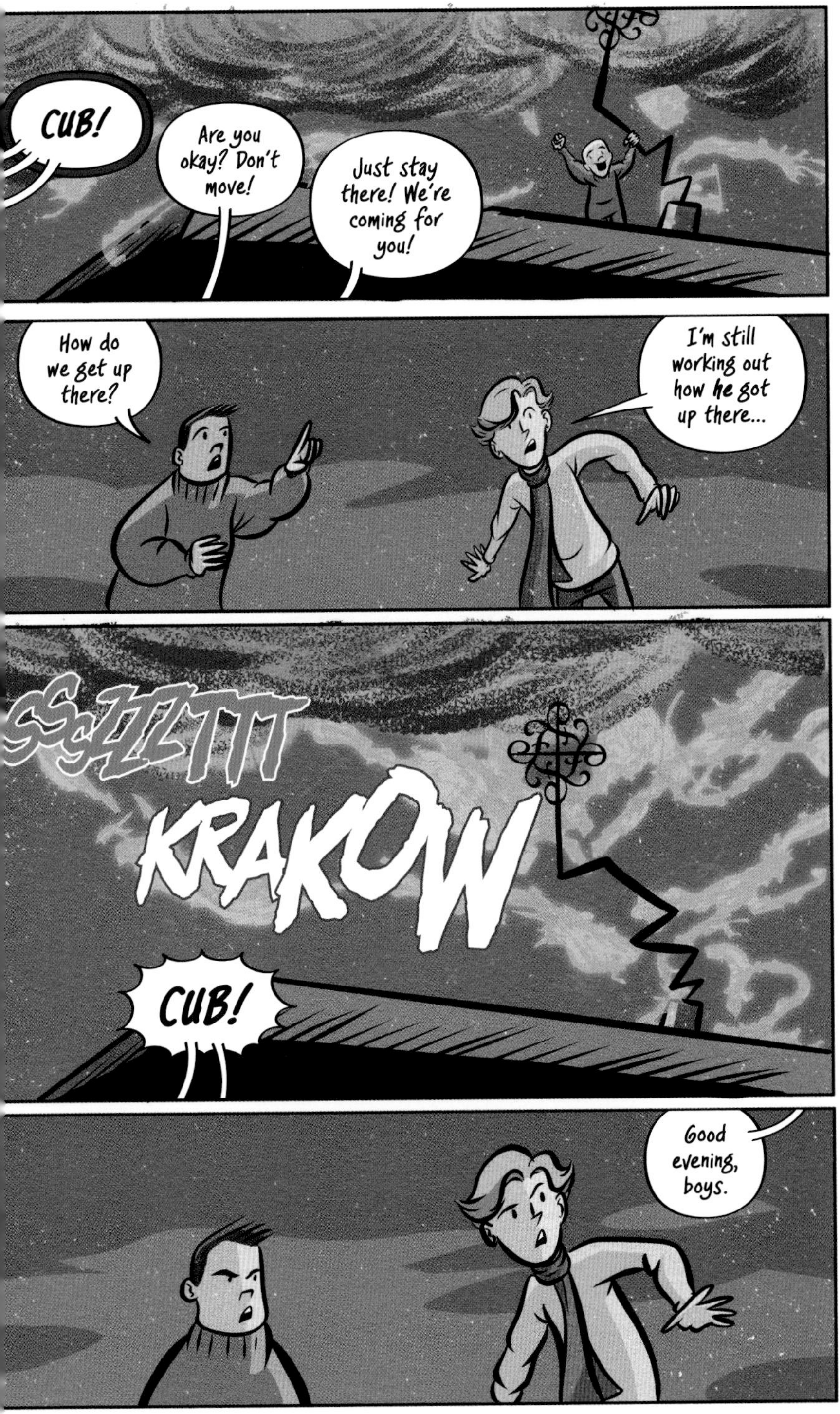
CUB!
Are you okay? Don't move!
Just stay there! We're coming for you!
How do we get up there?
I'm still working out how he got up there...
SSSZZZTTT
KRAKOW
CUB!
Good evening, boys.

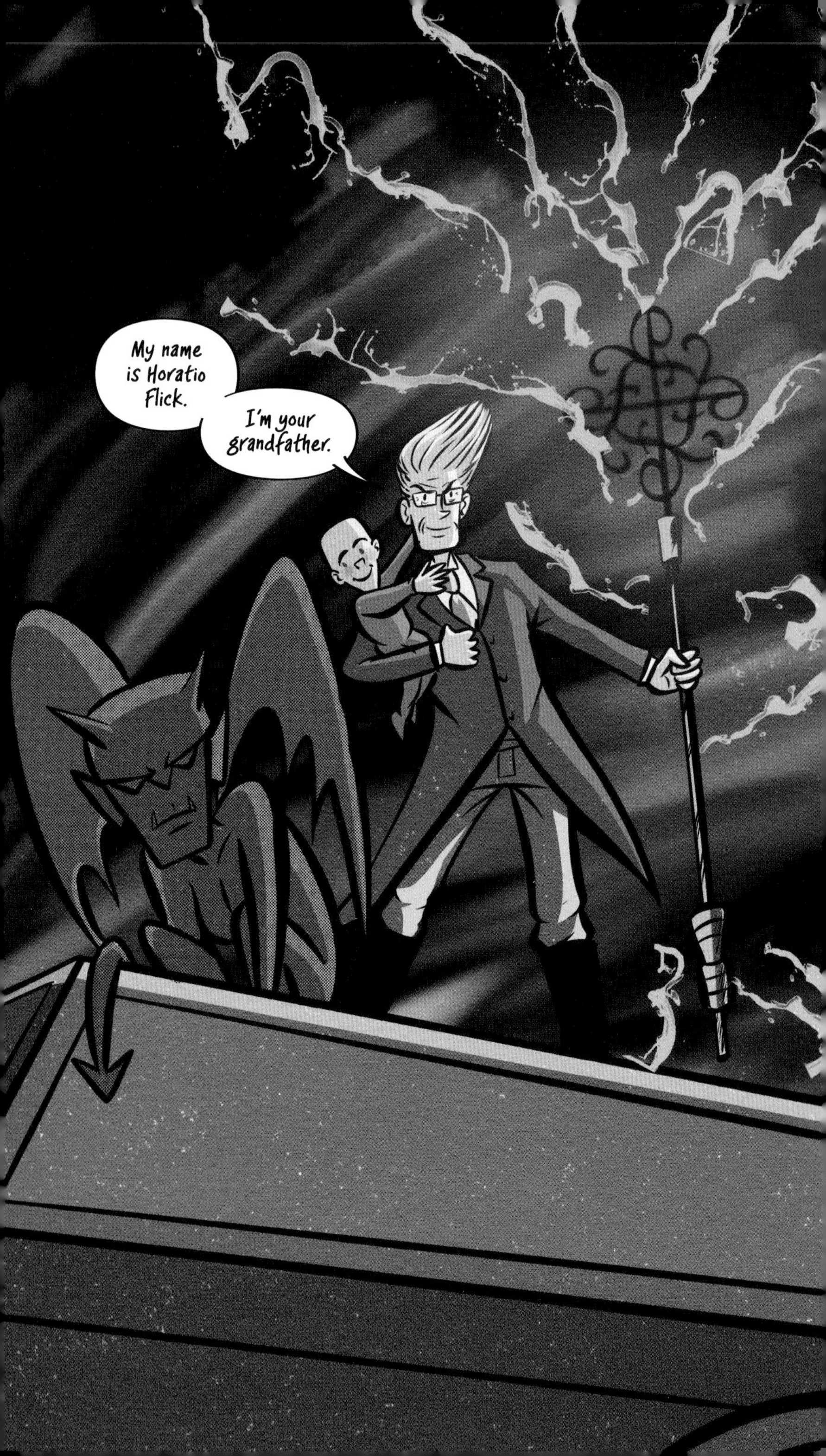
My name is Horatio Flick.
I'm your grandfather.

CHAPTER
9

THE SPACE OF A BLINK

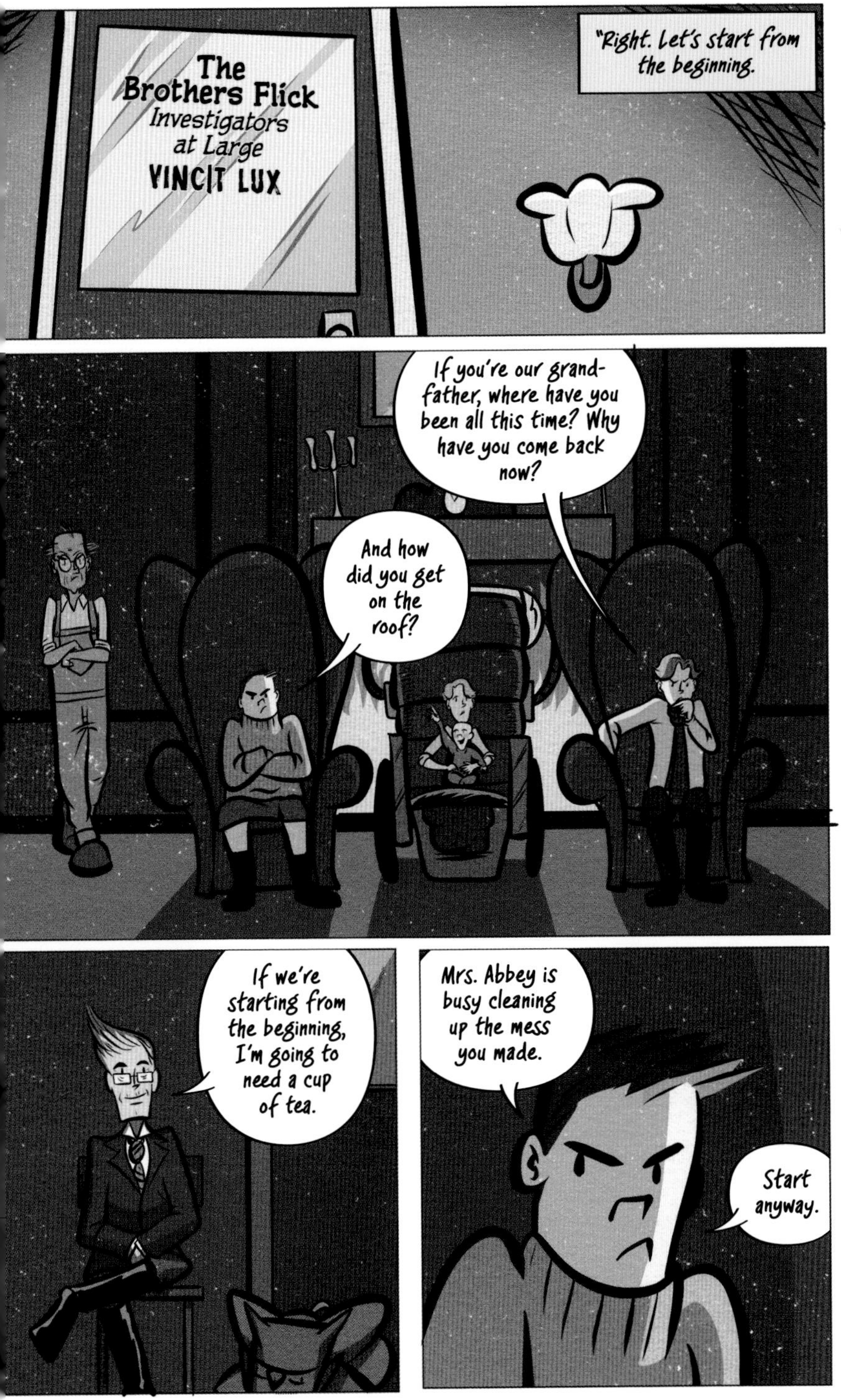
The Brothers Flick Investigators at Large VINCIT LUX
"Right. Let's start from the beginning.
If you're our grandfather, where have you been all this time? Why have you come back now?
And how did you get on the roof?
If we're starting from the beginning, I'm going to need a cup of tea.
Mrs. Abbey is busy cleaning up the mess you made.
Start anyway.

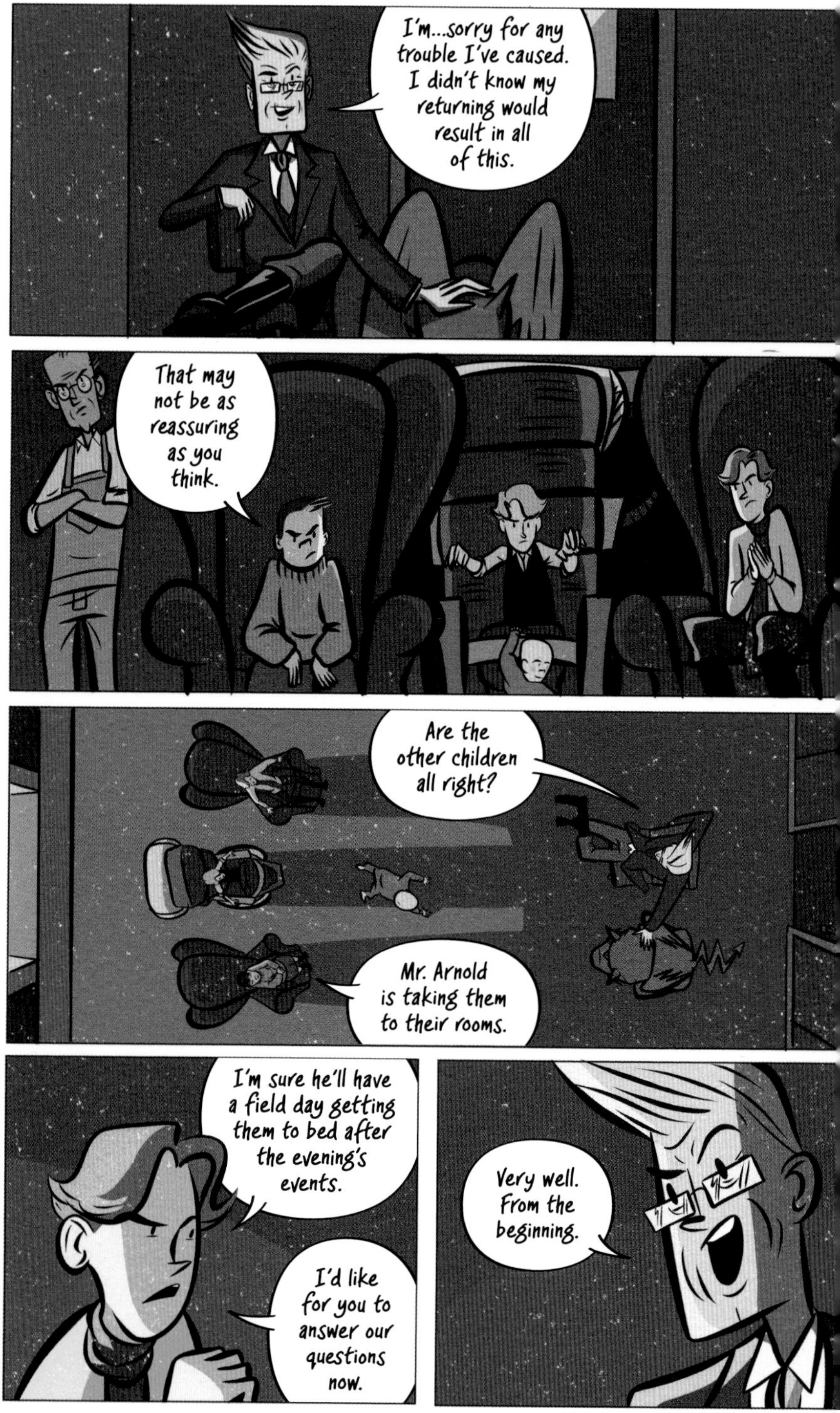
I'm...sorry for any trouble I've caused. I didn't know my returning would result in all of this.
That may not be as reassuring as you think.
Are the other children all right?
Mr. Arnold is taking them to their rooms.
I'm sure he'll have a field day getting them to bed after the evening's events.
I'd like for you to answer our questions now.
Very well. From the beginning.

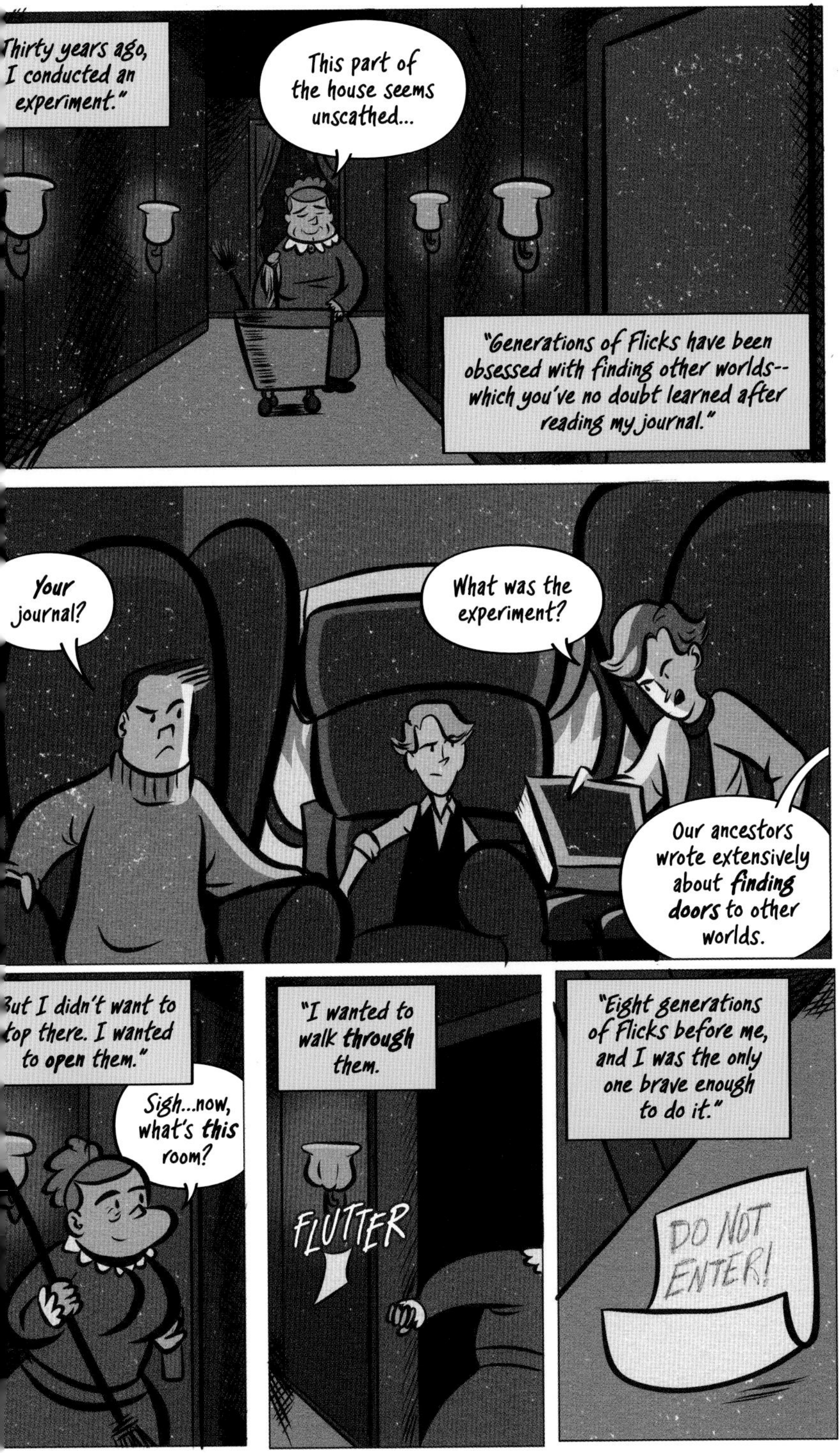
Thirty years ago, I conducted an experiment."
This part of the house seems unscathed...
"Generations of Flicks have been obsessed with finding other worlds--which you've no doubt learned after reading my journal."
Your journal?
What was the experiment?
Our ancestors wrote extensively about *finding doors* to other worlds.
But I didn't want to stop there. I wanted to open them."
Sigh...now, what's *this* room?
"I wanted to walk *through* them.
FLUTTER
"Eight generations of Flicks before me, and I was the only one brave enough to do it."
DO NOT ENTER!

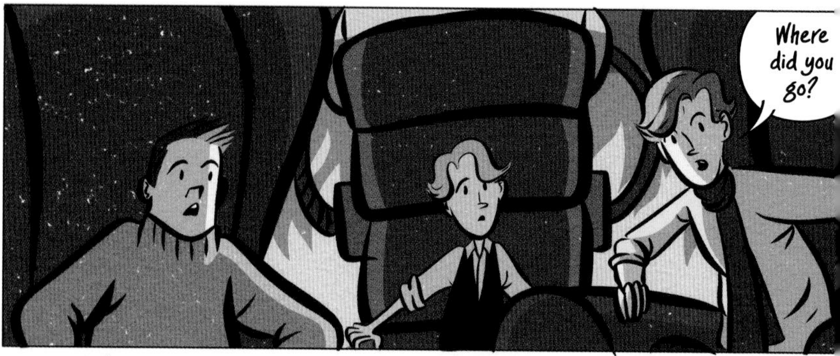
Where did you go?

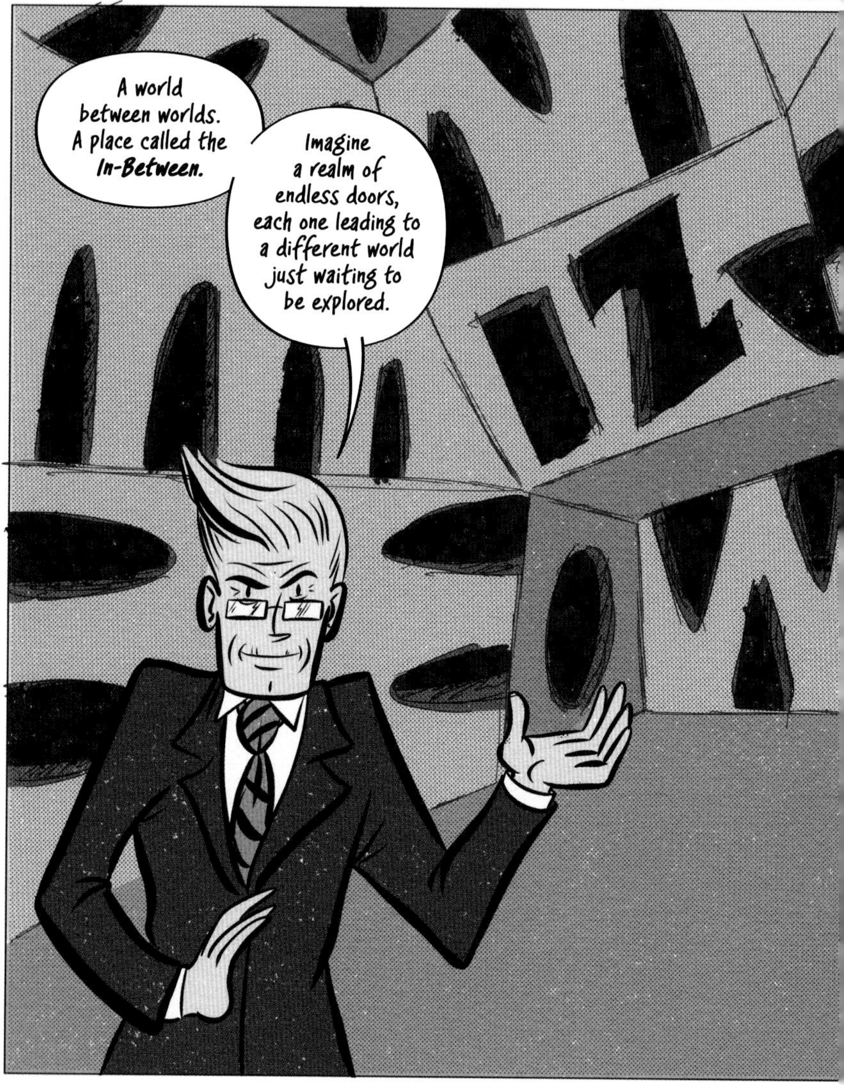
A world between worlds. A place called the *In-Between.*
Imagine a realm of endless doors, each one leading to a different world just waiting to be explored.

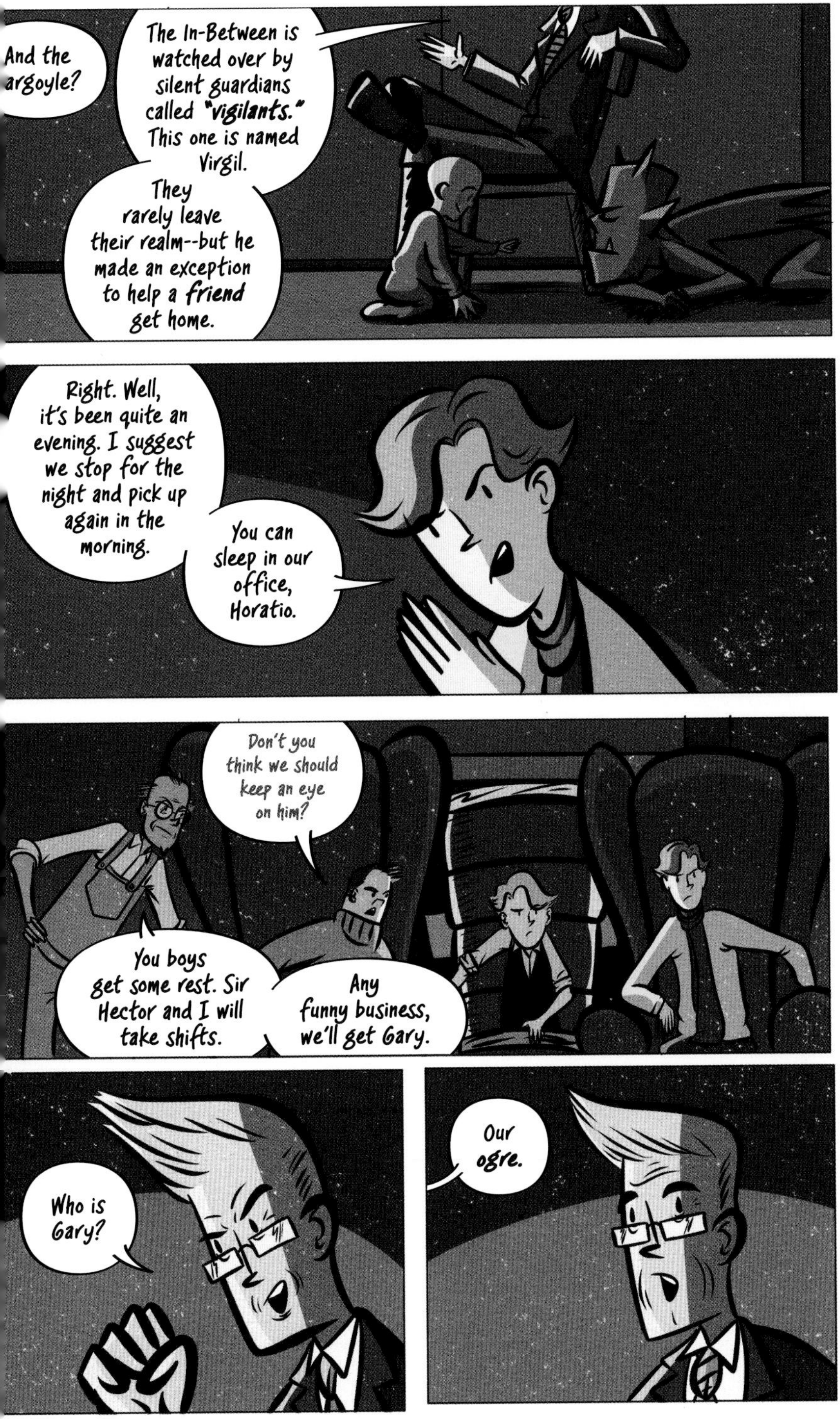
And the argoyle?
The In-Between is watched over by silent guardians called "vigilants." This one is named Virgil.
They rarely leave their realm--but he made an exception to help a friend get home.
Right. Well, it's been quite an evening. I suggest we stop for the night and pick up again in the morning.
You can sleep in our office, Horatio.
Don't you think we should keep an eye on him?
You boys get some rest. Sir Hector and I will take shifts.
Any funny business, we'll get Gary.
Who is Gary?
Our ogre.

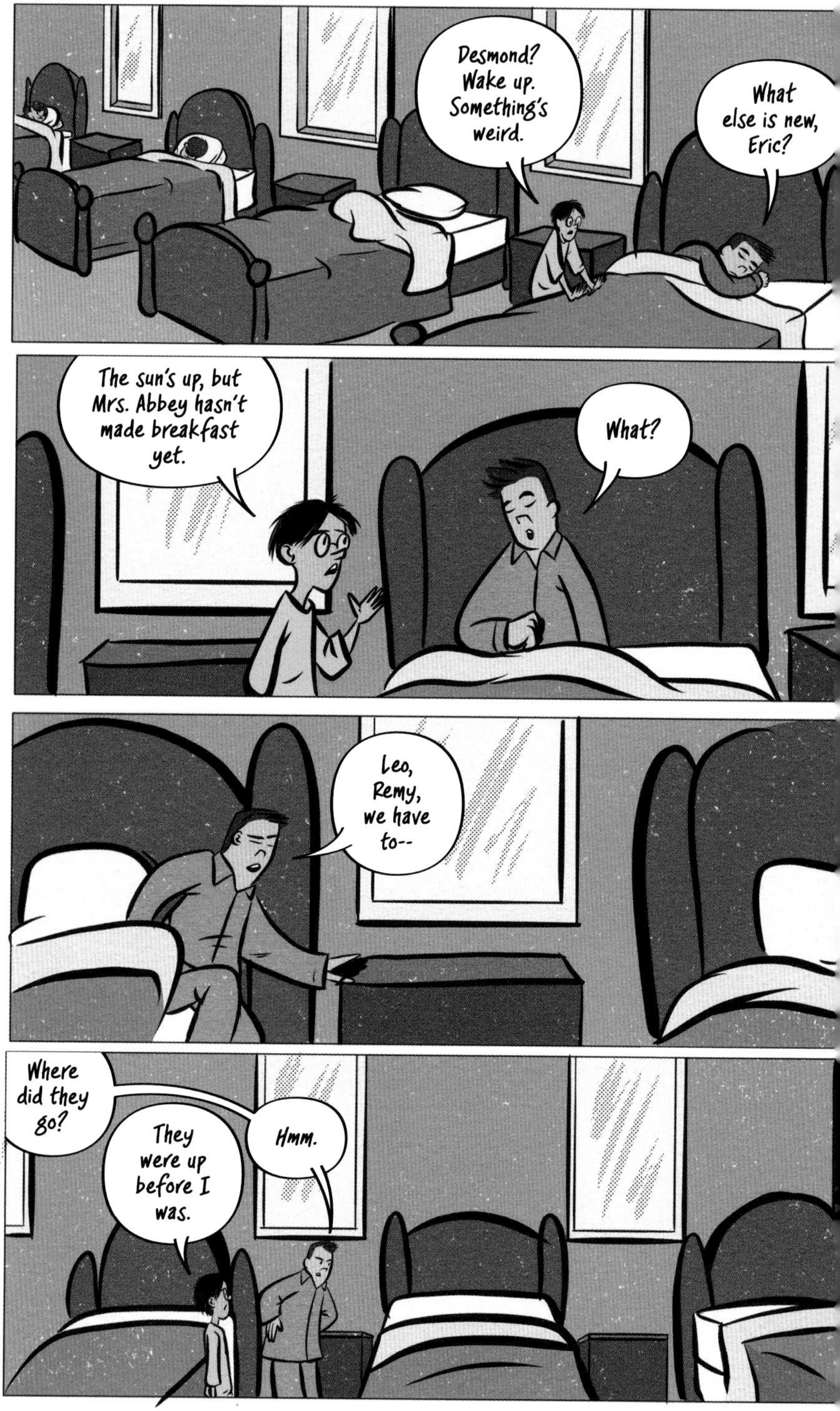
Desmond? Wake up. Something's weird.
What else is new, Eric?
The sun's up, but Mrs. Abbey hasn't made breakfast yet.
What?
Leo, Remy, we have to--
Where did they go?
Hmm.
They were up before I was.

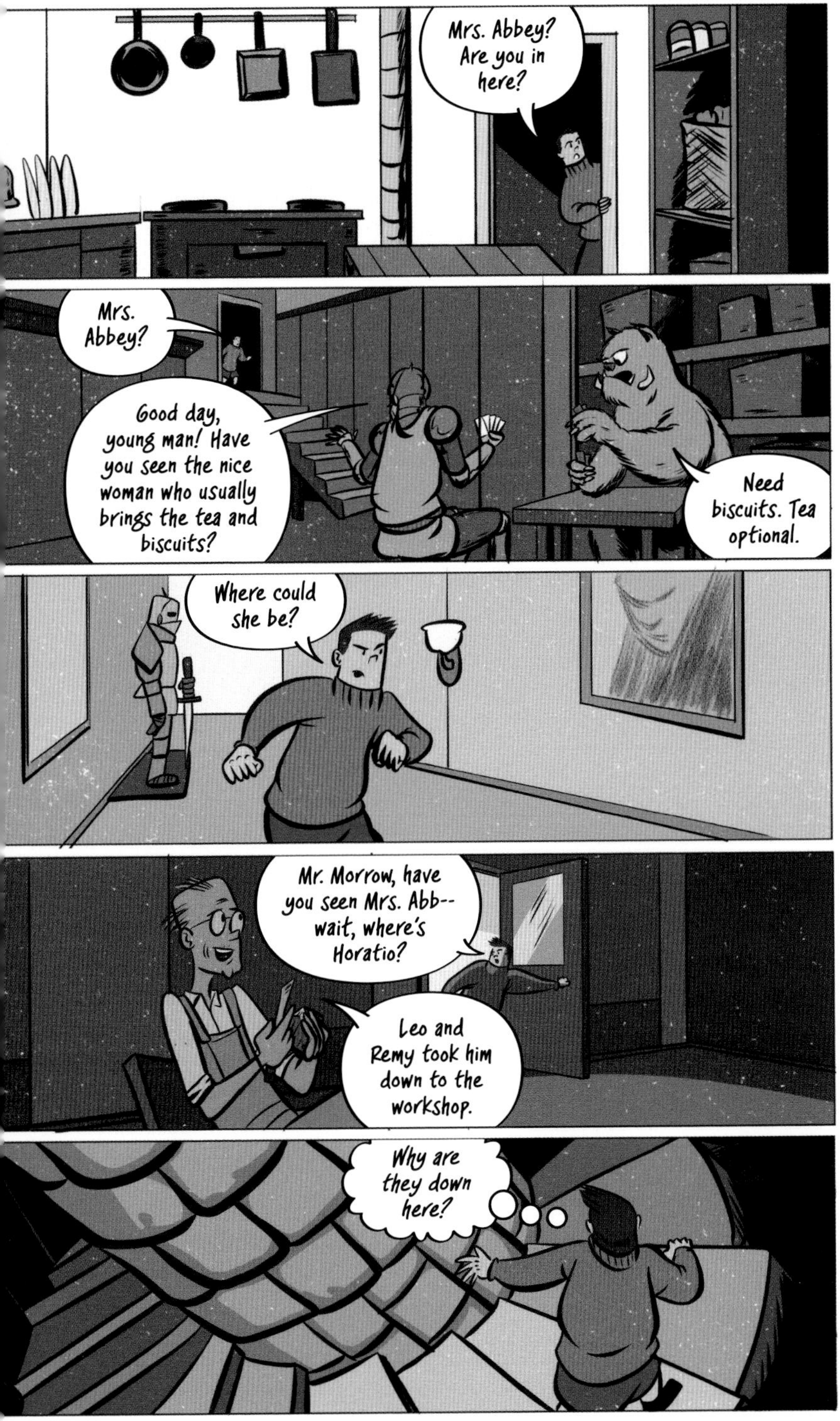
Mrs. Abbey? Are you in here?
Mrs. Abbey?
Good day, young man! Have you seen the nice woman who usually brings the tea and biscuits?
Need biscuits. Tea optional.
Where could she be?
Mr. Morrow, have you seen Mrs. Abb-- wait, where's Horatio?
Leo and Remy took him down to the workshop.
Why are they down here?

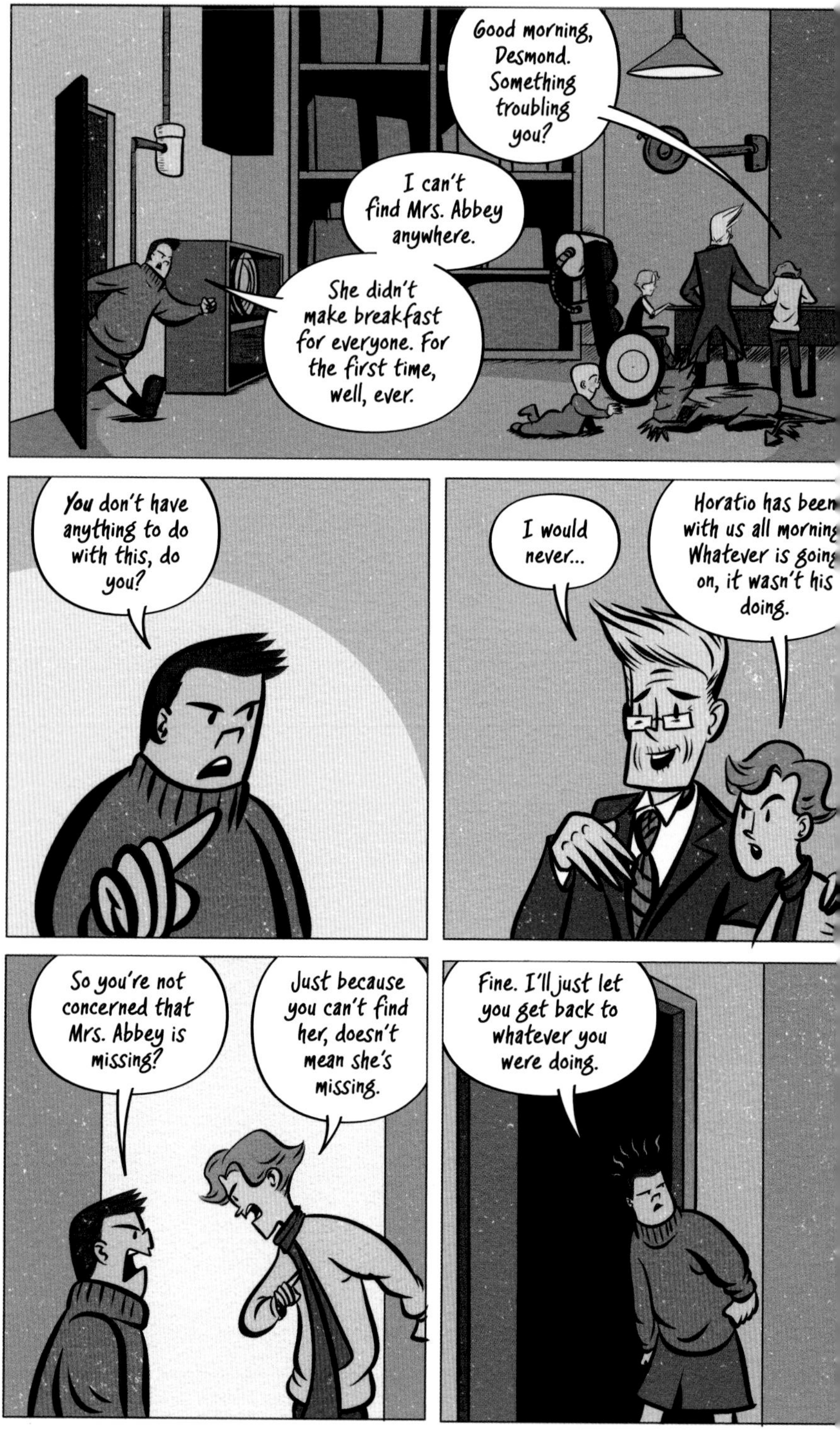
Good morning, Desmond. Something troubling you?
I can't find Mrs. Abbey anywhere.
She didn't make breakfast for everyone. For the first time, well, ever.
You don't have anything to do with this, do you?
I would never...
Horatio has been with us all morning Whatever is going on, it wasn't his doing.
So you're not concerned that Mrs. Abbey is missing?
Just because you can't find her, doesn't mean she's missing.
Fine. I'll just let you get back to whatever you were doing.

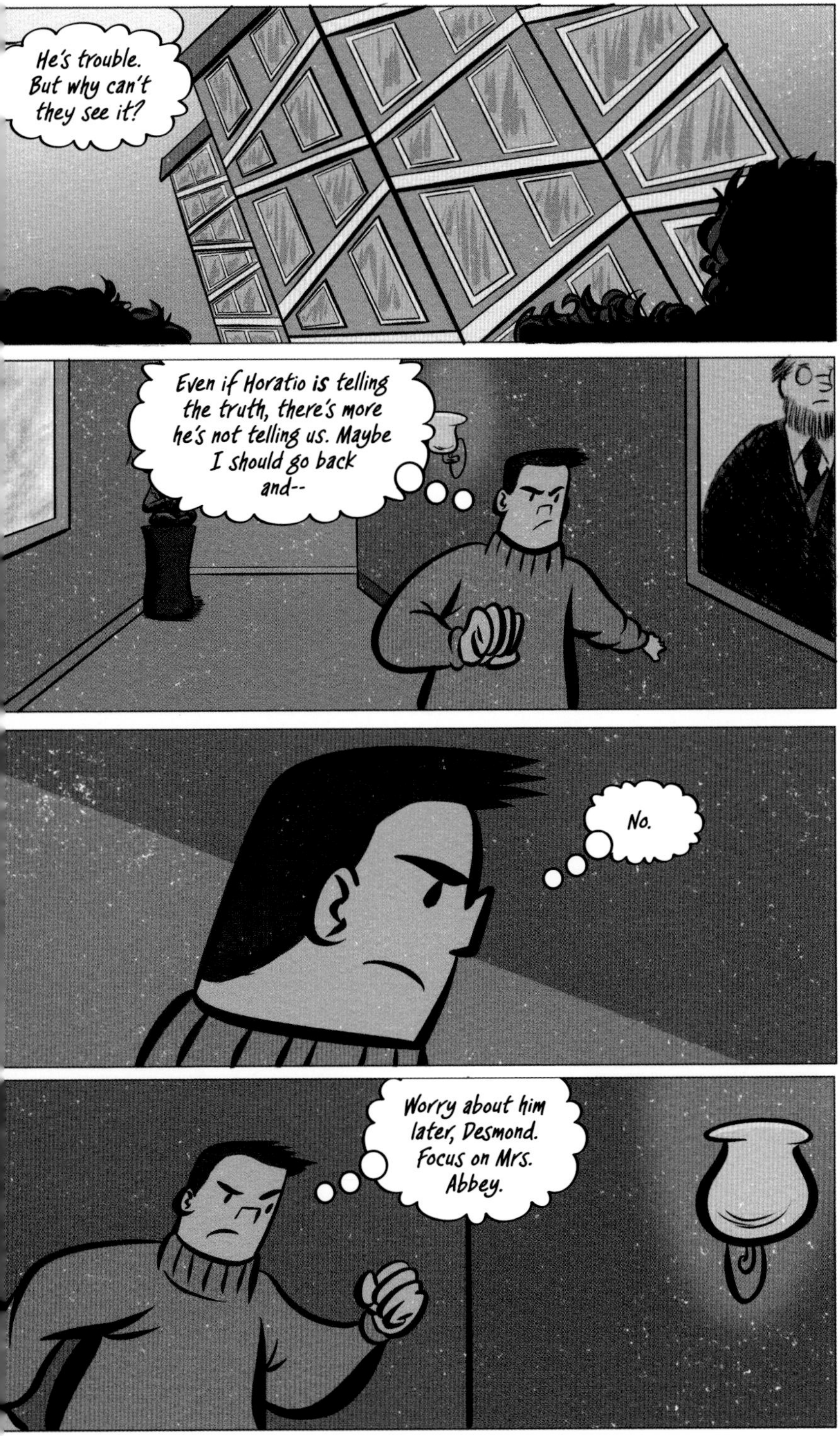
He's trouble. But why can't they see it?
Even if Horatio is telling the truth, there's more he's not telling us. Maybe I should go back and--
No.
Worry about him later, Desmond. Focus on Mrs. Abbey.

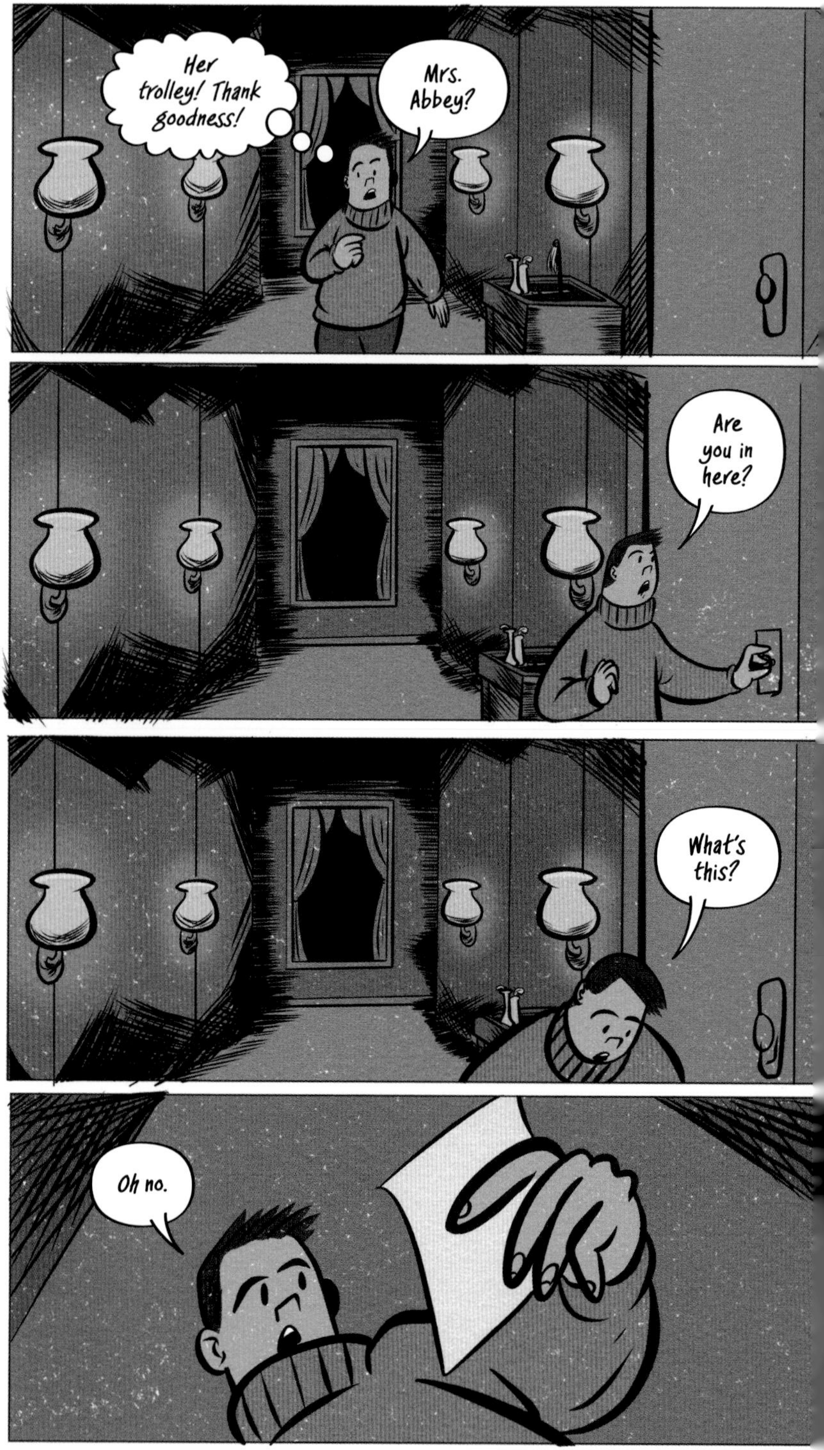
Her trolley! Thank goodness!
Mrs. Abbey?
Are you in here?
What's this?
Oh no.

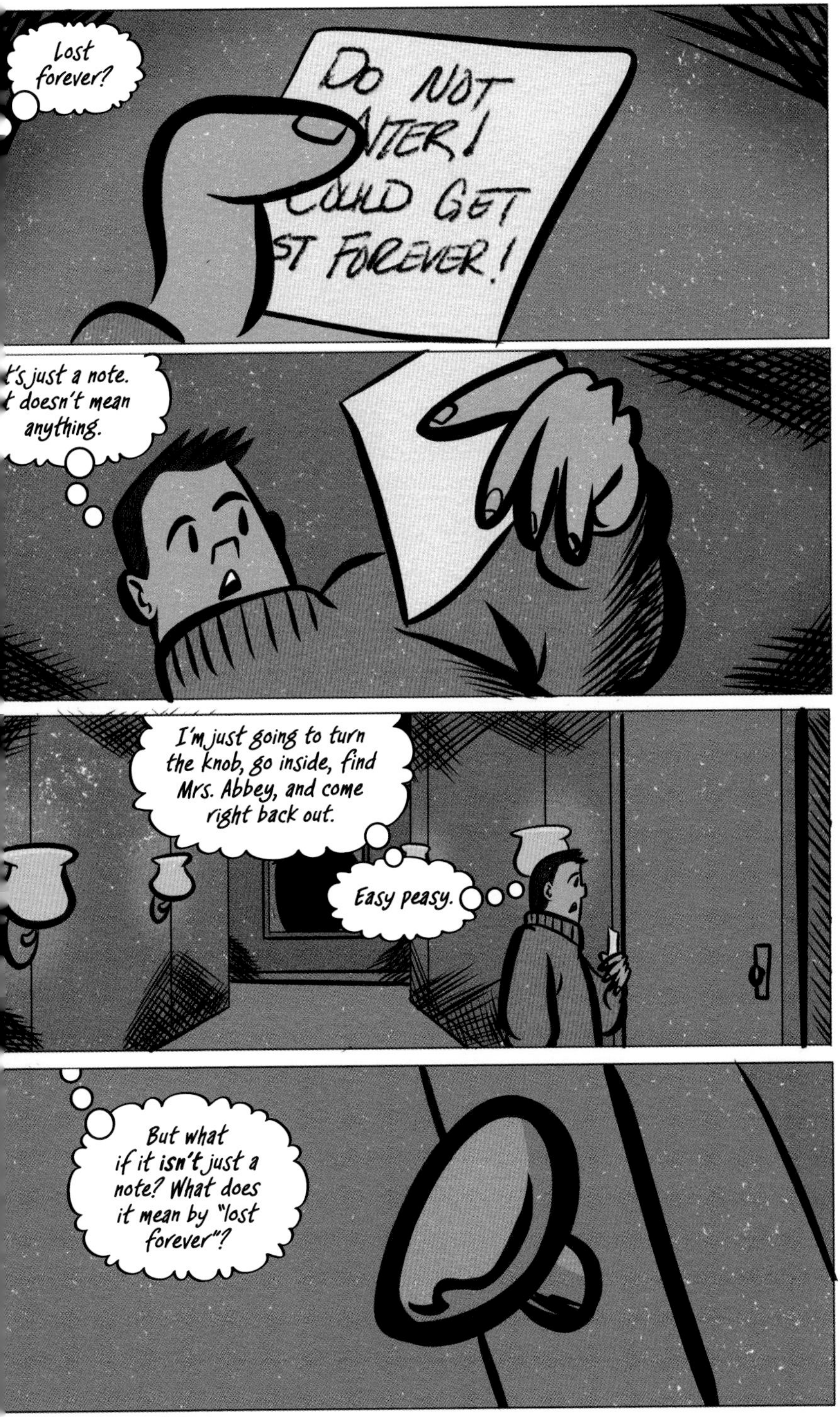
Lost forever?
DO NOT ENTER! COULD GET ST FOREVER!
t's just a note. t doesn't mean anything.
I'm just going to turn the knob, go inside, find Mrs. Abbey, and come right back out.
Easy peasy.
But what if it isn't just a note? What does it mean by "lost forever"?

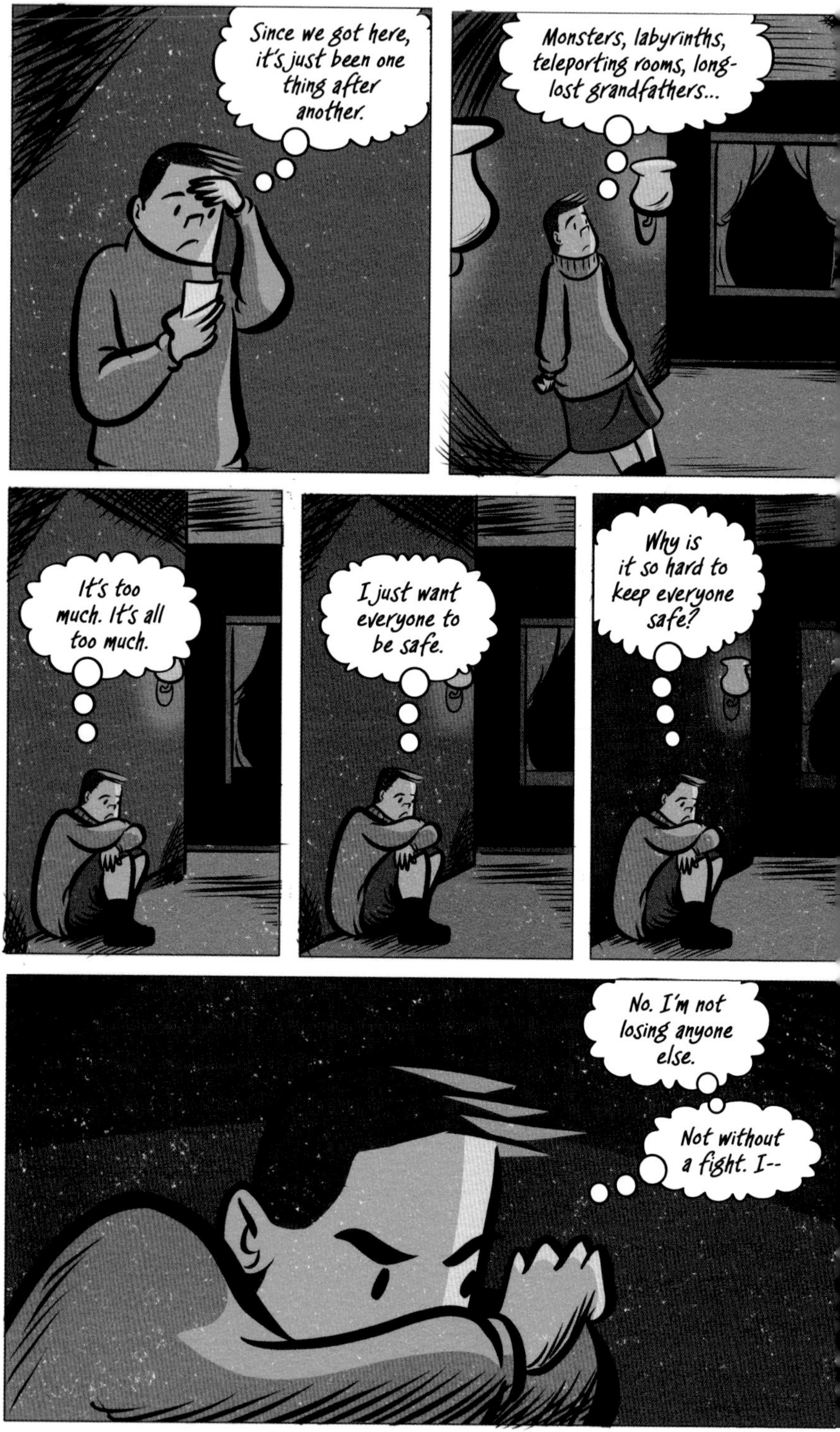
Since we got here, it's just been one thing after another.
Monsters, labyrinths, teleporting rooms, long-lost grandfathers...
It's too much. It's all too much.
I just want everyone to be safe.
Why is it so hard to keep everyone safe?
No. I'm not losing anyone else.
Not without a fight. I--

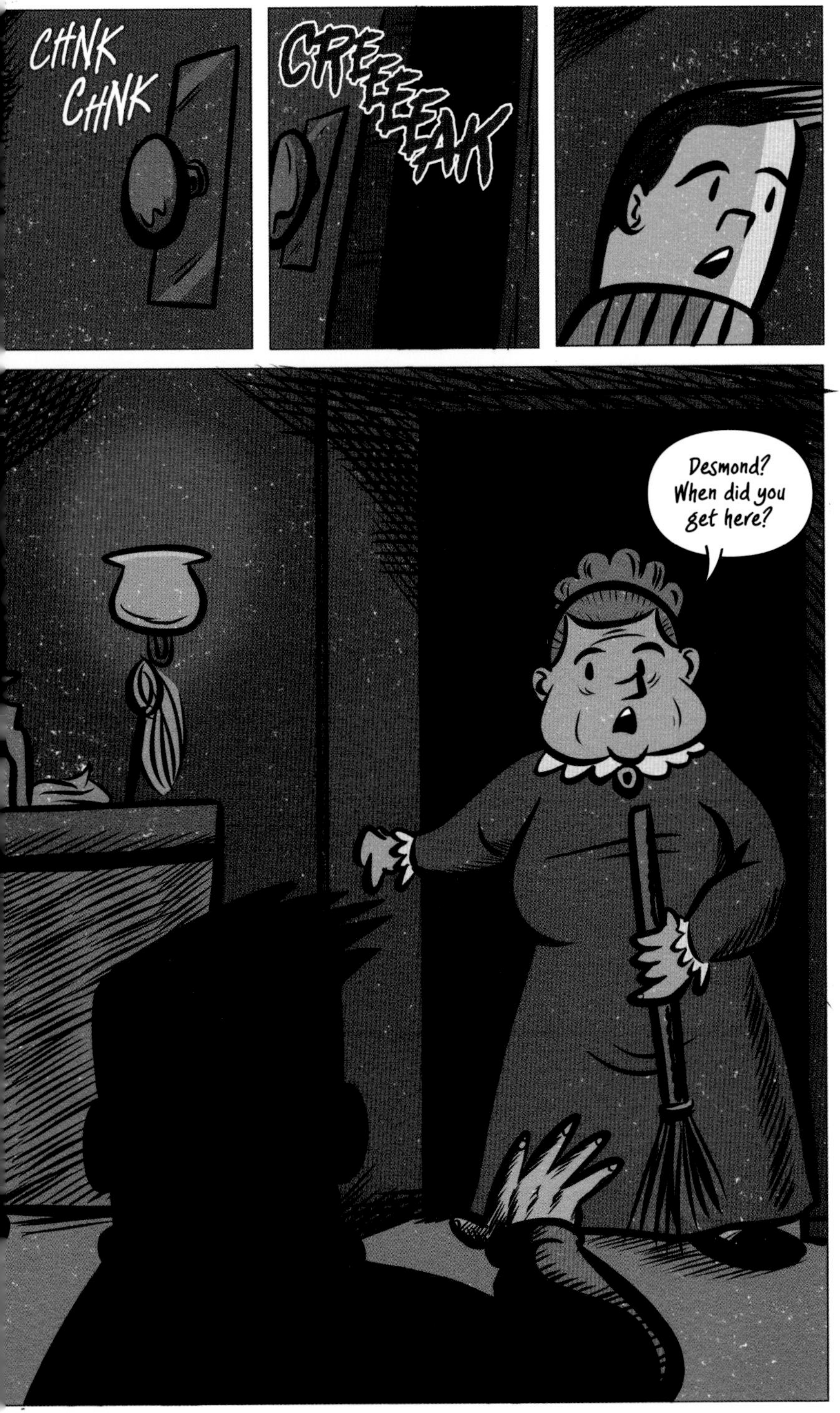
CHNK CHNK
CREEEEAK
Desmond? When did you get here?

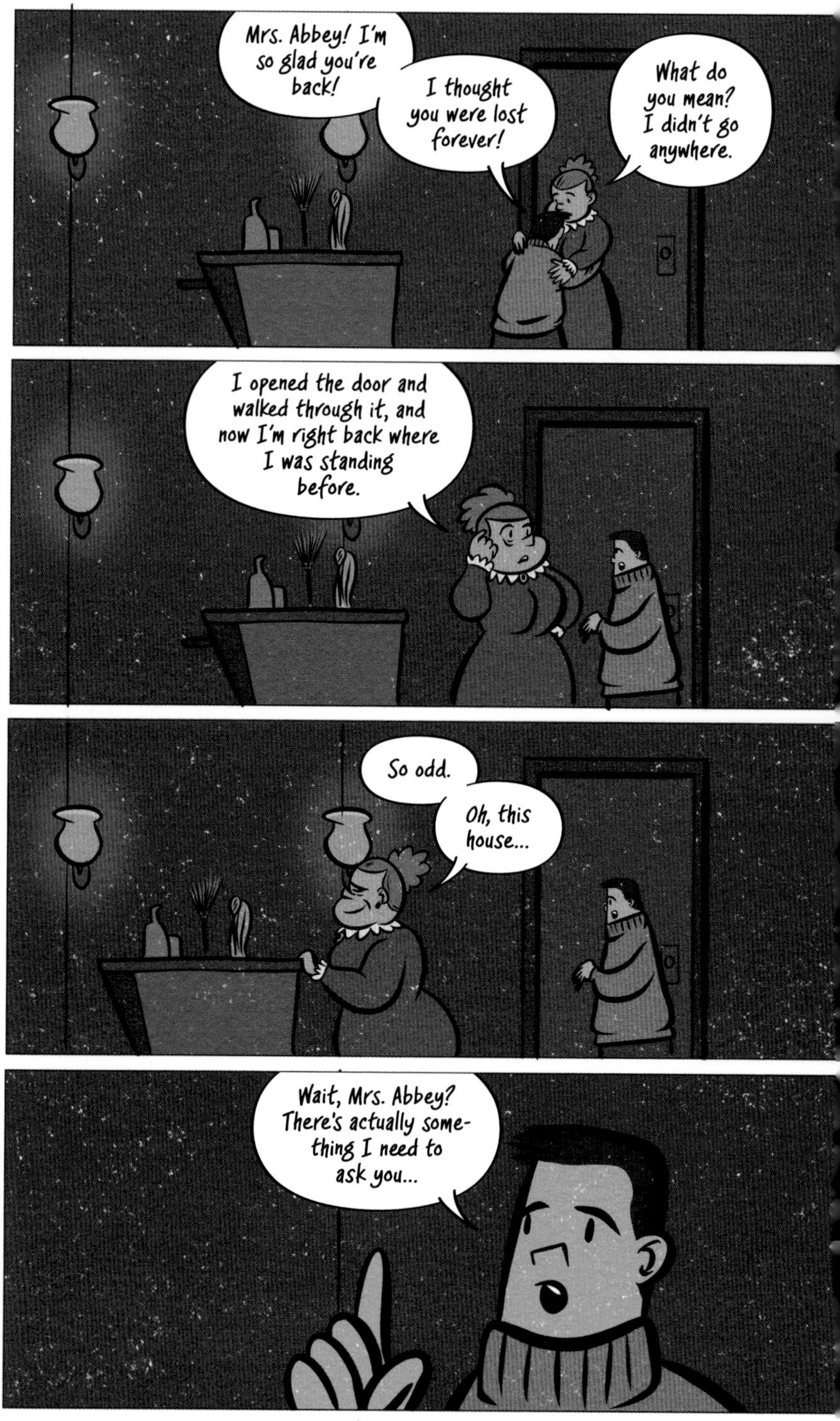
Mrs. Abbey! I'm so glad you're back!
I thought you were lost forever!
What do you mean? I didn't go anywhere.
I opened the door and walked through it, and now I'm right back where I was standing before.
So odd.
Oh, this house...
Wait, Mrs. Abbey? There's actually some-thing I need to ask you...

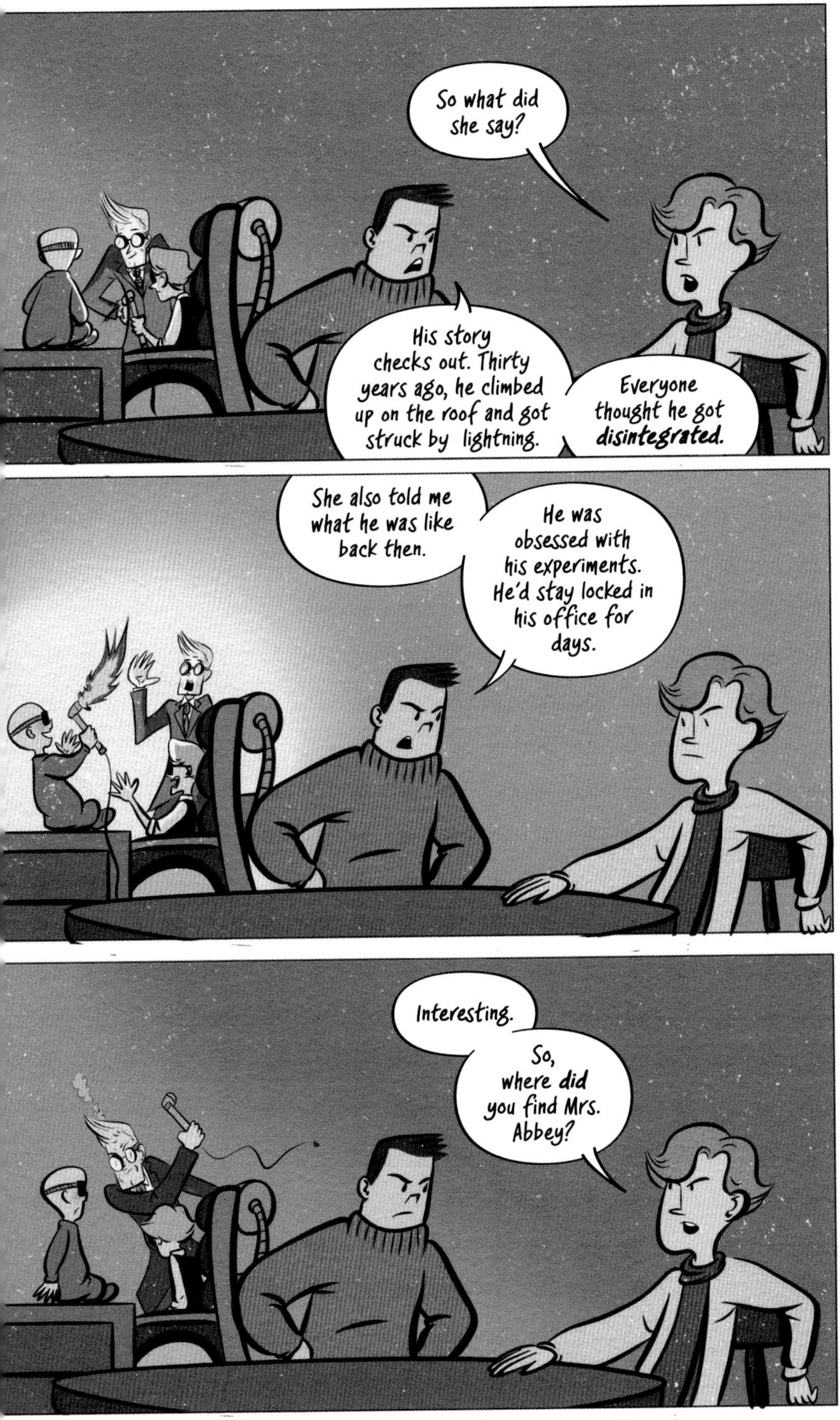
So what did she say?
His story checks out. Thirty years ago, he climbed up on the roof and got struck by lightning.
Everyone thought he got **disintegrated.**
She also told me what he was like back then.
He was obsessed with his experiments. He'd stay locked in his office for days.
Interesting.
So, where did you find Mrs. Abbey?

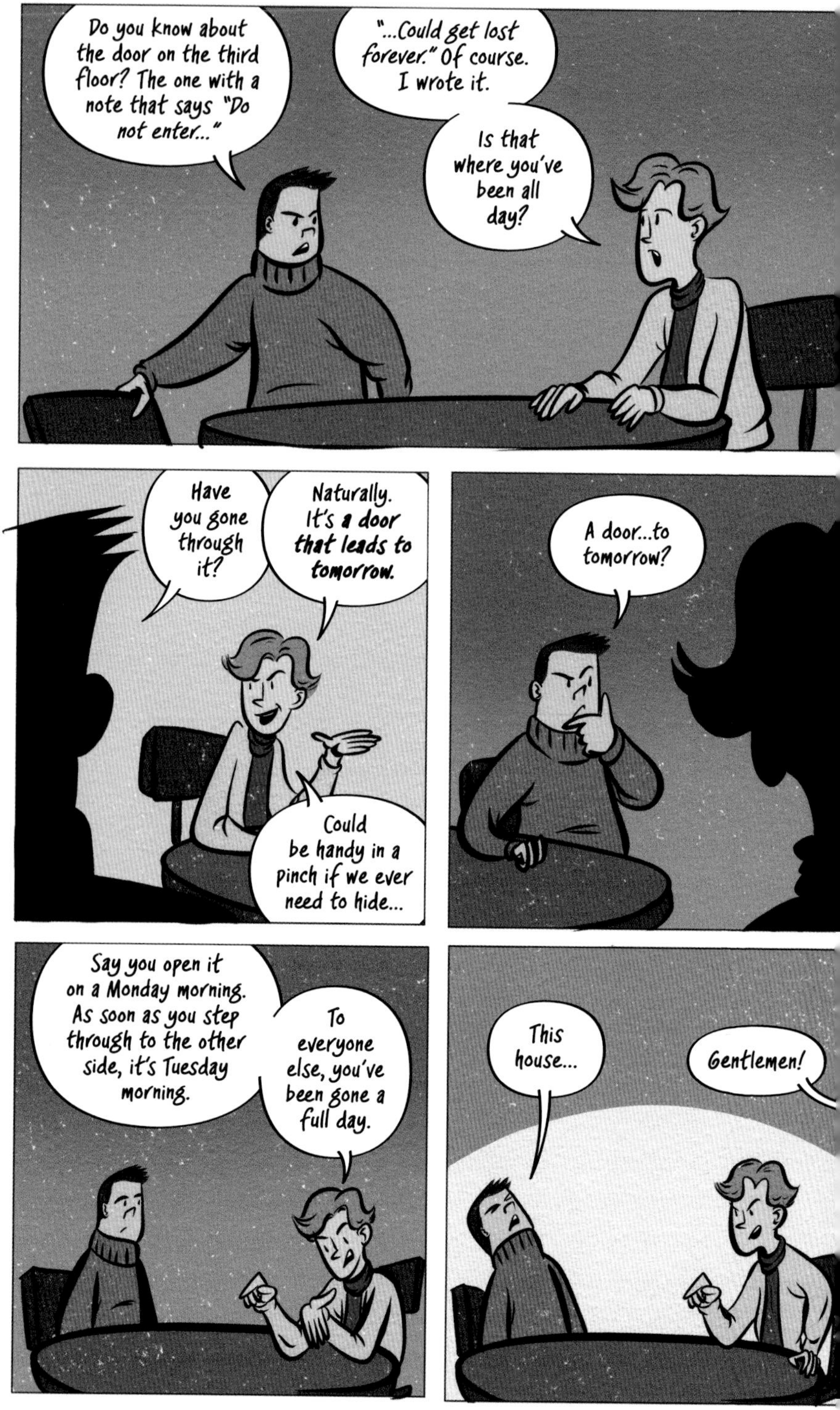
Do you know about the door on the third floor? The one with a note that says "Do not enter..."
"...Could get lost forever." Of course. I wrote it.
Is that where you've been all day?
Have you gone through it?
Naturally. It's **a door *that leads to tomorrow.***
Could be handy in a pinch if we ever need to hide...
A door...to tomorrow?
Say you open it on a Monday morning. As soon as you step through to the other side, it's Tuesday morning.
To everyone else, you've been gone a full day.
This house...
Gentlemen!

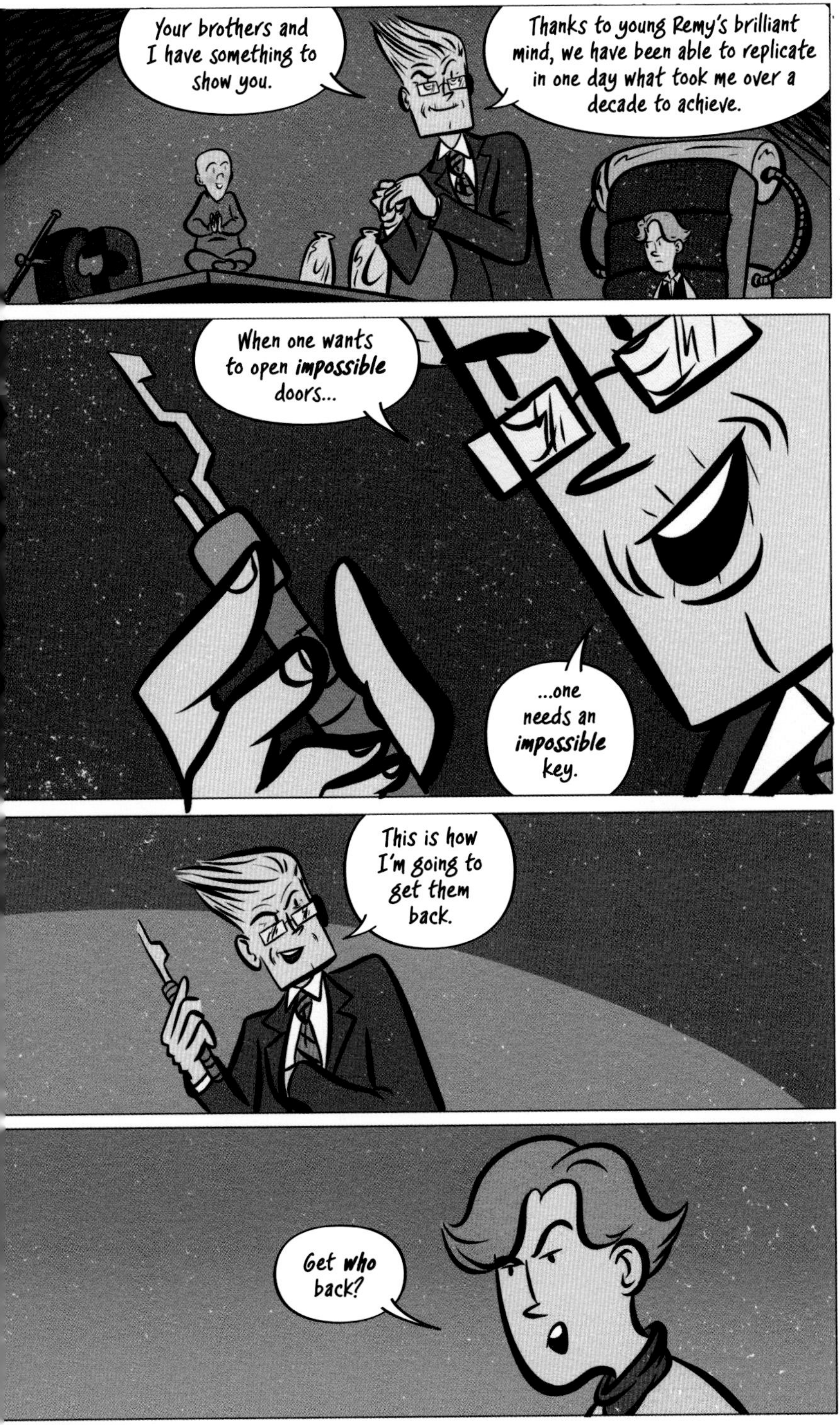
Your brothers and I have something to show you.
Thanks to young Remy's brilliant mind, we have been able to replicate in one day what took me over a decade to achieve.
When one wants to open *impossible* doors...
...one needs an *impossible* key.
This is how I'm going to get them back.
Get *who* back?

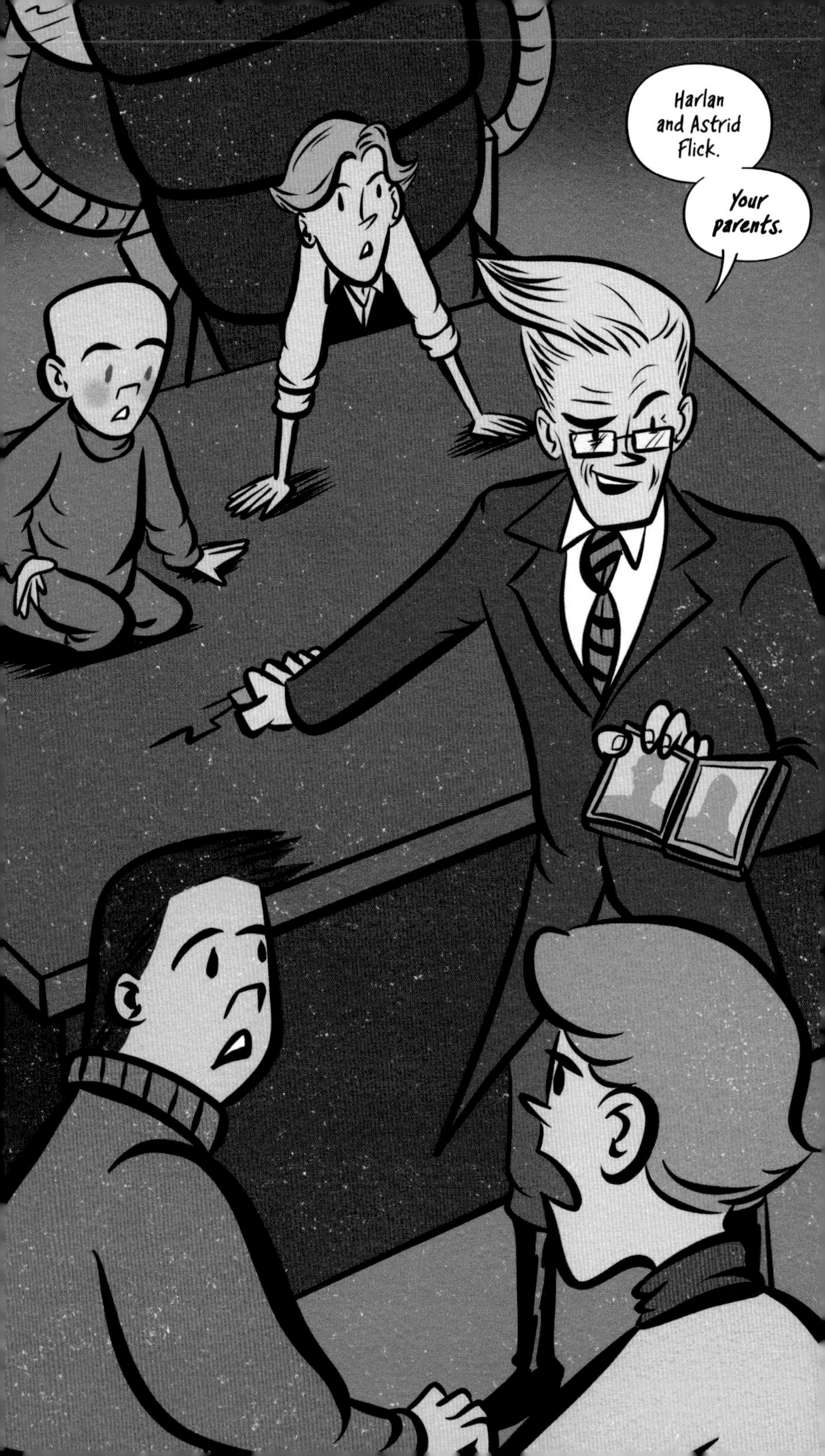
Harlan and Astrid Flick.
Your parents.

CHAPTER
10

THE OTHER SIDE OF FOREVER

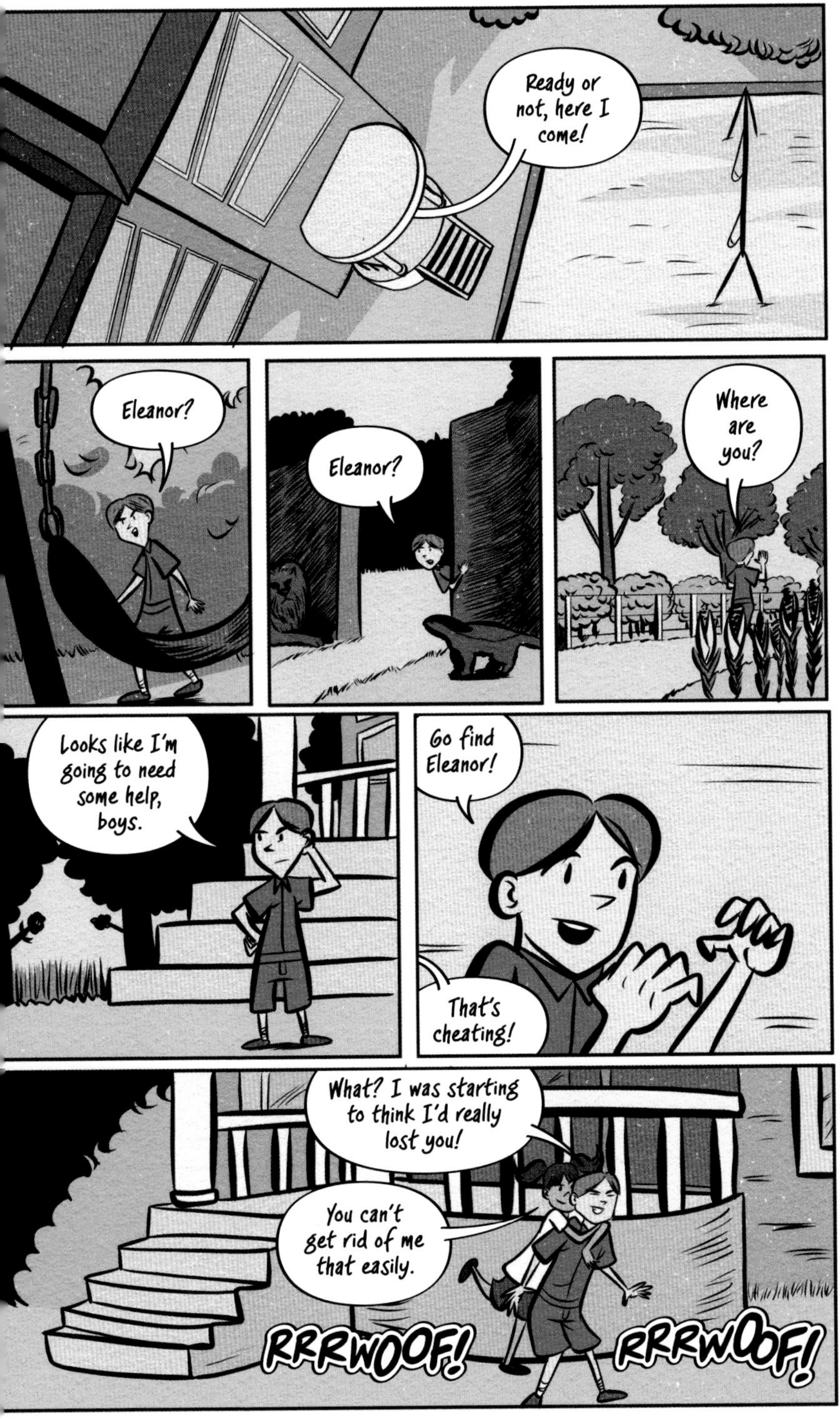
Ready or not, here I come!
Eleanor?
Eleanor?
Where are you?
Looks like I'm going to need some help, boys.
Go find Eleanor!
That's cheating!
What? I was starting to think I'd really lost you!
You can't get rid of me that easily.
RRRWOOF!
RRRWOOF!

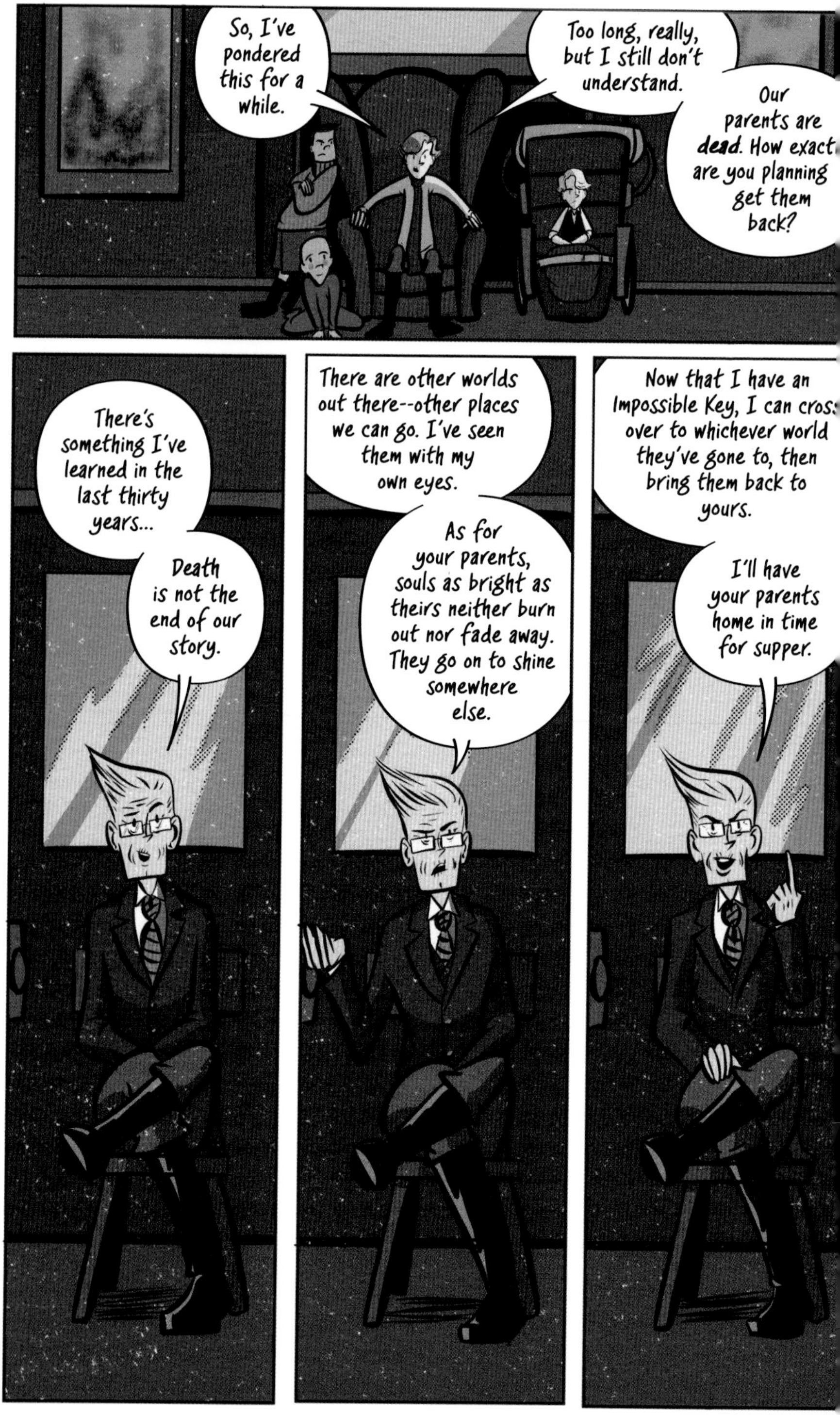
So, I've pondered this for a while.
Too long, really, but I still don't understand.
Our parents are **dead**. How exact are you planning get them back?
There's something I've learned in the last thirty years...
Death is not the end of our story.
There are other worlds out there--other places we can go. I've seen them with my own eyes.
As for your parents, souls as bright as theirs neither burn out nor fade away. They go on to shine somewhere else.
Now that I have an Impossible Key, I can cros over to whichever world they've gone to, then bring them back to yours.
I'll have your parents home in time for supper.

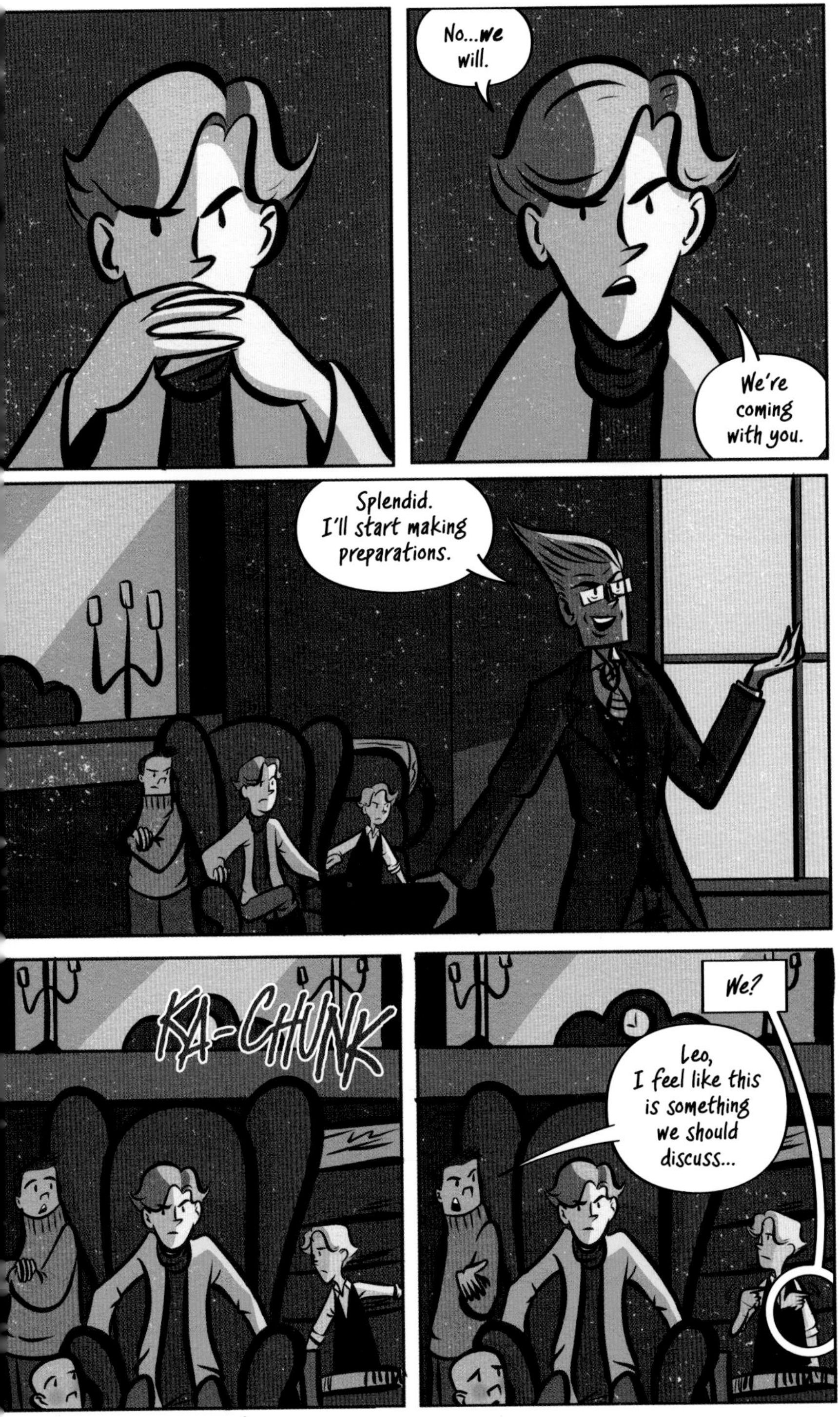
No...we will.
We're coming with you.
Splendid. I'll start making preparations.
KA-CHUNK
We?
Leo, I feel like this is something we should discuss...

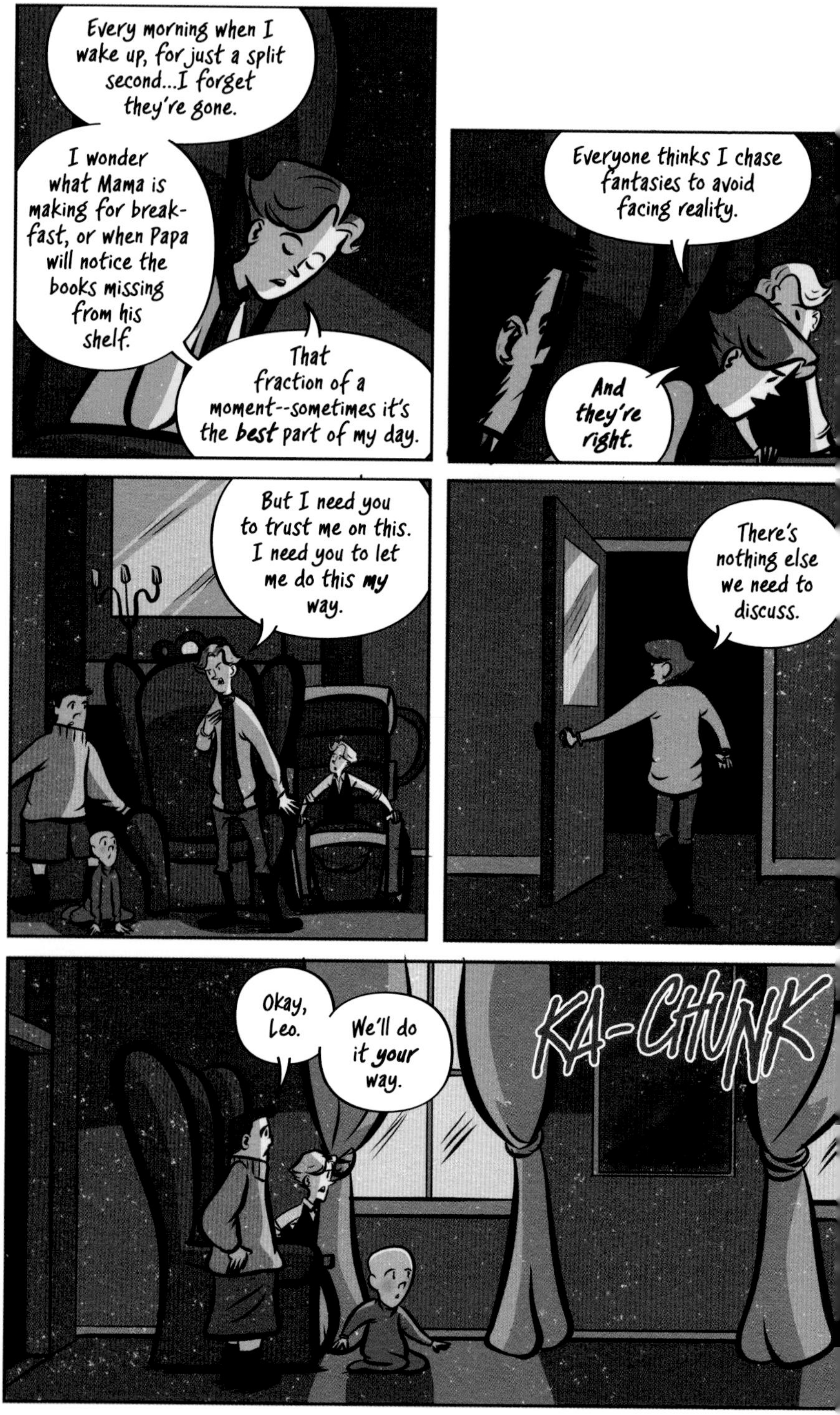

Every morning when I wake up, for just a split second...I forget they're gone.
I wonder what Mama is making for break-fast, or when Papa will notice the books missing from his shelf.
That fraction of a moment--sometimes it's the *best* part of my day.
Everyone thinks I chase fantasies to avoid facing reality.
And they're right.
But I need you to trust me on this. I need you to let me do this *my* way.
There's nothing else we need to discuss.
Okay, Leo.
We'll do it *your* way.
KA-CHUNK

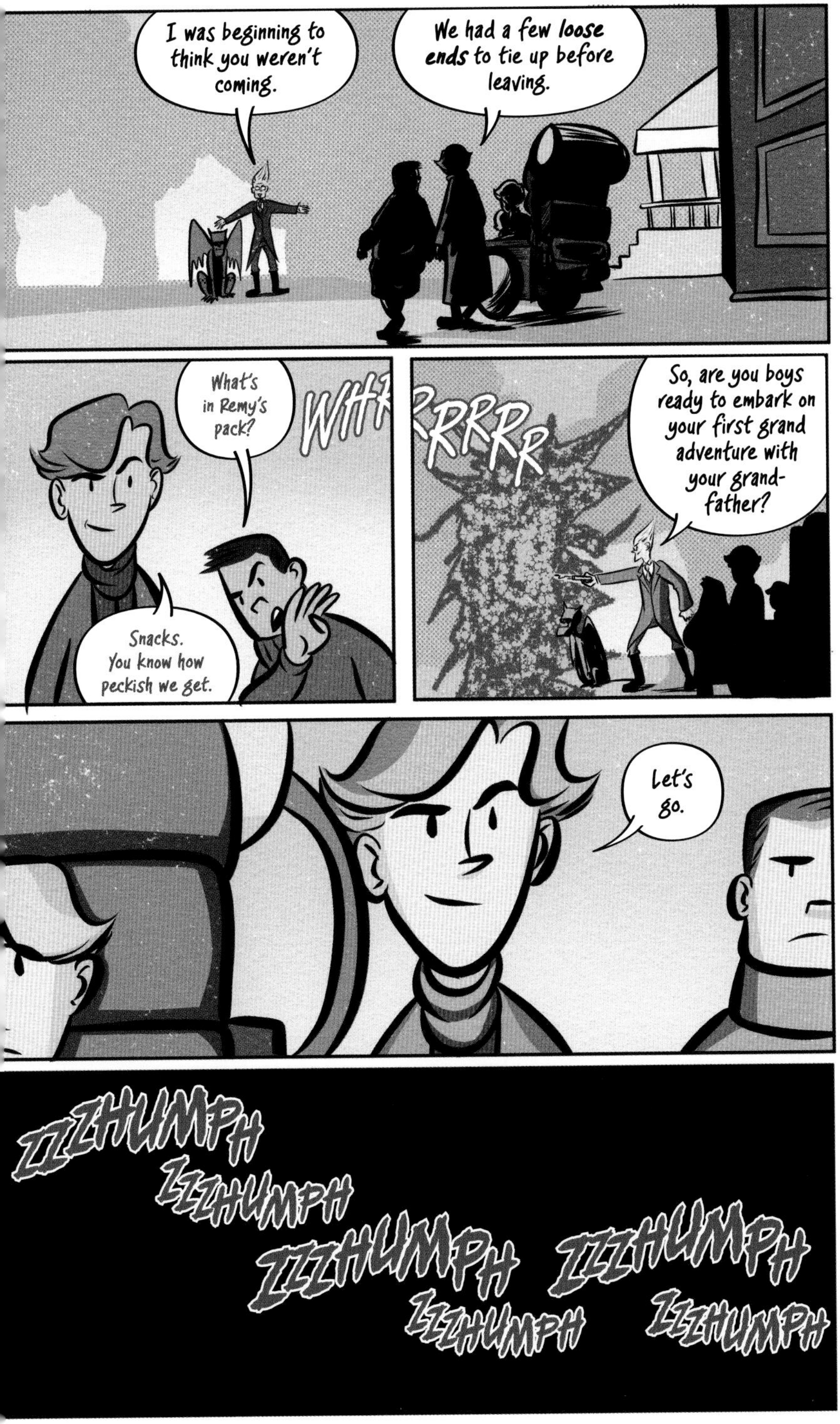
I was beginning to think you weren't coming.
We had a few loose ends to tie up before leaving.
What's in Remy's pack?
Snacks. You know how peckish we get.
WHRRRRRR
So, are you boys ready to embark on your first grand adventure with your grand-father?
Let's go.
IIIHUMPH
IIIHUMPH
IIIHUMPH
IIIHUMPH
IIIHUMPH
IIIHUMPH

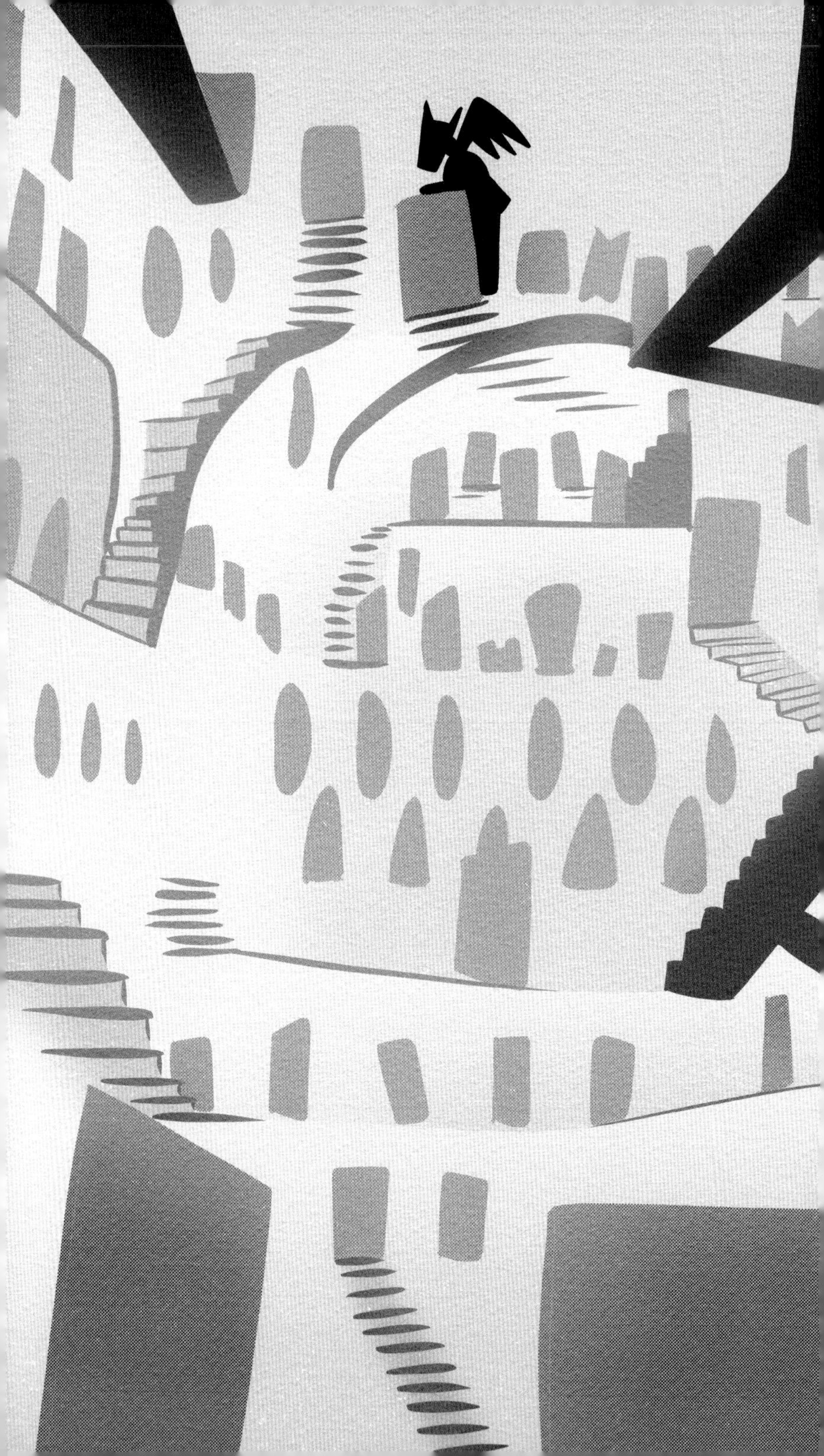

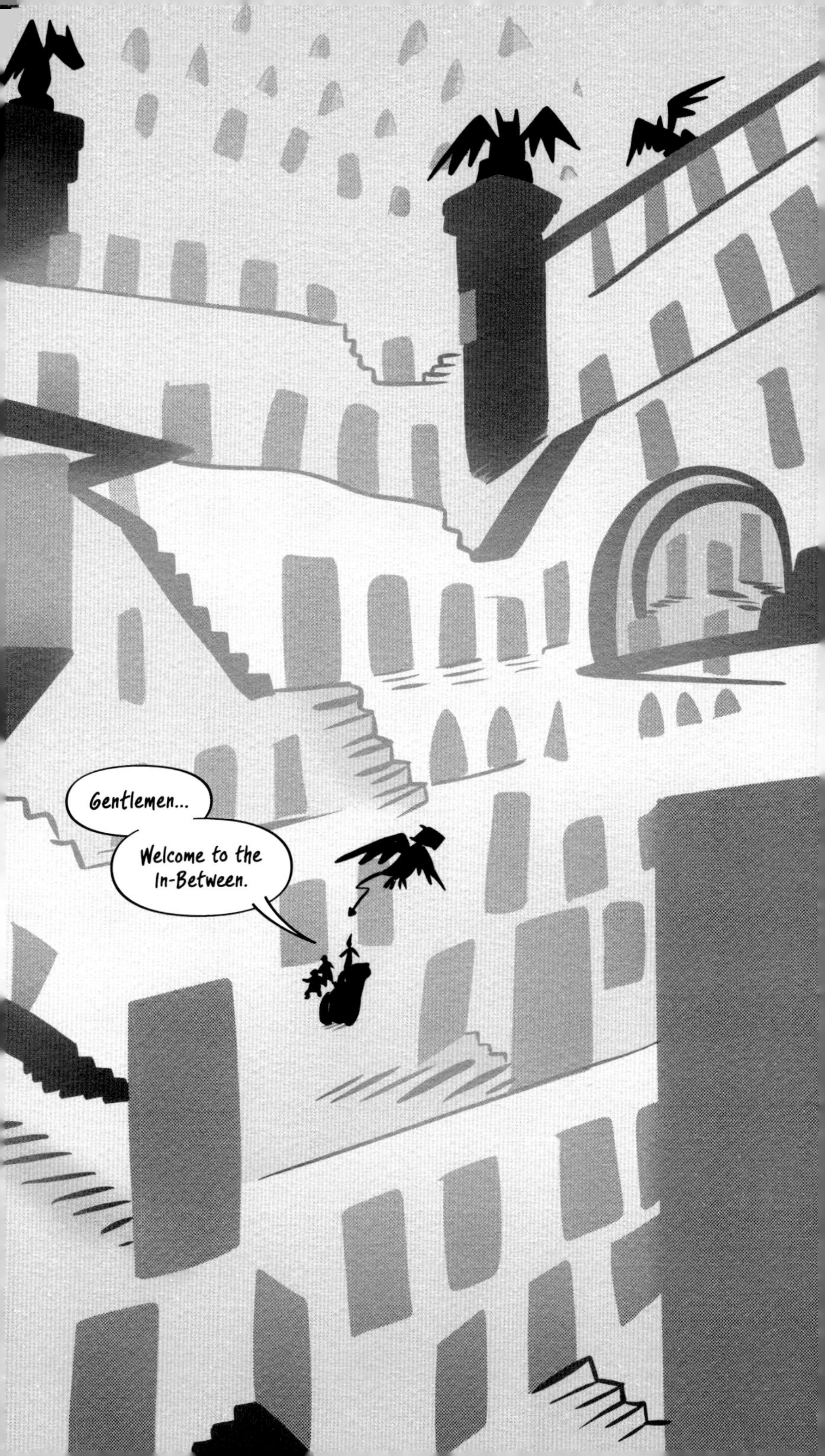
Gentlemen...
Welcome to the In-Between.

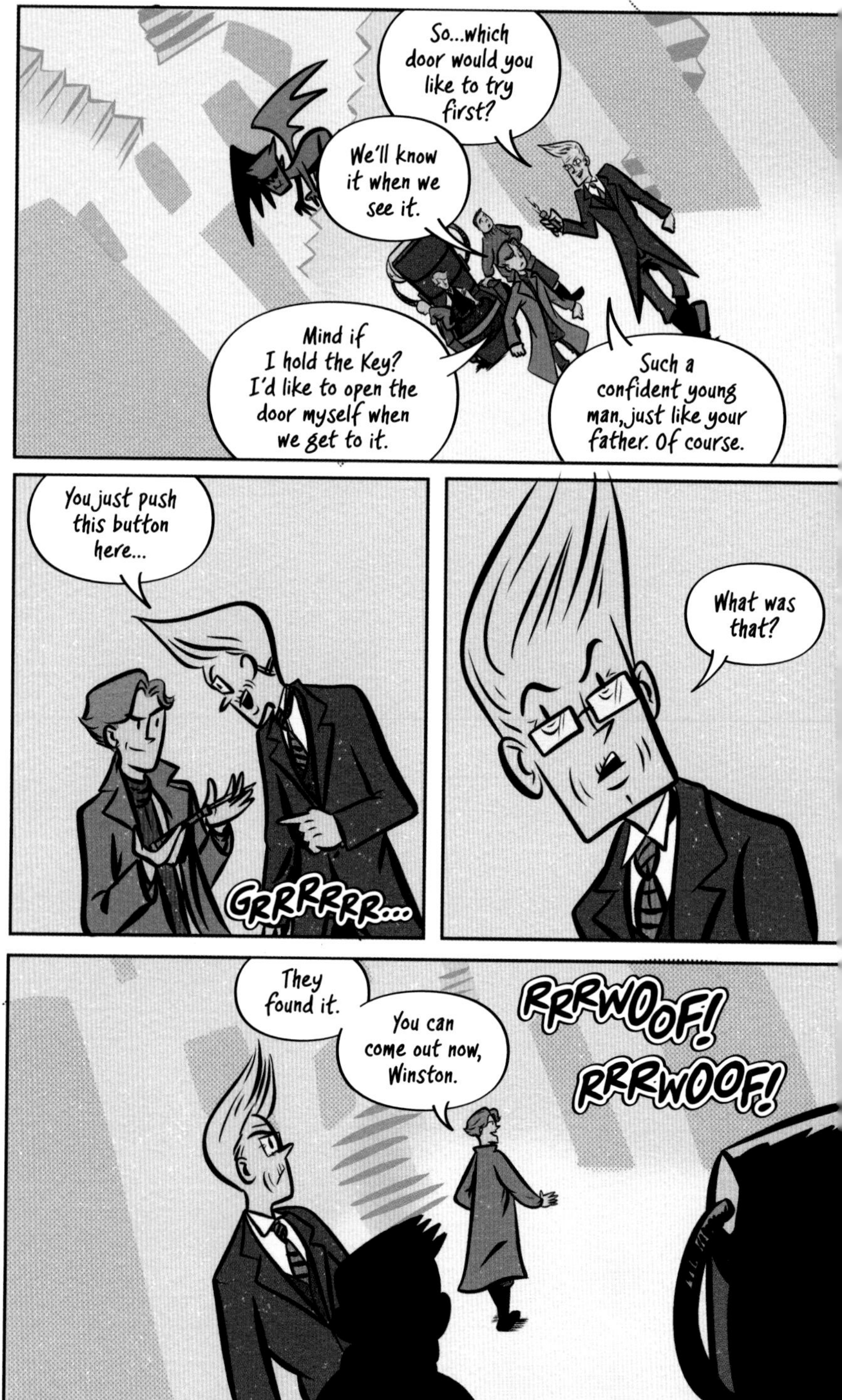

So...which door would you like to try first?
We'll know it when we see it.
Mind if I hold the Key? I'd like to open the door myself when we get to it.
Such a confident young man, just like your father. Of course.
You just push this button here...
GRRRRRR...
What was that?
They found it.
You can come out now, Winston.
RRRWOOF!
RRRWOOF!

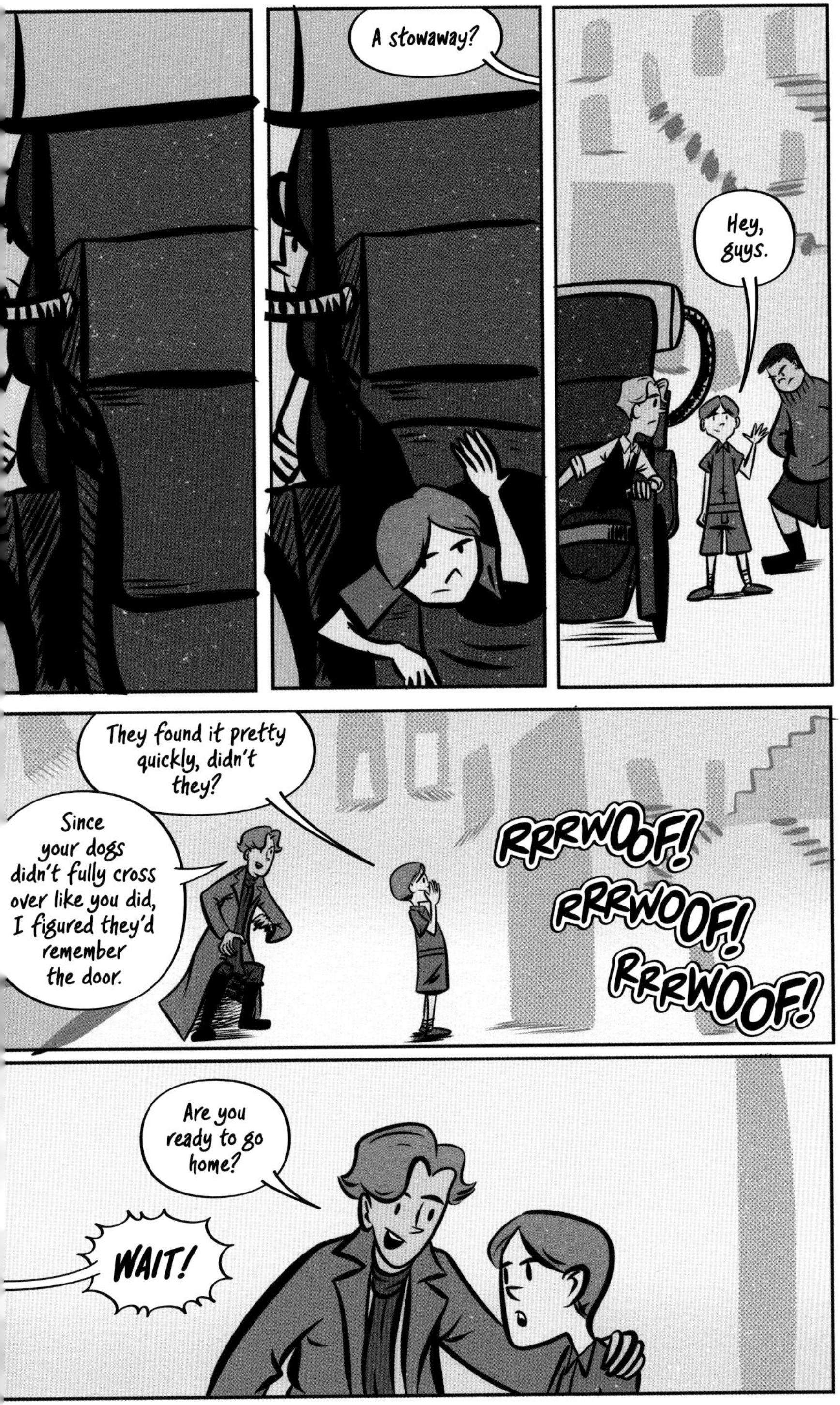

A stowaway?
Hey, guys.
They found it pretty quickly, didn't they?
Since your dogs didn't fully cross over like you did, I figured they'd remember the door.
RRRWOOF!
RRRWOOF!
RRRWOOF!
Are you ready to go home?
WAIT!

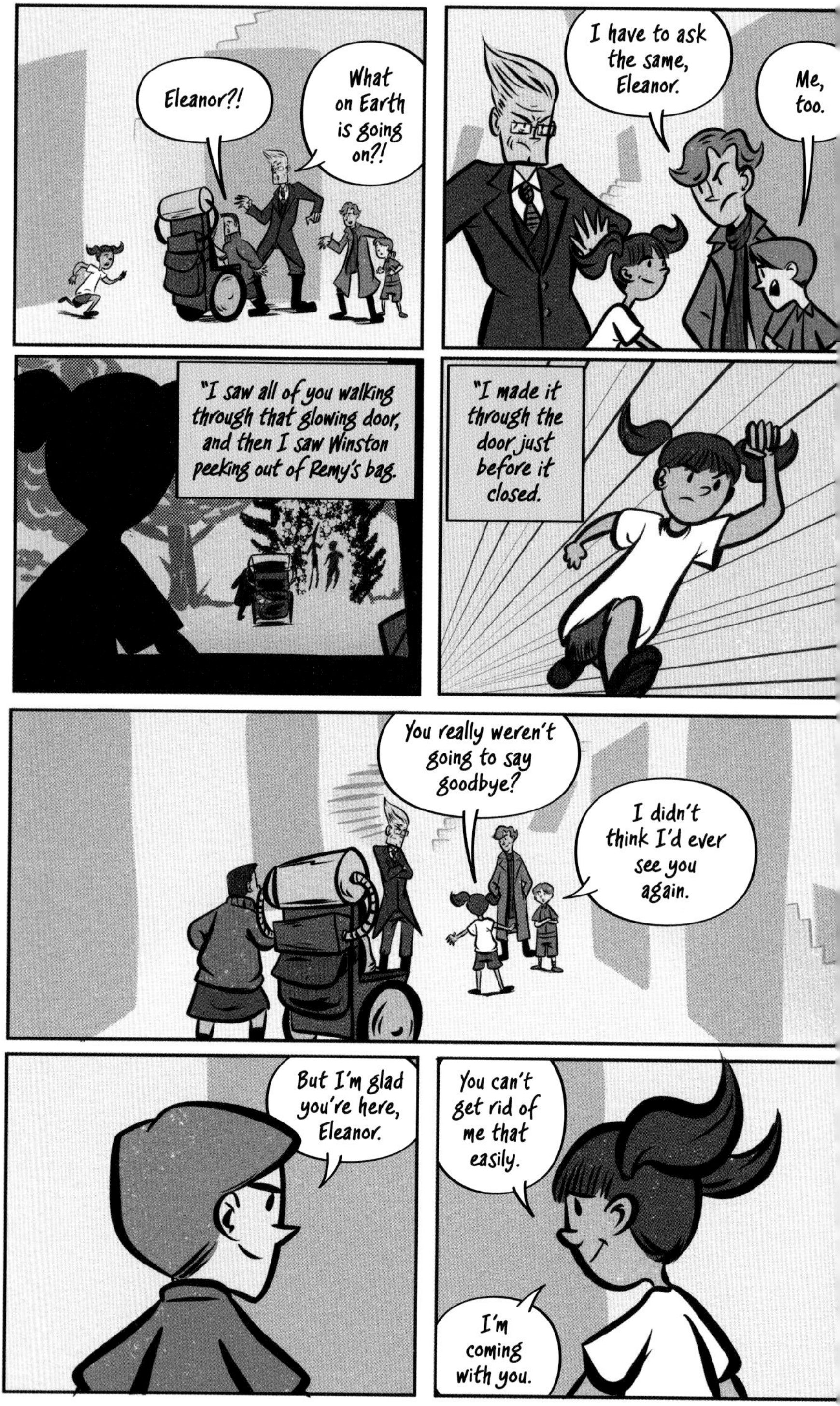
Eleanor?!
What on Earth is going on?!
I have to ask the same, Eleanor.
Me, too.
"I saw all of you walking through that glowing door, and then I saw Winston peeking out of Remy's bag.
"I made it through the door just before it closed.
You really weren't going to say goodbye?
I didn't think I'd ever see you again.
But I'm glad you're here, Eleanor.
You can't get rid of me that easily.
I'm coming with you.

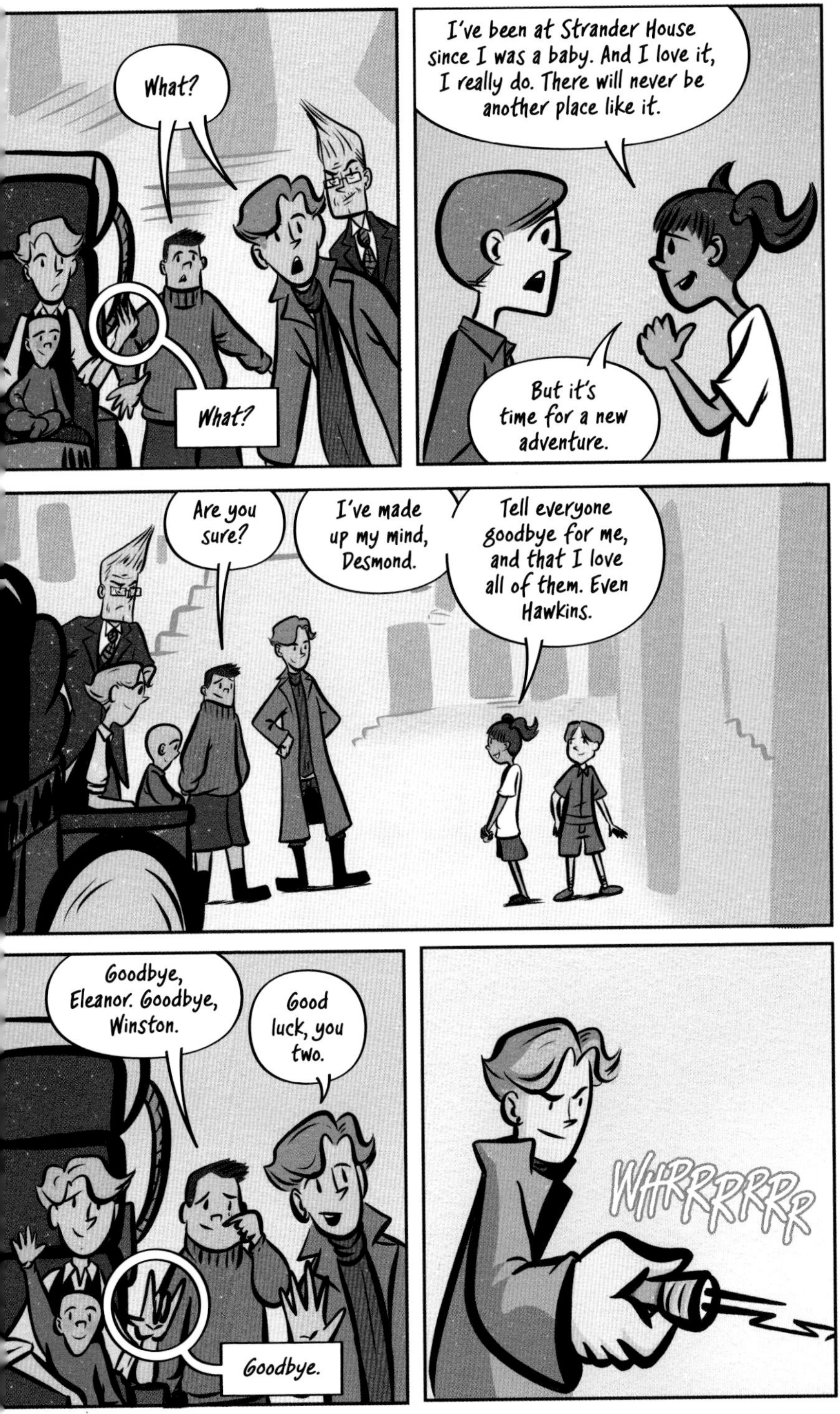
What?
What?
I've been at Strander House since I was a baby. And I love it, I really do. There will never be another place like it.
But it's time for a new adventure.
Are you sure?
I've made up my mind, Desmond.
Tell everyone goodbye for me, and that I love all of them. Even Hawkins.
Goodbye, Eleanor. Goodbye, Winston.
Good luck, you two.
Goodbye.
WHRRRRRR

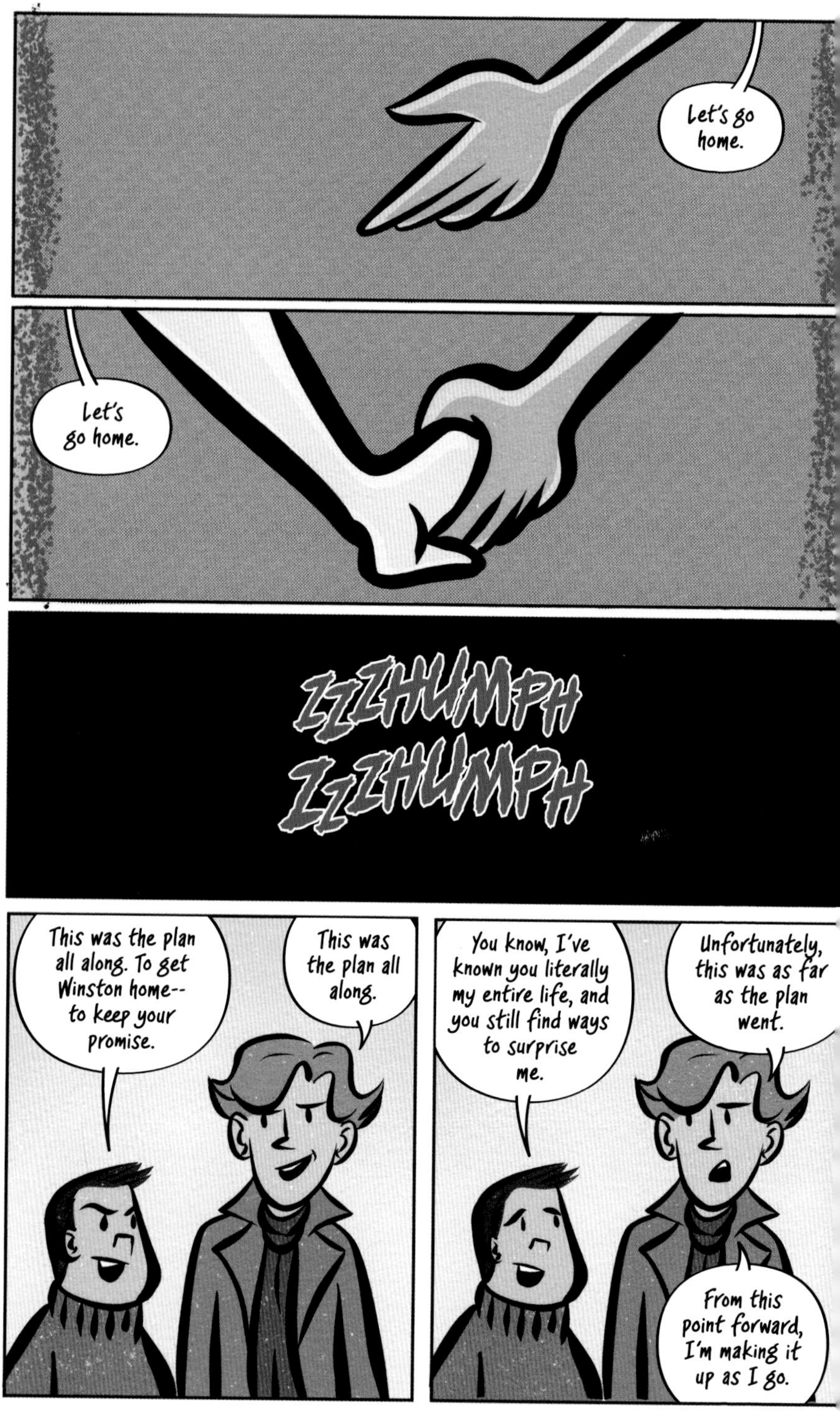
Let's go home.
Let's go home.
ZZZHUMPH ZZZHUMPH
This was the plan all along. To get Winston home-- to keep your promise.
This was the plan all along.
You know, I've known you literally my entire life, and you still find ways to surprise me.
Unfortunately, this was as far as the plan went.
From this point forward, I'm making it up as I go.

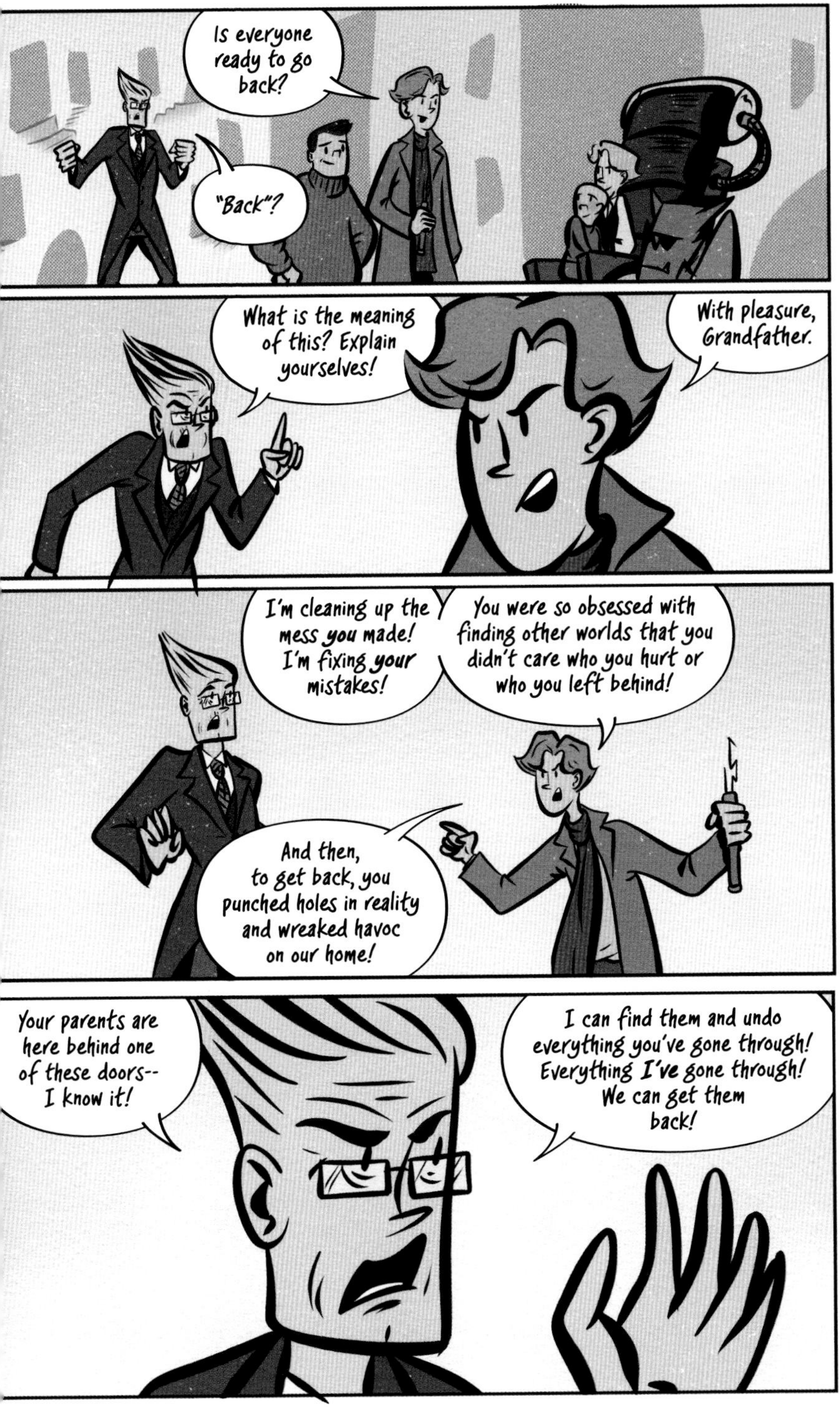
Is everyone ready to go back?
"Back"?
What is the meaning of this? Explain yourselves!
With pleasure, Grandfather.
I'm cleaning up the mess *you* made! I'm fixing *your* mistakes!
You were so obsessed with finding other worlds that you didn't care who you hurt or who you left behind!
And then, to get back, you punched holes in reality and wreaked havoc on our home!
Your parents are here behind one of these doors-- I know it!
I can find them and undo everything you've gone through! Everything *I've* gone through! We can get them back!

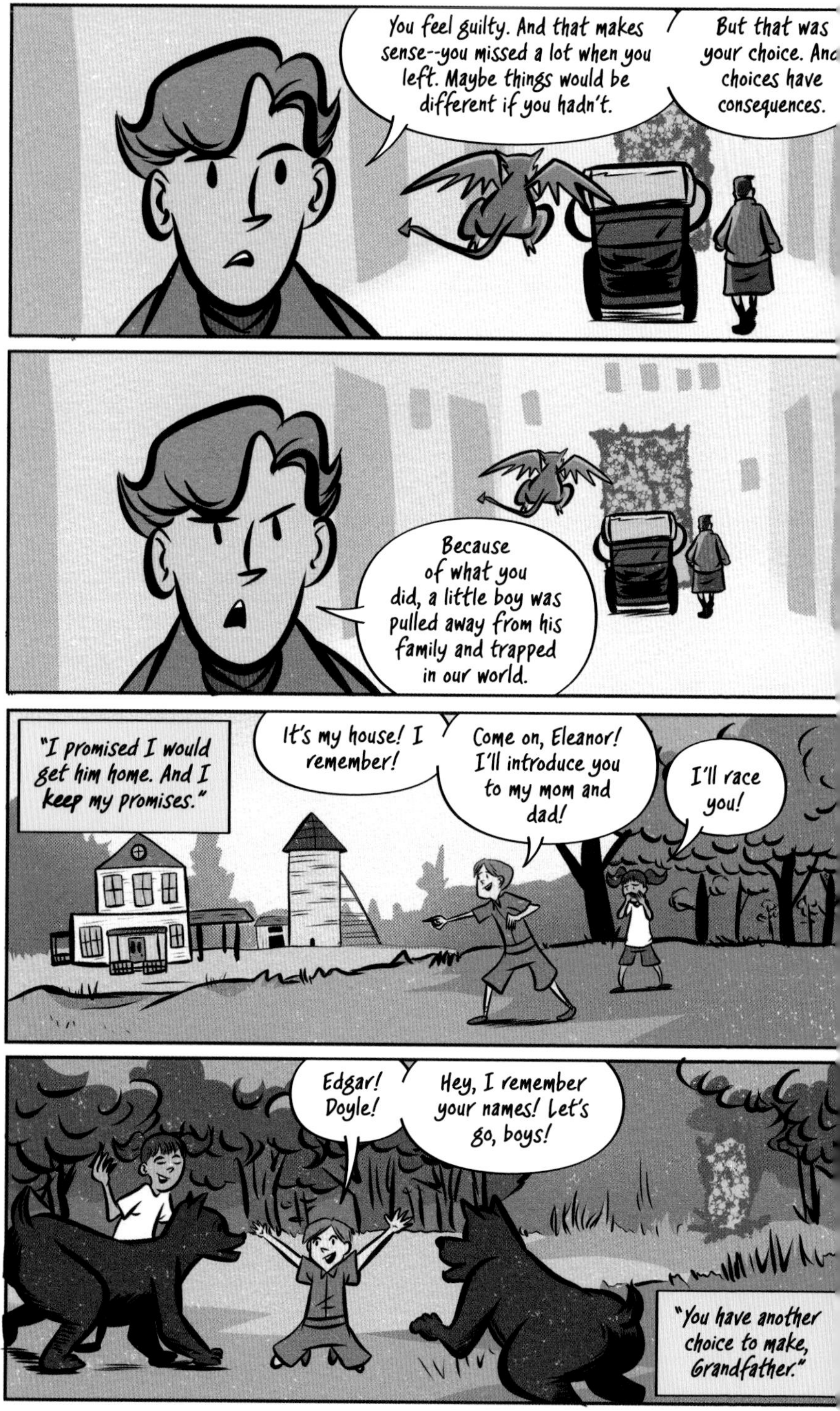

You feel guilty. And that makes sense--you missed a lot when you left. Maybe things would be different if you hadn't.
But that was your choice. And choices have consequences.
Because of what you did, a little boy was pulled away from his family and trapped in our world.
"I promised I would get him home. And I keep my promises."
It's my house! I remember!
Come on, Eleanor! I'll introduce you to my mom and dad!
I'll race you!
Edgar! Doyle!
Hey, I remember your names! Let's go, boys!
"You have another choice to make, Grandfather."

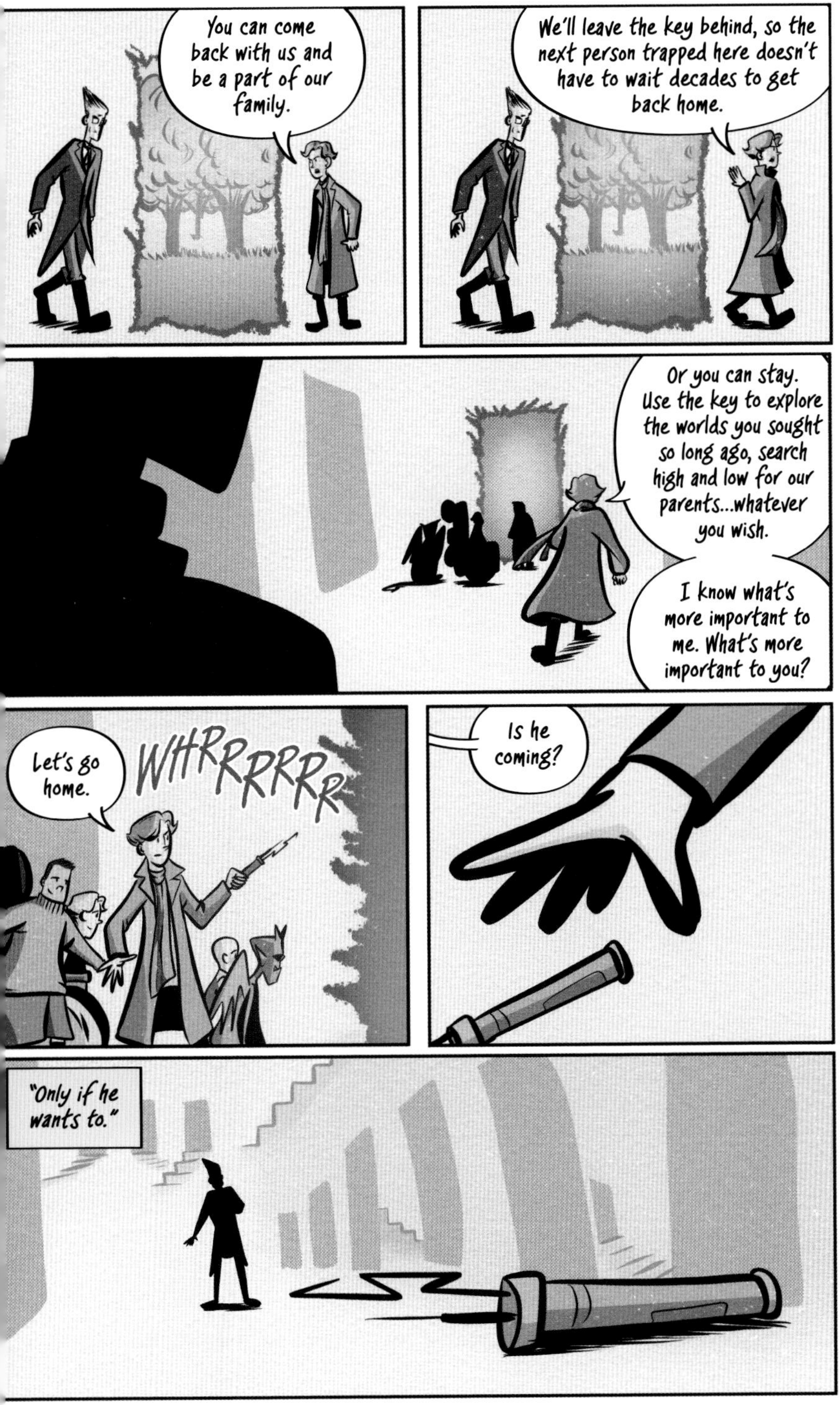
You can come back with us and be a part of our family.
We'll leave the key behind, so the next person trapped here doesn't have to wait decades to get back home.
Or you can stay. Use the key to explore the worlds you sought so long ago, search high and low for our parents...whatever you wish.
I know what's more important to me. What's more important to you?
Let's go home.
WHRRRRRR
Is he coming?
"Only if he wants to."

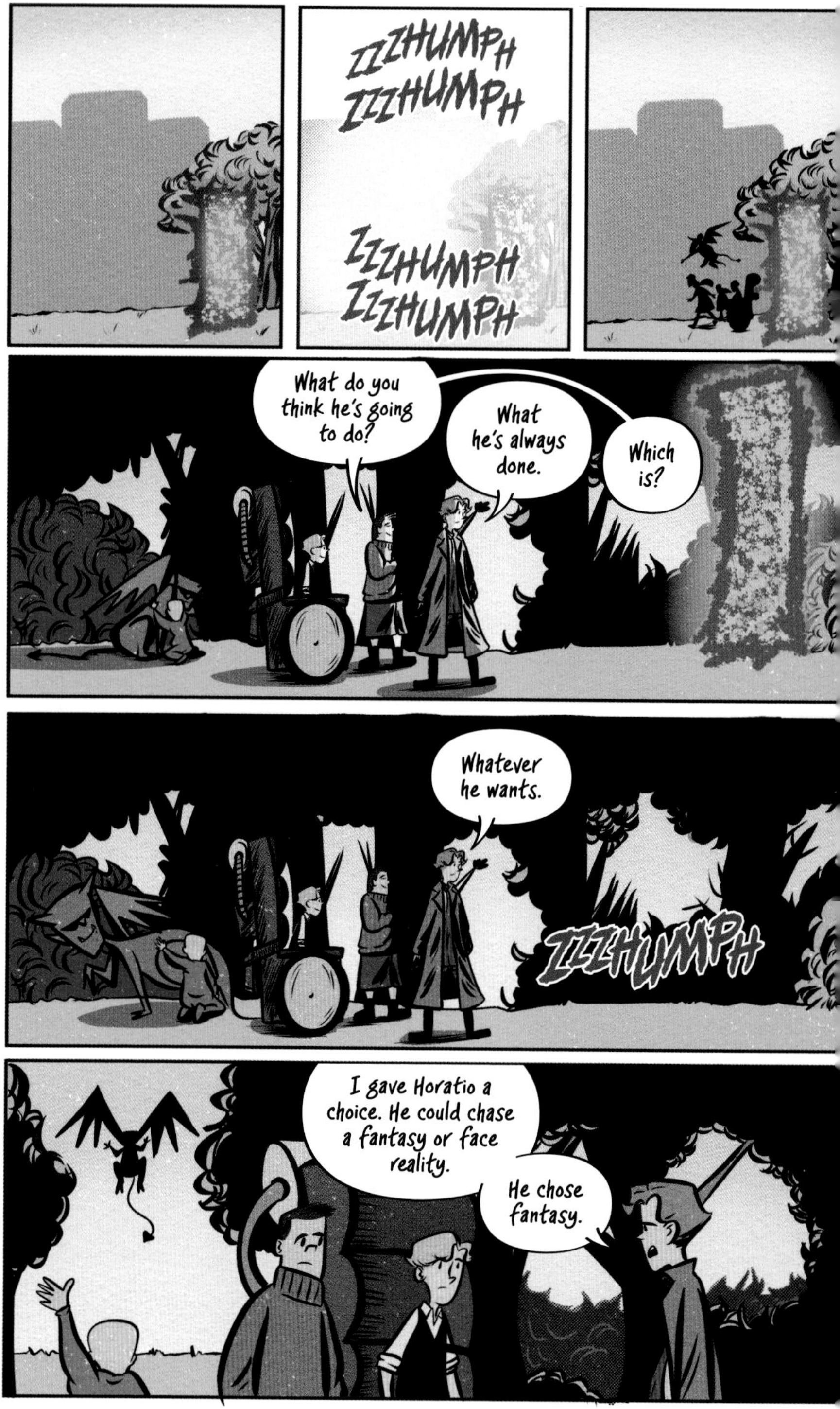

ZZZHUMPH
ZZZHUMPH
ZZZHUMPH
ZZZHUMPH
What do you think he's going to do?
What he's always done.
Which is?
Whatever he wants.
ZZZHUMPH
I gave Horatio a choice. He could chase a fantasy or face reality.
He chose fantasy.

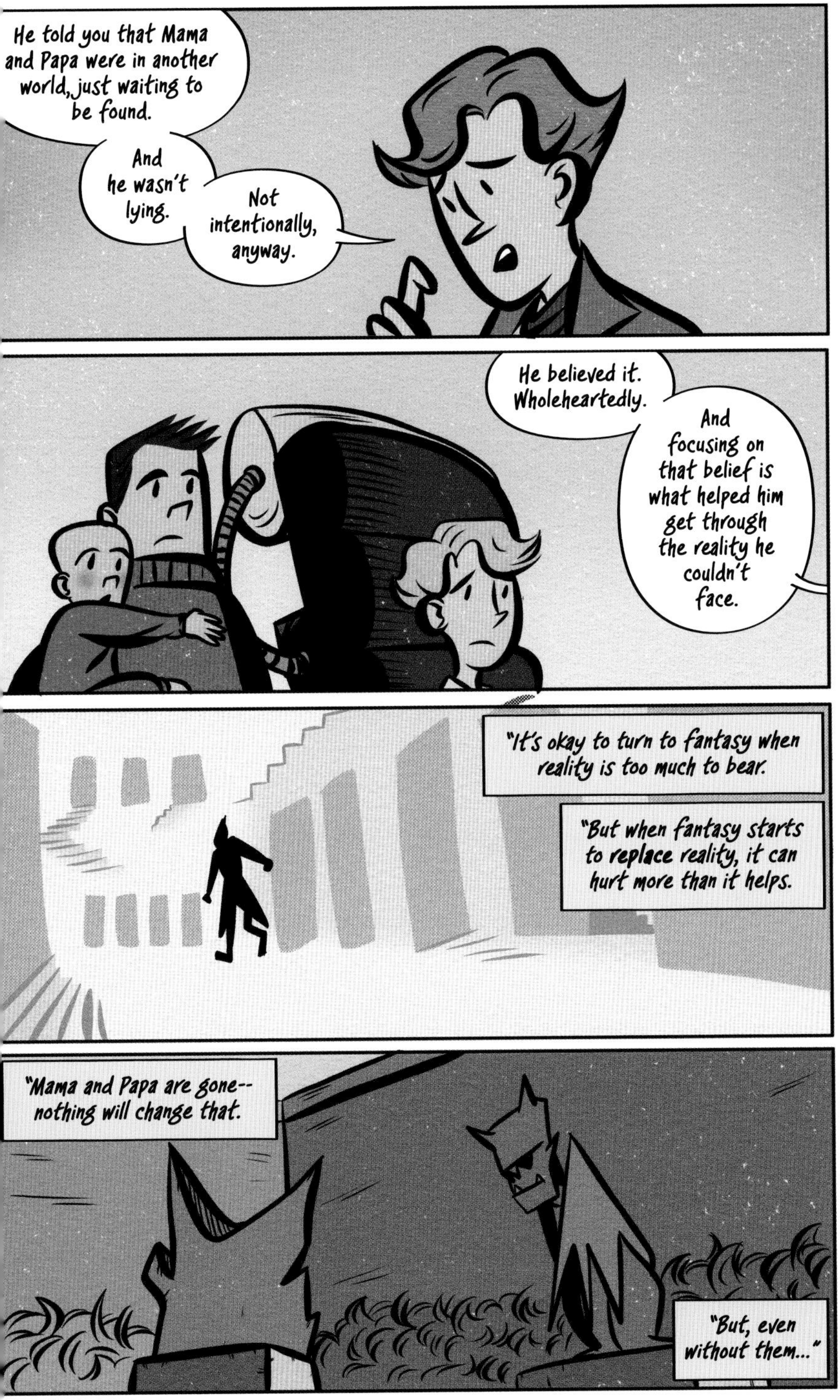
He told you that Mama and Papa were in another world, just waiting to be found.
And he wasn't lying.
Not intentionally, anyway.
He believed it. Wholeheartedly.
And focusing on that belief is what helped him get through the reality he couldn't face.
"It's okay to turn to fantasy when reality is too much to bear.
"But when fantasy starts to replace reality, it can hurt more than it helps.
"Mama and Papa are gone--nothing will change that.
"But, even without them..."

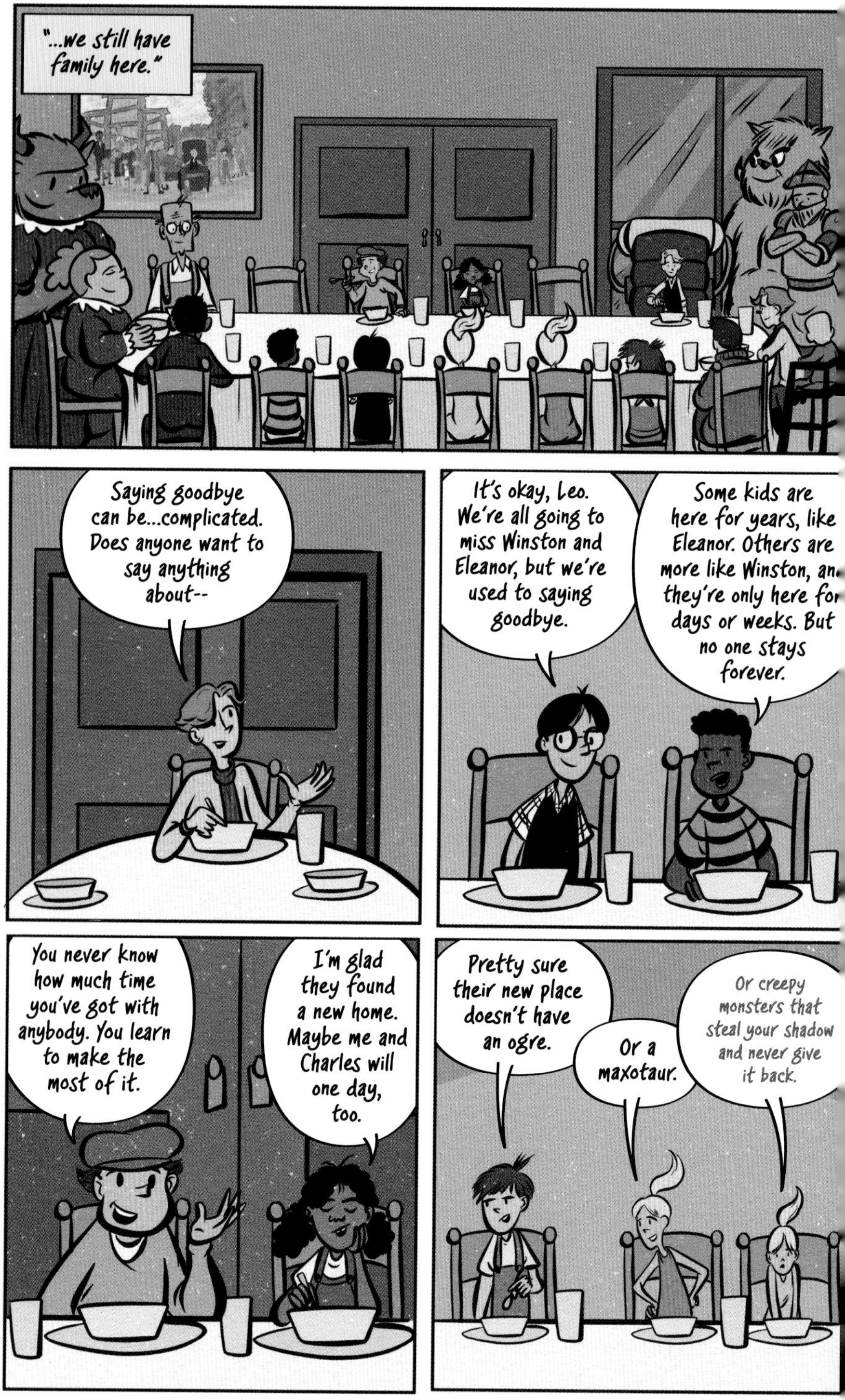
"...we still have family here."
Saying goodbye can be...complicated. Does anyone want to say anything about--
It's okay, Leo. We're all going to miss Winston and Eleanor, but we're used to saying goodbye.
Some kids are here for years, like Eleanor. Others are more like Winston, and they're only here for days or weeks. But no one stays forever.
You never know how much time you've got with anybody. You learn to make the most of it.
I'm glad they found a new home. Maybe me and Charles will one day, too.
Pretty sure their new place doesn't have an ogre.
Or a maxotaur.
Or creepy monsters that steal your shadow and never give it back.

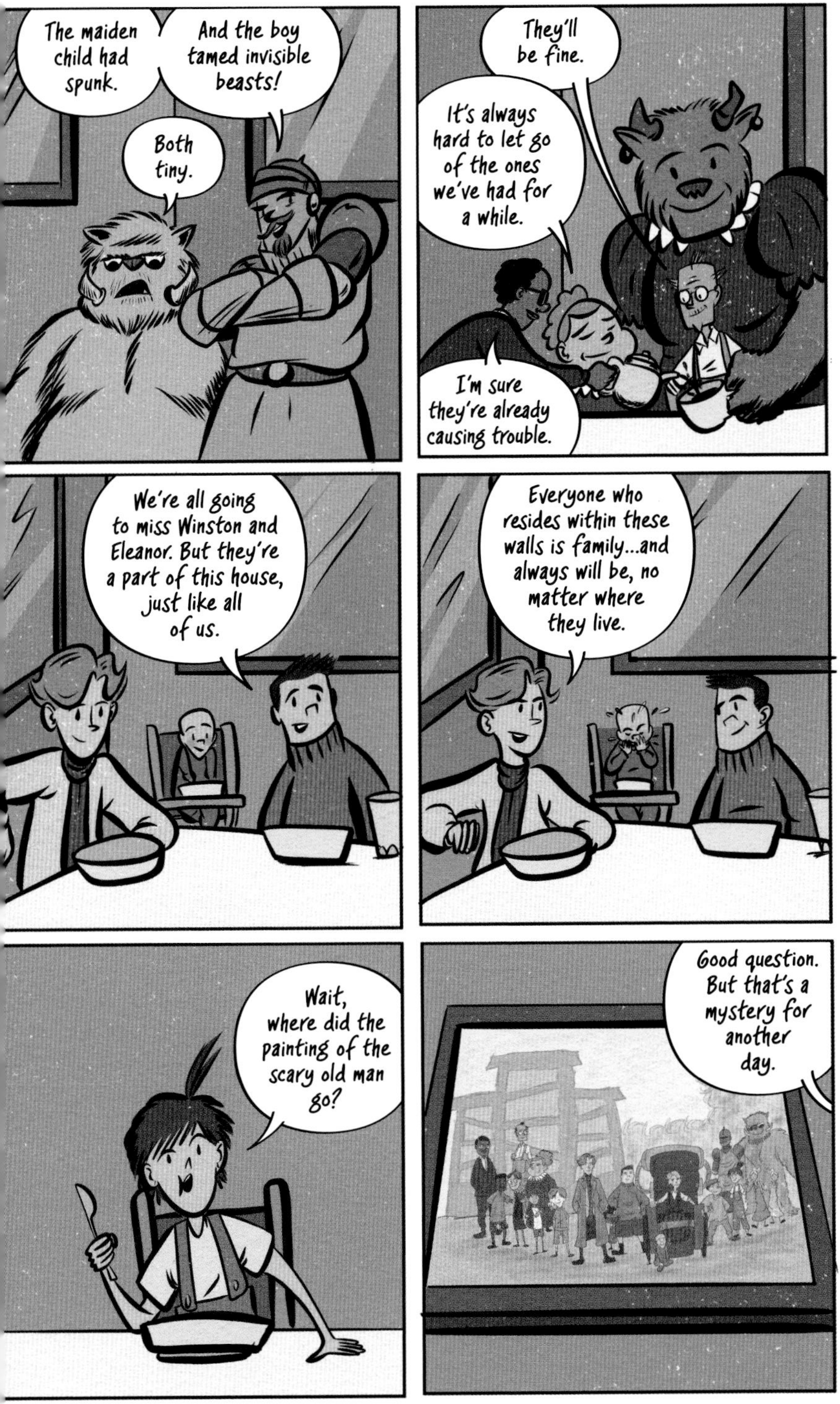
The maiden child had spunk.
And the boy tamed invisible beasts!
Both tiny.
They'll be fine.
It's always hard to let go of the ones we've had for a while.
I'm sure they're already causing trouble.
We're all going to miss Winston and Eleanor. But they're a part of this house, just like all of us.
Everyone who resides within these walls is family...and always will be, no matter where they live.
Wait, where did the painting of the scary old man go?
Good question. But that's a mystery for another day.

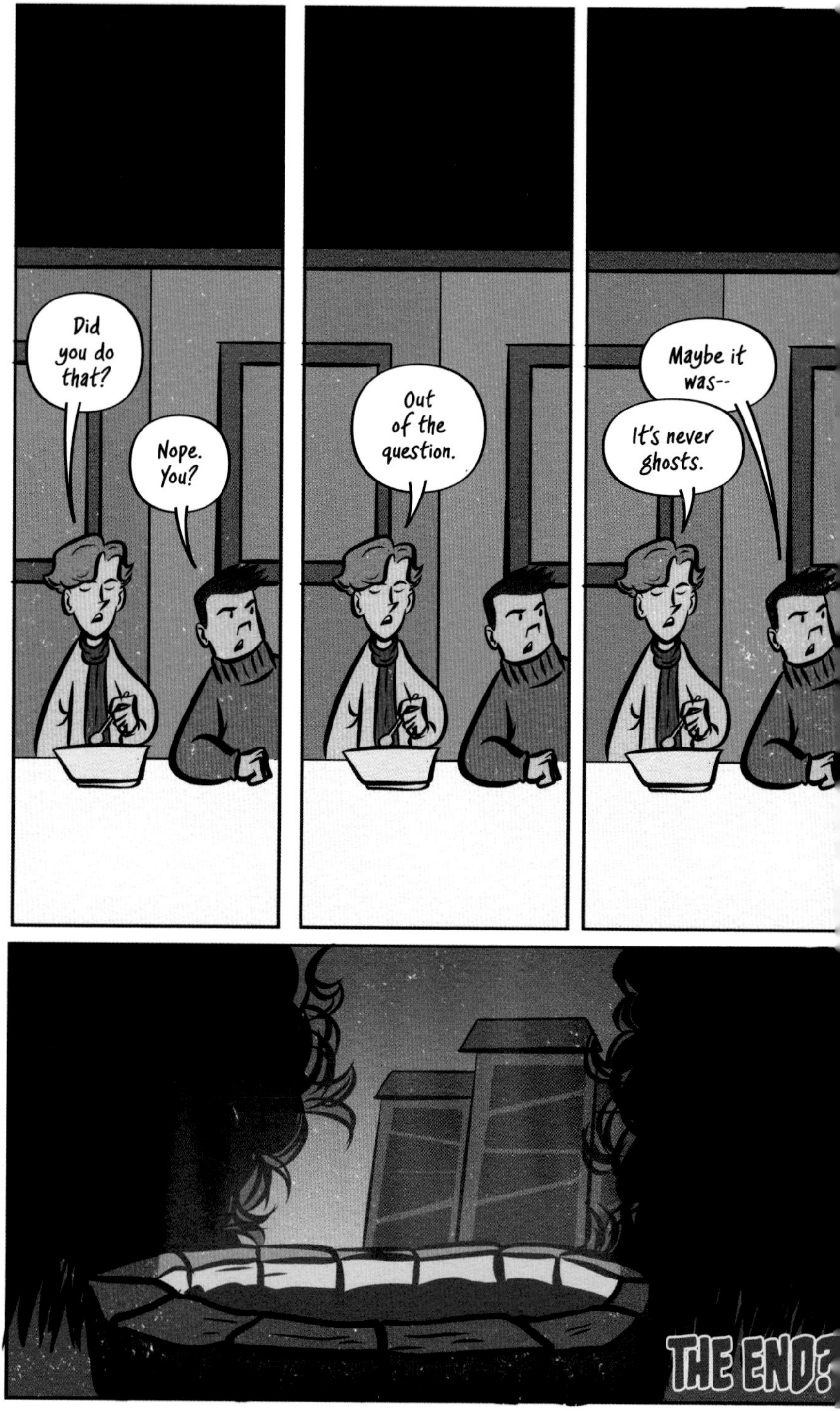

Did you do that?
Nope. You?
Out of the question.
Maybe it was--
It's never ghosts.
THE END?

EPILOGUE

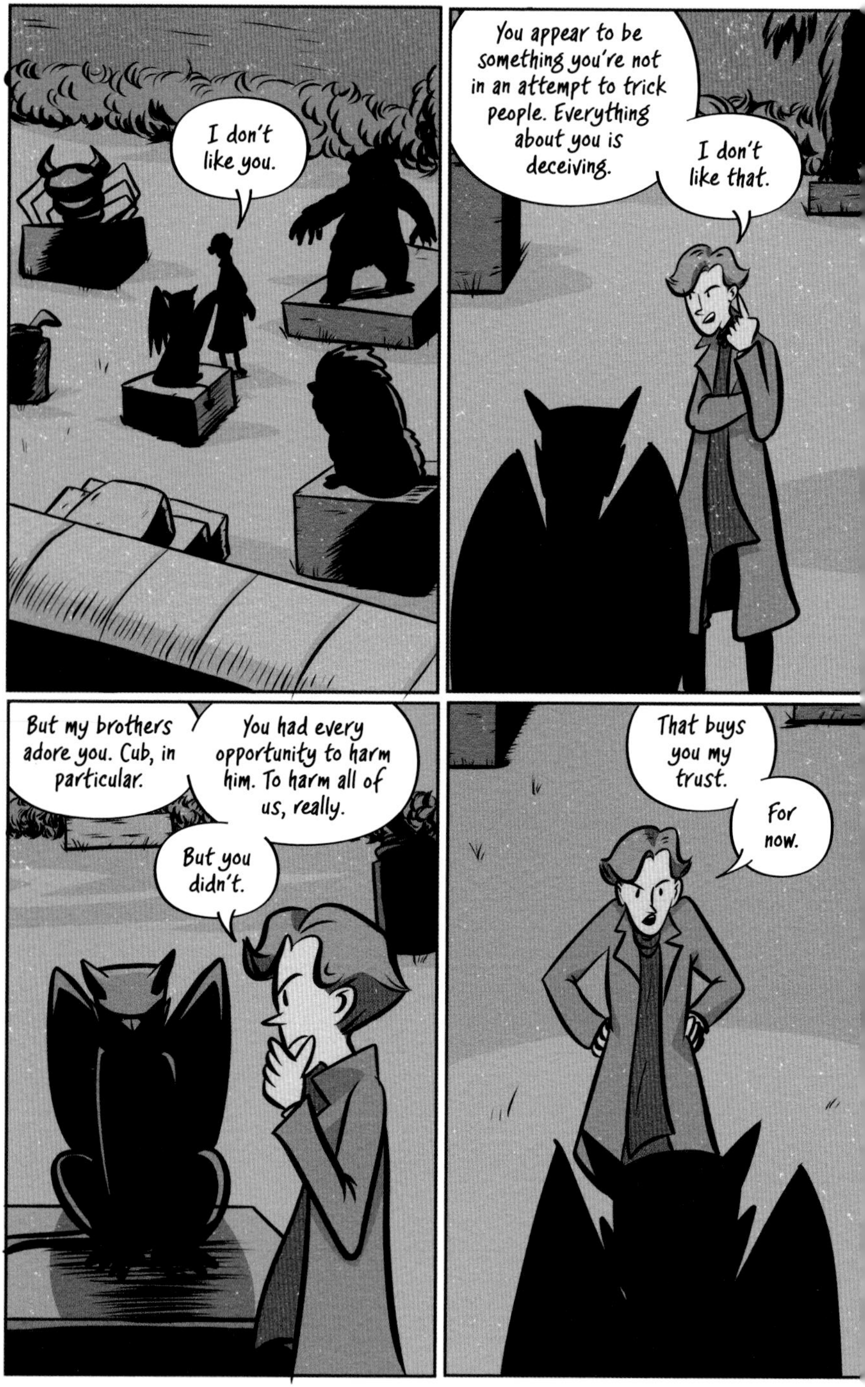
I don't like you.
You appear to be something you're not in an attempt to trick people. Everything about you is deceiving.
I don't like that.
But my brothers adore you. Cub, in particular.
You had every opportunity to harm him. To harm all of us, really.
But you didn't.
That buys you my trust.
For now.

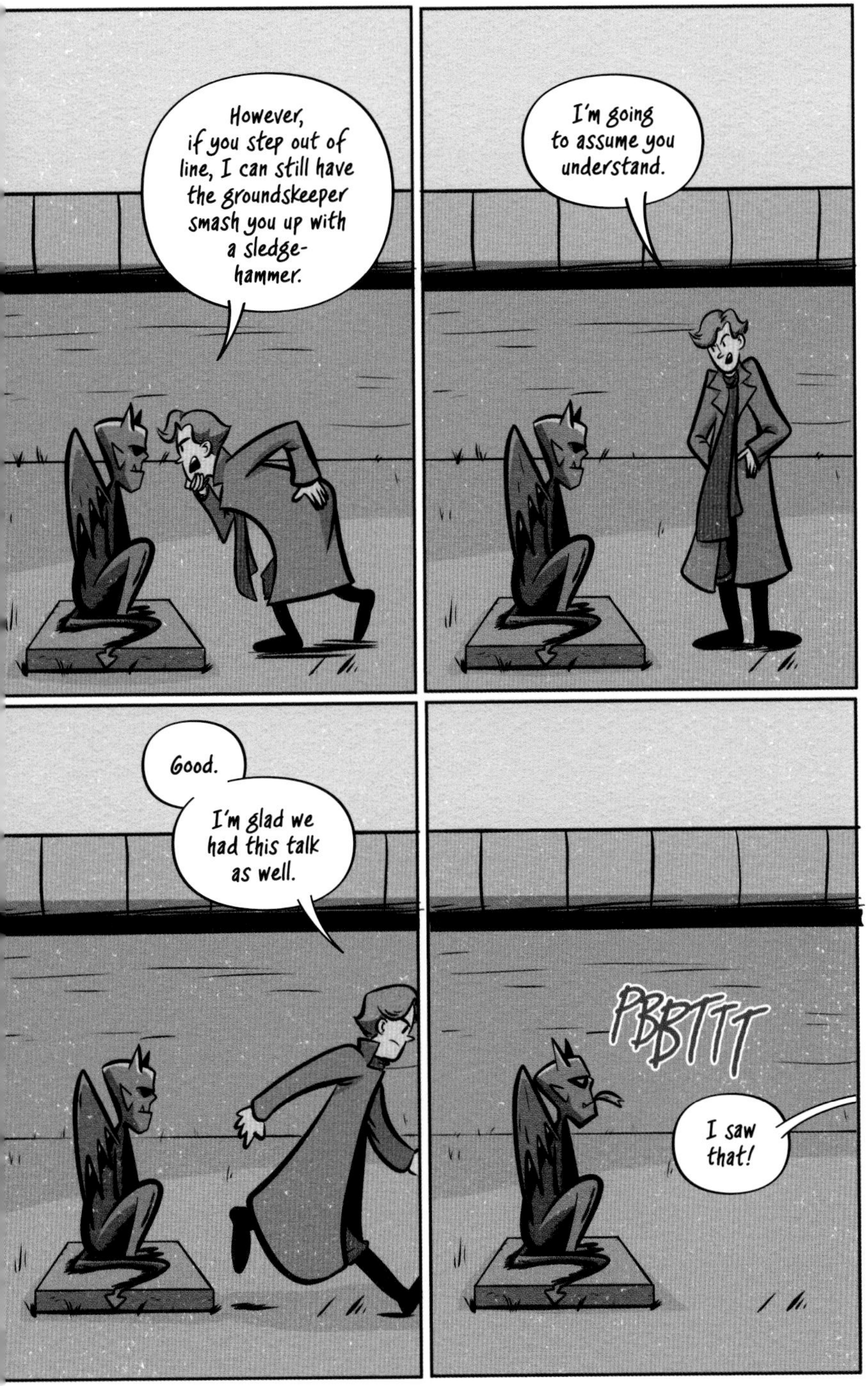
However, if you step out of line, I can still have the groundskeeper smash you up with a sledge-hammer.
I'm going to assume you understand.
Good.
I'm glad we had this talk as well.
PBBTTT
I saw that!

AUTHOR'S NOTE

Liam Eliot Haddock, my oldest son and the inspiration for Leo, died on June 9, 2019 at the age of nine. Writing this book began as a fun way to mix two things I love dearly: fantastic stories and my delightful children. After his death, the book took on a new purpose. It was a way for me to see him after I no longer thought that would be possible. It was a place where his wit and his spirit could live on and continue growing, as safe and as sound as the story would permit. Lastly, it was a way to share him and his brilliance with the rest of the world. I hope you're more ready than I was.

RYAN HADDOCK

RYAN HADDOCK

has wanted to write books since he was six years old. Drawing from his enduring love of science-fiction, fantasy, and comics, his greatest ambition is to write the kind of stories his eight year old self would read with a flashlight under the covers long after his parents thought he had gone to bed. Ryan resides with his family in a town known for ridiculously fast internet and a jingle about a train.

NICK WYCHE

is an old man who lives on a mountain and draws funny pictures whenever he can.

DAVID STOLL

has an affinity for clear storytelling, dynamic layouts, and childish hijinks, so this was the book for him! He's Denver-based, and can be reached on all social media @stollcomics.

WHITNEY COGAR

is a comic colorist and illustrator from Savannah, GA. She contributed colors to the two-time Eisner Award-winning *Giant Days* (BOOM! Studios), the *Steven Universe* comic series (BOOM! Studios), and Lucy Knisley's *Peapod Farm* series (Random House). She enjoys building punchy, rich enviroments in her work and designing enamel pins.

JIM CAMPBELL

is a twice-Eisner-nominated letterer who lives and works in a small English market town that has a lovely pub at the end of his street. Mostly, he works from home and not in the pub. Mostly. As well as books from Wonderbound, his work can regularly be found in 2000AD, and in titles from Aftershock, BOOM! Studios, Dark Horse, Image, Oni, Titan, and Vault.

WONDERBOUND

Find these titles and more at readwonderbound.com

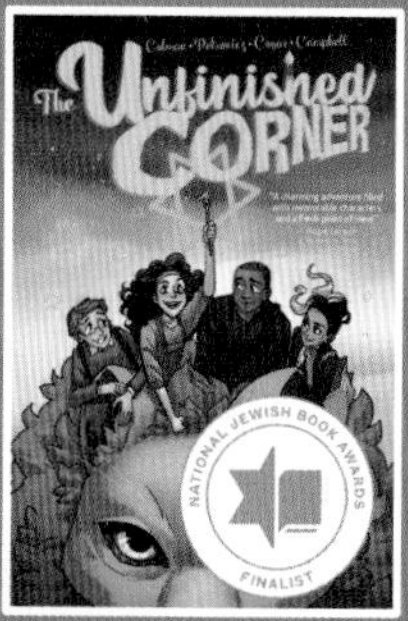
The Unfinished Corner
National Jewish Book Awards Finalist

THE UNFINISHED CORNER

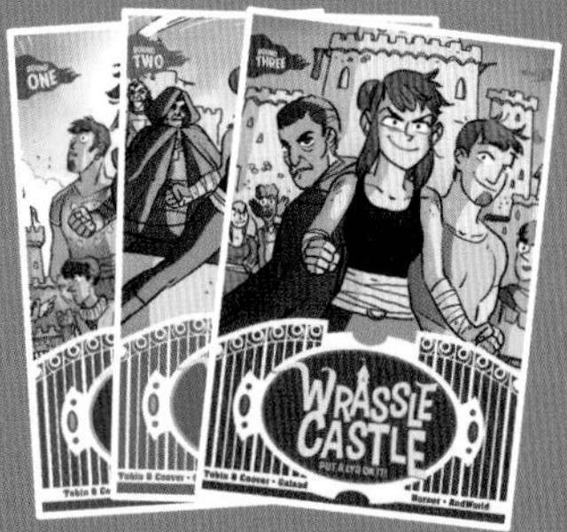
ONE
TWO
THREE
Wrassle Castle
Put a Lyd on It!

WRASSLE CASTLE: BOOK 1, LEARNING THE ROPES

WRASSLE CASTLE: BOOK 2, RIDERS ON THE STORM

WRASSLE CASTLE: BOOK 3, PUT A LYD ON IT!

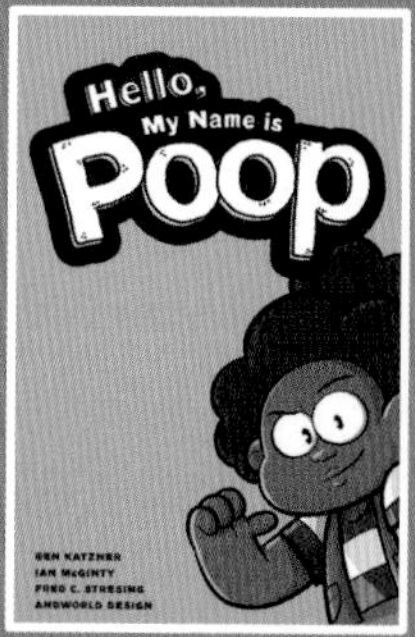
Hello, My Name is POOP

HELLO, MY NAME IS POOP

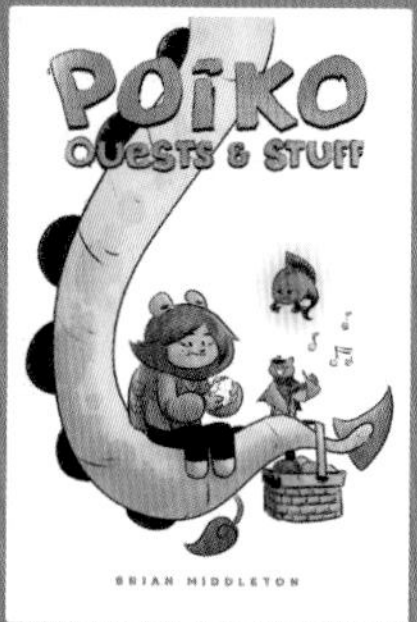
POIKO
Quests & Stuff
BRIAN MIDDLETON

POIKO: QUESTS & STUFF

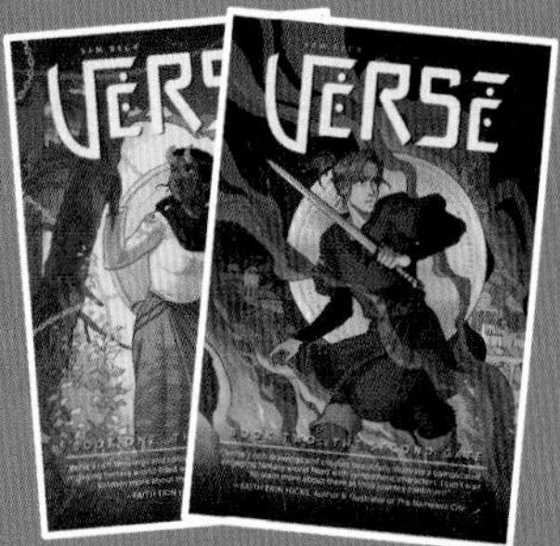
VERSE
VERSE

VERSE: BOOK 1 THE BROKEN HALF

VERSE: BOOK 2 THE SECOND GATE

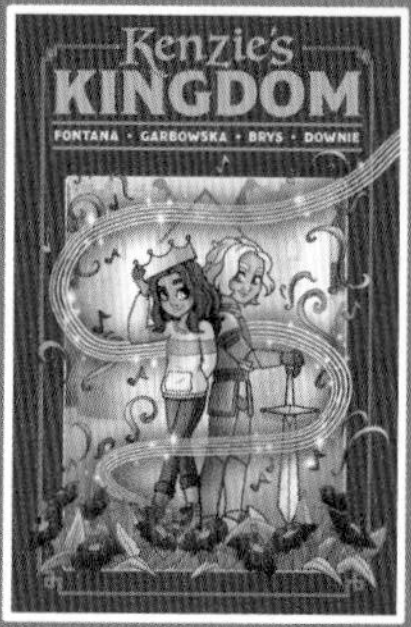
Kenzie's KINGDOM
FONTANA • GARBOWSKA • BRYS • DOWNIE

KENZIE'S KINGDOM

COMING SOON!

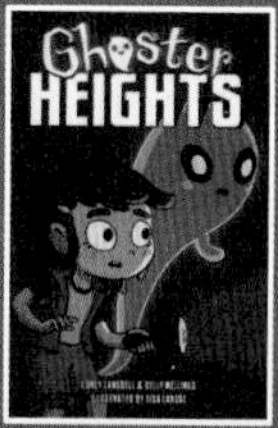
Ghoster Heights

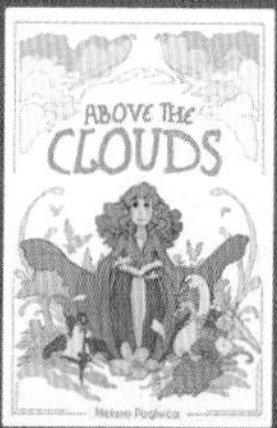
Above the Clouds

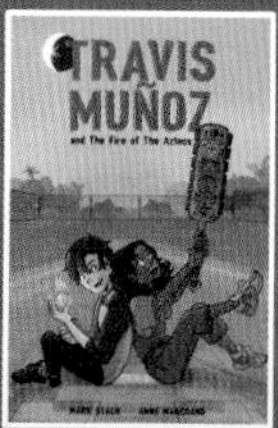
Travis Muñoz

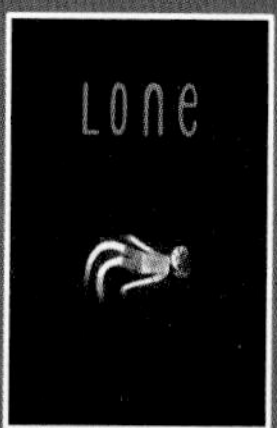
Lone

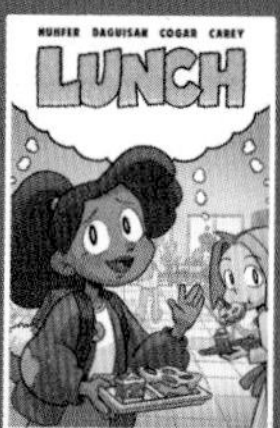
Lunch